DARK VISIONS

JAMES BYRON HUGGINS

WILDBLUE
PRESS

WildBluePress.com

DARK VISIONS published by:

WILDBLUE PRESS
P.O. Box 102440
Denver, Colorado 80250

WILDBLUE PRESS is registered at the U.S. Patent and Trademark Offices.

ISBN 978-1-947290-49-5 Trade Paperback
ISBN 978-1-947290-48-8 eBook

Interior Formatting/Book Cover Design by Elijah Toten
www.totencreative.com

DARK VISIONS

For Sarah
My heart
My daughter
My reflection
The torch shall pass to you
As it should, my love

ONE

Sitting upon a bough, the raven watched.

In the dying of the light the little boy swung slowly from the tree, his body broken, a noose around his neck. And at the edge of the forest a car burned and the raven watched as flame rose from the heat like hate rising from the heart of the sun.

The raven and the boy were together as the fire burned and burned and began to fade in the last of the day but still the raven did not move. It stayed upon the bough and did not leave the boy alone until the sun had descended and was gone.

The raven watched as the boy was claimed by the darkness of the night. It watched as the fire smoldered and the smoke vanished in the evening gray that overcame the day. It watched and it watched and it watched and it watched until something else had begun to burn in the dying of the light …

Fire rose in the raven's eyes.

* * *

Joe Mac felt the gray November cold more completely than he'd ever felt it before because he could no longer see the leaves fade from rust to gold or gaze upon the skeletal silhouettes of trees etched against the gray November sky.

Now he lived in the world of the blind, so feeling the cold was all that remained. The rest was darkness and he would inhabit this darkness until the day he died and they buried him in the dirt and this darkness.

The raven came as it always came; it descended with the sound of enormous wings to land with a thunderclap on the home Joe Mac had built for it.

Three years ago they met as Joe Mac was first learning to live in the world of the blind. The raven had come to him every day as he sat alone in the back of the barn, and Joe Mac named him "Poe" after the old poem. And every evening they would sit together in the back of the barn in Joe Mac's eternal night.

Poe did not rise or even seem to notice the familiar Mrs. Clemens as she approached, but then Poe rarely flew away when someone came close. Rather, he seemed to know the exact distance for danger and ignored anything else.

Mrs. Clemens brought Joe Mac his supper – an act Joe Mac reckoned to her uncommon human kindness – and spent a moment to inquire about his health. But Joe Mac sensed something different in Mrs. Clemens tonight. Her steps were halting and seemed to wander before she laid a hand on his shoulder.

Lifting his face, Joe Mac asked, "What is it, Mrs. Clemens?"

Mrs. Clemens shuffled, and Joe Mac felt the strength lessen in the hand; it was not much of a change, it was true, but a hand with little strength is even more revealing when what little strength it possesses is diminished ever more.

Joe Mac repeated more sternly, "What is it, Mrs. Clemens?"

"Oh," moaned Mrs. Clemens, "it's horrible, Mr. Joe Mac. Just horrible. Oh, god, I don't know how to tell you."

"Just say it."

She faltered, "It's about your grandson, Mr. Joe Mac. It's about Aaron. The poor thing disappeared from daycare today."

Joe Mac's left hand tightened on the arm of the chair. "How could they lose a four-year-old boy? Have they called the police?"

"Your poor daughter has called everyone! We're all scared to death something terrible has happened!"

With a shrill cry Poe erupted into the night sky as Joe Mac stood pulling his wool coat more tightly across his chest; he snapped his cane to length. "Why didn't someone tell me about this earlier?" he demanded.

"They've been too busy searching for him, Mr. Joe Mac! They've looked everywhere! And you can't even ..."

She let the sentence die.

"Take me to my daughter," said Joe Mac. "And compose yourself, Mrs. Clemens. We don't know that anything terrible has happened. Compose yourself! Stay calm. And take me to my daughter."

TWO

"Here's the case file on that little kid."

Jodi Strong raised her eyes as the file was laid upon her desk. The veteran New York City detective, Thomas Grimes, who delivered the file pulled up a chair and leaned back, folding hands on his chest.

"What do you want with this thing, Jodi?" Grimes asked and didn't attempt to conceal either his curiosity or confusion. "There's already a million cops on this, and we got twenty cases of our own to work."

"I took the original call last week when I was in uniform," said Jodi. "I interviewed the daycare workers, the mother, the father. And then they found the little kid but he was already dead. Just like the others."

Grimes spoke in a weary monotone, "Jodi, it was your case when you were in uniform. It was your case when you took the missing person report. But you got promoted to detective three days ago, and it ain't your case no more. It belongs to the task force and you ain't on the task force, neither. So what are you doing?"

Jodi shook her head, "Grimes, I know it's always a mistake to get personally involved in a case but –"

"Then don't."

"But that scene at the house really shook me up," Jodi continued. "I saw the little boy's room. I saw his picture. I felt like I knew him. And then he ends up … like he ended up." She slapped the file. "I'm tired of this psycho!"

Grimes sighed, "Jodi, the FBI has a thousand people on this. We've got about a million. One more cop ain't gonna make no difference in this. And we need you *here*."

Jodi made a slight sound as she sucked breath through her teeth. Then she said, "He's made a mistake, Grimes. They're just not finding it. Nobody's perfect."

"Well, this psycho is pretty close to perfect because right now the task force guys tell me they don't have a clue. One of 'em told me they're no closer to catching him now than they were four years ago."

Jodi opened the file and leaned back; "Aaron Roberts. Four years old. Abducted from the playground of his daycare. His body was found one hour after sunset –"

"Same as the rest of 'em."

Jodi continued reading as Grimes stood and leaned over her desk.

"Jodi," he began in a patient tone, "listen to me; I'm glad you made detective. I think you're a natural. But you're wasting your time. Whatever mistake this guy made ain't gonna be in no file. There's no fibers, no hairs, no prints, no DNA. There's no witnesses, no video, no tracks." He pointed toward the door. "This guy has killed twenty-four people, and he could walk through that door right now and confess to everything we've got and we wouldn't be able to pin him to a single thing. He doesn't take anything. He doesn't leave anything. He has no motive. He has no face. He has no name. *He's a ghost.*"

"Excuse me."

Jodi lifted her face to see an exceeding large man standing on the far side of her desk at the same moment she realized he was blind.

The man was slightly less than six feet but built like a brick. His body seemed one uniform size from his linebacker shoulders down through his barrel chest to his waist and weightlifter legs. His head was a square granite block set on a short neck. His white hair was standard military high-and-tight. His arms were heavy and the hand holding the cane was thick with strong-looking fingers although he held the shaft with a fisherman's touch.

Jodi was instantly curious why the man's presence gave her a palpitation of alarm. There was certainly nothing obviously threatening about him. And yet an aura of doom seemed to cloak him even more than the knee-length undertaker coat or the impenetrable black glasses; it occurred to Jodi that his appearance could not have been more unsettling if he'd been wearing a black funeral veil over his face. In all he reminded Jodi of a Texas tombstone she'd once seen that read, "*As you are, I once was. As I am, you will be...*"

Jodi whispered, "Good god ..."

Grimes turned, gaped, and grabbed one of the man's blacksmith arms. "Joe Mac Blake! I haven't seen you in years, Joe! How ya been, man?"

"You're lookin' at it," said Joe Mac. "They still got you in robbery, Grimes?"

"Same 'ol same." Grimes theatrically lifted a hand toward Jodi as she rolled her eyes; *he's blind, you dolt.* "Jodi, this is ex-homicide detective Joe Mac Blake. Joe is a legend! Joe, this is Detective Jodi Strong. She's the newest member of the team." A laugh. "Well, this is a blast from the past, buddy. What are you doing downtown, man?"

Joe Mac lightly tapped the desk with his cane. "Got a seat for me?"

"Sure." Grimes pulled up a rolling chair. "Sit down."

Joe Mac felt, found the chair, and sat. He turned his face toward Jodi, "Nice to meet you, Jodi. Grimes is a good man. He'll help you get the lay of the land around here, but it won't take you too long." He paused. "Can one of you tell me who's handling the Aaron Roberts case? He was the little boy that got killed last week."

"Officially that case belongs to the task force," said Jodi. "He's another victim of a serial killer we've been trying to catch for a long time."

"The Hangman?"

Jodi stared, then, "We've been ordered from on-high not to use that phrase, but, yeah, it was 'The Hangman.'" She glanced at the file. "But as it happens, Joe, I've got a copy of the file right here."

Joe Mac lifted his face. "Have you had a chance to look at it?"

"No. I just got it. What can I do for you, Joe?"

"Aaron was my grandson." Joe Mac's face was stone. "I know I can't contribute to the forensics, but if you have any personal questions about Aaron, maybe I could help you out a little bit."

Jodi stared. "I'm sorry for your loss, Joe."

"Appreciate it."

After expelling a long breath Jodi said, "Look, Joe, they've got a task force briefing in about twenty minutes. Why don't you come with me? The FBI will be there along with Captain Brightbarton. He's in charge."

"I don't have a badge anymore."

"You're with me. You'll be okay."

Joe Mac rose, his hand moving his cane.

"Let's go."

* * *

Joe Mac knew he was seated in the third row from the back, the second chair from the right side of the room. He'd been here many times during his thirty-five-year career as a New York City uniform patrol officer and then as a gold shield homicide investigator, and he knew every line of this place.

He also knew that the front few rows would be filled with investigators and uniform patrol supervisors. The next rows would contain FBI personnel. And the last few rows would be filled with forensics experts, psychologists, and people like himself.

Captain Steve Brightbarton announced, "All right, gentlemen, you've all had a chance to review the forensics on four-year-old Aaron Roberts. As of this moment we can confirm that Aaron was killed inside that warehouse. The suspect used blunt force trauma to break all his bones – the same thing he did to the other victims – and then he hung him by a noose around his neck. Same as the rest. Forensics says the tool used in the attack was a club coated in bronze, so keep your eyes open for a plain-view search. Crime Scene didn't recover any DNA. No hairs. No fibers. No prints. Not even any touch-DNA. We don't have him on video. We have no witnesses. The car was stolen from a police impound lot, and that's all we got. At this time I'll turn it over to FBI Special Agent Jack Rollins."

There was little to hear besides the rustling of clothing as Jack Rollins stood and Brightbarton took a chair.

"Afternoon," Rollins began, "you all know me. But for the uninitiated my name is Jack Rollins, and I am the Special Agent in charge of the FBI task force. Everything Captain Brightbarton just told you is accurate. I'll only add that the murder of Aaron Roberts is consistent with the twenty-three murders preceding this, so confidence is high that we're dealing with the same suspect. As usual, the suspect left nothing behind. The rope he used was standard clothesline that you can purchase at any hardware store. He torched the vehicle with a half-gallon of gasoline inside a one gallon milk jug armed with a two-dollar, off-the-shelf egg timer so we have no prints, no fibers, and no DNA.

"We have nothing further on a description. We know he uses disguises, and we have him on traffic cameras as an old man, a young man, a poor man, a rich man. The only thing we know for sure is that it's a man. We have isolated no salient physical characteristics that would make him easier to identify. He could be me. He could be you. All we can tell you is that we believe he's a white male in his mid-thirties. He's about six foot, 180 pounds. He very, very strong physically, and we believe he has a superior IQ. So our strategy is for the NYPD to continue their stop and frisk strategy of any and every person of interest. We want you to continue priority patrols and stakeouts of secular daycares, church daycares, schools, malls, playgrounds, parks. Meanwhile, we at the FBI will continue to work forensics and continue our enhanced surveillance of every name the computer spits out. Now, we do not know if this psychopath is armed but, of course, you know to approach him as if he is." He paused. "I know I certainly will. And now I'll turn this over to Dr. Marvin Mason. He's assistant senior anthropologist for New York's American Museum of Natural History. He also has a doctorate in archeology, and he is continuing to work with our Division of Behavioral Science to keep an up-to-date profile on this guy. So, Dr. Mason? Would you, please?"

The chamber was subdued, which allowed Joe Mac to hear Dr. Mason's soft steps and then the microphone was turned, apparently to accommodate his height.

"Thank you," said Mason.

Imperceptibly Joe Mac nodded; yeah, from the depth of his voice Mason wasn't big, but he wasn't a lightweight, either. Joe Mac estimated him at a few inches less than six feet, about 170 pounds. His accent was native Long Island.

"All I can tell you is what I've already told you," Dr. Mason began. "As you know, this subject takes the time to break every bone in a victim's body, and then he hangs them by the neck from a tree. We've done extensive research, and we have found this manner of human sacrifice, or punishment, to be so prevalent in ancient cultures that we can't isolate any specific cult or religion or sect or civilization as the primary instigator. He could have taken it from the Jews or the Gaelic tribes or the Vikings or various Asiatic cultures. All we can say is that we believe you're looking for an individual who kills in this highly methodical manner because he is motivated by some kind of pathological religious psychosis." He paused. "We know you guys are working hard, and all of us at the museum want to help. But that's all we've been able to come up with. There's just nothing exotic enough about what's he doing to narrow it down to any one culture or religion. It's barbaric and savage. But it's not exotic. Throughout recorded history it's something that's been done by almost everybody."

Jodi said, "Dr. Mason?"

Mason paused. "Yes?"

Beside Joe Mac, Jodi stood; she was leaning on the chair before them. "Doctor, how long is he going to keep this up?"

"We believe he's going to keep it up until you catch him or kill him."

"Why do you say that?"

"Just like we don't know what kind of obsession is motivating him, we can't say with any certainty when this obsession will be fulfilled," Mason answered. "I think it's safe to say that you're dealing with someone who is very smart and very cautious but also completely insane and I see no reason why he will stop doing what he's doing."

"History doesn't suggest a motive?" Jodi asked.

Mason sighed; "The closest thing we've found to a motive are rituals used in turn-of-the-century Europe to destroy werewolves." He cleared his throat. "In Europe, when they caught someone they suspected of being a werewolf, they would put them on a rack, break their bones, hang them, and set them on fire. They did the same thing to people suspected of witchcraft. Even in this century. Even in this *country*. But we don't think he's doing all this because he suspects someone of being a werewolf or a witch. We think he's doing it because he's afflicted with a bizarre religious psychosis that is totally beyond the understanding of any sane person and probably beyond his understanding, too. We don't think even he knows why he's doing what he's doing. He doesn't know why he's doing it, but he can't stop himself. That's how crazy we think he is."

"But why do you insist it's a religious psychosis?" Jodi pressed.

"Because breaking someone's bones and hanging them from a tree are traditional religious punishments. Both of them are in the Bible. Both of them are in the Koran. Both of them are in the Torah. In a nutshell, they're universal religious means of punishment for someone breaking a religious law regardless whether that law comes from Yahweh or Allah or Shiva. Does that answer your question?"

Jodi nodded, "Yes, thank you."

FBI Special Agent Jack Rollins stood – Joe Mac heard the scrape of chair legs – and asked, "I'm sorry but I don't know your name Detective –?"

"Detective Jodi Strong, sir."

"Are you on the task force?"

"No," Jodi answered firmly. "I worked the original missing person call on Aaron Roberts when I was in uniform."

Hesitation.

"I see," said Rollins. "Well, the fact is that we don't know any more about who killed Aaron Roberts than we know who killed the rest of the victims, detective. We know this guy's methods. We have no idea who he is or why he's doing this."

"I understand," said Jodi.

She sat.

Joe Mac followed Mason to his chair on the back of the dais and listened as Brightbarton approached the podium.

"That's it, gentlemen," said Brightbarton. "Check your boxes at the end of shift for any updates. And remember: Approach this guy with the most extreme caution. And that means approach him with your gun *out* and shoot him graveyard dead if he even *looks* at you funny. Be careful out there. Dismissed."

Joe Mac didn't move as everyone rose and began filing out the three doors. He lost contact with any presence on the podium in the mulling of footsteps and conversation like one might lose sight of an eagle against the sun. He did know that Jodi hadn't moved. Neither had she opened the file she'd brought from the office. He would have heard the rustling of paper, and there wasn't any.

"I checked up on you," said Jodi.

Joe Mac's voice was a soft growl; "When'd you have time to do that?"

"When I went to the bathroom. You're a legend."

Joe Mac revealed nothing.

"The lady in the bathroom told me that you solved over a thousand homicides. She said you were a detective first grade with a gold shield, and you were one of those real guys always out there, always hunting. Then you lost your eyesight when you rescued that little boy from that house fire. And I know it sucks – I mean, don't get me wrong; I would never say I know *how much* it sucks – but you did save that little boy's life. And I bet you're still a great detective."

Joe Mac lifted his chin. He seemed to hear better that way; he didn't know why. He didn't care. It worked, and if anything worked at this stage of his life, it was good enough. "Are you thinking you could use some help?" he asked.

By the scraping in her seat Joe Mac knew she turned. "Well, Joe, you knew Aaron. And I've already talked to your daughter. She's in no shape to help me or anybody else right now. So what do you say we ride out to that daycare center and take a look around?" She stood. "Anyway, the daycare's right down the road from your daughter's house. And you live close by, don't you?"

"I live in the barn out back," said Joe Mac. "They sort of turned it into an apartment." He shrugged. "It's good enough."

"Then let's take a ride, Joe. If nothing else, I'll take you home."

Joe Mac stood.

"Bring what you got on this case."

* * *

Joe Mac didn't need eyes to know exactly where they were at any moment. His soul knew this terrain by neurological imprint. He imagined that he might have driven much of it by himself even now.

"I don't know if I told you how sorry I am about Aaron," Jodi said – the first time she'd spoken in her squad car. "I know that nothing is fair in this world but this truly wasn't fair in an ungodly, horrible way that should be damned to Hell."

Someone once said the greatest sound is silence, but Joe Mac couldn't remember who it was. He only knew he had nothing to say until Jodi finally turned the squad car slowly to the left and announced, "Here we are, Joe."

She parked and Joe Mac could feel her stare.

"You ready for this?" she asked.

Joe Mac nodded and opened the door.

"Let's do it," he said.

He extended his cane though he hardly needed it; he could remember every inch of this daycare since he'd seen if often enough when he could still see; it was a compact one-story building with three wings like a *T*. There was a playground with brightly colored plastic equipment out back. It was surrounded by mesh fence about four feet high that had a gate leading into the building. There was one exterior gate on the left. The entire facility was a half-acre surrounded by pines.

Joe Mac had already moved to the front of Jodi's car as she walked up and said, "Do you remember the layout?"

"Yeah."

"Wanna go up to the fence?"

"All right."

Joe Mac had no problem negotiating the sparsely occupied parking lot. He felt the curb with his cane and stepped up knowing the feel of grass beneath his feet; it was a half-inch deep with dry ground beneath. He estimated three steps to the fence, and he was right. He placed a hand on the top of the steel mesh and lifted his chin.

He became aware that he was waiting for … something ….

"Those pine trees back there," said Jodi. "Do you think he could have come in through those? They would have hidden him from view until he came right up to the fence."

"He could have." Joe Mac turned his face toward the back acreage as if he could still see. His voice was faint. "Still green up top. Thick enough. Dead pine needles don't make a sound when you walk on 'em … Yeah. Let's go back there. I know the crime scene boys went over it but it won't hurt to do it again."

"I'm game," Jodi said, and they turned to walk along the fence line.

The front easement had been mowed up to the steel mesh, so Joe Mac didn't have to worry about weeds. Then he felt Jodi's hand at his left elbow, guiding him gently, and he wasn't offended. Guiding a blind man by a light touch at an elbow was something people just seemed to do by instinct.

Joe Mac was accustomed to the drag of his cane on grass; it was much different than the steady, balanced, light touch he used on concrete. He had to lift it higher and touch more quickly; it was more like stabbing fish than the smooth side-to-side he normally used.

Joe Mac estimated twenty steps to the end of this fence line, and he was right. They turned to the left and resumed walking when Jodi said, "I think he used this side. The other side faces the road, and I don't think he'd use that. He'd have to stop his car on the road, jump out, run up to the fence and try to grab one of them. And the kids would have probably run away from him, screamed for their teacher, and they would have called for a unit. He would have never been able to get out of the area before one of us caught up to him. I think he knew that."

"You're right," said Joe Mac. "He wouldn't do that."

"This guy doesn't leave anything to chance." Jodi's voice took a tinge of impatience. "Sometimes it amazes me how crazy people can be so smart when it comes to killing other people. It's almost ... cosmic."

They reached the section furthest from the building, and Joe Mac said, "Stop here. What do you see?"

Jodi said, "Well, this is the farthest point of the fence, and they don't mow the grass back here. It's about waist high right up to the playground. But it's been stomped down a little by the search party."

"How big was the search party?"

"It wasn't all that big. There wasn't enough time to organize a big search party or even get the word out. Aaron was reported missing at three in the afternoon, and they found his body at seven-thirty." A pause. "If he'd been missing for a whole day I'm sure we'd have had thousands of people walking the woods out here. But all they had that day was a few cops and some neighbors. Then they found Aaron's body beside that warehouse, and there was no more reason to look."

"Keep moving," Joe Mac motioned. "Keep looking down. Tell me what you see. It doesn't matter what it is."

They strolled and Jodi began "Looks like we got one rabbit hole ... Rabbit tracks ... There's a fresh mole hill ... A coke can ... "

"Bag it."

"Got it."

They continued.

"We got another mole hill ... A blue leaflet ... Bagging it ... A candy bar wrapper ... Bagging it .... I don't know why those guys didn't bag all this stuff ... Amateurs ... I should have come back here myself, but I was at your daughter's house ..."

"I appreciate it. Keep looking."

"I don't think this is going anywhere, Joe ... This coke can and candy bar wrapper look really old ... I don't think they have anything to do with what happened ..."

"Never assume anything, kid. Keep going."

"Okay ... Well, there's some kind of dead thing ... Looks like it used to be a bird ... There's a piece of white string ..."

Joe Mac stopped. "What?"

"What?" Jodi repeated.

"A what?"

"A string?"

"Did you say 'white string?'"

"Yeah. It's white."

"You wearing your gloves?"

"Yeah."

"Pick it up."

Jodi led him to the wood line, bent, and straightened. After a pause, she said, "It's just an ordinary piece of white string, Joe."

"Follow it."

After a moment, Joe Mac felt a tug on his arm. "This is kind of tricky, Joe. Stick close to me. It ..." They took several steps, "... it leads into the woods."

"Just follow it."

Jodi suddenly stooped and stayed low for a long time. "That's it," she said. "That's the end of it. It doesn't go any further."

"What's beyond this wood line?" he asked. "Can you see?"

"Yeah. Way back there. There's a field."

"Take me to it."

By Joe Mac's count it was thirty-seven steps to the field – his entire life existed now in how many steps it was from anything here to anything there. They stood for a long time and Joe Mac knew they were in the open because the trees no longer shielded him from the wind and he could feel the sun on his face.

"Anything?" he asked.

"Joe," she said with noticeable consternation, "what am I supposed to be looking for in an empty field?"

"Just tell me what you see."

"Well," he heard her hands slap her thighs, "I don't see anything but grass, Joe. And … whoa. I can see your daughter's house from here. It's about a half-mile away. Maybe a little more. Hey, is that your little green barn back there?"

"I reckon. Unless they got two barns."

"It's cute." Jodi took a moment. "Okay, the only other thing I see back here are some crows circling something on the other side of the field. Something must have died over there. Probably a coyote or a rabbit. Nothing else would –"

"Crows?" asked Joe Mac.

"Yeah. They look like crows."

"Take me over there."

They began across the high grass, and Joe Mac got the hang of it pretty quick; he'd do fine unless he stepped in a hole. Otherwise he could move as easily as Jodi seemed able, and then Jodi grabbed his arm; "Hold it, Joe. Yeah. I can see what it is."

"Is it a dead animal?" asked Joe Mac.

"Looks like it."

"A dead cat?"

Silence.

"Joe? How could you *possibly* know that it's –"

"Is it a dead kitten?"

"God Almighty. Yeah, it looks like it used to be … a kitten."

"How long has it been dead?"

"Uh … well, I'm not really an expert at decomposition, Joe, but it looks to me like it's been dead about a week. I don't know what those crows think they're eating, but there's not much left."

"So why are they circling?"

Jodi paused. "It looks to me like this really big crow is getting the rest of them all worked up over the bones. He's, like, herding them. Or something."

"Bait," Joe Mac stated with a bitter frown. "The string. A kitten. Aaron didn't go to the fence to see a man. He was taught to run from strangers. He walked over to see a kitty cat tied to the end of a string. The man was hiding in the grass. Then, once Aaron was distracted, this guy rushed up, snatched him over the fence, and ran off with him. Quick as that. He snatched the cat up, too, but threw it down after he was clear. He probably didn't think it was important enough to take the cat. He didn't think anybody would put it together. Or maybe Aaron was putting up a good fight, and he needed both hands." His teeth gleamed. "Yeah. That was probably it. He would have taken the cat, too, but Aaron was putting up a good fight and so he killed the cat. Broke its neck. Tossed it."

"Why didn't he just leave the cat at the daycare?"

"It's too obvious. And it's probably a trick he's used more than once. If it got in the papers he'd have one less trick."

Silence and sadness seemed to overlay them, and Joe Mac could faintly hear Jodi's movements. He knew she was standing with arms crossed, staring. He didn't feel like saying anything, either, as she whispered, "How horrible."

"Yes."

Her shriek cut the air, and Joe Mac heard her jump back. She gasped before she exclaimed, "That crow flew right over my head!"

She reached down as if to pick up a rock.

"Wait," said Joe Mac.

"What!"

"Is it a big crow?"

"Biggest crow I ever saw, that's for sure! God bless! That thing scared me to death! It could have parted my hair."

Joe Mac took a slow half-turn toward the tree line. He simply stood until he heard the familiar caw and he nodded. "And you say the crows led you here?"

"What?"

"The crows? They led you to the bones?"

"Actually, it was just that really big one. The one that scared me. He was circling around the bones real high, sort of herding the other crows down over the cat. I think he's like ... their leader. I mean, if crows have 'leaders.'" Suddenly she jumped back. "Look out, Joe!"

Joe Mac heard the familiar, powerful wings as Poe soared over him low enough to touch and listened until Poe was gone. Then he started forward.

"Look for some foot prints."

* * *

"Yeah!" shouted Captain Steve Brightbarton as he swung a fist through the air. "The psycho finally made a mistake!"

Jodi turned at the edge of the roped-off crime scene to see Joe Mac standing like a black harbinger of death in the middle of the field; the gigantic crow rested on the ground beside him like a faithful servant. She turned and walked forward, and when she reached Joe Mac she was curious that the crow didn't fly away.

It simply stood where it stood.

Staring at her.

"They've made casts of two shoe prints," she said. "They're way outside the earlier search grid. That's why the neighbors didn't find them, although I don't think they would have put it together anyway. They say the crow led them back to where he musta' parked his car." She hesitated. "Now that we've got a footprint, we might be able to trace the brand of shoe. If we're lucky, it's exotic. If not, we'll just run down everybody wearing Nikes. We might be looking at a billion suspects, but we'll know he's *one* of them."

"What are the prints like?" asked Joe Mac.

Jodi expelled a long breath. "They look to me like some kind of tennis shoe. Maybe a size ten or eleven. Like I say, the guys don't know what brand, yet, but they'll know by tonight." She looked at the crow, which was placidly staring back at her with almost-human ambivalence. "Do you two know each other?"

"You mean Poe?"

"It has a name?"

"Doesn't the Bible say everything has a name?"

"I don't know," said Jodi. "I don't read it, anymore."

"Maybe you should." Joe Mac paused. "Maybe we both should."

"He sure is the biggest crow I've ever seen."

"He's a raven. They're bigger than crows."

"He's almost as big as an *eagle*."

"That's what my daughter says."

Jodi knew she was scowling; it was fascinating how the thing held her gaze like a cat might do – never blinking, never looking away. It seemed to know she was curious about it and was returning the sentiment.

"He looks like the devil," she said.

"My daughter says that, too."

"Is he a pet?"

"Just a friend."

"He's a strange friend."

"Old men have strange friends."

Jodi turned toward the crime scene, arms crossed. "Well, like I said; he must be their king or something because he was herding the others over the bones of the kitten. I would have never looked over there if it hadn't been for him."

Joe Mac turned stiffly from the scene. "Take me home, if you would. Crime Scene can handle this without us. I want to check on Pamela before it gets too late."

"Sure."

As Joe Mac turned, the raven lifted off, and Jodi kept glancing up to see it circling them as they meandered across the field and through the woods and into the parking lot. And when they reached her vehicle, the raven came down with a formidable, utterly unafraid descent to land solidly on the roof of the squad car.

For the first time since she'd met him, Jodi saw Joe Mac smile. He reached up with his free left hand, and the enormous raven took two fearless steps toward him and hopped onto his forearm with a steel-vice grip. It bent its fearsome head – its hooked beak seemed sharp as black iron and much more frightening up close – and Joe Mac affectionately smoothed the glossy blue-black feathers.

"Go on," said Joe Mac.

At the words the gigantic raven erupted into the sky with a grace and fearlessness that struck Jodi with instinctive amazement. She had never seen such a powerful creature explode upward with such utter confidence and grace. She muttered, "You two really are friends, aren't you?" She realized she was gaping. "Did you say he's a wild raven?"

"He comes when he wants. Goes when he wants. Seems pretty wild to me."

"And he's not scared of people?"

Joe Mac opened his door. "Why would he be scared of people? You can't even get close to him unless he lets you."

With a grunt, Jodi opened the door.

"Yeah. I wouldn't be scared of anything, either."

* * *

Jodi waited at the entrance of Joe Mac's humble barn as he tapped a path back from his daughter's house. She wasn't surprised that the crow – wait, it was a raven – had circled over Joe Mac all the way over there and all the way back. What surprised her was that the raven seemed to have identified her individual car and could determine the difference between her squad car and all the other squad cars cruising to and from the crime scene.

Joe Mac stopped at the door and turned.

Jodi asked, "How's she doing?"

"She's been sleeping. It's gonna take her a long time." He felt for the lock using his forefinger as a key-guide. "They say you don't ever get over it. One day you just get up and start moving. But when you bury a child a part of your heart crawls down in that grave with 'em and stays there."

"Yeah," Jodi responded. "I lost a brother. But I know it's not the same. Not even close. Nothing compares to losing a child."

"Sorry about your brother."

"So am I. Drugs. We let him down, I guess. The whole family."

Joe Mac opened the barn door. "Come on. I'll make you some coffee. I learned how to do all that stuff where they rehab blind people."

"Fancy."

"Nuthin' but the good life."

Entering what was obviously a revamped barn Jodi saw – with a single glance – a recliner, a double bed, a plate of food on a small kitchen table, and Joe Mac's entire wardrobe strung along the far wall; it was a typical barn layout with added shelves and a bathroom slapped onto the back.

"You like to keep things simple, huh?" she asked.

"I got a roof. I got food. I got a bed. What more do I need?"

He began to clang around in his kitchenette as Jodi lifted and opened a lawn chair. She didn't feel the need to inform him that he only had one recliner. He knew, anyway, so she could deal with it if he could. She asked, "How come you were never assigned to this case? Seems like you would have been chief investigator for a serial killer like this."

"He wasn't killing people back then," Joe Mac called. "I retired six years ago. Back then he wasn't even a blip on the screen. It was only after I got hurt and put out to pasture that he started racking up a body count." He pulled two cups off a plywood board. "You bring the file in from the car?"

"It's right here."

"I want you to read it to me."

"The whole thing?"

"The whole thing."

"So you're gonna lend me a hand, Joe?"

He turned. Stared. "I guess that's up to you. I want to find who killed my grandson. And I can't do it by myself." Jodi saw a deep pain solidify his face. "I don't think nobody else would have me, no way."

Jodi felt a grimace. "Well, I think you've still got a few good moves left in you – you and your buddy. What's his name?"

"Poe."

"Yeah. Poe. What do you say we team up? We don't wanna leave Poe behind, do we?" She laughed. "I mean, he came in handy today, didn't he? Who knows?"

She meant it as a joke but wasn't surprised that Joe Mac didn't laugh. "Yeah," he said. "Who knows? Crème and sugar?"

"Plenty of both. Still got your gun?"

At that he did laugh and turned back to the coffee. "Why? You want me to carry? You can just tell me to shoot high or low."

She sat in the lawn chair and opened the file. "If we find this guy, I'll tell you to shoot high and low and everything in between. Frankly, I think Professor Mason is right. We're gonna have to kill this guy. He's not gonna stop. He's not gonna quit. He's not gonna give up. He'll die first."

"Yep," said Joe Mac. "I've taken down a few like that."

"Did you kill 'em?"

Joe Mac returned with two cups.

"Nobody wants to get planted," he said. "But the truth is that everybody gets what they ask for if they ask long enough. One way or the other."

* * *

It was late when Jodi tiredly finished reading the file, although Joe Mac was leaning forward in his recliner, hands clasped, chin uplifted, jaw set; he seemed as alert now as he had been six hours ago.

"Well, that's it," she said.

Joe Mac muttered, "Sunset."

She blinked. "What?"

"Sunset. You say each child was found shortly after sunset?"

"*Everybody* was found after sunset. And there are twenty-four victims to date. Some are old. Some are middle-aged. Some are kids. Some are men, women. But yeah, they were all found after sunset on the same day they were taken or the next day." Jodi stared over him. "What are you getting at, Joe?"

"But the kids were found immediately after sunset on the same day they were killed, right?"

Jodi considered. "I don't know. I'd need all the files to be sure." She continued staring. "Come on, Joe. What are you getting at? They were all found after sunset. What difference does it make if they were found the same day or the next day?"

Joe Mac was the image of a stone Buddha before he said, "This don't make sense." He was silent. "Serial killers target a specific kind of person. Young girls. Young men. They don't just kill Tom, Dick, and Harry. They have a preferred target. Or they take targets of opportunity. Like kids parking on some deserted dirt road. Or some old person in a nursing home who's already at death's door, and they decide to carry 'em across. But there's never been a case of a serial killer killing everybody that he comes across just because they're there." He paused. "Is that what they assume they're dealing with?"

Blinking slowly, Jodi said, "I haven't read all the files, but, yeah, I think that's what the task force assumes."

"They're wrong," Joe Mac frowned. "This guy ain't gonna break the mold. He has a preferred target. We just don't know what it is."

"So why is he killing every kind of person?" Jodi asked.

"Static."

She gaped and stared. "Static?"

"Yeah. Static. He's killing all kinds of people because he wants to muddy the water." Joe Mac took a long time, breathing deep. "Think of it like this: If this fool targeted old people, then every son and daughter out there would throw up an iron curtain around every old person in the country. If he was targeting young girls, every young girl out there would be carrying a pistol in her purse. Their daddies would make sure of it. If he was targeting four-year-old kids, daycares would be hiring armed guards. Mothers would be carrying shotguns out in the open. He'd never get close to another little kid in his life. Same with the others. It don't matter what group it is. But if his true target was a single group, and he didn't want anyone to know what group that is, then he would just kill all kinds of people. That way nobody would know who to protect. And you can't protect everybody."

"Is that what he's doing?" asked Jodi quietly.

"Yeah,"" Joe Mac nodded slowly. "That's exactly what he's doing."

"How can you be sure?"

"Sometimes you just have to trust your instincts, kid. Proof comes later."

Jodi paused. "So what do we do?"

"We need the files. All of them. Can you get your hands on them?"

Jodi sank back into the lawn chair, blinking. "Uh … well, I'm not on the task force. I'd have to go to Brightbarton and … and I've only been a detective for three days, Joe. I seriously doubt that he's going to let me see the case files."

"You found the cat, didn't you?"

"Well, yeah, but …"

"We'll go to him in the morning."

"Have you seriously considered the possibility that he might just be killing people at random?" Jodi offered. "I mean, wouldn't that be kind of diabolical? He doesn't kill anybody he knows. He doesn't really have a motive. He doesn't take anything, doesn't leave anything. He'd be almost impossible to catch."

Joe Mac's jaw tightened. "I don't believe in random any more than I believe in 'evil for no reason.' There's *always* a reason. It might be subconscious. But there's always a reason. There's always a motive. We just gotta figure out what it is." His breathing was measured and deep. "Who found the bodies?"

"How would I know?" Jodi closed the file. "Joe, you're asking me about all of the cases and I don't have all the case files. I do know that somebody anonymously called in the location of Aaron's body. That's how we found him so fast."

"The killer called it in because he wanted him found right after sunset." Joe Mac's frown deepened. "For some reason, it was important to him."

"Joe, you're making leaps in logic that I can't keep up with. We don't know that the killer called it in. You're assuming that, and you just told me to never assume anything."

"I also told you to trust your instincts."

"*Logic* is better than instinct, Joe. You can't prove instinct in court. You can't get a search warrant with instinct." Jodi leaned forward, concentrating her tone, "You can't get a *conviction* with instinct."

"Yeah. What do I know? Thirty-five years on the job. Solved a thousand homicides. How many hours, now, you been a junior detective?"

Jodi blew out a long breath. "Fine. But we don't have enough information to make any moves. We need the files. All of them. Instinct or not."

"The captain can give 'em to us."

"But will he?" Brightbarton didn't say anything about us attending the briefing, but what is he going to say when I tell him I want to be on the task force? I've been a detective for, like, *five minutes*. He'll laugh me out of his office."

"You found those footprints, didn't you? He's probably going to thank you and give you whatever you want."

"Yeah. Right." Jodi ran her hair back. "Okay, Joe, I'm going home. I'll pick you up at lunch. Then we'll go to Brightbarton and ask for the files and hope he doesn't die laughing."

"All right."

She stood lifting the file, her purse.

"Joe," she said wearily, "why are you doing this? I mean, I know Aaron was your grandson, and you probably loved him more than your own life. And, yeah, you were a great detective. And you still are. But back then you could defend yourself when you were on top of a bad guy, and now you're blind. And you gotta know this psycho is gonna come after us if he thinks we're closing in on him. So tell me, do you have a death wish?"

Joe Mac laughed, "A death wish? Never thought of it like that."

"Well?" Jodi paused. "Do you?"

"I ain't in no hurry to stay," said Joe Mac. "I ain't in no hurry to leave. That's it, I guess."

Jodi turned toward the door.

"*This* is gonna be a lot of fun."

* * *

Outside, Jodi walked in a daze of exhaustion and, for no reason she understood, glanced up at the tree beside her car. She was either too tired to care or some part of her simply expected it, but she felt no surprise to see the raven sitting on a branch.

Wide awake, it was staring down, and in the light of the moon Jodi suddenly and truly appreciated the enormous size and sheer beauty and strength of the majestic wings, the regal bent of its head, its proud breast. She appreciated the awesome power and unbroken will that emanated from it in a darkness deeper than the night.

"Hey, Poe," she smiled wanly. "Your buddy can't see his hand in front of his face. But you can see forever, can't you?"

She pulled open the door and Poe didn't move and she paused, one foot inside, a hand on top of the car, gazing at the Maltese image.

"You do look like the devil," she said quietly. "But this guy's the real thing. Can you see that, too?"

The raven stared.

* * *

Murder was such a simple thing.

Kidnapping was far more complicated because the risk of witnesses increased deplorably with each moment it took him to disorient, secure, and carry his victim to the vehicle and put them in the trunk. And each second that he did not absolutely control contained chance. And he hated chance.

He slowly, quietly crept down the side of the elderly man's house, his outline hidden from the road by high hedges that the man grew along the wall. If the old man had been more careful about his life, he would have cut the hedges to the ground; they were a burglar's dream. But the old man was not cautious.

Although it had only been a week since he killed the little boy, he felt it was prudent to kill again as soon as possible for two reasons.

First, he had been killing at an almost regular rate of one victim per month, and no pattern was good. It might inadvertently reveal something about his routine – maybe even something subconscious. So if he killed again within two weeks it would force the FBI profilers to reconfigure their psychological profile of him, and that alteration possessed no down side. The more wrinkles he could throw into their profile, the better. Second, he needed to insert as many variations into his missions as possible as quickly as possible. That would be another wrinkle the FBI profilers wouldn't like but couldn't dismiss.

The old man slowly rose from his recliner and slowly approached the door when the bell sounded. He casually approached the foyer without a weapon. He was obviously off-guard, relaxed and confident inside his own home. Then he answered the door, and the man simply stepped forward to punch the taser into his chest.

With a shout the old man fell.

He casually stepped over the body and closed the door. It took five seconds to zip-lock the old man's hands behind his back. Then he duct-taped his mouth and zip-locked his ankles. After that he straightened, staring around. He took a minute to study his surroundings recalling the rules; *take nothing, leave nothing* ...

He was not concerned about fibers he might take with him on his clothing or shoes. As usual, he would destroy his shoes and clothing in the stolen vehicle when he torched it. Then he would put on clean clothes and take his secondary vehicle.

Before the night was done, he would drive into the short-term parking garage at the airport where restricted air space prevented police or FBI helicopters from following. Then he would switch to his third vehicle – his primary vehicle – and begin sanitation procedures to insure he was alone.

Only then would he begin home.

He bent and effortlessly lifted the old man onto his shoulder. The stolen LTD was within twenty feet of the door. He checked for witnesses, saw none, and walked swiftly forward. He roughly dumped the old man in the trunk, slammed the lid, and in twenty seconds was cruising at a slow and lawful speed.

He had purposely left the front door ajar; he wanted this discovered as quickly as possible. It would frustrate the FBI, and it would divert attention from the murder of the little boy. And if no one was Good Samaritan enough to check on the old geezer's welfare then he would call the police himself with another anonymous report.

Forbidding the unpredictable, he would reach his destination within the hour, and this one would be dead within another hour. Simple as that.

A little work, a little sweat, and it was done.

And he would be home before sunrise.

Nothing to it.

THREE

"What do you mean we don't have the same files as the FBI?"

Expressing her anger with career-ending courage, Jodi wasn't hesitating to vent her indignation to Captain Steve Brightbarton, chief of the NYPD task force assigned the solemn duty of apprehending "The Hangman."

Jodi had picked Joe Mac up with lunch, and they arrived at the station within the hour. After familiar greetings were exchanged between Joe Mac and Brightbarton, the captain invited them into his office where Jodi took the fore and asked Brightbarton if they could be attached to the task force.

To Jodi's surprise Brightbarton readily admitted that they'd earned a place on the team when they found the shoe prints. Jodi didn't tell him that they'd have never found a thing but for the assistance of a very strange bird.

Jodi continued, "Do you mean to tell me that the FBI files are better than our own files of our own murders?" Brightbarton began to reply before she added, "Is that even legal, captain? Can they even do that to us?"

"Of course they can do that to us, junior," Brightbarton replied in a weary monotone. "They're the FBI. They can do anything they want. And where is it written that they have to share every piece of intelligence with us, anyway?" He gestured toward the "war room." "They don't share everything with us. We don't share everything with them. That's just the way it works. Always has. Always will."

Jodi stood with one arm akimbo. "What happened to 'working together?'"

"We work together, yeah, but they don't absolutely trust us, and we don't trust them *at all*, so we're always playing this game." There was a pause and Joe Mac felt the captain's stare. "Been a while, Joe," he said finally. "I meant to come out and see you a few times but ... you know how it is."

"Yeah," Joe Mac stated, flat. "I know. So when did they give this to you?"

"About a year ago."

"Gonna see it through?"

"I doubt it. I got two more months before I've got my thirty-five. Then color me gone, baby. Florida here I come. Warm weather. Umbrella drinks. Naked women. I'll take it all day long. And I ain't *never* coming back to this town."

"The good life, huh?"

"At least it'll be better than *this* life." He paused. "So what are you doing with junior, here?"

Joe Mac motioned to Jodi. "She told you. She took the missing person report on my grandson, and she wants to follow up." He shrugged. "I figured I'd ride along. Maybe offer a little advice. What's the harm?"

A long silence.

"That's it, huh? How come I don't believe you?"

"What else can I do but give advice?" asked Joe Mac. "You know I'm blind as a bat. I can't carry a gun. I don't have arrest powers. I'm not even bonded anymore. All I can do is sit and listen and tell her what I think."

"Can't she just call you at the end of the day? Like Dear Abby?"

"It won't hurt nuthin' for me to ride along with her, Steve. And you know how it works. Sometimes you have to be there."

Brightbarton's laugh was tragic. "You have no idea what you're asking, buddy. You honest-to-god have no idea."

"Why don't you tell me?"

There was a shifting; Brightbarton had leaned forward. "All right, Joe. Listen up. This guy ain't no joke. Not even the FBI is willing to send normal agents after him. They're gonna send Hostage Rescue if they ever have him cornered. You listening?"

"I'm listening."

"So what are you gonna do if you stumble into him? I don't know if you've checked lately, but you're *blind*, Joe. This guy could pull out a piece, walk right up to your face, and blow you away, and you wouldn't even see it coming. Or are you gonna put your life in the very uncertain hands of Little Ms. Junior Detective, here, who's never been in a gunfight in her entire life?" Brightbarton shifted. "Have you ever even *pulled* your gun, Jodi?"

"Well, I –"

"No! You haven't!" Brightbarton answered. "I checked with your supervisor! You've mostly been doing paperwork for the goons downtown."

"I don't plan for us to get that close to him," said Joe Mac. "If I get a feeling, I'll call you, and you can send SWAT."

Brightbarton made a sucking sound with his teeth before he stood and walked around to the front of the desk. "You know that's not the point, Joe. The point is that you're asking for my blessing to go after this guy. And this psycho makes Charles Manson look like Billy Graham. He'll come at you with a gun, a hammer, and a noose. And what you got? You got an old blind man's cane. That's all you got. And I wouldn't exactly call that a fair fight. And you say you're just here to observe? Well what if he don't care if you're just here to observe? What if he takes it kinda *personal* that you're looking to plant him?"

Brightbarton cursed before adding, "Son, you need to get it straight who you're dealing with before you put *her* life in danger. This guy is The Devil! One of his victims was a six-month-old baby boy! And you expect me to let you, a blind man who can't find his face with a map, wander around asking questions about where to find Satan himself?

Don't you care about living or dying? Don't you know what this psychopath will do if he thinks you're on his trail? If he doesn't kill you outright – which he ain't gonna do! – he'll break every bone in your body and hang you from the neck until … *you … are … dead.* And there's not a thing you'll be able to do about it! You'll be at his mercy. And this guy can't *spell* 'mercy.'"

"You've read all the files?" asked Joe Mac.

"Yeah, yeah," Brightbarton leaned back against the desk. "I read every one of them a thousand times. I take my job seriously."

"What else can you tell me?"

Brightbarton replied with unconcealed frustration; "So you don't intend to take my advice? You intend to go after this guy, anyway?"

"I guess so."

"Well you're gonna die, Joe."

"Everybody dies."

"Yeah, but not everybody gets in line for it."

"So what else you got?"

With a tired sigh Brightbarton continued, "You were at the briefing. I can't add anything to it. He's in his mid-thirties. He's white. He's smart. He's strong. He doesn't take anything. Doesn't leave anything. We got no clues, hairs, or fibers. He doesn't have any motive that we can understand. He doesn't seem to be associated with any of the victims in any way. He uses a different car, a different disguise every time. We find the cars later, but he torches them, so we don't have any prints or DNA. He kills old people, young people, black, white. He seems to choose victims at random, so we can't predict where he's gonna strike next. There's no pattern that we can see."

"Were all the victims found shortly after sunset?" asked Joe Mac.

"Not all of them. Some weren't found 'till the next day. But we've thought about that connection with sunset, and

I don't think it means anything. It just took longer to find some than it took to find others. That archeologist seems to think religion has something to do with it but, personally, I think he's just an overdressed bookend. He doesn't know any more about how to be a detective than Little Ms. Moffat, here."

Joe Mac heard a step in the door as Brightbarton said, "Hey, Jack."

FBI Special Agent Jack Rollins replied, "Sorry, captain, I didn't know you were busy."

"That's all right. What can I do for you?"

"We got another one," said Rollins.

Brightbarton hesitated. "Another kid?"

"No, I understand it's an old man. But he was killed the same way. Bones broken, and then he was hung in a tree. It's way north of the city, so the state has jurisdiction. But it's one of ours, for sure. I'll have a file for you by the end of the day."

"All right," said Brightbarton. Then he added, "Jack, I want to introduce you to Detective Jodi Strong. She's an addition to the NYPD task force."

There was a significant pause before Rollins remarked, "Welcome to the team, Detective Strong."

"Jodi."

"Jodi. Just call me Jack."

Jodi must have nodded because she said nothing. Then Brightbarton added, "And this is an old friend of mine, Joe Mac Blake. Joe was the best homicide man this city ever had – the best homicide man *any* city's ever had." He grunted softly, "Joe's retired – a line-of-duty incident, but we think he might be able to help out as an advisor."

Rollins must have been staring, but Joe Mac wasn't certain until the FBI man said, "Welcome you to the team, Joe. I don't mean to use a cliché, but it's never been more true than now: We need all the help we can get."

"We won't get in your way," said Joe Mac.

"Don't worry about it. If there's anything I can do for you, let me know." There was a faint shuffling in the door. "I'll get that file for you, Steve."

"One question," said Joe Mac.

Rollins answered, "Yes?"

"Can you set us up a meeting with that professor of archeology?"

"Of course. When?"

"Soon as possible?"

"Sure. I'll call Detective Strong's cell when I've got a time." A pause; clothes rustling. "Jodi. Joe. Be careful."

"Thanks, Jack," said Jodi.

He was gone.

Nobody spoke for five seconds, and Joe Mac was carefully following every conversation up and down the hallway to make sure – as much as possible – that the FBI agent had truly departed. Finally, Brightbarton said, "What was that, Joe? I just told you that that egghead is useless."

Joe Mac considered his words and said, "I don't know. There's something about what he said." He paused. "Or didn't say. I want to talk to him."

"About what?"

"I'm thinking that he might be onto something. I just don't know what it is." Joe Mac turned his face to the side as if he were watching. Then he said, "We need the files." A pause. "And we need a desk."

Brightbarton stood, and Joe Mac heard him lift a box; he set it down solid. "Here's copies of everything, Strong. Good luck. You can use Sanders's old office. Turn left out the door. Second door on the right." He sniffed. "All I can say is this guy's a ghost. Personally, I think he's got specialized training. Probably Rangers. Special Forces. Delta. Who knows?"

Joe Mac said nothing, but then realized that his image must be far more disturbing than he knew because Jodi asked, "Joe? What's wrong?"

"I'm thinking he's too good," said Joe Mac.

Stillness lasted until Jodi asked, "Are you thinking he might be a cop?"

Joe Mac frowned, "He's somewhere in the floor plan. And I don't think we're going to catch him by chasing him. We're gonna have to figure out where he's going next and lay up for him. That's why we gotta figure out what his motive is. When we understand why he's choosing them, we'll catch him."

Brightbarton muttered, "Joe, we've looked for motive a million times, and all we've come up with are a lot of hair-brained theories with nothing to show for it. Now, I'm sure he does have *some* kind of crazy motive. But it's incomprehensible."

"Nah, we just don't comprehend it *yet*." With each breath, Joe Mac was feeling more at home. "Have you cross-checked the victims?"

"Son, the computers have cross-checked *everything*."

Brightbarton sat; "There's nothing that links them, and we have, believe me, cross-checked where they shopped, where they got their food, their clothes, their insurance, their groceries. We've looked at where they bought their pillows and pets and everything else they ever bought. We checked their phones and computers for possible links and came up with nothing. We checked anniversaries and parents and genealogies and every other thing. Some went to church, but some didn't. There's no thread that ties them together except for the fact that they were all on this guy's list." He took a moment. "I can't figure it unless he's just picking them at random. And that means his next victim could be anybody at any place at any time and that's gonna be a nightmare."

He was quiet before he exclaimed, "What am I saying? It's *already* a nightmare. We might as well tell everybody out there to just carry a gun wherever they go. And that would include everywhere they go *inside* their own house because this guy could be your husband, and some poor wife won't have a clue."

Joe Mac stood. "You ready, kid?"

"I'm ready." Jodi walked to the desk, and Joe Mac heard her grunt as she lifted the box. He knew it was a lot heavier than most people would suspect.

Jodi walked past him.

"No, thanks. I got this."

"I'm blind."

"And crippled, too. Yeah, I can see that."

* * *

Sanders had understandably left almost everything in his office.

Joe Mac didn't blame him. Sanders had been looking at this office every day for the last twenty years. Now that he had reached the age of blessed retirement, he didn't want a single thing in his new life to remind him of the old. He wanted to make as clean a break from police work as possible in both his world and mind.

"At least he didn't leave his gun and badge," Jodi remarked as she methodically unloaded the box.

"Nah," said Joe Mac, "your gun and badge is cut and dried. There's a little man at a desk in an empty room. You hand him your badge. He tosses it in a cardboard box. Then, if you want, you can keep your leather and your piece. You just have to pay for it. He takes two minutes to explain your pension and benefits and that's it."

"No going away party?"

"Not even a watch."

"What'd they give you after thirty-five years on the job and being injured and losing your eyesight?"

"A ride home."

"Pigs."

Her cell phone rang, and she answered. "Strong." There was a moment before she replied, "Right. Five o'clock at the museum. We'll be there. Thanks, Rollins. Yeah, we'll let you know what we get. Later."

Joe Mac lifted his head and found the scents and sounds of the building more familiar than the scents and sounds of his own home. But that wasn't hard to understand. He had spent far more time in this building over the past thirty-five years than any home he'd ever had. In a sense this building *was* his home. And he discovered himself following every conversation hovering in the open door with a sense of déjà vu.

If he'd been in on the discussion, he could have advised them on the best judge for the case and what to expect from forensics. He could have told them what the CODIS used by the FBI was likely to contain in terms of DNA. He could have told them what the Shooting Review Board was going to say over a rookie shooting his daughter dead when she came home in the middle of the night, surprising him. He had been in on all these conversations a million times. He'd worked a thousand shootings involving rookies and veterans, and he could almost predict the Review Board's decision for any crisis that might come down the pike. But he was getting distracted by problems flowing through the door and reined in his mind.

"What do you see?" Joe Mac asked; he had taken a seat in a folding chair, and Jodi was sitting at the desk.

"I'm looking through these files to see how many of these were reported by anonymous callers," Jodi answered. "It looks like fifteen were reported by whom we assume is the killer since he wouldn't leave his name. The rest were reported by family or strangers who obliged us with their names and addresses, so I guess you're right. If they're not found fast enough, he calls it in."

"Separate the ones that weren't hung from a tree."

"I already have. Four weren't hung."

"That's not what I said."

She paused. "Then what did you say?"

"I said to separate the ones that weren't hung from 'a tree.'"

With an audible sigh, she began sifted through files, rattling pages with the sound of rapid searching and reading. After only one minute she said, "Okay. Seven of these were hung from beams, rafters, or steel girders located inside or outside warehouses, old buildings, condemned houses – places like that. No real pattern that I see. Oh, and one was hung from a chandelier. That's fancy." She hesitated. "That means sixteen were hung from trees."

"What about the children?"

"All the children were hung from trees."

"You already checked, huh?"

"First thing I did." Jodi leaned back in Sanders's creaky old chair. After a moment, she said, "So you think this guy is hiding his true motivation – which is to kill an unknown but particular group – by killing all the rest of these folks, too? And that's why he didn't bother to hang every single one of them from a tree? He just wanted to hang them as quick as he could and get out of there to confuse us?"

"It's an idea," Joe Mac answered with a ponderous tone. "What other groups were hung from a tree?"

Joe Mac waited until she said, "Okay. All the black males. All the women. All the children. All the white males under the age of thirty-three. So it could be any one of those groups. It can't be the older white males because those are the ones he hung from any convenient pillar or post."

"All right," Joe Mac murmured. "That gives us a place to start."

"Joe, I respect you, but that's all this is – a pretty lame place to start. In these files, there is absolutely nothing to back up this idea." She paused and Joe Mac could imagine her turning the chair, so she could gaze out the window. "Where are we even gonna begin looking for this guy? He could be anywhere!"

"Motive," said Joe Mac. "We need a motive."

"Joe," said Jodi with exasperation, "this guy's motive is nowhere in sight. We only know that he broke their bones and hung them and that goes about as far as a flying ashtray when it comes to motive." She muttered something indistinct before, "Okay, so it's a "religious" motive. But Good God! There's a by-god-zillion religious motivations and psychoses and pathological religious reasons to kill someone if that's what cranks your tractor. *That* doesn't get us anywhere, either."

"First, we find out *why* he selected them. Then we find out *how* he selected them, and when we find that we'll find *him*."

"Yeah, yeah, Joe, you keep saying that. But so what if we understand that his motive is religious? What does that get us? It could still be one of a zillion people with a bazillion different religious motives. Like this guy is the only religious nutcase in town? Have you been to a mental asylum lately? *Everybody* in there is religious! They're also crazy as a soup sandwich! Determining that this guy is selecting people because he has a religious psychosis is not what I would call progress."

"We'll see," said Joe Mac. "What time is it?"

"It's time," said Jodi. "Let's go to the museum and see what kind of dead end *this* egghead can lead us down."

* * *

Although she had been here a dozen times, Jodi was always impressed by the New York City Museum of Natural History.

It was a colossal monument to Greek architecture – a work of art in itself – with an aura of genius in the exacting precision of the stonework, the commanding colonnades, the wide, welcoming steps that led to majestic twin doors twenty feet high. It was wired with every alarm system known to mankind, although Jodi could think of nothing anyone would be likely to steal from this cavernous repository of petrified bone, prehistoric images of *Homo sapiens* along with uncountable dinosaur relics and more.

There were vast ethnographic and archeological collections that boggled the mind plus examples of textiles, coinages, thrones, headdresses, weapons, shields and every other remnant portraying the evolution of the human civilization.

Some of the hypothetical archeological displays revealed highly evolved civilizations that virtually dominated the Earth, and yet nothing was known of them. The only clues that existed were tidbits of steel weaponry discovered more than three thousand years before the Hittites popularly invented steel in Palestine. And one mysterious civilization – a kingdom which even now remained unnamed – had discovered the secrets of creating glass, of hot and cold running water, of determining the dates of droughts or monsoons by the mere rotation of the Earth and stars more than 6 thousand years BC. And Jodi herself had been stunned to see the fossilized footprint of some type of humanoid being that radiocarbon-dated to 420 million years BC. Before that eye-opener, she thought – like most people – that Australopithecus, man's earliest ancestor, dated to a mere 4 million BC. It had been a moment when Jodi accepted the fact that science knew virtually nothing. Instead, science was just a constant unfolding of inexplicable fossils and "gravitrons" and every new "discovery" only led to another mystery.

Gently guiding Joe Mac's left elbow, Jodi mounted the long-ranging steps of the museum and walked through the outer doors; there was another set of metal doors that were shut at night but were open during the day. Then they were inside the castle-like hall of the edifice, and Jodi recognized Marvin Mason, the young archeologist, as he approached with what seemed a genuine smile.

Jodi shook his hand.

"Thank you for coming," Marvin said. "Why don't we talk in my office?"

"That'd be great," Jodi nodded.

It took a surprising fifteen minutes to negotiate the maze of overpacked closets, lockers, and hallways – Jodi understood quickly that the geniuses behind all this science cared very little for fancy offices – to finally sit down with Marvin in what Jodi would have otherwise guessed to be the basement.

She gazed over the surroundings. "So this is your office, huh? I hate to say it, but it looks more like a warehouse for petrified dino bones."

Marvin laughed, "That's actually what it is." He shrugged, "I'm not far enough up the pyramid to merit a grown-up office. But, in a few years, who knows? I'll probably get a real desk instead of a sheet of plywood and two sawhorses."

"I guess all the money is out front?"

"Yeah." Marvin leaned back in his chair. "The board is dedicated to putting out the best displays, research projects, books, and whatever else for the public. And that doesn't leave much for desks or – to be honest – a decent salary. You'd probably be shocked at how much money I don't make."

"Believe me, I'm a cop; I wouldn't be shocked."

Jodi noticed that Joe Mac had somehow found a chair by himself and was sitting and listening with that now-familiar rapt expression – chin up, dark glasses aimed vaguely at the ceiling, both hands lightly clutching his walking stick in front of his barrel chest. She added, "This is Detective Joe Mac. He's an advisor, so that makes him a lot like you, I guess."

Marvin said politely, "Hello, Detective Joe."

Joe Mac nodded.

Jodi: "Marvin, you said that these murders are like the historical murders of various cults. Can you explain that to me with a little more detail?"

"Sure," Marvin answered. "First, executing someone by beating them and hanging them by the neck has been done by, well, practically every religion and cult that has ever existed. That's why I can't single out any one of them. It's so thoroughly prevalent throughout history that it's practically ubiquitous."

Jodi asked, "Well that doesn't get us anywhere, does it?"

It wasn't really a question.

"Nope," said Marvin. "It doesn't. I'm sorry."

"So what can you tell me that might be useful?"

By Marvin's expression he was taken off-guard by the question. His eyes wandered to the left, right, and back again before he said, "I don't really know, Jodi. From all I've seen this could be the work of some Judaic sect or a form of execution used by the Druids or some other ancient Gaelic group. It might even be an old Irish punishment. I mean, I'm sorry, but to ask me to single out any particular group is like asking me to tell you who invented the wheel." He stared. "I have no idea."

This was going even worse than Jodi had feared, and her hopes had been pitifully low to begin with. She glanced at Joe Mac just as he shifted, aiming his face fully toward Marvin. "Talk to me about the sunset," said Joe Mac. "Why is it important for someone to be hung from a tree after sunset?"

Marvin seemed happy to finally have an answer as he said, "Ah, yes. Practically every culture that has ever existed has believed that hanging someone in a tree past sunset would curse them in the next world. The Greeks, Romans, Gaelic tribes, Jews – they all believed that." He seemed unable to stop himself from adding, "People think the Romans weren't superstitious. But the truth is the Romans were ridiculously superstitious. Yeah, they would hang people from a tree to curse their immortal souls. They would bury human sacrifices *alive* in the Forum Boarium to appease their various deities. The Roman army even carried sacred chicken coops into battle, so that auguries could interpret victory or defeat from the grain that fell from the mouths of hens. You don't call *that* superstitious?"

"That's very interesting, Marvin," said Jodi, "but let's try and stay on-point, shall we?"

Marvin's mouth quirked. "Sorry."

"It's all right. Let's get back to this superstition about being hung from a tree after sunset. You say the purpose was to curse someone?"

"Right."

"To curse his *soul*?" asked Joe Mac.

"Or his spirit," Marvin answered in an abruptly vague tone. "Or his chance of life in the next world. Actually, we're not sure. The only reason we even know it was a curse is because the ancient Jews recorded that much in their letters. And there's also evidence to believe that the Druids did it to curse someone's soul. Or spirit. But the Druid evidence is a lot less definitive." He paused. "*A lot less.*"

Joe Mac suddenly frowned as if he'd found a clue. "Didn't the Jews and the Druids live a pretty long way from each other?"

"Oh, yeah. Two thousand miles. At least."

Joe Mac leaned slightly forward. "So why do you think they both thought hanging someone from a tree after sunset would curse them in the next world?"

"Well, we don't know exactly *why*," Marvin stated with decidedly less conviction. "The Druids never wrote anything down, so we don't know all that much about them. Their beliefs, their rituals, their social structure, their entire culture was passed down by oral tradition. It supposedly took someone years to memorize it. But since they wrote nothing, they left us with nothing to study so we've got a whole lot of questions and not a whole lot of answers."

"That's not exactly correct, Mr. Mason," announced a voice from the doorway. "Answers may be written with bone as eloquently as with a pen."

Jodi turned to see a man enter the office. He was well over six feet tall, maybe two hundred pounds. His jet-black hair was aristocrat-white at the temples and his face was aquiline and severe. His blue eyes scintillated in the half-light of Marvin's basement, and he had the comport of a king. He nodded courteously at Jodi and waited, hands close to his sides; his effortlessly perfect poise indicated refined training at a very young age. In fact, everything about him hinted at a privileged upbringing and superior intelligence.

"Oh, hello, Professor Graven," Mason said as he stood. He extended a hand toward Jodi. "Let me introduce you to Detective Jodi Strong and Detective Joe Mac. They've been assigned to the task force."

Professor Graven beamed as Jodi rose and extended her hand. He held it gently but firmly for a moment; "I am pleased to meet you, Detective Strong, Detective Joe Mac. I am Augustus Graven, director."

"Nice to meet you," Joe Mac nodded "I'm just tagging along with Detective Strong, there, in her investigation."

"Excellent," said Professor Graven. "We are always available to assist the police." His brow hardened. "But, unfortunately, I'm not certain at all that we've proven ourselves useful in this matter."

"You're the head honcho?" asked Joe Mac.

"In a manner of speaking," Professor Graven smiled. "But in my current position I do far more bookkeeping than science. In fact, it's been years since I've chaired a research project. Now I am mostly a glorified fundraiser."

"We were discussing a possible motive for this serial killer, professor," said Marvin. "Would you like to contribute? The detectives think that if they can understand the killer's motive they'll be closer to catching him."

Professor Graven slowly nodded with a frown. "Perhaps. What motive are you considering?"

Marvin: "I've been suggesting that the killer's motive is almost certainly religious in nature because almost all the victims were hung from a tree after sunset. All their bones were broken, and both these things are historically associated with religious execution."

"Were all the victims Jewish?"

"Uh, no. About a third of them."

Professor Graven regarded Jodi with something akin to compassion as he said, "If that's the direction you're taking, Detective Strong, have you and Detective Joe Mac considered members of Jewish ethnicity?"

"Actually," Marvin muttered, "I was about to suggest the Druids."

"Oh," Professor Graven gestured, "forgive me. Please, proceed."

Glancing over all of them, Marvin continued, "As I was saying; Ancient Israel hung people after sunset to curse them. But they didn't always break all their bones, so it doesn't completely fit. The Druids, however, did both on a much more consistent basis. They'd almost always break a victim's bones and then hang them before they finished them off."

"Hmm," mused Professor Graven, "that's an intriguing theory, Dr. Mason. But it involves an inference that may not be correct. We do know without question that the Druids were a singularly savage lot who practiced shockingly barbaric forms of execution. But we don't know whether they did it on a consistent basis."

Swiveling in his chair, Marvin reached over and removed a large book from a shelf as he said, "Of course you're right, professor. I was only referencing the pictographs Crawford discovered in his dig at Boshov that showed Druids breaking a victim's bones and then hanging them from a tree. They're unlike anything I've ever –"

"Yes, you're correct," Professor Graven nodded. "I'm familiar with Crawford's discovery. It is quite fascinating. But I'm not certain about his inferences. A single pictograph is not enough to denote a consistent practice. Or even a consistent belief. I would be a bit more recalcitrant about making conclusions until more evidence is unearthed."

Marvin half-tilted his head to the side, then focused on Jodi. "Well, to be more accurate, detective, everything I'm telling you is just 'a best guess.' But if the Druids did regularly break someone's bones and then hung them from a tree until the sun went down, it would be consistent with other ancient civilizations who did the same things for the same reasons." He glanced at the professor. "The only civilization that consistently wrote down the full-blown rules of their history and culture were the Israelites. And even they were a bit vague about certain things of major importance. For instance, we don't know when Israel immigrated from Egypt into Palestine. They wrote about it, but they didn't write down the name of the Pharaoh at the time of the Exodus. And nobody has ever definitively nailed it down." He shrugged, lifting both hands. "Ancient history is as much guesswork as provable fact."

"To expatiate on that critical point," Professor Graven began, "history is often nothing more than interpreting the meaning of material that has accidentally survived a great deal of rain and dirt, so archeologists are very wary about drawing conclusions."

Jodi asked, "So if what you do is mostly guesswork, why is the FBI even using you to draw a psychological profile?"

"I honestly don't know," Marvin responded instantly and – Jodi had to admit – humbly. He added, "All I know is that the FBI came to me for advice and who's gonna say 'no' to the FBI?"

Joe Mac asked impatiently, "What significance is there in beating someone or breaking someone's bones? Historically speaking, that is."

Professor Graven: "Various scraps of historical Roman literature claim that breaking someone's bones would cripple them in the next world just as hanging them from a tree until sunset would curse their immortal souls to eternal darkness. And, yes, breaking the bones of the condemned and hanging them from a tree was a belief of the Romans, the Israelites, the Gaelic Empire. All three nations appear to have held identical superstitions."

No one seemed eager to speak.

The professor frowned, "My friends, let me offer you a word of warning. Before you – as investigators – attempt to apply your considerable intelligence to the interpretation of these ancient rituals you must remember that our modern modes of regarding punishment or death or sacrifice or right or wrong cannot be applied to the primitive mind."

"Why is that?" asked Jodi.

Professor Graven replied without hesitation: "Because the primitive mind was self-possessed within the metaphysical environment of its time and, hence, does not easily lend itself to modern interpretation."

Joe Mac: "Could you give me that in English?"

Professor Graven continued, "Think of it thusly: We are the product of our metaphysical environment and the science in which we live. Likewise, primitive man was also the product of his metaphysical environment and the science in which he lived. But our science would be regarded by primitive man as the forbidden witchcraft of alien beings just as we would regard their science as the barbaric Voodoo of base savages. And just as our science varies greatly from their science, so do our diametrically opposite ideas for what probably constitutes metaphysical truth. Primitive man would have never understood the impotent foolishness of wearing a rosary or worshipping god within a temple or church. And modern man will never understand primitive man's singular devotion to worshipping the moon atop a pyramid of human skulls. In the same way, no modern mind can definitively deduce *why* primitive man practiced human sacrifice. The true motive is quite simply beyond us. It was part of the science of the world in which primitive man lived, and we do not. All we can do is take our best guess as to why he practiced such a thing and hope that further archeological evidence will be discovered to verify our most strenuous attempts at objective analysis. And so, if you are searching *ancient* man's 'motive' for breaking someone's bones and hanging them from a tree to discover a *modern* man's 'motive' for breaking bones and hanging someone from a tree, you have to remember that the motive of the primitive mind and the motive of the modern mind can be diametrically opposite despite the fact that their actions are exactly the same."

There was a pause.

Joe Mac said, "That's English, huh?"

"You did mean to say 'human sacrifice?'" Jodi asked. "Breaking someone's bones and hanging them from a tree was a form of human sacrifice?"

"Yes," Professor Graven answered, "ancient man did practice human sacrifice in such a manner. Archeology can answer that question with a comfortable degree of reliability. But *why* ancient man practiced human sacrifice in such a manner is a question we cannot answer. And that is the answer you seek, is it not? The motive for doing this?"

"Yeah," said Jodi. "What was the motive?"

"It is logical to infer that the motive was to appease a god," said the professor "But gods vary from culture to culture. Nor do we know 'why' it would appease such singular gods. We don't even know *for certain* that appeasing a god had anything to do with it. All we know for certain is that they did these things. The 'motive' is another question entirely, and we don't have a clue what his motive was so if you're searching out the motive of an ancient man to understand the motive of a modern man for doing the very same thing you might want to seriously rethink your investigative technique.

There is simply nothing in psychology or anthropology that would support your approach."

He bowed formally to Jodi, nodded to Marvin. "And now, good friends, if you'll forgive me, I must return to my duties. Dr. Mason, I'm confident you will extend to the detectives every courtesy. And if either of you wish to meet with me at another time please do not hesitate to call. I remain at your service."

Marvin nodded and Graven disappeared into the museum. When he was gone, Marvin said, "Professor Graven is actually the last word on the Druids. And a lot of other things as far as that goes. He's really the one you should be talking to."

"You're doing great, Marvin," Jodi smiled tightly. "So, did the Druids use altars or temples for human sacrifices, or did they just hang everybody from a tree?"

Marvin hesitated. "Why are you so focused on the Druids?"

"Because the Israelites didn't break someone's bones and hang them from a tree with the notion of human sacrifice," Joe Mac stated.

Marvin raised his arm. "But didn't you just listen to what the professor told you about motives? He said —"

"We heard what he said," stated Jodi. "But we gotta work with what we got, ya know? We need a motive whether it's right or wrong because right now we have *nothing*."

Joe Mac enhanced on that; "Listen, Marvin, while the Jews might have beaten people to death or stoned them to death, it was always because they broke some kind of law. It wasn't for the sake of 'murder.' But 'murder' is what this psychopath is doing. He's not 'punishing' people. He's just murdering them."

"How do you know that?" asked Marvin.

"Because these people had nothing in common," answered Joe Mac. "These people had completely different life styles. There is no similarity, no connection, so this is cold-blooded murder. And that's what these Druids did for whatever ungodly motive, so what do you know about the Druids?"

Marvin assumed a dejected aura; "Well, again, we don't know hardly anything about the Druids. And I'm not trying to insult you by being smug or anything." He paused for a breath. "We know that the Druids had what we refer to as 'gathering places.' We don't know what else to call them. But they didn't use altars, so we don't know anything about their ceremonies. We do know they worshipped deep inside forests – something that, incidentally, scared the crap out of the Romans. Anyway, we think the Druids worshipped Nature, so they obviously thought that Nature should be the place where they worshipped. Or so we *presume*." He paused. "Then they were wiped off the face of the earth around forty-two BC by Julius Caesar in a military campaign that stretched from Spain to Great Britain."

Jodi: "You mean none of the ancient Druids survived?"

"Ah, well, there's speculation and ... and *rumors*." Marvin seemed to consider. "Some people believe that a handful of the ancient Druids did survive the massacre of Julius Caesar by hiding out in Ireland. And that theory sort of holds water because the Roman Empire never set foot in Ireland. A lot of historians also speculate that the descendants of those Druids were eventually 'absorbed' by the medieval Knights Templar in Great Britain and had more than a little bit to do with construction of the Rosslyn Chapel. And, not surprisingly, there's substantial archeological evidence to back that up."

"What evidence?"

"Many of the engravings in the Rosslyn Chapel are clearly Nature-based, and the Druids specifically worshipped the gods of Nature." Marvin began counting off his fingers; "There's 'The Lady in the Lake' engraved on a wall of the chapel. And 'The Lady in the Lake' is indisputable proof that the surviving Druids exerted at least *some* influence among the relatively modern Knights Templar. Then there's the 'Green Man.' He was also an ancient Celtic vegetation god – a god of the Druids. And there's the 'Prentice Pillar,' which is basically a string of dragons nibbling at the fruit of the 'Tree of Life,' and that pillar is obviously Druidic. But the most fascinating Druidic influence to me is the –"

"Wait," Joe Mac broke in, "the 'Tree of Life' is in the Bible."

"Yeah," Mason gestured, "but the 'Tree of Life,' was a Druid belief at least three thousand years before the Bible was ever written, so the question becomes: Who stole what from who? You know what I mean?" He pointed to a stack of scrolls. "The Druids predate Israel and the Pentateuch by at least three thousand years. And some very eminent scholars conjecture that they predate Israel by more than *five* thousand years. But, either way, the Druids *theoretically* had an elaborate system of worship way before any other known civilization.

"Most scholars believe the Druids even built Stonehenge." Marvin waved at a stone engraving. "And, for all we know, they did. In fact, everything about the Druids – their belief system, their culture, their gods, their religious rituals, their scientific accomplishments and technology – everything they knew or practiced or passed down from generation to generation in oral tradition was in existence for at least five thousand years before a single letter involving Ra or Shiva or Yahweh or Allah or Zeus was ever written. I mean, the comparatively 'new' religion of the Hebrews might have shocked Egypt when it emerged, but it was just a red-headed stepchild to the ancient Druids. Even Ra, the thousand-year-old god of Egypt when the Israelites migrated to Palestine, was a *recent* development to the Druids." He paused, mouth a tight line before adding, "What I'm trying to say is that the Druids did it *first*. They *invented* the concepts of gods and immortality and human sacrifice and epitaphs and iconography and pictographs. They even invented a calendar based on their religious precepts instead of the moon and stars. But the most fascinating Druidic influence in the Rosslyn Chapel is–"

"Yeah, yeah, I got it," said Jodi. "But you're missing my point, Marvin. Again."

He paused. "What's your point?"

Jodi leaned almost nose to nose. "Marvin, I'm asking you all this because I want to know if there could be some kind of ape-crazy Druid running around killing these people to appease his god. You see what I saying? Appeasing your god is a *motive*, and that's what we're trying to find. If we can find his motive, we can find *him*."

"Oh. Sorry." Marvin straightened and gazed about as if he'd forgotten where he was. "Well, since you ask – yeah, there's a modern version of the Druids that don't make a secret of their existence. But how much they have in common with the ancient Druids is a mystery to me. Most scholars think that modern Druids don't have anything at all to do with the ancient Druids because the knowledge of the old Druids died with them. Sort of like the knowledge we lost when they burned the library at Alexandria, you know? But then some say that the knowledge of the original Druids was preserved within a secret society that stretches all the way back to the days of Julius Caesar. And I've heard it said that this … society … is hidden within the hierarchy of a dozen nations. And only they know who they are."

"What do you think?" asked Jodi.

"Honestly?

"No, Marvin. Lie to me."

"Sorry." Marvin leaned closer. "Okay, I think the secret knowledge of the ancient Druids has been preserved within this society for more than two thousand years. And to even be a part of this society you have to be born into it. I think they're very powerful. They're very rich. And I do mean 'stupid rich.' In fact, they've been ridiculously, filthy, stupid rich since the day they retreated to Ireland. I think that when

Caesar attacked them the Druids just took their wealth, which was literally a mountain of gold, and hid themselves among the royalty of various nations. And since then they've carried on quite comfortably."

"Marvin – Dear Lord – Marvin, is it even *possible* that some modern member of this 'secret society' of ancient Druids has gone completely insane and is killing people in accordance with ancient Druid beliefs to make his god happy?"

"I doubt it."

"Why do you doubt it, Marvin? It's the only thing that makes sense. It's the only thing that might explain why this psycho is killing people in this arcane fashion."

He focused on Jodi's angry face as he added, "Listen, Jodi, you're approaching this from the wrong angle. You're considering all Druids to be ... uh ... 'crazy.' But the Druids were the intellectual elite of the Gaelic Empire. They were revered for their knowledge of science, of politics, and rituals, and gods, and competing mythologies and the science and cultures of bordering nations as far away as Egypt and China and Greenland. They were even renowned for their expertise on war and tactical thinking, so I don't see how any 'modern Druid' would allow himself to go insane and start killing people for no reason! Just like I don't see how a society as intelligent as the Druids could have been wiped out by something so primitive as a military campaign orchestrated by that egomaniac Julius Caesar. I think the Druids would have found a way to survive inside a secret society."

Jodi slammed her hand on the plywood desk. "Marvin! You're still missing my point! I'm not talking about 'all' Druids! I'm talking a Druid who's a few colors shy of a rainbow, ya know? A Druid who's all foam and no beer? A Druid whose cheese slid off his cracker? A Druid who looks in the mirror and says, 'Good Lord! Isn't it *amazing* how crazy I really am?'"

"Yeah, I get it," said Marvin.

"Wait a second," said Joe Mac. "Marvin, tell me more about this secret society of ancient Druids. What do you know about them?"

Marvin stared blankly, then, "I see where you're going with this, Joe. You think a modern Druid who is part of this secret society might be killing these people for some kind of 'secret reason,' right?"

"Right," said Joe Mac.

"All right," Marvin put his face in his hand, then began: "Okay. Well, is there a logical reason to believe that there is really a 'secret society of ancient Druids' active in our modern world? Yes, there is. Why? I'll tell you why."

Jodi droned, "Please take your time, Marvin."

"The Druids and the Knights Templar designed everything with a back door – a way to survive no matter what. The Knights Templar were supposedly wiped off the face of the Earth in the fourteenth century. But I can't see how an organization as brilliant as the Knights Templar didn't design an elaborate escape plan that they were constantly prepared to use if they were utterly doomed. I mean, that's just forward thinking. And the Druids and the Knights were renowned for their forward-thinking. So I think *both societies* survived just by packing up their gold, relocating, and carrying on under the guise of some untouchable rich dude in a foreign land. I mean, how hard can it be to hide out for a few centuries when you've got an obscene fortune in gold?"

"All right," Jodi allowed, "so, *presuming* that this is one of these 'ancient Druids' and he's gone insane, how is he choosing?"

"His victims?"

"Yeah. His victims. Why didn't he come after you instead of Aaron Roberts?" Jodi was increasingly beginning to feel like she was on the verge of something. "What separates his chosen victims from you and me? Is it some anagram in their name? Is it a constellation? A comet? Some sort of planetary alignment? Something the FBI overlooked? Think about it, Marvin. He's got to be using some kind of protocol."

"Why do you say that?" Marvin asked with surprising confidence. "He might just be picking people at random. He might just be listening to 'the voice of god' like the Son of Sam did with his dog. And the Son of Sam killed a bunch of people, too. Happens every day. Especially in *this* city." He looked around. "Really, in the balance of things, the Long Island Serial Killer has probably killed more people than this guy. I don't understand why there's not a task force out on *him*."

"There is. But we're not on it because we can only chase one psycho at a time." Jodi sighed tiredly. "No, he's not selecting people at random. I agree with Joe. This guy has a process for choosing who to kill. It might even be an unconscious process – something he's not aware of – but he's got *some* kind of criteria for selection."

Marvin gazed away before he said, "I can't help you there. I've read the case files myself and I've looked for a pattern, but I can't find anything."

"It's not in the files," Joe Mac stated from nowhere. "If it was in a file the computers would have found it. Marvin?"

"Yes, sir?" said Marvin.

"Drop the 'sir. Do you know any Druids?"

"Sort of," Marvin replied. "Don't get me wrong. I don't know any Druids of the 'Ancient Order.' But I think I might know some modern Druids of … well … the 'modern order.'

"I want a sit-down with one of them," Joe Mac stated.

Marvin's face turned from Joe Mac to Jodi. To Joe Mac. Back to Jodi. Then he leaned forward and whispered to Jodi, "Is he serious?"

Jodi rolled her eyes. "He's blind, Marvin, not deaf. He can hear you better than I can, and he's on the other side of the room."

"Do I not look serious to you?" asked Joe Mac not unlike an undertaker.

Marvin wiped his palms on his coat. He gazed around absently as if searching for something he couldn't remember. Then he said, "Okay. I'll ask Professor Graven. He'll know. But you should remember that these people take their … uh … what they do … seriously. I don't know if they'll talk to you. In fact, I doubt it."

"They'll talk," stated Joe Mac.

Jodi laughed.

"All right." Marvin picked up the phone. "Like I say; I'll ask the professor. You want to wait or should I call you after I find out?"

Joe Mac stood, tapping the floor.

"Call us."

Jodi was on her feet and at Joe Mac's side, her hand on his elbow as they began to cross the room. But at the door she turned.

"Marvin?"

Marvin lifted his face. "Yeah?"

"Don't tell them why we want to talk to them." Jodi watched for a reaction; there was none. "Just tell them that we need to talk to them, and you don't know why. I don't want you any closer to this than you already are."

At that, Marvin understood.

His mouth drew into a tight line.

"Yeah," he said quietly. "I understand."

FOUR

Sounds of the city literally smothered Joe Mac as he stood at the top step of the Museum of Natural History.

He had been here many times but he had never noticed the trickling sound of water in the storm drain at the street. He had never heard the faint click of a nearby traffic control box or the cooing of pigeons on the museum roof so far above; the noises he'd always noticed before had been the obvious – the sound of cars, people, sirens, and the roar of jets overhead. But now he heard all that and more; he heard the much lesser sounds that moved and shifted and whispered within and beneath the stones and the street.

It was noticeably colder, and the wind had a thickness that provoked Joe Mac to lift his face. He sniffed and said, "It's gonna rain."

"Yeah," Jodi answered, ruffling through her purse. "That's what the weatherman said last night."

"It's getting cold."

"The weatherman said that, too." She finished what she'd been doing. "Has losing your eyeballs turned you into a barometer?"

"Looks like it."

"You hungry?"

"No. But we can eat if you want."

"Come on." She tugged his elbow and they began to walk. "I know a good place right near here. And they make good coffee, too. 'Bout like Starbucks. Only cheaper. You can at least have a cup of coffee with me."

They walked for five minutes when Joe Mac realized this was the first time he'd been on a city sidewalk since he'd lost his sight. He was surprised, if not shocked, that he had little or no problem threading a way through the milling crowd. And he was tempted to tell himself that it was because he was so alert and perceptive, but he knew that wasn't the truth. On the contrary, the truth was that nobody wanted to crash into a blind man on the sidewalk, so they were doing gymnastics to get out of his way.

Jodi said, "You know, Joe, despite all that big talk I'm not sure that religion has anything to do with this. I don't care if it's the Druids or the Jews or the Baptists. And I know what I said about motive, but I think the odds are even that this guy is just totally insane and doesn't have any motive at all. He just gets off on it. That's his motive."

"Anything is possible, kid," said Joe Mac. "But I've worked a lot of murders. And I've never worked one where the killer didn't have a motive."

Joe Mac stopped and raised his face; he had heard a familiar cry among the pigeons and sparrows. He knew Jodi was alternately studying him and then whatever he might be listening to, but Joe Mac said nothing. He was certain he had heard a familiar caw somewhere in the flood of birds flowing like a river over the square.

"What is it?" Jodi asked.

"See anything up there?"

He waited until Jodi remarked, "Nope. What am I looking for?" Another pause. "What! You think Poe's up there? You think he followed us all the way here?"

"He's followed me to other places," Joe Mac replied. "Ravens have a facility for memorizing cars and faces. That's why they can pick you out of a crowd. Or pick out your car on the freeway."

He knew Jodi was still searching rooflines.

"Almost like a human being, huh?"

"Better than a human being. They got better eyes."

"Huh," she began, "well, I don't see Poe. But if Poe doesn't want to be seen nobody's gonna see him, that's for sure." She tugged his elbow. "Come on. Let's get something to eat before I dry up and blow away. And you should eat something, too. I have a feeling we're gonna have a long night."

Joe Mac fell in beside her, lightly touching the sidewalk.

"At least we won't be alone," he said.

Jodi took a dozen steps before she mused, "I wonder if Poe is gonna be like a guard dog. You think he'll warn us if we're in danger?"

Joe Mac grunted.

"I bet we find out."

* * *

It was a nice evening to spend at a sidewalk café enjoying the kind of coffee you get once or twice a year. Joe Mac set down his cup on the table with, "You're right. This is good coffee. You oughta bring me here more often." And he laughed.

Jodi found herself smiling, "You don't get out much, do you?"

"Not much."

Jodi had the impression that Joe Mac – the dark glasses, immobile face, black coat concealing his whole body – was a lot like a sphinx; there wasn't much to read. She asked, "Do you like it out there in the barn? Just you and Poe?"

"I ain't got no complaints. I've always liked farms."

"Me, too," said Jodi. "I was raised on a farm in West Virginia. I still talk kinda country. My friends are always laughing at the way I say things. I guess I got it from my father." A smile came to her slowly. "You kinda remind me of him, Joe."

"Yeah?" he laughed. "How so?"

"Oh, he was a no-nonsense kinda guy, too. He always took care of business before anything else. But he was funny when he wanted to be. And he was kind. He taught me a lot." She blandly watched people passing. "Then I came to

New York for college and ended up staying. But part of me is still on that farm. Always will be, I guess."

"Your father sounds like he was a good man."

"He was." Jodi found herself staring.

"So," Joe began with what seemed like genuine concern, "the spook part of this don't bother you none?"

Jodi laughed out loud, "Are you kidding me?"

"No," Joe Mac scowled. "What do you mean?"

"Didn't you just hear me say I was from West Virginia?"

"Yeah. So?"

"Joe! I'm from West Virginia! Do you not know how much spooky stuff we have in West Virginia?"

"Tell me."

"Oh, my," Jodi knew she was smiling; she couldn't help it. "Where to begin?" She took a moment. "Okay, well, over in Mason County we've got 'The Moth Man.' He's actually sort of famous. They even made a movie about him. He's supposed to be about ten feet tall, he's got red eyes, and flies like a bat. He can also tell you your future. But it's generally a terrible future. Then over in Taylor County we have 'The Headless Horror.' He's been riding his horse out of the woods holding his head in his hand and scaring drunk rednecks back into church for about a hundred years. Some say he used to be an ol' Primitive Baptist preacher who just did it to scare people out of the evils of drinking. And I can believe it. Then, in Nicholas County, we have the dreaded 'Yahoo.' He's kinda' like a really tall version of Bigfoot – only meaner – and no chicken coup is safe. And last but not least we've got the much-ballyhooed 'Lizard Demon,' and he is very greatly feared across five counties of mostly swamp land. I even took part in a night-time hunt for him when I was sixteen – me and my duck-gun." She laughed again. "Joe, if you're looking for ghosts, goblins, witches, or dead guys walking through the hills at night all you have to do is come to West Virginia. We got it all. And I grew up around it, so Druids don't even get a blip on my radar screen. When these brave cow-tippers can rank up there with 'The Moth Man' or 'The Headless Horror,' then we got something to talk about."

Joe Mac was chuckling, "Yeah, kid, I think you're gonna do all right."

Jodi paused a long moment, studying Joe's stoic countenance, before she said more seriously, "Tell me something, Joe. If you don't mind."

"Sure."

"Were you ever married?"

After a moment, Joe Mac nodded, "Yeah, we had forty-one years together. I was … happy. And I guess she didn't mind me too much, neither." A pause. "She died a while back. That's when I moved to the barn. Sold my house. What about you?"

"Ah," Jodi sank deeper into her chair, "I've had bad luck with guys. My dates have been mostly pigs, drunks, losers, wimps, or just plain crazy. It's got me to the point that I don't trust anybody. Or I don't trust my feelings." A pause. "I don't know. I don't dwell on it. It's too depressing." She felt it necessary to add, "I really don't understand it. I'm a nice person. I think I'm even a nice cop. I don't abuse my authority. I'm fair to everybody. I treat people like I'd want them to treat me. My friends said I wasn't tough enough to be a cop. But I think you can do this job and still be a nice person." She paused. "Most of the time."

"You can be," Joe Mac nodded ponderously. "The secret to doing this job is to own the job. Don't let the job own you."

Jodi continued to watch. "What do you mean?"

Joe Mac made a growling sound and shrugged. "I mean that at the end of the day your soul still belongs to you whether you pull the trigger or not."

"Whether I pull the trigger or not? Wow. That's kinda cryptic."

Head bent, Joe Mac laughed, "When the time comes, you'll understand." He raised his face. "Let's get back to the precinct. Go over those files. Marvin might not even call us today. Might not call us 'till tomorrow."

Jodi stood and lifted her purse onto her shoulder. In a moment, they were ambling down the sidewalk to a much thinner crowd. They had traveled two blocks when a vague premonition compelled her to glance over her shoulder. They walked yet another block when she reached into her purse and wrapped her right hand around the grip of her Glock.

A sweeping blue-black shape as large as an eagle suddenly blocked out the sidewalk and the city beyond as Poe landed directly in front of them.

"Hey, buddy," laughed Joe Mac.

Jodi smiled, "Hey there, Poe! What ya been doing, big guy?"

With a deafening shrill Poe exploded from the sidewalk and barely cleared Jodi's head. She spun to see Poe quickly close the distance to a nearby tree and when he reached it he began diving behind it, screeching, and in seconds a figure ran from behind the tree futilely trying to swat Poe with a hand. In another moment, the man rounded the far corner and was lost from their view but not from Poe's view; the last image Jodi caught of Poe, the gigantic raven was savagely tearing at the man's head with his beak and talons.

A high-pitched scream carried from down the block.

Only then did Jodi realize she was holding her Glock in plain view; she'd drawn it when the man emerged from hiding.

"Joe?" she said. "I think somebody's stalking us."

"Good."

"Why is that good?"

"It means we're on the right track. If nobody was paying any attention to us, I'd be worried." Joe Mac turned his head as if he could see. "Best keep your eyes open."

"Nobody's stupid enough to attack two cops."

"The problem, kid, is that stupidity looks exactly like courage to a fool when he's getting paid enough."

"*Hey!*" shouted Jodi.

A big figure rushed them from between two cars and – without question – Joe Mac turned into it and threw a sledgehammer fist that hit the man dead in the chest.

Jodi ripped out her Glock for a clear shot.

"*Joe get out of the way!*"

With a look of shock the man staggered up and Jodi saw a knife in his hand but Joe Mac was standing solidly between her aim and her target. And in the same breath, with Joe Mac standing hard, both hands raised in fists, the man turned and ran fast and low, evading any chance Jodi had at a clear shot. In seconds he was twenty cars away and kept moving until he cleared the distant gate and was gone.

"*Damn!*" yelled Jodi, raising her gun above her head in both hands. "I wasn't gonna kill him, Joe! I just wanted to question him!"

Joe Mac's teeth gleamed angrily. "He was just a punk." He sniffed. "He don't even know who hired him. Just like that fool behind that tree." A pause. "We ain't close enough yet for this crew to bring out the big guns. But we're on the right track."

"We still could have questioned him, Joe! We gotta do this by the book!"

With a frown Joe Mac rumbled, "I shoulda' told you already. I must be getting senile. But you ain't gonna end this one doing it by the book. There won't be no interrogations. There ain't gonna be no arrests." He paused. "When you confront something that is truly evil, you've got two choices. You let it go. Or you kill it."

Jodi's cell phone rang and she fetched it. "*Yeah!* Wait! I'm … I'm sorry! Yes, this is Strong. Great. Wait a second." She pulled out a notepad and pen. "Okay, go ahead." When she was finished, she closed the pad and looked at Joe Mac.

"We got us a real Druid. He's out on Long Island. He said he'll see us around midnight."

Joe Mac asked, "Is midnight the witching hour?"

At the last word, Poe landed with a thunderclap on the fence to Jodi's side, and his eyes were instantly darting across the sidewalk and street and cars. Jodi saw his fearsome black talons were covered with a red wetness that looked an awful lot like blood.

Jodi muttered, "Is midnight the witching hour, Poe?"

With a powerful clap of his magnificent wings, Poe erupted into the air and in seconds was soaring in slow circles above their heads. It was the classic formation a bird of prey takes over the dead.

"I guess so," she whispered.

* * *

It was almost midnight when Jodi parked the car on a rise overlooking the address Marvin had given them.

They were in north Westchester County and deep in the countryside that had been the birthplace of a thousand ghost stories over the centuries. It didn't escape her attention that this was once was a region made famous for witches and witch hunts as well as the notorious and regretful scandals that followed the puritanical bloodshed.

For the most part Joe Mac had been surprisingly talkative during the two-hour ride. He had told her a dozen stories of how he had solved the most difficult murders of his storied career so that Jodi felt she was the recipient of an *ad hoc* education in homicide investigation worth more than the police academy and the FBI mentorship combined. But when Joe Mac suggested they park at a distance and study their intended destination instead of just driving through the gate "like a couple of amateurs," she began to wonder why and finally asked, "So what am I supposed to be looking for, Joe?"

"Does this place have a gate?" Joe Mac asked.

"Yeah, it's got a guardhouse and a gate. I see one uniformed guard. Can't tell if he's armed. The place looks like forty, fifty acres. One house is visible, but it's just a bunch of lights behind the trees. Looks like a rich person, for sure." She lowered the binoculars. "And the snow is really beginning to pick up. I'm not joking. We might not be going back to the city tonight if this don't let up."

"What time is it?"

"Fifteen 'till twelve. Almost midnight."

"That's close enough. Let's go on in, then. And I know you're probably great at interviewing people, but listen to me for a second."

"Another lesson?"

"You bet. Now, we don't know what we've got, so if you start feeling like backing out and coming back later with ten more detectives, just say you're ready to go and we'll leave. One: Never push a bad situation. Two: If it *feels* wrong, it *is* wrong. Back out. We can come back with more men. Got it?"

"Got it."

"Otherwise, just be yourself. We don't know that these folks have anything to do with this. And, far as I know, there ain't nothing illegal about hugging trees, so let's not get antagonistic unless there's a reason." Joe Mac's face was bent slightly forward, the broad corners of his mouth turned in a frown.

Suddenly Jodi knew but asked, "Joe? Are you carrying a gun?"

"You bet."

Jodi almost laughed, but the gravity of it stopped her. Then she asked, "What do you plan to do with it?"

"Nothing. I'm blind. But if it comes down to it, I'd rather have it than not have it."

"Okay," Jodi laughed.

"One more thing," Joe Mac added.

"Yes, Obi-wan?"

"No matter what happens – no matter what he says – act like you already know it. If you show surprise, he'll know that he holds the cards." Joe Mac half-turned his face toward her. "Act like we're just here to confirm stuff. Got it?"

"Got it. But why?"

"It's psychological. If they feel they can pick and choose what to tell us, that's exactly what they'll do. And that's the same for anybody. It's instinct. Nobody likes to go buck naked commando. But if they're convinced that we already know the score and we're just here so they can help themselves before things get ugly, then they'll tell us everything they know. So let him do most of the talking. And don't ask a lot of questions. A question lets him know what we *don't* know."

"Okay," Jodi said, biting her lip. "You ready?"

"You're the boss."

"Yeah. Right." Her cell phone rang. "Wait a minute." She answered and heard Rollins: "*Where are you guys?*"

"Rollins?"

"*Yeah. It's Rollins. Professor Mason told me you guys went to Westchester to interview someone who's in some kind of coven or cult. Is that what you're doing?*"

"Marvin told you that?" Jodi exclaimed. "I told him not to talk to anybody!"

"*Yeah, but that didn't include me, did it?*"

Jodi glanced at Joe Mac and didn't like what she saw. "No," she said finally, "that didn't include you."

"*So who are you guys talking to?*"

With a sigh, Jodi said slowly and distinctly, "We're up here in Westchester. We're going to interview someone inside a local cult who we think might know something about the murders. We don't need any backup. We're not in trouble. And we'll let you know what we find as soon as we get back. Okay?"

"*Yeah. Okay. Let me know one way or the other.*"

"All right. Bye."

She hung up and waited for Joe Mac to speak but he didn't.

He didn't have to.

Two minutes later Jodi stopped at the decidedly royal gate, and a guard walked up with a faint wave and a smile. Jodi raised her badge, "Detective Jodi Strong and Detective Joe Blake. I believe we have an appointment?"

"Yes, ma'am; you're expected."

The guard stepped back, clicked a remote, and the gate opened. Then they slowly wound their way through fast-gathering snow to what loomed up as a Mediterranean-style mansion on a hill. They got out and Jodi knocked.

As they waited, Jodi turned, gazing up. "Good grief! It's really coming down! Can you feel it? We might have to find a hotel or a restaurant for the night. I don't have any snow chains, and we'll never get down this mountain without them."

Joe Mac said nothing, so she glanced over to see him standing at the edge of darkness. Unmoving, he was a singularly melancholic image cloaked in black from head to toe, his black walking cane in his black-gloved hand; she didn't think *anyone* would answer their door if his Charon-like form was all they saw, so she positioned herself in front of the peephole.

The door opened, and a man in a white shirt and khaki pants stood holding a glass of red wine. He smiled a becoming smile; "Hello! I'm Anthony Montanus. And you would be Detective Strong and Detective Blake?"

"Yeah, I'm Jodi." She motioned. "And this is Detective Joe Mac Blake. He's an advisor. May we come in?"

Montanus stepped aside. "Of course. May I offer you something?"

He soundlessly closed the door.

"Sure," said Jodi. "Some wine?"

"Chardonnay?"

"Yes, thank you."

"Scotch if you got it," said Joe Mac.

"I do indeed. Please take a seat by the fire. It's getting cold out." Perfectly relaxed and courteous, Montanus stepped to a cupboard and began pouring drinks. "I was quite fascinated when Professor Mason called this afternoon. I hope that I can be of some service. Do you take ice in your scotch, Detective Blake?"

"It's just Joe," said Joe Mac. "Yes, thank you."

Jodi felt a thrill of alarm. "What did Marvin ... I mean, what all did Professor Mason tell you?"

"He said you wanted to talk to someone familiar with local groups who adhered to ancient Celtic beliefs," Montanus answered without any hint of suspicion. "I told him that I would be more than happy to talk to you."

"Oh," Jodi said before she could stop herself. "Professor Mason told us that you might be a little reluctant to talk. He was actually kinda hesitant to call you at all."

Montanus laughed, "Yes, some Druids are unreasonably secretive. But I'm not one of them. Neither was my wife." He delivered a glass of wine and a scotch. "Cheers."

Jodi toasted. "Thank you."

The wine, she had to admit, was exquisite; it was the kind of wine people pay high dollar for but never enjoy. "This is excellent, Mr. Montanus."

"Tony, please. Thank you." He smiled, "I'm not one of those people who pay five hundred dollars for a bottle of wine, keep it in the cellar for fifty years, and then die without ever having enjoyed it. I'd rather enjoy all the things I can afford while I'm alive and leave nothing undone, unsaid, or unsung." He laughed. "And, now, I did get an indication from Marvin that this was of a rather serious nature. Am I right?"

Joe Mac said flatly, "You're right."

"I thought so."

Everything Jodi heard and saw indicated that Montanus's relaxation was genuine because he quite simply behaved as if he had nothing to hide. Then he stunned her with, "This is about all the murders that have taken place in the city over the past four years, isn't it?" He waited, watching Jodi's face. "These murders that the press attributes to 'The Hangman?'"

Never act surprised ...

Jodi closed her mouth; those words from Joe Mac could not have been spoken at a more appropriate avenue. She was convinced she'd prevented herself from revealing anything. That is, unless Montanus read the split-second she bit her lip.

"Yes," she said. "How did you know that?"

"I've been expecting a visit from the FBI or the police for some time," Montanus continued with a sip. "But I don't mean to presume. Why don't you ask me whatever it is you want to know?"

"What do you know about the murders?" Joe Mac asked.

"I don't think I know anything at all that would help you solve the crimes," Montanus said slowly. "I presume – something I hate to do – that you suspect the culprit of these crimes is someone familiar with Celtic beliefs. That's a simple presumption. But you might also suspect that it's someone associated with the Druids. And while that might very well be true, it won't be anyone in our group."

Joe Mac seemed to absorb that before he asked, "Why not?"

Montanus sighed as if he'd had this discussion many times; "The peace-loving members of my particular Druidic group have had this discussion among ourselves many times. It was also a deep suspicion of my late wife." His brow hardened as he continued, "The people in my group have long suspected that someone with beliefs tied to Gaelic traditions was executing these innocent people in some demented belief that they are at war with the Hebrew god. We've kept our suspicions to ourselves until now. But perhaps the time has come for me to tell you what we think."

Joe Mac said nothing, but Jodi felt it was time to ask, "How many people are you talking about? I mean, how many people are in your particular group?"

"Oh," he mused, "perhaps thirty. Maybe a few more."

"And this is like a religion?"

"No, no," Montanus shook his head, "it's just a reverence, you might call it, for Nature. There are no gods or demons or angels or principalities that might damn you for all eternity. It's simply a Nature-based way of trying to live harmoniously with the world." He concluded with some emphasis, "We do not sanction violence. We never have."

Joe Mac: "But you folks have suspected that these murders were somehow associated with a Druid? Why is that?"

Montanus reclined deeper into a genuine leather lounge chair. "Well, it was this madman's preferred method of murder that was the first clue. To break someone's bones, to hang them by the neck from a tree until after sunrise; those are ancient Jewish punishments. And the ancient Druids literally waged war against the ancient Jews. That was the primary logic behind our suspicion."

Jodi asked, "But how does that automatically bring this suspect into relevance with a Celtic-based group?"

"Not just any Celtic-based group," Montanus noted, finger uplifted. "I'm speaking specifically of the *Druids*." He took a deep breath. "Stone engravings that have been unearthed in parts of ancient Gaul suggest that the Druids executed those of Hebrew linage in exactly this manner. You see, the Druids were very well educated. In truth, they were the leading artisans and scholars of their time. They were quite well versed in Latin as well as Hebrew. And they were very well acquainted with Israel's god just as they were familiar with the Pentateuch and its various punishments. And they consequently used these Jewish punishments against captured Jews for the express purpose of cursing them in the eyes of their own god. But I don't mean to digress. Aren't you here to ask me if I know of any local Druid who might be capable of carrying on a one-man war against the Judeo-Christian god?"

"That's close enough," stated Joe Mac. "So what do you know?"

"I, myself, know nothing. But my late wife had some considered suspicions. And there are others in my group who have advanced opinions. They believe that the person you're looking for is a Druid who follows ... well, 'an ancient path.'"

"I'm sorry about your wife," said Joe Mac plainly.

Montanus nodded, "Thank you." He paused. "Yes, she died only recently. I'm still ... adjusting. As is ... natural."

Frowning, Joe Mac nodded.

"So," Montanus continued, "as I was saying, I agree with what my wife thought. But not all Druids are the same. My group happens to be peaceful. But Cathren believed that there's ... uh ... an *underground* Druidic group in this area that is very much prone to extreme violence. And there's no way of knowing, of course, but one of those Druids might be crazy enough to carry on a military campaign against the god of Israel. He would have to be somewhat insane, of course, but it *is* possible."

Jodi asked, "What else did your late wife think?"

Montanus turned a meditative gaze to the fireplace. "She believed that this hidden group of Druids is very dangerous – not only to nonbelievers but to fellow Druids. In fact, I'm not entirely convinced that my wife's death was an accident. But the local police did an investigation and ruled it accidental."

"If I might ask," Jodi began, "what happened?"

"She died in a fall down the stairs."

Jodi paused. "I see."

"In any case," Montanus continued, "if these people believe they are following the ways of the ancient Druids then they are very, very dangerous indeed. And I don't think they're going to fall down like a bunch of whipped dogs when you catch up to them. If I were to take a guess, I'd say you're facing a very tightly knit group and they have some kind of enforcement arm. I don't know what police would call it - a soldier, an assassin – but it's somebody who knows what he's doing and he's probably been hurting or killing people for a long time to protect this group. Plus, I can guarantee you that he's not afraid to die any more than he's afraid to kill a rabbi, a rich man, or a police officer." He glanced at Joe Mac. "Truth is, he's probably already killed police officers. And he has backers – people who make sure he has weapons and cars and places to stay. Killing people is probably all he does. And I hate to repeat myself, but my guess is that he's very good at it."

Joe Mac said flatly, "If you don't mind me saying it, this ancient Druid stuff sounds a little far-fetched."

Montanus responded without any apparent offense, "When you discuss Gaelic belief systems, especially the Druids, you'll hear about groups and cults of every size and color. Some of them are like the late sixties flower children and some are just downright Satanic. And they hold theories that run the gamut between a scholarly analysis of ancient literature to unbelievably ridiculous speculations and fantasies that range all the way from aliens to Moonbeams of the Larger Lunacy. It's always been like that when people discuss the Druids because so little is known about them."

Jodi commented, "I thought you were a believer."

"I'm more of a scholar," Montanus said, relaxing. "I trust that archeology has revealed enough information about Celtic beliefs to give us a rudimentary understanding of Druidism. But not everyone is as careful as I am. Some people call themselves Druids and literally just 'make things up.'"

Joe Mac scowled, "If what you say is true, how do we find this guy?"

Montanus was clearly confused before he hesitantly said, "I don't know. But there's an old woman who might be able to help you. I haven't talked to her in a long time, but she was a good friend of my wife. And I think she's vaguely familiar with a group that believes they're the direct descendants of the ancient Druids. And I do mean 'the blood descendants.' They believe that so-and-so of the old Druid Empire was their great, great granddaddy. They also believe that all that old, forbidden Druid knowledge has been passed down from generation to generation within their 'circle' and they're the 'wielders of the secret flame,' so to speak. And I don't mean to accuse anyone, but it might be the group you're looking for."

"You've never dealt with them yourself?" Jodi asked.

"No," Montanus emphatically shook his head. "I've never been personally exposed to them at all, and I don't care to be."

"And your late wife?"

Montanus paused. "I don't believe so. My late wife, Cathren, was Celtic ,and she believed in a kind of oneness we should all seek with Nature. And some would call that Druidism. But there was nothing violent about it. There's no blood, no sacrifices or bones or amulets or graveyard ceremonies. It's simply a philosophy of finding a oneness with …well … all living things. But it's a philosophy of peace. I can't see my wife ever associating with any of them. She would have considered them repulsive."

Something – and Jodi didn't know what it was until she looked at Joe Mac – had suddenly snatched her attention.

Joe Mac had moved to the edge of his lounge chair, both hands wrapped around his cane. And where his left ear had been aimed at Montanus, now he had turned his head a bit further so that he was listening to something else. With a glance, Jodi confirmed that Montanus didn't notice Joe Mac's shift of concentration.

With an effort, but unable to totally withdraw her attention from Joe Mac, she asked, "Where can we find this woman, Tony? I need to talk to her."

Montanus stood and stepped toward a table that ran along the wall; "I believe her name and address were in Cathren's organizer." He lifted the book. "Cathren kept everything in this book – all her addresses and phone numbers and notes. And this old gal we're talking about has an unusual name. so it shouldn't be hard to find. It's something like Critiani –"

Glass shattered and Montanus spun with a scream into the table. He was still on his feet as Jodi ripped out her duty issue Glock nine-millimeter searching instantly for the location of the shot, and then more glass in the rear door disintegrated in a fuselage of bullets that tore through the frame of the entrance – a weapon on fully automatic fire – and slammed into Montanus until he bellowed and fell face-forward to the floor.

Jodi only peripherally realized that Joe Mac had hit the floor as she fired into the dark outside the house.

"*Joe! Are you hit!*"

"*No!*" Joe Mac roared and surged to his feet. He turned to the shattered glass door and staggered forward until he found the wall. "What did you see?"

"Just trees!" Jodi changed clips. "This is *not* good! It's pitch black, and my flashlight's in the car!"

"Call for help!" Joe Mac shouted as he hauled what Jodi saw instantly was a big Springfield 1911 out of his coat. She knew it wasn't police issue and would never be police issue in New York City because a bullet from a .45 could blow a hole through two or three people and keep going to hit a few more – not a weapon you used in a densely-populated area no matter how good a shot you were.

"Is there a deck!" Joe Mac shouted.

"No!" Jodi managed as she snatched out her cell phone. "It's a patio and then a flat backyard and nothing but trees!"

Another machine-gun blast smashed into the wall beside the door.

"*Stay down, Joe! He's trying to kill you!*"

"Where's the muzzle flare?" he shouted back.

"Inside the tree line!"

"How far are the trees?"

"A hundred feet!"

Joe Mac moved out the door, and Jodi barely glimpsed him at the edge of darkness and light. He stood for a moment, the .45 tight in his right fist.

Then he rushed forward …

And disappeared into night.

* * *

If the ground was flat, Joe Mac was confident he could cover fifty yards in seconds, so he moved as fast as he could before slowing at what he judged to be the final few yards, one arm stretched out, fingers alert to any touch. Then he felt freezing cold leaves and snow and ducked, moving closer to the trunk of a tree.

He put his chest to the trunk and turned his ear to the woods.

Nobody can walk on snow without crunching each step. It didn't matter if you were a master assassin with an AK-47 or a half-blitzed wino with a bottle in each hand. So, if this guy was trying to retreat through these woods, he'd be making a racket with every step. And the faster he moved, the more noise he'd make.

Joe Mac heard quick crunches in the snow at his nine o'clock.

"*… He's inside the wood line, but he's moving perpendicular … He's heading straight for the road and that means he ain't got no backup … It's just him and me …*"

Joe Mac knew that if Jodi couldn't see past the tree line from the house, then the darkness was complete and you can't shoot what you can't see.

He moved perpendicular to the house, feeling his way from tree to tree. The ground was mostly level, but he picked his feet up high and set them down evenly so as not to twist an ankle or fall, which would be a crashing sound that this shooter couldn't help but hear. He had made it a good hundred feet by his own reckoning when he heard a step almost shockingly close and Joe Mac spun and fired the .45.

A voice cried out.

"Ninety feet! ... He's on snow! ... Still inside the tree line ... He's not using a flashlight because it'd give away his location ... He can't move much faster than I can in this mess, and he can't move at all without making a sound ..."

Joe Mac closed thirty feet then he took a solid one-hand hold on the pistol, feet shoulder length apart, his ear turned in the direction of the last sound, face down. He reached out with his free hand and found a thick tree trunk; he'd need it after he fired.

A moment ...

A moment more ...

Joe Mac stilled his breathing, listening close.

Crunch.

Joe Mac fired.

Instantly shots from a fully automatic weapon returned as Joe Mac spun behind the tree he'd already found. He heard bullets whiz by at twenty, ten, and five feet and some hit the tree. Then the firing ceased and Joe Mac didn't wait; he was quickly out again and moving forward. He ignored the sound his own steps were making.

"... Listen close! ... Concentrate on the snow ... You know his direction ... He's trying to make it back to the road ..."

The attacker seemed to be moving more quickly. His steps were no longer separated by an anxious pause. In fact, he seemed to be running as well as someone could run in the darkness and trees and ice.

Joe Mac was moving imprudently fast until he smashed his face into a tree that his sweeping left hand had missed and he staggered, reaching reflexively to his forehead to sweep away blood or sweat.

"... *Forget it!* ... *He's getting too close to the road!* ... *The trees are going to start thinning!* ... *Take a shot while you can!* ..."

Stepping away from the tree, Joe Mac fell into a wide stance and held the .45 in a firm two-hand grip. He didn't move at all. Didn't breathe. He waited until he heard another step and fired six rounds from the .45; he laid down a figure eight pattern so that nothing within that field of fire could escape without being hit.

In the sulfur-thick air and with the smoke burning his throat and eyes, Joe Mac reached quickly into his left-hand pocket and found one of three spare magazines. He dropped the spent clip from the .45 and, after feeling that the magazine wasn't backwards, slid it in the grip. Then he dropped the slide and waited, again unmoving, again holding his breath, again poised to hear the faintest sound.

He heard a moan and some staggering.

Joe pulled the trigger seven times at the sound of the staggering and speed-changed clips. Then the forest was ghostly silent but for the ringing in Joe Mac's ears.

Moments stretched and Joe Mac tried to ignore the heat rising from his coat. He swept a hand over his face and didn't bother to determine whether it was sweat or blood chilling him to the freezing wind. He'd know when he returned to the house.

Or he'd be shot dead out here, and it wouldn't matter.

An engine roared to life.

Joe Mac turned to his left and moved as quickly as he dared. Within five steps he was aware of limbs lifting from his body and knew he was in a clearing. He also heard a car approaching fast and he raised aim at where he surmised the road would pass; he didn't know what else was in front of him but he intended to shoot, anyway.

The roar grew loud and coarse and then it soared through a location about forty yards out and six feet about Joe Mac's shoulders.

Joe Mac fired seven rounds until the slide locked but the roar continued down the road as more gunfire erupted in the night. Then that firing ceased as well and Joe Mac could hear the engine climbing away. It rose on this road and then through the gate of the subdivision where more shots were fired.

Within thirty seconds there was only rolling echoes.

Joe Mac realized that Jodi must have gone out the front of the house and fired every round she had as the car passed. And he wasn't surprised that neither of them managed to kill the driver or disable the vehicle.

It was a lot harder than most people knew to disable a car with a pistol. Most bullets just bounced off the windshield, anyway, unless you were lucky enough to hit the same centimeter-size hole twice. That is, unless you were firing some buffalo-strength .50 caliber that could crack the engine block. And, last, any car equipped with no-flat tires would keep rolling no matter how many bullets you put into them.

Joe Mac heard a call …

"*Joe! …. Joe! … Where are you!*"

Joe Mac wiped his face. "Over here!"

He didn't move after that because he had no idea where he was standing. For all he knew he was poised at the edge of a bluff. Then he heard a familiar sound and raised his face, waiting. Another second, and Poe landed on the ground before him.

The raven shrilled, flapping angrily.

Joe Mac nodded, "I know. He got away. I wish you could have followed him for me, buddy."

Poe erupted into the air as Jodi came running up. She was panting as she reached Joe Mac, and he knew she was bent double with her hands on her knees. She made a series of gasps before she managed, "Did you hit him?"

"I don't think so," Joe Mac shook his head. "You?"

"I put …Whew! Give me a second!" She walked a few steps. Then she turned back and managed, "I think I put a few in his car! I don't know! There's no street lights in that section of the road. Oh, man! I've gotta get in shape! Anyway, I don't know. To be honest, I don't know if I hit anything or not."

"Let's get back to the house."

They took a few steps.

"You call for somebody?" he asked.

"The sheriff. They called an ambulance."

"All right."

When they reached the house Joe Mac heard a sheriff's radio and knew a deputy was already in the driveway calling for backup.

"Wait," Jodi said and Joe Mac knew she was removing her badge and holding it high. "Over here! Don't fire! We're police officers! We're police officers! We're coming to you!"

Joe Mac didn't need to be told that the deputy was a rookie. As he and Jodi began talking excitedly about what had just happened, neither of them had the presence of mind to go inside the house and make sure the crime scene was secure.

"Hey," Joe Mac finally said, "you two need to do this *inside* the house while you secure the scene."

"But nobody's in there," said Jodi.

"He might have a *cat*," Joe Mac said. "He might have a dog. And a dog or a cat will disqualify a crime scene for a prosecutor as fast as anything, so get in there. Both of you!"

As Jodi began to turn, Joe Mac snatched her arm.

She jumped. "*What*!"

"Grab his wife's organizer and hide it in your bag before backup gets here," Joe Mac said, low. "And don't let that deputy see you do it."

She was so close Joe Mac felt her breath.

"Done."

FIVE

After standing over Montanus' red form – the blood had completely transformed his white shirt into a bright scarlet sheet – FBI Special Agent Jack Rollins lifted his face with an incredulous gaze. "And you're telling me this man didn't have anything important to say?" he asked dully. "Are you kidding me?"

Neither Jodi nor Joe Mac replied.

"Well?" Rollins pressed. "What did he know? And why aren't you telling me? Is this a police versus FBI thing? Because I'm not here to debate what belongs to who! I want to catch whoever did this!" He pointed toward the entrance to the subdivision. "You do know the guard at the gate is dead, don't you? Your boy is on a killing spree!"

Jodi said slowly, "Mr. Montanus told us that he didn't know anything that would help us." She gestured sadly to the body. "But he obviously did."

"What else did he 'obviously' not know?" Rollins placed hands on hips. "Come on, Strong! I checked you out! Your last supervisor said you have total recall for these things! Tell me everything that he said!"

Jodi inhaled deeply. "Well, we asked him if he knew any local cults that might be good for these murders, and he said he might know one. Then he got up to get some more wine and somebody shot him through the back door. After that …" She lifted her hands with a shrug, "… it was a whole new ball game. We went after the bad guy. There was a fairly dramatic running gunfight in the dark. The guy got away. And here we are."

Rollins angrily stepped over the body, closing the distance. "People can lie to a cop all day long, Strong, and they're not breaking the law. But it's a federal crime to lie to a federal agent. And that goes for cops, too, so I'm gonna give you one more chance to rethink your answer. What did this man tell you that got him killed?"

Joe Mac stepped forward with a frown: "He didn't say *anything* that got him killed, Rollins! It's what he was *about* to say that got him killed! But he never got the chance." He thumbed a hand at the glass door. "And I'm betting whoever was standing outside that door heard every word. They were probably using a laser or wolf ears. And if ol' Montanus there had clammed up, he'd probably still be alive. But he was cooperating with us. And I think he would of give us a name, too. But he never got to it."

"Well, what *did* you get out of him?" Rollins asked.

"He told us that a local cult was probably responsible for our murders," Joe Mac answered gruffly. "But that's all we got."

Rollins' displeasure was evident in the entirety of his face, his posture, and his stare. For a long moment, he said nothing. Then a voice made him turn.

"Well, well, well, well," Captain Steve Brightbarton said as he descended the short steps into the living room. He bent as if staring Montanus in the eye before he said "Yep, this is something different. What makes you say that the hitter who did this is the same psycho we've been hunting in town, Joe? This is not exactly his MO."

"Montanus, there, was killed before he could give us the name of 'The Hangman,'" said Joe Mac. "But he was about to. I'm pretty sure of it."

"Hmmm." Brightbarton straightened and focused on Jodi. "Did you guys get any kind of look at the shooter?"

Jodi shook her head. "It was too dark."

Turning squarely, Brightbarton stared at Joe Mac's thick black glasses. "What about you, Joe? Did you get a look at him?"

"I was tying my shoe," said Joe Mac.

"Uh huh." Brightbarton stared around the room before he said, "Okay, boys and girls, what's the operational status of your weapons? Let's do this by the numbers."

"Sir, I fired ten out of seventeen rounds in one clip," said Jodi. "I put in a new clip with seventeen rounds, and there's one in the chamber."

Brightbarton simply stared at Joe Mac and then leaned closer: "Don't even try and tell me you didn't pull a piece."

Finally, Joe Mac muttered, "I mighta' fired a couple a' clips."

"Might have? Well, I ain't even gonna ask you if you hit anything. I don't expect you'd know. In any case, turn your weapons into crime scene before you leave. They're gonna have to run ballistics." He focused on Jodi. "Detective Strong, you'll pick up a new piece tomorrow morning from the armory. Joe, you're gonna have to dig something else out of your shoe box." Brightbarton paused. "Since you're just 'an observer.'"

"You bet."

Brightbarton stared down again. "Looks like ten rounds center mass, not one of 'em thrown. That's pretty good shooting. Looks like our boy has some serious skill sets. Probably got trigger time in Iraq or Afghanistan, and now he's on the private market."

"Look at this, captain," said Jodi. She presented an empty cartridge case. "We found a bunch of these out back."

Brightbarton held it up to the light. "A seven-six-two by thirty-nine. I'm guessing an AK on full auto?"

"Yeah," answered Joe. "It looks like you're gonna have to upgrade your profile, Agent Rollins. You've been plowing the wrong cantaloupe patch."

"What's that mean?" asked Jodi.

With a groan Rollins smoothed back his blonde hair, which had been tousled by the gathering snowstorm. Finally, he said, "Yeah. This is gonna add a wrinkle or two." He paused. "Or three."

"Is there a problem?" asked Jodi.

Joe Mac motioned with his cane. "The FBI profile wrote this guy up to be a wildly unstable religious psychopath. Now they're gonna have to upgrade him to a fundamentally stable military operator because it takes a boatload of training to hit a man on fully automatic fire. And this honcho put ten rounds through Montanus' chest at fifty feet inside two seconds with one fully automatic burst." He nodded. "Yeah. That takes a lot of disciplined military training and then some because no normal man can do that even *with* training. It takes a good touch – sort of a natural born killer thing. And it upgrades the FBI profile from an 'unstable religious psychopath' to a meat-eating, highly functional Oklahoma cowboy with profoundly twisted religious delusions. It means the FBI's spent about a billion dollars over the last four years looking in all the wrong places. They should have been pulling military files instead of church registers and asylum rosters."

Jodi found herself staring at Rollins who suddenly seemed none too happy. His expression intimated that it was even worse than Joe Mac alluded, but she opted to keep her mouth shut. This was her first shooting and the last thing she wanted to do was say something foolish. She wasn't even certain whether they would be keeping her on the case now that she'd fired her weapon.

"I suppose neither of you are hurt?" Brightbarton asked mildly, staring from Jodi to Joe Mac. "I didn't think so. But as a formality both of you go to the hospital and get some air. Then go home. I'll see you in my office with your PBA representatives tomorrow morning at eight. Meanwhile I'm 'suspending' your normal period of suspension following a shooting. I need both of you on this case. I think you're too close to breaking this, and I can't have you sidelined. Any questions?"

Joe Mac shook his head.

"No, sir," said Jodi.

"Good." Brightbarton looked at Rollins. "Anything you want to ask 'em before I send 'em to the hospital?"

Gazing down, Rollins shook his head.

"All right. Get out of here."

In minutes they were inside Jodi's car, and she was still puzzled at the aftermath of the shooting. She kept wondering if she'd done something wrong. "Is this what usually happens after a shooting?" she asked.

"Yeah, basically," Joe Mac answered glumly. "First, they ask you the status of your weapon. Then they collect your weapon and send you to the hospital to get some oxygen and get checked out. They can't ask you any questions about the event until your PBA representative is present, so they usually schedule your interview for the next day. And then, after all that, you're usually suspended until the investigation is complete. But, like he said, he 'suspended our suspension.'"

"He has the power to do that?"

"Sure," Joe Mac shrugged. "The only person he answers to is the assistant chief or the chief. And Brightbarton's not gonna have any problems with them. Not on *this*. Their careers are on the line, same as his."

Jodi laughed lightly as she started the car. "Rollins sure didn't look happy. I wish you could have seen his face. He's *mad*."

"It don't take a big man to carry a grudge."

"Why should he hold a grudge against us? We didn't do anything to him." She pulled onto the road; the snow had been heaped into the ditch by a snow plow worker that Jodi would thank in her prayers. "That's kinda petty, don't you think?"

"We've made progress where he couldn't, and he knows it," said Joe Mac. "Plus, it's gonna look real bad for him if the podunk NYPD manages to solve a major crime that a hundred FBI special agents couldn't crack. Might even get in the way of his next promotion."

"Good grief," Jodi grimaced, "I don't mean to hurt the guy's *career*. He's a good agent as far as I can tell. It's just that I want to solve this case."

"He knows that, kid; I wouldn't worry about it." Joe Mac rolled down the window. "And Brightbarton thinks you're a good cop, or he would have come down on you a lot harder than he did. He thinks you got potential."

Jodi gaped. "He does?"

"Yeah."

"Really?"

Joe Mac laughed. "You're still on the case, ain't you? That's because he believes in you. That's because he trusts you to do the right thing."

Jodi moaned, "That's so nice of him."

Joe Mac's head bent, his smile lasting. Then, "All right. Let's get to the hospital. We both need some air."

After they were headed down the mountain, Jodi reached into her purse and pulled out Montanus's organizer. She ruffled the pages, glancing down as Joe Mac turned his head, clearly listening as he asked, "You sure that deputy didn't see you lift it?"

"I'm sure."

"Don't look through it right now. Keep your eyes on the road. I'll make some calls when we get to the hospital."

Jodi found herself staring between the road and Joe Mac's expressionless countenance and finally asked, "You're gonna call this old woman *tonight*?"

"No. We're not contact her until after you pick up your new piece in the morning, and we make statements. But I'm gonna call some guys tonight to watch over her, so that nothing happens to her before we get there." He turned his head as if to gaze out the window. "They won't mind."

Jodi asked, "Cops?"

"No," he shook his head. "I don't want any more cops in on this. Somebody blew this rendezvous tonight, and it had to be Montanus or a cop. Nobody else knew we were coming." He concentrated. "If it was Montanus, it could have been one of a hundred people he talks to on a regular basis, and he has no idea they're stabbing him in the back. Might have been the same person that set his wife up to die. And if it was Rollins, it was Rollins himself or somebody he talks to on a regular basis."

"What about Marvin? The archeology guy?"

Joe Mac's face scrunched. "He just don't seem good for this. I think he's just an honest egghead."

"But you really think it could be Rollins?" Jodi realized her mouth was hanging open. "That doesn't seem credible to me."

"I don't know," stated Joe with a sudden undertone of weariness. "I can't see what he'd be getting out of it. He's a career man. He's got everything to gain and everything to lose. But I don't know who he's talking to." A pause. "It don't matter. When you're not sure whether a situation is good or not you back away and get another angle on it until you *are* sure. You don't push a bad situation. You remember that."

"Roger that," said Jodi. And after a moment, "You know, I'm learning a lot from you. You should be a teacher."

Joe Mac nodded, "One last time."

Jodi glanced over.

"One last time?"

Frowning, Joe Mac drew another .45 from his coat and rested the gun on his thigh, his head bowed. His voice was tired.

"One last time," he whispered.

* * *

"You can make it home all right?" Joe Mac asked.

Jodi pulled on her sweater and tossed the hospital gown in the hamper; it'd taken the hospital two hours to clear them for release "with medical permission" and this was the first chance she'd had to talk to Joe Mac since they walked into the ER.

"Yeah, no problem," she said. "What about our contact? Did you send some people to protect her until we get there?"

"Yeah. Some longshoremen who owe me. They're both bull throwers, so nobody's gonna bother her. Even so, we don't need to burn no time at the station tomorrow. We go in; you pick up your piece; we make our statements and hit the road."

"What about you?" Jodi asked. "They confiscated your gun."

"I got six more 1911s at the house."

"Good grief, Joe."

"What? You only got one gun?"

"Like I can shoot more than one at a time?"

"You'll learn." Joe Mac turned. "Let's get out of here. I'll walk you to your car. Then I'll hitch a ride."

"C'mon, Joe. I can take you home."

"I got a ride."

"Another longshoreman who owes you?"

"A reporter. He owes me, too. That's an art you need to cultivate."

"What's that?"

"Friends that owe you."

"They come in handy after an officer involved shooting?"

"I have a feeling you're gonna find out."

Jodi released a deep sigh.

"Me, too."

* * *

He dropped his blood-soaked coat and shirt on the floor and didn't bother to try and raise his right arm; he knew he couldn't.

The old blind man was either very lucky or very good. One of his shots hit him solidly in the chest smashing his ribs into splinters and sending him sprawling across that hateful frozen ground. But he had managed to stagger to his car. Then, as he was driving away, another bullet fired by the old man had struck the frame of the door, splintered, and fragments tore through his arm and hand and face.

He was bleeding badly enough to die, but he had already called the man, and the man told him that help was on the way. He knew he was in shock; it was the result of such massive blood loss. In fact, he had only barely managed to drive home and had not executed a single procedure to make sure he wasn't followed, so he couldn't trust his own judgment right now. The best thing – the *only* thing he should do was just sit here, keep pressure on the wound, and try to remain calm.

He ripped open a box of large gauze pads and pulled one out. Then he opened a pill bottle and swallowed two morphine capsules. Next, he pressed the gauze pad hard against his chest. He couldn't tape it into place with one hand, and so he simply maintained pressure. He was thirsty with a bone-dry thirstiness he knew would become maddeningly worse because blood loss would also cause dehydration. Then he would begin to feel cold because all his blood was leaving his body.

He'd been wounded enough times to know the exact sequence of events that would transpire all the way up to death itself. But he wouldn't die from this. They would be here soon, and the doctor would start an IV and sew up his wounds; the IV would restore his blood pressure and stave off shock; the sutures would stop the bleeding. And, in a few days, he would be on his feet.

He tried to remember whether he had left anything at the scene. He knew he had left the empty cartridge cases; there'd been no time to collect them. But he affirmed in his mind he had left nothing else.

Reviewing the scene in his mind, he had two vivid thoughts; he was still amazed that the old blind man had reacted so fast, and he was grief-stricken that he himself had failed.

His orders had been to kill them all, but when he swung aim to kill the old man he was already on the floor behind the couch and so he had failed to complete his mission. But, ultimately, it didn't matter; he'd have another shot at the blind man soon enough. And next time he would not miss.

The old blind man – Joe Mac Blake was his name – had made more progress in tracking and identifying him that a thousand FBI agents and ten thousand police officers combined in the past three years. But then he had made a mistake with Joe Mac's grandson.

No, he should have never left the dead cat at the edge of that field because they had found his tracks. And, while it wasn't much, it was still more than he had ever left at a scene and, in his mind, a grievous mistake.

Blinking sweat and blood from his eyes, he removed a Beretta semiautomatic pistol from his shoulder holster and held it loosely. He didn't know who would be emerging from the stairs into this basement but he would be prepared.

Steps moved across the ceiling above his head.

The steps reached the stairway and descended.

He flicked off the safety.

The man entered the basement wearing his habitual black, hooded coat, and he was trailed by the woman physician who was on constant call for these things.

She studied him without expression as she unhooked her bright red EMT bag and removed a suture kit. She also removed syringes and vials and a stethoscope. Then she approached him with a bland look of routine, and he knew he would be all right. He just needed a little rest. Then he'd be back in the game.

The hooded man bent and placed a firm but gentle hand on his shoulder, "Rest, brother," he said calmly. "We'll take care of you."

The man gently removed the bloody Beretta from his hand and slid it into his own coat. "I am here now. Everything is going to be all right."

"Yes," he nodded. "Thank you."

He paid no attention to the man as he walked behind the couch. He never heard a sound as the man – his friend, his mentor, his teacher – removed the Beretta from his coat pocket and leaned back over the couch.

He never felt the bullet that smashed through his brain.

* * *

After placing the Beretta in the dead man's hand the black-coated man straightened and gazed about the room. He removed his handkerchief and used it to pick up the man's cell phone. He cracked it open to remove the battery and then dropped them both in his pocket. Without looking, he asked the physician, "Did you touch anything?"

"No," she said, trembling. "Why did you have to kill him?"

"Because he left his blood on a tree," said the man. "They've sent a sample to CODIS for matching. And his DNA is indexed in CODIS." He inhaled deeply. "They would have found him by morning."

"Are you certain that his DNA is in CODIS?" she asked hesitantly.

"Yes." The man continued to study the room. "Also, the same car he used at the scene is parked in this garage. There is an idiot's trail of evidence from the scene to his car to this house. The police will very quickly connect him to the scene. Then they will come for him and arrest him."

"He would not have talked."

"That is not a chance I will take."

"But don't you have people inside the police department who can –"

"It's too late for my people to make this go away. And so, now, when they find his body, they will have their serial killer. And they will close this case."

She mechanically began reloading her equipment in the EMT bag. "It's a shame. He was a good soldier."

"He was a fool." The man turned his face to her, and the woman trembled. "Because of blood loss and shock, he made unforgivable mistakes. And if you make a similar mistake you'll die in the same fashion."

She took a deep breath before saying, "But, now, who will we send? We still have to deal with this last child."

"I'll take care of the last child," the man answered.

"Very well." She began to back away holding the EMT bag over her chest. "Do you need me for anything else?"

"No." The man pulled back the hood revealing dark hair tinged with white at the temples; his stern face was the mold of intellect and will. "The only thing that matters now is this last child," he whispered. "When he is dead, this is finished."

"And then?"

The man's brow hardened.

"Then our victory is assured," he said in a different voice. "And at the end of that day, and the battle is won, the sun will *not* shine again."

* * *

Walking toward his barn in the full dark Joe Mac knew he wouldn't sleep.

His mind kept turning the scene over and over like he might steadily turn a rock in his hand looking for clues as to what kind of rock it might be.

He knew they'd snagged a good line on this old woman, and he wasn't worried about somebody knocking her off before they reached her tomorrow, so, in truth, he should have been more relaxed. But he wasn't relaxed. He was still fired up from the gunfight with the smoke of gunfire on his hands and the sound of gunfire ringing in his ears. And he felt a whiteness in his blood that he hadn't felt in a long time.

He didn't even raise his face at the sound of an onrushing hurricane-sound and Poe landed lightly on his shoulder instantly pulling in his powerful wings. Poe dipped his head to touch Joe Mac's face with his beak, and Joe Mac said in a low voice, "Yeah. Let's go inside, buddy. It's cold out here, ain't it?"

"*Poe,*" said Poe in his human voice. "*Poe … Home …*"

"Ha. They say you don't know what your words mean. They're idiots. You know exactly what they mean, don't ya?"

"*Home,*" said Poe.

Joe Mac laughed gustily as he unlocked the barn door and Poe flew into the vast space to immediately find a familiar place on a wood lamp arching over Joe Mac's desk. And Joe Mac knew the raven would be awake all night. And he would be alert to the slightest sound, aware of the tiniest movement.

He had learned that Poe had a different call for every occasion. A 'caw' was affectionate. A 'cluck' was loving. A 'shrill' was a warning; it meant danger is near. A 'shriek' was his battle cry, and what Joe Mac considered to be his 'scream' was just pure rage.

Wearily Joe Mac dropped his heavy wool coat over his recliner and walked to the kitchen. He felt in the refrigerator for a pack of bacon and pulled out a piece. Then he tore it into greasy strips and laid them in a plate. Walking back to his desk, he laid the plate beside Poe with a cup of water and took a moment to smooth Poe's long feathers.

"You're a good boy," Joe Mac said and leaned his forehead into the raven. "Yeah, you need to stay inside tonight. The world is just … too cold for us no more."

Poe cawed softly.

With a nod, Joe Mac took a seat at his desk. He opened a drawer and pulled out another Springfield 1911. He removed the clip, cleared a round from the chamber, and disassembled it. Then he carefully laid the clip, the frame, the barrel, spring, plug, slide and slide lock on the big unused calendar beneath his hands.

He took a moment, silently counting.

"Okay," he breathed, "let's do it."

He grabbed the slide and slammed in the barrel, then the spring and plug. He locked the slide onto the frame and it took him two seconds too long to find the slot for the slide lock but he finally found it to lock the slide in place and he checked the safety. Last, he slammed in the clip, instantly racking a round.

Joe Mac turned his face to Poe.

"Seven seconds is too long," he said. "These are some mean ol' boys. You and me need to be ready."

Violently extending gigantic wings Poe bent and shrieked.

"I know you're ready!" Joe Mac laughed. "We're gonna both be ready!"

* * *

Statements the next morning were cut and dried since no dead body was recovered, but Brightbarton said, "I'm happy to let you know that you hit him solid, Joe. We found his blood on a tree, and we've already submitted a sample to CODIS. If we're lucky, he's in there. And if we're *really* lucky, he's our man, and this nightmare is about smash into a real bloody, biblical ending."

Jodi asked, "You sure it was Joe's shot or my shot?"

"It was Joe's shot," Brightbarton laughed. "The only thing you hit, rookie, was a couple of dangerous looking trees." He stared a moment. "Good thing you were there, though. Ain't no telling who them trees was just waitin' to attack."

Jodi rolled her eyes across the walls. "So is the FBI putting a rush on the CODIS? They're not gonna take their usual two months, are they?"

"Rollins told me he'd push it through in a couple of days."

Joe Mac stood. "Let me know."

Brightbarton leaned back in the squeaky wood chair; "So what's on the agenda today in case we roll snake eyes with the DNA?"

"We're following up a lead."

"Anything I should know?"

"Not right now."

Brightbarton took a long time before he said, "How do you figure this shooter knew where you guys were headed last night?"

Joe Mac shook his head. "I don't know. But I think I'm gonna play this one real close from now on."

"That's liable to put you in a bind." Brightbarton didn't say anything for a while. Then added, "What about you, Strong? You okay with playing Lone Ranger?"

"Yeah," Jodi said emptily. "I'm tired of this in-fighting. And nobody should have known where we were last night. Something's wrong."

"Something's always wrong," Brightbarton rumbled. "You just ain't been around long enough to know it." He paused. "All right. You two keep your cards close. But, Joe, if you got instincts on somebody, at least give me a call."

Joe Mac lowered his face.

Brightbarton emphasized, "*Just me.*"

"Man, you only got two more months before it's casinos and naked women," said Joe Mac. "I don't think I'm gonna do that."

"You'll do it or you and Strong are off the case. Right here. Right now."

Jodi stood and clapped her hands once. "If Joe won't do it, I'll do it!"

Nothing was said for the longest and then Brightbarton grunted, "Go on. Get out of here. Call me soon as you get something."

Walking down the corridor Jodi gently guided Joe Mac by the arm and said quietly, "You don't even trust the captain? Are you serious?"

"I trust him," Joe Mac rumbled. "But he's too good a man to get shot dead in this fiasco when he's only got two months to go. He needs to take sick leave and not even come in until he turns in his badge. That's what I'd do."

"No, you wouldn't. You'd go out guns blazing. Look at you right now. You're old. You're blind. You don't stand a chance if you have to go up against this guy in a standup fight. But here you are."

"I just want justice. But justice can be expensive. It can cost you."

"Cost you what?"

"Might cost you everything," Joe Mac said, brow hardening. "So, if you want justice done, you better make sure your own debts are paid up first." He paused. "Don't they say that justice starts at the House of God?"

"Yeah," murmured Jodi, "that's what the Bible says. But tell me something more to-the-point, Joe, since we're 'partners.'"

"What's that?"

"Do you have some kind of death wish?"

"Not that I'm aware of."

"Not that you're 'aware of.'" Jodi stared. "That's not exactly a 'no,' Joe."

"What are you worried about? You're not the one who don't care about dying."

"Because it's always the person who doesn't care about dying that ends up living! It's people like *me*, who are scared to death of dying, that end up getting killed. It's always people like you that live."

"Aw, don't worry about it. I ain't gonna let nothing happen to you. I'll die first."

"That's edifying."

As always Joe Mac caught every familiar sound and smell as they descended the reversing stairways to the first floor, and then they were on the street; Jodi guided him with an ever-gentle hand – he was learning to read her slightest touch – to the car.

"Hey, Poe," Jodi said. "You gonna follow us again?"

Poe shrieked; he was perched atop the squad car.

"Yeah, I know. You're ready for a fight," muttered Jodi as she turned her face to Joe Mac. "Don't worry, Poe, it's coming." She looked at Joe Mac. "Now we check out the old woman?"

"Yeah."

"Go on, Poe!" she said as Poe lifted off, wings smashing down with prehistoric strength.

Joe Mac asked, "You remember the address?"

"Yeah. It's way out on Long Island. Gonna take us a while to get there. We need to pick up anything on the way?"

"You got a Remington and an AR-15 in the trunk?"

"Standard issue, yeah. What about it?"

"Rack the shotgun and chamber the AR-15. We'll keep 'em up front with us." Joe Mac listened as she obeyed without objection; he heard her open the trunk, rack the Remington 870. Then she racked the AR-15 and walked back to her door.

"I got 'em," she said.

Joe Mac got in the car and closed the door as she handed him the shotgun; he placed it between them with the barrel pointed into the floor. He listened as she reached over the seat, laying the AR-15 in the back.

"I'm not even gonna ask what you plan to do with that," Jodi said as she started the car. "You think we might be walking into an ambush?"

"Yeah," Joe Mac grunted. "As a matter of fact, I do."

"Well, I'm wearing a backup in addition to the Glock I checked out this morning." Jodi smoothly weaved her way into traffic. "I got a nine millimeter Beretta in a shoulder holster, a .38 six-shot in my purse, and my Glock on my waist. If that's not enough firepower we're probably dead anyway. What about you?"

"Same as last night," Joe Mac droned. "But I want you to know something,"

"What's that?"

"If things start lookin' dicey, I want you to back out whether I go with you or not." Joe Mac waited, but she said nothing. "I can handle myself just fine without you. And one of us is gonna have to call for help. So if I tell you to get out, do it with no questions. You understand?"

"I'm not afraid, Joe."

"I know you're not afraid. But I'll be a dead man if you don't do what I say. You're gonna have to trust me."

Jodi was silent a long time. "All right," she said finally. "But if I think you're just sending me outside so I won't get hurt I'm gonna be mad."

"That's all right," Joe Mac nodded. "Where'd you get the extra guns?"

"I've got friends, too. Last night I called my old uniform partner and he brought me two backups this morning."

"Better to have 'em and not need 'em than –"

"*I know*," said Jodi. "Is Poe gonna follow us all day?"

"Probably."

"Good."

"Why do you say that?"

"Because I think Poe's a better guard dog than any guard dog that ever lived. I also googled 'ravens' last night. Biologists say that ravens are the smartest animals on the planet."

Joe Mac laughed, "You did what?"

"I googled 'ravens.' Did you know that ravens have been tested by biologists, and they've determined that ravens are even smarter than chimpanzees and dolphins?" Jodi didn't wait for an answer as she continued, "Can you imagine that? That a raven is even smarter than a dolphin? Who would have guessed that? No wonder Poe can follow us everywhere we go. It's probably child's play to him. And if a guard dog can sense danger I guarantee you that a raven can sense danger ten times faster. Heck, I like having him around. If Poe does his shrill or whatever it is I'm gonna put my hand on my Glock without even looking. I don't know what's coming, but I'll be ready if Poe gives his warning."

Joe Mac chuckled.

"I'm serious, Joe."

"I know you are." He stopped laughing with an effort. "Oh, man, that's funny." He laughed some more. "Well, I'm glad you like him because I don't see no getting rid of him. I think he's with us to the end."

"I hope and pray," Jodi said quietly. "It also said that God always uses a raven to lead and protect his people."

Joe Mac was still. "Did it really say that?"

"Sure did."

He nodded.

"I believe it."

* * *

It was a sedate two hours down Long Island to the home of Critiani Morgan, the only name in Montanus' organizer that even came close to matching the name he'd been in the middle of mentioning when he was shot down.

Jodi drove past the address, turned around, and came back stopping the car a quarter-mile from the house. She put it in park and waited, staring until Joe predictably asked, "What do you see?"

Jodi began, "Well … not much. She's got a two-level colonial-style house. Baby blue. Lots of windows. Got some sheets blowing on a clothesline. Got a little maroon Honda in the driveway. I don't see her walking around. Must be inside."

"Nobody else?"

Jodi looked up and down the road but didn't see a single car. She checked the rearview mirror and said, "Nope. And I think I would have noticed if somebody was following us. They would have had to have turn around when we did."

"Does she have a porch?"

"Yeah. A big ol' screened-in front porch." A pause. "What? You want to interview her on the porch? Isn't it kinda cold?"

"Yeah, it's cold. She can put on a coat." Joe Mac was silent a long time. "All right. Let's go on up there."

"You gonna mention what happened to Montanus last night?" she asked as she pulled back onto the road.

"Not right off."

"Why not?"

"I wanna see how tight-knit these people are. I wanna see if she already knows." Joe Mac paused. "If she knows that he's dead, she'll know why we're here."

"And is this good or bad?"

"Depends of whether she's friendly. If she's not, she'll tell us everything she knows. But if she's one of them, we won't get anything out of her."

Suddenly Jodi exclaimed, "Uh oh!"

In the near distance a light green, beat-to-death, pickup truck leaving a trail of burning blue oil was roaring down on them.

"Heads up, Joe!"

"Is it a pickup truck?"

Jodi gaped. "How do you know that it's a —"

Sending gravel flying in a shower that peppered her squad car like bullets, the pickup truck had barely stopped when a burly, bearded figure bearing a pump-action shotgun leaped out of the passenger door and walked calmly forward.

He was six-and-a-half feet tall and pushing four hundred pounds. As tremendous as his arms and legs appeared at close range they paled in comparison to his kegger-beer gut stretching his 'Y'ALL NEED JESUS' tee shirt to the max. His wild head of hair descended to his shoulders beneath his 'CAT' bulldozer cap. Behind him, from the driver's door, came a nearly-identical shape carrying a gigantic Smith and Wesson .44 revolver.

As if Jodi had stepped on their mother's grave, they came to the front of the car and stood staring. The first one sharply racked the shotgun. The second one raised the .44 and held a steady aim at Joe Mac's head. Then the passenger leaned sharply closer, squinting at Joe Mac. He reared back with a gut-shaking laugh and came down again. "Joe Mac!" He dropped the shotgun to one hand and punched the driver. "It's Joe Mac, Bobby!"

"Bobby" leaned closer, peering, then a huge smile divided his chest-level beard. "Joe Mac!" he shouted and came around to Joe Mac's side as the second one walked to Jodi's window, the shotgun low in his hand. He leaned down to Jodi's window and said, "Well, hello, little lady! I'm Ronnie! And that's Bobby!"

"Officer Jodi Strong," said Joe Mac loudly, "I'd like to introduce you to Ronnie Kosiniski and Bobby Kosiniski. Or as they are known far and wide – The Kosiniski Brothers."

"Nice to meet you, Officer Strong," smiled Ronnie Kosiniski.

"Nice to meet you, little lady!" called Bobby Kosiniski. He slapped Joe Mac's shoulder. "How you doin,' hoss! We kept an eye out for ya, but we ain't seen hide nor hair. She ain't even been outside but to hang them sheets."

Joe Mac asked, "Graveyard dead, huh?"

"Quiet as a church."

"Good," Joe Mac nodded. "That's real good." He took a deep breath. "All right, I appreciate you boys helping me out. We'll take it from here. Oh, and by the way, how's your pa doing these days?"

"He's hanging in there," Bobby replied.

"Tell him I said hello."

"We will and … Well, we heard about your grandson, Joe. We're real sorry about it." Bobby's deep beard dropped in a frown. "If you do some payback, let us know. We'll keep a couple of shovels in the back of the truck."

Joe Mac nodded, "Thanks, Bobby." He leaned toward Jodi. "Hey! Ronnie!"

Ronnie bent, "Yeah, Joe?"

"There's a chance I might need some taxi service," Joe Mac continued. "I'd get a real taxi but there might be some gunfighting."

"Just give us a call, hoss! We'll pick you up and take you around."

"Appreciate it."

Ronnie Kosiniski abruptly focused on Jodi.

"Are you married, little lady?"

Jodi smiled, "YES!"

"Ah," he growled, "all the good ones is always taken."

Jodi grimaced. "I'm sorry."

"Nah, that's all right, girl. But if you give him nothing but tail lights and dust one day you know where to find me, right?"

"Right," laughed Jodi.

"Good enough! Let's go, Bobby!"

Bobby let go a final punch to Joe Mac's shoulder. "You take care, hoss! You call us if you need some backup. We'll come running!"

"I will," said Joe Man. "Thanks, boys."

"You bet."

In another moment, and leaving a cloud of blue smoke, the Kosiniski Brothers were well down the road and still gathering speed. They'd only been gone almost thirty seconds when Jodi looked timidly at Joe Mac. "Wow," she said. "So that's the Kosiniski Brothers, huh?" She found herself smiling. "They're colorful, I'll give them that."

"They're good people." Joe Mac said, curt. "They're the kind of people that won't let you down in a pinch – no matter what. They may not look fancy, but they got heart. And I'll take that over fancy any day of the week."

"And twice on Sunday," said Jodi. "So? We ready?"

Joe Mac nodded, "Let's do it."

Two minutes later Jodi knocked on the door and an elderly black woman with white hair slowly opened the wood door and walked out onto the porch. But she left the screen latched as Jodi raised her credentials; "I'm Jodi Strong with the New York City Police Department, ma'am. Are you Mrs. Critiani Morgan?"

Her gaze and face were plainly suspicious.

"Yes," she replied. "Can I help you?"

"Mrs. Morgan, can we please speak with you?" Jodi read more than suspicion – she saw genuine fear. "You're not in any trouble, Mrs. Morgan. We just want to ask you a few questions."

Critiani Morgan looked to Joe Mac's shadowed shape standing beside the squad car and focused again on Jodi as she asked, "What's he here for?"

"He's my partner," Jodi smiled tightly.

After another long moment Mrs. Morgan slowly unhooked the screen door and stepped back. "Come on in, then," she said.

Joe Mac entered, and they took a seat at a leaf-strewn wooden table. Then Jodi looked at Joe Mac and said, "Mrs. Morgan, this is Detective Joe Mac. He has a couple of questions for you. Is that all right?"

Mrs. Morgan took her time before she said, "I expect that's all right."

Joe Mac managed a smile with one side of his mouth, his face slightly uplifted, as he said, "Thank you, Mrs. Morgan."

"You're a *blind* detective?" she asked.

"I am," Joe Mac nodded.

"How can you be a detective and be blind?"

"'Cause I been arresting all kinds of these fools for forty years, ma'am, and I know a lie when I hear one."

A smile cracked Mrs. Morgan's face, and she leaned back in her chair. "You go ahead and listen to me, then. What questions you got?"

With a thrill of genuine alarm Jodi knew this is where it could go south in a heartbeat if Mrs. Morgan had something to hide. She was also deathly afraid that Joe Mac might attack this with a sledgehammer instead of a scalpel. Then Joe Mac said calmly, "I'm sad to tell you that a friend of yours was hurt last night, Mrs. Morgan."

Mrs. Morgan scowled. "Who might that be?"

"Mr. Tony Montanus."

A hand rose to her mouth, and Mrs. Morgan gasped, "Oh, no! Not poor Tony!" She looked again at Jodi. "What happened to him!"

"Them people attacked him at his house," said Joe Mac.

"No! No!" She followed, "Was he hurt bad?"

"I'm afraid so," said Joe Mac and morosely bowed his head. "He passed away last night at the hospital. The doctors couldn't save him." A pause. "They tried, but they couldn't save him. I'm sorry, Mrs. Morgan."

That was a lie, but Jodi surmised it didn't matter. Mrs. Morgan didn't know about the attack, anyway, and Jodi saw the wisdom of breaking it to her gently. Finally, Mrs. Morgan shook her head and said, "I've always been afraid of something like this happening. Ever since poor Cathren died I've been afraid of something like this happening."

"That's why we're here," Joe Mac nodded.

Jodi knew that Joe Mac knew absolutely nothing about the wife of Tony Montanus, but he was doing a good job acting like he did. And Jodi also realized in the same split-second that the death of the husband was linked to the death of the wife. She wasn't sure how she knew, but she was certain that she did.

Obviously so did Joe Mac as he continued, "I know you don't want no more of this terrible stuff happening, Mrs. Morgan. You seem like a good person. And you're tired of these people same as me." A pause. "I think something needs to be done about 'em."

"I do, too!" Mrs. Morgan slapped a hand down flat on the table. "I do, too!"

"Just point me in the right direction," said Joe Mac, lifting his chin. "I might be blind, but I can smell scum like this a mile away."

"Oh," she stretched a hand across the table, "you have to be careful with those people, Mr. Joe Mac. They're awful! They killed poor Mr. Montanus's wife, and now they done for him. Oh, they're terrible people!"

"I need a name!" Joe Mac boldly declared. "It's time!"

"Oh, lord!" she groaned. "They killed poor Cathren and now her poor husband! They've killed all kinds of good folks that know their secret!"

"I need a name!" said Joe Mac like a judge pronouncing doom.

Mrs. Morgan rested with both hands over her face a long moment. Then she rose with, "Wait here. I have to get my book."

Jodi said nothing as she disappeared into her house and then looked at Joe Mac whispering, "What are you talking about? What are we gonna do with a name? We can't just bust in on these people! We need to know what she knows! And you said you weren't even going to mention the shooting last night!"

Joe Mac turned his face. "Sometimes you just have to wing it. Like Poe."

"Oh, god!"

Mrs. Morgan came out the door and sat, quickly flipped through an address book. "There's a note in here that has a name on it. I kept it after Cathren died. I just knew I'd probably need it one day." She continued looking. "He's the only one I know by name. But Cathren told me there was a heap of 'em. She said she'd been keeping up with 'em because of what they did to that boy."

Joe Mac asked, "Is this the person that hurt Cathren?"

She answered. "He's one of 'em. But there's a bunch of 'em." She slowly shook her head. "I told Cathren not to mess with those people. I told her how mean they was. I said they were straight from the devil, and they are. They think they can just do anything they want to anybody they want. And most folks are too scared to say anything. But Cathren wasn't. She was going to the police after they disappeared that boy."

Joe Mac scowled, "You said that twice. What boy are you talking about?"

"Cathren was gonna report them to the police after they made that last little boy disappear out west of the city near that graveyard. I don't remember the little boy's name. But it was some little boy who accidently saw them coming out of some graveyard somewhere."

Joe Mac asked, "How did Cathren know about it?"

"A friend of hers told her about it. And then the friend ended up dying the next week in some kind of terrible accident." She made a distressing sound. "Those folks just seem to bring death on everybody they meet. It don't matter if you're a child or full-grown."

Joe Mac waited like a monument to justice, and Jodi barely dared to glance between them until Mrs. Morgan lifted a piece of paper.

"Here it is," she said in much a softer, and frightened, voice. "This is the name of the man that called Cathren two days before she fell down the stairs. But she didn't fall down them stairs! Everybody knows that!" She gazed at the name. "I kept it all this time because I felt that the good lord would make this day come 'round and somebody would do the right thing for poor Cathren!"

"Let me see," said Jodi and took the scrap of paper. She stared down. "Does this guy live in the city?"

"No. I think he lives out this way."

"Good." Jodi gently gripped Mrs. Morgan's hand. "Mrs. Morgan, I don't want you to tell anyone that we visited with you today, okay? We don't want you involved. Do you understand what I'm saying?"

"Yes," she nodded.

"That means that you can't even tell your friends," Jodi added gently. "You can't tell your family or your church or anybody else. You understand me, right? We were never here. You never talked to us. You don't know anything about us."

"*Oh!*" Mrs. Morgan cried.

Jodi had whirled in her chair, her hand already on her Glock, to see Poe tucking in his massive black wings that momentarily blocked out the sky. He had landed on the rail of the short stairway leading up to Mrs. Morgan's porch, and after he settled in, he raised his obsidian black eyes to focus directly on the old woman as if gazing into her soul.

"*A raven!*" Mrs. Morgan whispered. "Somebody gonna die for sure!"

Jodi noticed as Joe Mac narrowly turned his face to the sun. She couldn't see his eyes but she sensed they were open. Then with a shriek Poe erupted from the handrail as a black four-door sedan sped up to Mrs. Morgan's house with the windows rolled down.

Jodi dove into Mrs. Morgan shouting, "GET DOWN!"

Jodi sensed rather than saw Joe Mac hit the deck as the thin screen surrounding the porch vanished and the wooden wall of the house was tattooed with multiple lines of bullet impacts that continued for an unknown period of time because every second felt like a full minute. Finally Jodi lifted her head and saw, with horror, four men on foot, the sedan stopped in the road, and Joe Mac rising with his .45 drawn.

"Four men!" Jodi shouted. "They're spread out, Joe!"

Joe lurched into the lower wooden half of the porch and froze in a shooting profile. Jodi expected him to fire immediately but then he shouted, "Give me one on the clock!"

"Eleven o'clock!" Jodi responded and focused on the one on her far right.

They fired at the same moment although Joe kept firing in a tight pattern until the slide locked. He changed clips with a smoothness that was more instinct than skill as bullets tore through the porch. Strangely, where the wood was reenforced with wooden beams, the bullets failed to penetrate; it was something Jodi noticed with preternatural acuity and shouted to Joe, "Get behind a beam, Joe! Bullets don't penetrate! Stay down, Mrs. Morgan!"

Another fusillade tore through screen and wood panels, and as Jodi came up again to return fire she saw Joe's man dead in the yard. The other three were rushing forward, and Jodi took a lesson from Joe; she focused on the one in the middle and emptied the entire clip from the Glock. It was seventeen rounds fired in a tight pattern.

She saw the man go backward with a shout just as she saw something else blast its way through the smoke-filled ditch roaring into the melee like the wrath of God. A shotgun blast from the passenger side sent one attacker flying backwards as the last attacker spun and was running to barely evade the second shotgun blast. Then Bobby Kosiniski was out of the pickup truck, arm leveled with the massive Smith and Wesson .44 as the man fled, and Bobby didn't hesitate to fire. The impact was – as Jodi expected – enormous and hurled the attacker forward ten feet before he landed on his face, skidding to a stop. Then the driver of the sedan obviously decided that discretion was the better part of valor and was speeding from the scene, vanishing into smoke and dust.

"WAIT!" screamed Jodi as Ronnie and Bobby Kosiniski raced back to the pickup to give chase. *"Don't go after him!"*

Bobby bellowed, "But we can still get him!"

Quite unnecessarily, Ronnie added, "We saw that car coming this way and knew something was wrong with it! That's why we –!"

"FORGET ABOUT THAT! You two get in your truck and get out of here! Get out of here NOW! You won't be in any report! *Now go! VANISH! DO IT NOW!*"

Ronnie and Bobbie Kosiniski obviously knew the drill, and Jodi didn't have to ask who taught them as Joe rose to his feet. He stood hunched, head bowed. Listening. He nodded as he heard the pickup tear through the yard, back across the ditch, and down the road.

Moaning, Mrs. Morgan was attempting to rise. She had a hand on the table, which was remarkably untouched, and had risen to one knee. "Oh, my lord," she groaned, "They're gonna kill all of us …"

Jodi sheathed the Glock and helped the elderly lady to her chair. She hugged her for a moment before separating to say very calmly, "No, Mrs. Morgan. We're going to stop these people before they hurt anyone else."

"But who will protect me?" Mrs. Morgan asked. "They'll be back! I know they will!"

"We're going to put you some place safe," said Jodi. "Don't you worry about that. Can you pack a suitcase?"

Mrs. Morgan was nodding, "Yes, I think so …"

"Then pack a suitcase. We're putting you up in a nice hotel with a few police officers guarding the door until Detective Joe Mac and me arrest these people. Okay?"

Mrs. Morgan walked on shaky legs towards the door, her hands visibly trembling, "Okay. I'll be ready in a minute."

Jodi knew it'd be a lot longer than "a minute" before they could transport the old woman to a safehouse or a safe hotel room. She could already hear sirens approached and walked to Joe Mac. She gently put a hand on his shoulder, "How ya doing?"

"Ha," Joe Mac smiled. "You askin' *me*?" He turned his face toward her. "How many did you get?"

"I got one. You got one. The Kosiniski Brothers got two. The one driving the car got away."

"Why is that?"

"I didn't want Ronnie and Bobby getting involved in a rolling gunfight on the freeway. The Kosiniski Brothers are too valuable an asset to burn. I'm gonna tell the captain we did all the shooting."

"Then you better get the shotgun from the car and fire off a round into the ground before those sirens get here. And collect whatever shotgun shells the Kosiniski brother used. And make up some story for the tracks of their pickup."

"I'm on it."

"Good girl."

* * *

Only Brightbarton displayed an aspect indicating that he just *totally* believed Jodi's hack-eyed story of how they were attacked by "unknown" persons for "unknown" reasons and then someone driving down the road lost control, veered into the firefight, might have returned fire, and quite obviously fled the scene "in reasonable fear for their life."

Seated, his elbow on the table, his chin on his hand, Brightbarton merely raised a gaze as an investigator stepped into the porch. "No ID, no keys, no nothing," said the detective. "Not a one of 'em has as much as a hamburger receipt. We'll have to run their prints and facial ID. We might get lucky."

"Do it," said Brightbarton dully. He turned a gaze to Joe Mac, who was leaning against a stout beam. He gestured to the ten cops meandering around the porch. "Could I please have a little privacy, gentlemen?"

No objections. They vanished like ghosts. But Special Agent Rollins remained in place and didn't look like he was in a mood to move.

"That means you, too, Rollins."

Very reluctantly, Agent Rollins walked to the bullet-torn screen door as he tossed over his shoulder, "If their lies don't hold up to ballistics, I'll see both of them in a federal prison. And just to remind you, federal prisons don't grant parole."

He was gone.

With a deep sigh Brightbarton eventually asked, "The Kosiniski Brothers just happened to be passing by?"

Jodi blinked. "I didn't mention the Kosiniski Brothers."

"The brothers got two of 'em," answered Joe. "Then I got one and Jodi got one. Her story will hold up to ballistics. The rest is just smoke. Confusion. Blinded by the light. She 'kinda' saw this. She 'kinda' saw that. Rollins can save his federal parole for himself."

"Why is that?" asked Brightbarton.

"Cause he's getting high on my list of things to do."

There was a long silence. Then, finally, Brightbarton asked, "Are you serious?"

"I am."

"'Cause he knew you were here?"

"And only the killer could have known we were here."

"Or someone who knows the killer."

"Yep."

Brightbarton's frown was deep and pronouncing.

Jodi had, of course, seen cops break the law in small incidents, knew the oft-necessary times to "forget" a minor crime, and had "bent" the law more than a few times herself. But to see someone of Captain Brightbarton's royal stature talk about sending an FBI agent to a federal prison and basically cover up a shooting incident involving four dead men reached a new water mark for police discretion.

"And how would Rollins know where you might be?" asked Brightbarton.

"'Cause I told him we might be coming out this way."

"A blue dye operation?"

Joe Mac nodded slowly.

Tiredly, Brightbarton looked at Jodi as he said, "A blue dye operation is when you put dye in a stream, rookie, and then watch to see where it comes up downstream. Usually it's done with false information, but the truth works just as well. It's one way of finding a mole."

Jodi pursed her lips.

With a groan Brightbarton stood, folding his legal pad. "You two will turn in your hot weapons to Crime Scene. Don't worry about your backup weapons. You're probably gonna need them. Then go to the nearest hospital, get some air, and be in my office at eight tomorrow morning with your reps to answer some questions. Whether you want to continue your investigation for the rest of the day, that's up to you. I'll see to Mrs. Morgan's safety. We'll put her in a hotel with a man at the door."

"Last time we were in a live shooting incident you told us to go home until you interviewed us the next morning," Jodi noted. "Now you're saying we can keep working until tomorrow?"

Brightbarton's mouth parted and his brow hardened in the look of someone incredulously watching a zombie rise from the grave. Then he said, "Little girl, you're neck deep in an investigation that might see you dead before tomorrow morning whether you're working it or not. If it was me, I'd like to spend my last hours going after whatever scumbag just signed my death warrant." He shrugged, "Even if I die going after him, at least I won't go down like some kind of meaningless nobody that don't own the job because I didn't have the guts to make the hard call." A stare. "A call like *this*."

Without any readable aspect, Brightbarton walked away and out the screen door. After a brief pause, Jodi focused on Joe Mac.

"What, exactly, does that mean, Joe?"

Joe sighed heavily before he said, "It means that when you go up against true evil, it's justice that you need to decide. Not the law." He paused. "It means that, sometimes, what pulls the trigger is … something bigger than you."

* * *

Back in the squad car it took less than a minute for Jodi to run an NCIC check on the name, but it came back negative on active warrants. Still, she got an address, and it was on a stretch of Long Island inhabited exclusively by the I-don't-want-to-be-bothered.

"You know this area?" she asked.

"Yeah, I know it," said Joe Mac. "Been out there a few times. Not too many people. And nobody's on the beach this time of year. You get in trouble on that strip and you might as well be on the moon. You sure you're up for this?"

"Yeah. Of course."

"Let's go, then."

Jodi pulled onto the remarkably empty road and began cruising before she asked, "What are we getting into, Joe? I mean, that old woman made it sound like these psychos kill people all the time and get away with it. Is this the Mafia?"

"No. This is a lot worse."

"So what are they?"

"I don't know. You'll have to give me a few minutes with What's-His-Name."

"Jacob Statute."

"Give me a few minutes with Mr. Jacob Statute, and I'll see if I can't get him to answer a few questions."

Jodi kept glancing from the road to Joe Mac's hardening face. "Joe?" she began. "Joe, if you beat him to death, we'll never find out who killed Aaron. You're gonna remember that, right? When we get there?" A pause. "Joe? Are you listening to me?"

"I ain't gonna beat him to death," Joe Mac rumbled. "I'm gonna practice the golden rule. Do unto others as they do unto you."

"That's not the golden rule."

"It's good enough for who it's for."

* * *

The house of Jacob Statute would more appropriately be described as a "hovel" in comparison to the vast estates that ran the length of Long Island. Not everyone on the island lived palatially but Jacob Statute had a house that Jodi quantified as a "shed."

It was set back much closer to the road than the usual Long Island mansion where privacy was a high – and expensive – priority. If Jodi hadn't suspected Statute of attempted murder she would have guessed that he lived in a guard house.

With Joe Mac at her side, his hand shoved deep in the pocket of his coat, Jodi knocked rapidly and waited. When no one answered, she walked to the garage and opened the door. Inside was a dark blue Ford Taurus with a shattered front windshield and bullet holes along the left side. The passenger side window was also blown out.

Jodi pulled her Glock.

Walking to the driver's side window, she saw the seat was heavily soaked with blood. Looking in the back seat, she saw an AK-47.

"We got blood and a rifle, Joe."

Joe Mac nodded and removed his hand from his coat; he held a Springfield .45. "Come on," he said and signaled with the pistol. "We're going in."

"We're not gonna wait for backup?"

"I want a chance to question him before they get here. Let's go."

Jodi returned to the front door and knocked again, but there was no answer, so she kicked it with all her might; the stout oak door didn't move an inch as she staggered back.

"Whoa!" she exclaimed.

"Let me try," said Joe Mac.

He grabbed the door knob with his left hand, his arm outstretched. Then he surged into it with his shoulder and the door was blasted open with a thick portion of the splintered door frame falling like a tree.

Jodi was in the door quick, scanning left and right before she saw blood on the floor. "We got blood," she said. "It leads down the stairs. Looks like a basement."

"I'm behind you."

Descending slowly, Jodi reached the basement floor to see a man lying across a couch. Blood coated his entire body and there was a bullet hole in his right temple. A gun was still in his hand, and Jodi almost holstered her weapon, but remembered her training.

She scanned the room, insuring they were alone, then cuffed him before she told Joe Mac, "He's dead. A bullet through his right temple. Looks like a suicide."

"Look around before you call it in."

Jodi began searching the low coffee table set before the couch, and there was nothing but two bloody panels of a shredded bullet proof vest, a bottle of morphine tablets, and an open box of large gauze pads.

"What do you see?" asked Joe Mac.

"Well, first; he was wearing a ballistic vest, but that hog-leg .45 of yours blew a hole clean through the front *and* the back panel. There's a dark blue Navy peacoat on the floor soaked with blood. There's a second full-size Beretta 92FS laying on top of it. The left sleeve of the coat is torn up real good. Looks like shrapnel. I guess one of us did hit him in the car." She put on her surgical gloves and searched the coat. "No cell phone."

"Check the rest of the room."

Jodi walked further and began searching cardboard boxes and drawers. She found a lot of carpenter and mechanic tools, a high stack of maps, a reloading machine, empty cartridge boxes, various types of gunpowder, caps, and a small arsenal of weapons.

"We've got maps," she commented. "Lots of maps."

"Keep the maps."

"Okay. We've also got tools, and it looks like he was a survivalist. He's got a whole arsenal of rifles, shotguns, pistols, all kinds of ammo. He's got a big, wooden crate of what look to be genuine military hand grenades. Some vests still in the box. He's got a first-rate EMT bag complete with bandages, tape, splints, whatever you might need. Then we have a whole lot of different kinds of unused tennis shoes still in the box, all size ten." She was still. Then, "Why do you think this guy killed himself? This guy was a survivor; he had everything he needed to hang on for a while. And surely a scumbag like this would have a nurse or a vet or even a real doctor on call."

Joe Mac was standing with his face slightly raised.

"Keep looking."

Jodi opened a closet; "Oh, man, Joe; I wish you could see this."

"What is it?"

"There's some kind of Satanic-looking robe. It's black with some ... very ... intricate gold embroidery. There's a big circle – like a tunnel – and inside that circle is a crescent moon and thirteen stars with a bunch of lines joining them in a constellation or something. I don't know astronomy. Or astrology. Whichever it is." Joe Mac heard her moving around before she continued with, "There's some Exorcist masks – demon masks. Linda Blair on a really bad hair day. We've got half a dozen Rambo knives. We've got ... wow ... We've got what look to be genuine human skulls, Joe. There's ... seven ... complete skulls. The jaws have been wired at the hinge by someone who – it looks like – knew what they were doing. And there's, like, black and red leather straps around the neck like they hang these things up for Christmas."

"Are they fresh?" asked Joe.

"*Fresh?*" Jodi asked. "How is god's name do you determine whether a human skull is fresh or not?"

Joe paused. "Go on."

"We have every stylish working girl's dream – your beautiful *Belk* necklace of human finger bones strung together on a red and black-beaded Catholic rosary *sans* crucifix – so elegant. And, finally, we've got the proverbial cherry on top of the cake. He has what I swear to god is a human heart preserved in a pickle jar of what has to be formaldehyde. Oh, my god, how … awful." She took a moment. "Jesus, Joe, this is decadent, man."

"I get the picture. Take another look at the dead guy."

She walked back and bent. "It's a contact wound. Powder burns. Typical five-point starburst. If he didn't do it himself, someone sure knew how to make it look like a suicide. And he must have trusted them because he had a .38 backup on his ankle." She stepped back, still staring. "It looks like a suicide to *me*. And I'm pretty sure it's gonna look like a suicide to everybody else. But you don't believe it, do you?"

Joe Mac frowned, then shook his head.

"No," he said. "I guess I don't."

She removed her cell phone. "Time to call it in?"

"Go ahead."

It took her less than ten seconds to make the call.

"Now what?" she asked. "He wears size ten tennis shoes, so this is gonna be our man. He's the one that killed Aaron. And he probably killed the rest of them, too. But I bet you there's not a thing in this house that ties him to any crime scene. He burns everything."

"He's just part of it," said Joe Mac. "He's the arm but I'm after the head, now. I want whoever's behind this."

"So this isn't the end of the road?"

"No, but you can see it from here."

"Well, you can count me in." She looked up, studying the rafters. "I'm gonna go put these maps in the unit and wait for a local."

"Call Brightbarton. Tell him what you've got."

"You mean what 'we' got?"

"I'm just an observer."

"Yeah, right; you staying down here?"

"For a minute." He moved his head toward the staircase. "Go on. Make sure you tell Brightbarton."

Jodi ascended the stairs more quickly than she intended and wondered if the blood and the tension wasn't beginning to affect her. She wasn't aware of any conscious fear, but she was aware of the possibility that it could be beneath the surface and rising.

Still, she knew the job: She would wait for the locals, give them the story, and let them handle it. It would be entirely up to Brightbarton whether he wanted the NYPD Crime Scene Unit to respond, but she was confident that the FBI would send their best forensics people and take charge of the whole scene.

Walking into the sea fresh air was a rush and for a moment Jodi simply stood on the porch, gun in hand, staring at the blazingly bright, beautiful blue sky which seemed another universe compared to the dark, bloody pit below her. And she felt a distinct desire not to go back down the stairs but wasn't worried about her nerve. She wasn't even close to folding. Then she wondered why Joe Mac had chosen to stay with the body.

Half-turning her head, she almost entered the house again but thought better of it.

Whatever he was doing, he wanted to do it alone.

* * *

Head bowed, Joe Mac listened.

He could hear the hot water heater spinning. He could hear the wind rising. He heard his own heartbeat.

The smell of blood was strong, and Joe Mac doubted this man would have lived whether someone finished him off or not. The .45 had worked like it was designed to work – a single big round to put a man down. That's why it was invented. A .45 was usually a one-shot stop but there are no guarantees in life.

Not for anything.

He was keenly listening for a car arriving in the driveway or steps on the floor above. He certainly didn't' want to be caught executing an illegal search and seizure outside their jurisdiction but estimated he still had a little time.

Doubtless, whoever killed this guy already removed everything from his coat and pockets. Almost anyone would possess the presence of mind to do something that simple and essential. But there were other places to hide things – places Joe Mac had only learned about after thirty years of searching people who were professionals at hiding things.

He'd sent Jodi upstairs because he wasn't sure what he would find, and he didn't intend to drag her to where he was willing to go. It would all depend on what he found. If it was something neutral, like a clue, then he'd share it with her. But if it had a name, then he would go it alone. She was a good kid; he wouldn't let her be party to murder.

He found the body, the leg, and felt down until he reached the boot. Joe Mac pulled off his right boot, searched inside it, then twisted the heel; it didn't move. He removed the other boot, searched inside, then twisted the heel.

The heel rotated ninety degrees.

Inside the hollowed-out heel was what felt to Joe Mac like a plastic tab. and then he realized it was a tightly folded sheet of paper wrapped in cellophane. Almost as soon as he dropped it into his pocket Joe Mac twisted the heel back into place and stood.

He would be pushing his luck to stay down here any longer, so he carefully found the stairs and began climbing. And almost as soon as he reached the plateau, the front door opened and Jodi was speaking to someone in a subdued voice.

"We'll take it from here," said the man.

Joe Mac nodded and continued out the front door. He tapped his way down the two-step rise to the sidewalk and along the driveway as other cars arrived. In another few moments he was innocently sitting in Jodi's squad car.

The driver's door opened and Jodi sat. She took a moment, apparently staring at the parade of officials arriving and entering. "Brightbarton said NYPD isn't going to respond because the FBI is already on its way and there's already too many chiefs on this island. So what'd you do down there?"

Joe Mac removed the paper from his pocket.

"What's this?"

Jodi unfolded it and was silent: "I really can't tell you, Joe. It looks like some kind of weird map."

"A map?" Joe Mac turned his face. "What kind of map?"

"I said it was 'a weird map.'"

"Chose another adjective."

"A *really* weird map."

"I think you're missing the point."

She laughed. "There's a bunch of dots running in one direction from what I assume is a road. The dots go to a box that's inside what looks like a bell. Or maybe it's a hill. And there's a name – *Fortinus*. Then the dots run in a completely different direction for a long ways. Eventually the dots reach four small circles that sort of box in, or square off, a big circle. And inside this big circle there's a smaller circle right in the center." She was still and silent before she exclaimed, "*What is this thing?*"

Jodi twisted at a knock on her window. She rolled it down, and Joe Mac heard a voice; "Do you know whether the FBI is asserting jurisdiction in this case, Detective Strong? Our crime scene guys want to know before they start moving things around."

"Yes," Jodi replied, "the FBI is on its way, so if I were you guys I'd just secure the scene and not touch anything."

"Works for me."

She rolled up the window, and Joe Mac felt her stare.

"Now what?" she asked.

"Run *Fortinus* through the data base. You'll get the phone book, but let's see what we got to work with."

"And then?"

"Let's go to the museum."

"For what?"

"Let's see what Marvin can make of this map."

Jodi started the car.

"And round and round we go …"

* * *

Marvin's face lit up when he saw them approaching through the vast first floor of the museum, and he assumed a joyous posture until Jodi stuck out her hand with the map and said, "I got a bone to pick with you, Marvin."

He froze. "What did I do?"

"Who did you tell about us going out to see Mr. Montanus on Long Island last night?" Jodi put both hands on hips. "Tell me *exactly* who you told."

Quickly searching left to right Marvin replied, "I, uh, asked four or five staff members if they knew anybody who might talk to you guys about Druid activity." He shook his head. "Then I asked Professor Graven for the same thing, and he gave me a name. Why?"

"Because the guy's dead now! He was shot dead last night when we were trying to question him!" Jodi watched for a reaction; there was plenty. "I thought I told you not to talk to anybody else, Marvin. Did I not tell you that?"

"Yeah!" Marvin was electrified. "But I didn't think you were talking about people I work with every day! They're my friends! How did Mr. –"

"Not now," Jodi waved off the question. "But from now on you don't tell *anybody* what I tell you! Do you understand? People could get killed, Marvin! *We* almost got killed!"

Marvin seemed to be growing more upset by the second. "No! I won't! Oh, my god! I swear! I won't! Is the guy really dead?"

"Yes, he's dead." Jodi handed him the paper. "Tell me what this means."

Scowling, Marvin turned the paper this way and that. His brow was hard, and his jaw was set, and for a long minute Jodi didn't think he'd have any answer before he said, "Where did you find this?"

"At the home of the man who's been killing all these people. Do you have any idea what it means?"

"Yeah," Marvin said with confidence. "This is a place for human sacrifice." He opened his eyes wider. "For … a lot … of … human … sacrifice."

"Let's go to your office."

"Good idea."

Fifteen minutes later they were sitting in Marvin's makeshift office, and he spread the paper on his plywood desk. He took a large magnifying glass and went over the map inch by inch until he asked, "Where did you say you got this?"

"At the killer's house," said Jodi. "Out on Long Island."

"No way," he shook his head. "That's not the starting point for this map. This has a different starting point."

"What's it a map of?"

Joe Mac was sitting much closer to the desk than the first time he'd been inside the museum. It was as if he didn't want to miss a single syllable of what Marvin had to say. His face was lifted and he had both hands cradling his cane.

"Okay," Marvin began, "you see these small circles? These are what we call 'ritual shafts.' They're holes dug exactly twenty-five feet deep with stakes sticking up at the bottom. Druids used to throw people into the shafts as human sacrifices. Obviously, the person would land on the spike, get killed, and their bodies would stay down there."

Jodi pointed to the largest circle. "What's this?"

"This looks like a scale replica of Stonehenge," Marvin answered. "You've got five large trilithons surrounding by fifteen more trilithons. I don't know that Stonehenge ever had a spike in the center but, then again, neither does anybody else. Nobody even has an iron-clad theory on who built the thing."

Jodi said, "I thought the Druids built it."

"Yeah, people say that, but it's sort of a misnomer. Most archeologists agree that the people who built it lived in Britain around eight thousand BC, but the Druids didn't possess enough knowledge of architecture to have built it. You see, Stonehenge dates all the way back to a period of Europe when people existed just by hunting and foraging. They knew nothing about agriculture or keeping flocks. They hunted what they could kill and they picked berries or tomatoes or whatever else they came across to survive. But Stonehenge – as we know it – was built by a fairly sophisticated civilization that survived some kind of global holocaust and migrated into Britain around eight thousand BC."

After staring, Jodi asked, "What kind of 'global holocaust?'"

Marvin looked her in the eyes. "Look, there's *indisputable* archeological evidence that a devastating flood covered about one hundred-fifty thousand square miles of Mesopotamia around eight thousand BC. It was somewhere around the time that the last Ice Age retreated. You gotta think: Places like Great Britain or North America were buried under a mile of ice at the time. Then all that ice melted, the water table rose all over the world, and *lots* of places got flooded. I mean, it doesn't quite rise to the mythological 'Noah's Flood' that covered *the entire world,* but it sure covered the entire world *as they knew it.* They've even – and this was just recently discovered – found the old Black Sea shoreline four hundred feet beneath the surface of the current shoreline, and it dates to eight thousand BC."

"And this Ice Age flood was the global holocaust?" asked Jodi.

"Yeah," Marvin nodded. "Now, some scientists infer that the civilization that domesticated Britain and Western Europe were the survivors of that flood. Archeologists conjecture that this nation migrated north after the flood receded in search of greener pastures and eventually settled in France, Germany, and Britain. Some say they taught the indigenous food gatherers – or the earliest 'Druids,' – a better way of life. And there's no doubt that a civilization savvy enough to survive a *quasi*-global apocalypse would also be well versed in architecture, so there's every possibility that they might have taught the ancient Druids how to build Stonehenge. And, over time, the two nations just naturally merged into one single civilization."

Joe Mac asked, "How does any of that help us solve this murder?"

"Wait a minute, Joe," said Jodi. "Would these people who migrated north have been familiar with the Jews?"

"Sure," Marvin nodded. "They came from Mesopotamia. And there's evidence that the book of Job was written somewhere around that period. In fact, some archeologists hypothesize that Job is the oldest book in the world. Even older than Gilgamesh. Older than *anything.* But that's beside the point. To answer your question: Yes. Whatever civilization moved north after the flood would certainly have been familiar with the beliefs of bordering tribes and that would have included ancestors of Israel."

"Could Druids have come out of this civilization?" Jodi asked.

"No, the Druids have been in Britain since the world began. But then this secondary civilization migrated north after the flood and they 'absorbed' the primitive Druids along with many of their shamanistic rituals. And this mingling created a new form of Druidism that was both very intelligent and very savage at the same time. It's really the only way to describe how a group like the ancient Druids – a group that simultaneously operated at such a high level of sophistication while also practicing something as barbaric as human sacrifice – came to exist. This new civilization modernized the primitive Druids, but the Druids retrained all their gods and beliefs and rituals. Yeah, they became sophisticated enough to build Stonehenge, but they kept their more savage ceremonies – ceremonies like the *Wicker Man*. In fact, Caesar thought the Druids were so horrifying and savage that he was doing the world a favor by killing every single one of them."

Jodi sat back in her chair and stared for a long time at the map. "Stonehenge is in England, right?"

"In Salisbury, yeah."

"So if a group of Druids built another Stonehenge in New York State would it serve the same purpose?"

Marvin gazed up at the roof. "Well ... not really," he said at last. "The primary purpose of Stonehenge was astronomy because it rests on the fifty-first parallel. And I don't think any part of New York State rests on the fifty-first parallel, and that location is critical."

"So if this is a map to a local replica of Stonehenge," Jodi said slowly, "how do we use this map to locate it?"

"You'd have to know the starting point on the map," Joe Mac stated. "That's what that little house is for. It's the place where the map begins."

Jodi: "Could this place be underground?"

"Stonehenge is bigger than people think. It'd have to be a huge cavern. Do you have any idea where the starting point for this map is?"

Jodi had begun shaking her head before he was even finished. "No," she said dejectedly, "but if this thing is underground, I suppose the starting point is underground, too."

"You're supposing a lot," said Joe Mac. "Why don't we stick to what we know?"

Jodi struck the paper. "I know this is a map! I know this represents a replica of Stonehenge! I know the people behind Aaron's death are Druids, so I know that whoever gets together at this place with their 'Druid beliefs' are the same people who are responsible for killing twenty-four innocent people in my jurisdiction in the past four years! They may not have pulled the trigger, but they sure ordered it done, and *I know* that's bad enough for some serious payback, Joe!"

Joe Mac sat unmoving, his face slightly lifted to the light, before he said, "But we don't know where to start looking for this place. We need to get some answers out of one of these people, and that means we have to capture one of them. And the only chance we have of doing that is to get to their next target before they do. Then we set up, wait for him, and snatch him up when he comes in."

"That's great, Joe. But that only brings us back to the fact that we don't know who his next target is because we don't know how he's choosing them! We don't have a motive! For all we know his motive is that he's crazy and that means he's picking them at random!"

"He's not picking them at random," Joe Mac said, solid.

Jodi collapsed back in her metal chair, legs sticking straight out, arms hanging at her sides. She blew out a long breath and didn't move again. She saw only dust-caked gray metal racks and unorganized, black-pitted dinosaur bones.

Joe Mac said, "Marvin? What kind of astronomy are you talking?"

Marvin, who was bent in his chair, raised his face. "What?"

"What kind of astronomy did these Druids do?"

Marvin sighed, "Well, uh, that's a really complicated question. And I'm not sure that anybody knows the answer."

"Give it your best shot."

Marvin stared at a distant wall, removed a pipe from his coat, and leaned back. "Okay," he began, "the basic design of Stonehenge was to determine the dates for sacrifices by some kind of unknown –"

He struck a match.

A thunderous and bizarrely silent blast hit Jodi fully in the face and she was aware that she was in the air, the ground racing away beneath her even as dirt and dust rose from the floor enveloping her in a cocoon and then she suddenly stopped moving.

She dimly sensed she was sliding down a wall.

* * *

Way too slowly, Jodi realized she was sitting and holding a cloth to her face, and her head was hurting.

A lot.

She heard Joe Mac's familiar voice and gazed narrowly to the side simultaneously recognizing three things: first, Joe Mac and Captain Brightbarton were in a quiet conversation; second, she was still in the museum, but the surroundings were smoking; and third, firemen were casually roving to and fro.

Amazingly, Jodi also realized she was not in any immediate danger because no one was moving with any display of alarm. Instead, they all seemed to be treating this like a dead crime scene rather than a potentially explosive situation.

She wondered what had happened. Then an EMS guy came over to put a hand on her shoulder. "How you doing?" he asked.

"Fine," said Jodi on automatic pilot. "What happened?"

"A gas leak blew up," he answered. "But it was several street levels beneath you, so you guys didn't get burned. You did get hit by the concussion – the change in air pressure. But that only lasted a split-second, and the medics said you were just stunned."

"What about a concussion?"

"Both pupils are responsive. But I'd recommend you go to the ER and get an MRI. That's standard procedure."

Jodi stood. "Screw standard procedure. Thanks." She walked slowly to Joe Mac and Brightbarton and muttered, "I know Marvin's okay because neither of you look too upset. I also know this was another attempt to kill us. What I *don't* know is what *do* we know that makes us such a threat?"

Brightbarton stated, "We were just discussing that."

"By the way, how *is* Marvin?"

Joe Mac: "Like you said; he's fine. He got knocked out by the explosion. 'Bout like all of us. He's in a meeting with the director."

"Okay. Thanks." Jodi chose to sit down beside Joe Mac; she didn't wait, want, or care for an invitation to join this "strategy session" or whatever the hell it was. She figured she'd earned the right to join anything she felt like joining as far as this mess goes.

"Huh," grunted Brightbarton. "Well, as I was saying: You guys have stumbled onto something, and even you don't know what it is or why it's important. But it's something critical to these people." He hesitated a long time. "It could be a name. A location. Both." With a sigh he added, "You already have the clue to find this guy if you can only figure out what it is. With luck, you could close out this case before daylight."

"We ain't had too much luck," mumbled Jodi. Then, "Oh, man, I feel bad that I'm only now thinking about this. But did anybody else get hurt?" She fixed on Brightbarton. "Was there any collateral damage? As they so callously say?"

He shook his head. "Just you three. Possible concussions. Nothing serious."

"Okay."

"We're wasting time here," Joe Mac stood. "Where's Marvin?"

Brightbarton scowled, "He's upstairs. Why?"

Joe Mac shook his head as he moved forward. "We're not the ones who know what they're afraid of."

Jodi closed her eyes; she should have seen it coming.

"It's Marvin," said Joe Mac.

* * *

Remarkably, Marvin seemed to have recovered from the blast like a veteran World War II infantryman. He was covered in dust, a trace of dried blood marked his forehead, and a sling cradled his arm. And yet he seemed composed and alert as if getting blown up was an everyday thing.

"Hey," smiled Jodi. "Well, you look all right."

"I am," said Marvin, a nod. "And they told me you two were okay, so I came up here to give a ... what do they call it?"

"A debriefing?"

"Yeah. That." He rolled a shoulder with a grimace. "Not surprisingly, Professor Graven was relieved that we came out okay. But he was genuinely thrilled that none of the fossils were damaged. I've never felt more expendable in my life."

"Where is he now?" asked Joe Mac.

Glancing placidly around the room, Marvin replied, "I can't tell you. He's probably downstairs with the firemen."

Joe Mac pulled up a chair, and sat. "Marvin, we think you know something that these people don't want us to know. It's something that even you don't know is important, and they don't want you telling us because they think we'll put two and two together. Can you remember what we were talking about before the explosion?"

After slow blinks Marvin finally said, "I … I think so."

"Can you give it a try?"

Jodi preferred to stand, and so she leaned against a wall as Marvin said, "Uh … we were talking about the purpose of Stonehenge." He swallowed with difficulty. "Well, the most commonly held theory is based on the summer solstice. The entire structure was built directly on the perfect parallel, and the combination of the trilithons and fifty-six bluestones laid around two circles of trilithons was the most brilliant means of tracking the movements of the sun and moon. So, whoever built Stonehenge was aware of the 'Metonic' cycle, which is where both cycles of the sun and moon synchronize over a period of eighteen-point-six solar years with an error of only two hours."

"Stop right there." Joe Mac raised a hand. "So this thing was basically a means to tell the longest day, the shortest, the seasons and stuff like that? And they timed their human and animal sacrifices by this calendar, right?"

"Well … yeah. That's what most archeologists think."

"But we don't need Stonehenge to determine the seasons anymore," Joe Mac said. "We've got satellites that tell us when the solstice is gonna be here or what time the moon is gonna rise, so let's pretend for a moment these people who build this modern replica of Stonehenge – if that's what this map reveals – didn't build it with all these solar alignments in mind because they don't need it for that anymore. We've got telescopes for that. What would be the other reason for building it?"

"For rituals," Marvin said plainly. "That would be the *only* reason to build it. And there's good evidence to suggest that the original Druids were … well, let's just say they were 'primitive.' And human sacrifice, decapitation, and cannibalism were part of their everyday belief system. Then this nation from Mesopotamia joined them and it was far more knowledgeable about astronomy and apparently more dedicated to sun worship. So, consequently, the primitive Druids's practice of human sacrifice became a part of their sun worship and musical festivals, and, at that point, the die-hard, bone-deep serious ancient Druids were basically created. It was a merging of two radically diverse cultures – the sophisticated and the savage – and it worked in some kind of one-out-of-a-million magical way that stayed strong for eight thousand years."

"Did you say they held music festivals?" asked Jodi.

"Yeah," Marvin nodded. "There's theories that the artful design of Stonehenge was purposed so that the entire monument could be flooded with water to a depth of about six inches. Then two musical instruments would be simultaneously played on top of the water plain inside the trilithons, and the interplay of the music between the water and the stones would give the optical illusion of ... *of an invisible being* ... standing there." Marvin stared as if waiting. "I mean, it's just a theory. But it's got respected backers. Some people say that the musical allusion of an otherworldly being standing inside the stones is the only reason they held musical festivals at all. And that kind of makes sense. Not to digress, but Jimi Hendrix experimented with water and music, too. Hendrix would flood his sound stage, and then he'd record on top of the water. He said it was 'out of this world.'"

Joe Mac was frowning. "What purpose would that serve?"

Leaning back, Marvin said, "I have no idea. But anything is a viable theory with that place. I don't think they've even scratched the surface of what it was built to achieve." He gazed from Joe Mac to Jodi for ten seconds before he said in a sad voice, "But I do know this: If what you suspect is true, then you two are absolutely dealing with some very bad people who very likely practice human sacrifice, decapitation, and cannibalism *to this day.*" He paused. "Now I know you guys are cops, and you do this for a living, so you're not scared of these people. But I bet you they're not scared of you, either. I'm betting they'll kill you just like they've killed that guy last night and not give it a second thought. So, are you sure you want to go to the wall with these people? I mean, you're talking about an ancient culture that systematically killed tens of thousands of people by ritual sacrifice in an age where killing tens of thousands of people wasn't an easy thing to do!"

Face slightly bent, Joe Mac said nothing. It was Jodi who roused herself, brushing back her auburn hair from her forehead. Then she said, "Yeah. I do want to go to the mat with these people. Now, how do you think they're selecting their victims, Marvin? It has to be astronomy, right? Something the FBI computers didn't pick up?"

Marvin stared at the map. "I can't imagine something so complex that an FBI computer dedicated to astronomy wouldn't pick up. It seems to me that if this method of choosing people had anything to do with astronomy the computer would see it instantly. I know that a computer would pick up on it long before I would. I don't really know astronomy. I only know things I care about."

Joe Mac lifted his face. "Only things you care about." He paused. "The Druids cared about astronomy. They cared about their sacrifices. They cared about rituals. But they only cared about all those things because they cared about maintaining their power. And the greatest threat to their power was ... what?"

Marvin: "The Roman Empire."

"No," Joe Mac shook his head. "No army ever defeated a nation's spirit. We lost in Vietnam because you can't bomb nationalism out of an enemy. Kill them all day long, and they'll still be loyal to their faith. That's a truism; the only thing that can defeat faith is a stronger faith. But back then there were only two great faiths. There were the Druids, and there was Israel." He stared off. "Sometimes with these old civilizations the answer lies in numerology. What do you think, Marvin?"

Marvin hesitated. "Uh, well, that might make sense. But what kind of numerology are we talking? Numerology can be mind boggling."

Joe Mac continued, "Jodi, call up the birthdays of these kids and check them against Jewish holidays."

"This is insane," muttered Jodi as she hauled out her iPad. "Okay, the kids were born between June 6 and the first of November, and there's really nothing all that special on the Jewish calendar during that period. We have a minor holiday, *Leil Selichot*, or prayers for forgiveness, on September 16. We have a minor fast, *Tzom Tammuz*, on July 11. We have *Tish'a B'Av*, a holiday that commemorates the destruction of the two temples, on August 1. And Jesus was born in December, so he doesn't even count."

Jodi noticed that Marvin had frozen in a curious pose; he had a hand raised as if to ask a question, a single finger uplifted, but he didn't say anything.

"Marvin?" She stared. "Are you all right?"

"Uh," he began, "actually, there's no way that Jesus was born in December. I thought you guys knew that."

Jodi didn't move. "Marvin, how could I possibly know that?"

"Because it's obvious."

She didn't blink. "Would you please explain to me why it's so obvious?"

Marvin lifted his hands as if raising a cloud. "Look, it says in the Bible that Elizabeth, Mary's cousin, got pregnant exactly three months before Mary got pregnant, so Jesus was born three months after John the Baptist, his cousin, was born. Right? Okay. Now, Zacharias, who was the husband of Elizabeth, was serving as a priest during the course of Abijah, and we know by non-biblical sources when that was, so we know that Zacharias served as a priest between June 13 and June 19 of that year.

"Anyway, to sum it up, the Bible says that after Zacharias completed his service he went home, and Elizabeth immediately got pregnant. That would put the day of her conception somewhere near the end of June. So, if you add nine months to that, you have March. And that's when John the Baptist was born. And since John was three months older than Jesus, that means Jesus would have been born in June." He swept a hand across the plywood. "Anybody can figure *that* out."

Jodi began typing into her iPad. Her eyes flew over each file, opening and closing until she had all six cases displayed in letterbox. She began scanning, "Okay, all the kids were born between June 6 and September 27 in 2012. And Jesus was born in June, too. But what's special about 2012?"

Marvin muttered, "Don't ask me."

Typing, Jodi continued with, "Okay, the oldest child was born June 6, 2012. And June 6, 2012, was also the date of a 'Venus Transit.' That's a very rare eclipse that happens once every one hundred years, and it happens in a pair. Venus passes between the earth and the sun and then it does it again eight years later. Then it doesn't do it again for another one hundred years. And so, all these children were born the first year following that Venus Transit. But how and why does that unite them?"

"The star over Bethlehem when Jesus was born," said Marvin. "People would have mistaken Venus so close to the Earth as a giant star over the city."

"That's it!" Jodi screamed as she slammed her hand down on the desk and leaped to her feet. *"They think one of these kids is the Messiah!"*

Marvin had jumped back. "But which one?"

"They don't know which one! That's why they've been trying to kill all of them! These psychos have a list of kids who might be the Messiah, but they don't know which one it

is! And that's their motive! That's why they've chosen these children!"

Joe Mac coldly stated, "But they've been killing these kids for four years. If these Druids are so scared one of these kids is the Messiah, why didn't they kill all of them the day they were born?"

"They took their cue from Herod," said Marvin.

"What?" asked Jodi. "What does that mean?"

"When the so-called 'kings of the Orient' finally caught up to give Jesus their gifts, Jesus was almost two years old. The kings didn't find Jesus in a *stable*. The Bible says that when they caught up to Jesus, he was old enough to be following his mother around the house. And that's why Herod, the big honcho of Jerusalem, told his men to kill every child under two years old. Jesus wasn't a baby when the order was given to kill every child in the city because one of them might be the Messiah, so these Druids weren't exactly horrified when these children were born. They knew they had years before the Messiah would be a threat to them. They could take their time hunting him down. Plus, it's easier to kill a targeted group over a period of years. That way you can defuse the horror of the situation, get people to lower their guard. Plan more carefully. Stuff like that."

"There has to be another qualifier for this list," said Joe Mac. "The date of birth and this Venus eclipse isn't enough. A billion kids were born that year. Were these kids all born in the same city or hospital?"

"No," said Jodi. "They were born all over the world in different hospitals, and two were born at home."

"Relatives?"

"No relatives."

"How far back did the FBI cross-check the relatives?"

Turning her head, Jodi stared. Then she slammed the computer, jammed it in her bag, and surged for the door. "Not far enough!"

Joe Mac was on his feet and moving with surprising swiftness for the door. "Get your coat, Marvin. You're coming with us."

With a quick half-turn Marvin snatched his overcoat from the back of his chair and whirled it so that it settled on his shoulders like a cloak. He hurled his arm-sling aside. Then he followed them into the labyrinth of tunnels to pull beside Jodi, who was checking her watch.

"Why am I coming?" he asked, excited.

"Because that blast wasn't meant to kill *us*," said Jodi. "It was meant to kill *you*. We just happened to be there."

"Now what? We tell the FBI?"

"We only tell the FBI what they need to know. We don't tell them anything we don't have to tell them. It's just us."

"Are you serious?"

"Live or die, Marvin, it's just us." Jodi stopped and gazed up projecting her best game face. "Are you with me?"

Marvin's brow hardened as he stared down.

"You're not gonna have to look for me, Jodi."

SIX

Special Agent Jack Rollins turned as Jodi barged into the section of the department reserved for FBI agents and counsel. Behind Jodi, Marvin scurried forward, and Joe Mac stopped just inside the open door.

"Rollins!" shouted Jodi.

Rollins coolly took a sip of coffee as he slowly gazed over Jodi's dust-covered form; he focused for a longer moment on her thoroughly wrecked head of hair.

"I heard about the explosion," he replied finally. "But they said it was just a gas line, so I let the fire department handle it."

Jodi stated, "I need the genealogical printouts you did on the victims."

It only required Rollins a second to catch her meaning. "Jodi, we've been over those things a thousand times. None of the victims were related. And why are you still on this? You guys should be in the hospital after that gas explosion. And, by the way, I've got a crime scene unit and fifteen agents out on Long Island right now taking that guy's place apart. By tonight this thing is spam in a can."

"It's bigger than one man," Jodi answered. "And I'm sure the victims are related."

Rollins was a professional and professionals do not express surprise, confusion, or anger. He merely stared for a moment before he stated, "*Who*, exactly, is related? All of them? I don't find that credible."

"No," Jodi shook her head. "It's just the children."

"Just the children," Rollins repeated. "What about the rest of them?"

"The rest don't matter!" said Jodi but sharply raised a hand. "No. Wait. I don't mean that they don't matter. *They do matter.* But the adults were never the targets. The children are the real targets! The children have *always* been the real targets! The rest of the murders were thrown into the mix just to confuse us. The rest were just killed, so we would spend years chasing down dead ends and red herrings and wild turkeys that don't mean anything. They were killed so we'd spend months looking for motives and relationships and suspects that don't exist. You see what I'm saying? There was *never* a genuine motive to kill any of the adults! It wasn't somebody they knew! It wasn't anything they did! They were killed to muddy the waters, so we wouldn't see that the children were always the only true target!"

"That's a whole lot of killing just to muddy the waters," Rollins stated firmly.

Jodi bent her face forward and calmed her tone. "I know I'm right, Jack. I want to see the printouts you did on the children. I want to see their relatives."

Rollins took a sip.

"Okay," he said finally. "Come on."

He led them through a surprisingly quiet FBI office. Then he threw open the door of an unoccupied storeroom, and Jodi beheld tons and tons of printouts and files. Some printouts were stacked six feet high. Others were stacked in cubes as big as a full-size van.

"Oh, no," Jodi whispered.

"Yeah," said Rollins with a nod. "And as far as relatives go, we checked back until there was nothing else to check. I'd say we went back at least two hundred years on each of them and we didn't find a single connection. And that wasn't just the kids. That was all of them because that's what we were working with at the time. Now you're telling me this was just about the children? Okay, fine. But we didn't find any connection between the children, either. They had no relatives. At all. Period."

Jodi asked, "Where are the printouts?"

"How would I know?" Rollins swept out an arm. "They're in here somewhere."

Wearily Jodi pulled up a chair and sat. She leaned forward, forearms on her knees, hair draping her head. "I can't take this," she whispered. "First, we're cold. Then we're hot. Then we're right on top of that psycho, and he gets himself dead. Then we get shot up. *Twice*. Then we get *blown up*. And now we finally figure out a motive, and we get torpedoed with red tape. I can't take it anymore."

"Who was in charge of cross-checking relatives?"

Jodi raised her face to see Joe Mac standing beside her. He had somehow made it across the bustling room by himself. After a brief pause, Rollins said, "I almost forgot about you, Joe. You want the agent that did the cross-checking?"

"Yeah."

Rollins pointed. "Andy headed up the team. Hey! Andy! Come over here, would ya?" As he approached, Rollins leaned over Jodi. "His name is Andy Edison. He led the background search, so he'll know more than anybody else. He might even know where they put the files."

Jodi didn't raise her face. "Thanks."

"Hello," Special Agent Edison said as he arrived. "Can I help you?"

Joe Mac executed a grave half-turn into Edison. "We think that the children might be related. We were going to check printouts, but maybe you could fill us in."

Jodi stood. "Hi. I'm Jodi."

"I'm Andy." Edison bent his head forward, mouth in a tight line. He stood like that until he shook his head. "No," he said. "Not possible. We checked family trees as far back as they went, and I don't remember any of them sharing a single relative. And that wasn't just the children. That was all of them, so you don't need to go through the printouts again. There's nothing in them that ties any of the victims together. Including the children. I'm absolutely certain."

"What year did the records end?" asked Joe Mac.

"Uh ..." Edison closed his eyes. " ... I believe we were able to go back to about 1801. We lost paper on them a little before the Civil War."

Jodi blew out a long breath.

Joe Mac pressed, "About half of them were Jewish. Is that right?"

"Thirteen were Jewish. To be exact."

"Did you ever think that was unusual?"

"No," Edison shook his head. "This is New York. If someone is going to go on a killing spree it's almost a sure thing that a fair number of victims are going to be from Israel or Spain or Germany. Or Mars."

Jodi was standing with one hand on a hip, gazing to the side, and there must have been something in her stance because Rollins asked, "God Almighty, Jodi. What's wrong? The guy's dead. It's over."

"I told you, Jack. Jacob Statute didn't work alone. He's *never* worked alone. He's part of a very dangerous group, and they're not finished."

Just when Jodi didn't think she could be any further shocked, the ineffably stately Chief of Archeology for the American Museum of Natural History, Professor Augustus Graven, stepped to the fringe of the circle. After respectfully staring across each of them Graven asked, "Could I be of service?"

Jodi blinked. "What are you doing here, professor?"

Professor Graven bent his head. "After I was confident that none of you were injured in the gas explosion, I responded to an FBI request to study evidence seized from the suspect's house this afternoon. They thought it might be Celtic in origin." A humble gesture. "It's been my honor to informally assist Dr. Mason in advising them for some time now. But I have no official connection to the case."

Jodi squinted at the skulls and robes laid across several long tables. "Does any of it relate to a Druid ceremony?"

Graven nodded once. "My background in forensic anthropology indicates that the heads were severed by a single blow. And concerning the Druidic practice of decapitation, there is the *oppidum* of the *Saluvii at D'entremont, Provence*, where there is a pillar of sculptured human heads and the discovery of fifteen human skulls severed in the exact same manner. But, then, the cult of the head and skull was a widely exercised Celtic means of worship dating back to the sixth century BC and was not necessarily limited to the Druids."

"So how can you say this is not a Druid ritual?"

"I did not mean to infer that it was *not* executed during a Druidic ritual, Detective Strong." Graven stared sternly. "I am only saying that there is no means of *proving* this was done during a Druidic ritual and not another Gaelic ceremony."

"But what about the robes? The staff?" Jodi had begun tapping her foot. "Are those not robes worn by Druids?"

"I don't know," Graven replied. "There are no trustworthy literary references to the design of ceremonial Druidic robes or staffs. The closest references would be eighteenth century drawings which may or may not be accurate at all." He paused before adding almost apologetically, "You must remember that archeologists are limited to making their best guess based only on materials that can endure burial for centuries in the harshest geological conditions – conditions that rapidly destroy books and clothing. We simply have no authoritative literary references and no surviving relics that we can use for comparison except the few engravings captured in badly eroded stone or tremendously degraded bronze. And those are very vague images indeed."

Joe Mac stepped forward, "Just what can you tell us?"

Graven turned to stare across the far table. "I can say that whatever cult severed those heads – and it *is* a cult – was either intentionally or unintentionally following the ritual mode of decapitation practiced by ancient Gaelic societies.

But I cannot affirm that this was performed during a Druidic ceremony."

"Huh," Joe Mac grunted. "It looks like archeologists can't really determine a whole lot of anything at all."

"That is a fair statement," Graven stated comfortably. "Archeologists can almost always determine *what* was done. But we can almost never tell you *why* it was done. We can almost never tell you if this was a frightening religious ritual or a friendly tribal practice. We cannot tell you if this was a curse of damnation executed only on the most terrible of enemies, or a purification ceremony reserved only for the most beloved of family members. For all that archeologists can infer, there is a great deal more we cannot infer. And yet it is exactly this thirst to solve these mysteries that is the great lure of scientists to the profession of archeology. And – I might add – to science in general."

"Thank you," said Jodi and grabbed Joe Mac's arm. "This is useless. Let's get out of here."

"Just a second." Joe Mac turned fully into Professor Graven. "You used a fancy word. I believe it was *oppidum*. What is that? A temple?"

"It's one of many Latin words for 'sanctuary.'"

"So the Druids were big on sanctuaries?"

"No," Graven said without expression. "As familiar with the idea of a sanctuary was to the civilizations of Rome or Egypt, the concept of a sanctuary was equally alien to the Druids. They simply never conceived of worshipping their deity inside the walls of a manmade structure. Yes," he continued, "to a Druid, the only proper sanctuary was a vale hidden in the deepest woods where they might commune undisturbed with the spirits of the forest and the earth. And since there are no verifiable Druid sanctuaries in the annals of archeology, I am inclined to believe that that particular fragment of Druidic lore is true. But a few structures have been uncovered that did have *some* kind of purpose for Druids. We simply don't know what they were."

Jodi asked, "What about Stonehenge?"

"Yes,' Graven nodded, "yes, indeed, there are many who incessantly allege that Stonehenge served some type of purpose for the Druids, but there is no physical evidence of it. And most archeologists give the notion no more consideration than the notion that Moses genuinely parted the Red Sea. But, then, the world of archeology is replete with two phenomena: One is the propensity of many to base their theories on nothing but physical evidence. The other is the propensity of many to base their theories on fantasy-fueled inclinations to see the world *as they wish it was* instead of the world *as it truly was.* Any indulgence to either extreme is always a mistake."

Joe Mac asked, "So you're saying it's real unlikely that the ancient Druids ever used Stonehenge for rituals?"

Professor Graven shrugged, "I'm saying – and quite frankly, I believe – that there is no physical evidence to suggest that the Druids ever used Stonehenge *at all.* Not even for astrological purposes. But that is not to say that the Druids *did not* use Stonehenge. I am only saying that there is nothing to prove that the Druids *did* use Stonehenge."

"Back to zero, huh?" Joe Mac's face opened in a smile. "That's a lot like detective work, professor. It don't matter none what you know. It only matters what you can prove."

"Exactly," agreed Graven.

"The only wild card in that philosophy is that some people don't really need proof," Joe Mac added. "Just 'knowing' is enough for revenge."

Jodi noticed Rollins scowling.

"As a law enforcement officer, that doesn't make sense," Rollins stated with a tinge of irritation. "You can't get a conviction with conjecture, intuition, the Voice of God, or hairs standing up on the back of your neck, Joe. There has to be *proof* before you can take someone to court. And society will never justify vigilantism." He paused. "A man who takes revenge by murder is looking at *the* judgment."

Joe Mac slowly turned and began tapping his way across the room. "There a judge for dead folks, ain't there?"

"Yeah," said Rollins. "So?"

"So I guess it all depends on whether you're ready to be judged."

After staring, Rollins muttered, "Yeah. Okay. Whatever. Hey, Jodi, if you're gonna keep on this case, what do you need from me?"

"I'll let you know," Jodi said and joined Joe Mac. As they walked, Jodi was quite surprised that she wasn't crying just for some miserable stress relief.

It wasn't the stress of the investigation. It wasn't the stress of being promoted. It wasn't even the stress that her last day in uniform involved the murder of a little boy. She actually didn't know what it was – specifically – but she felt like giving in.

"Where we going now?" she mumbled.

Joe Mac said, "We might have had the answer all along. Do you remember what Mrs. Morgan told us about Cathren Montanus?"

"No. What'd she say?"

"She said that Mrs. Montanus had been gathering information on this group before she died."

"And you think she kept the information in her house?"

Joe Mac turned his face into her. "If she's like everybody else I know she kept it in that book you stole."

"But we already looked at the book, Joe."

Joe Mac shook his head. "We didn't look *at* the book. We looked for one name that was *in* the book, and it's not the same thing. We're gonna give that book another look."

Blinking some clarity into her mind *and* her eyes, Jodi quickened her pace.

To say she felt energized would have been a vast overstatement. Rather, it was just that the infinitely dreary, energy-sapping, depressing cloud that overshadowed her mind and soul lifted a little bit at the hope that they weren't completely beaten in something that meant so much to so many. It was true; many were dead and beyond caring. But there were children and mothers and fathers and sisters and brothers grieving the loss of someone they'd cherished. And not *every* victim on this hideous list was in the grave just yet, so Jodi felt that she and Joe still had the chance to save someone.

"I'm glad you're with me, Joe," she said. "I couldn't do this without you."

"You never know what you can do until you get up and try," Joe answered. "I do it every day."

"Do what?"

"Find some kind of reason not to lay down and die."

"Do you think that'd make you happy?"

"I don't think it'd make me more miserable."

Outside the station, Jodi turned to Marvin who was faithfully following every step. "Okay, Marvin, this is where you go home." She smiled tightly. "You don't want to be a part of what's coming. And I'm assigning some friends of mine to hang with you. Just to make sure you stay safe."

Marvin's brow hardened as Jodi pointed.

He turned his head to see a pale pickup truck with two bearded giants that grandly lifted a hand in hello. "They're friendlier than they look," Jodi commented. "They're gonna stay with you day and night until I say otherwise. But you might have to help them blend in."

"Uh ... well ... I have a lot of work to do in the basement. It's way out of sight ... of normal people."

"They'll fit right in."

"What about you?"

"I don't know. This might take a few days."

"I'll sleep in my office." He raised a faint gesture to the empty night. "I don't have anybody at home, anyway. I haven't had anybody at home in ten years. And in *my* office who's gonna notice a few more bodies laying around?"

Jodi couldn't help but smile. "I'll be calling you when this is over, Marvin. One way or the other."

Marvin nodded with a smile.

"I'll be waiting."

* * *

When they arrived at the Jodi's isolated squad car, she looked across the parking lot, the sky, the buildings.

"I don't see him," she said.

"He's up there," Joe Mac lifted his chin. "Somewhere."

After they settled into the car Jodi retrieved the stolen organizer from her gun range daypack and turned on the overhead light. "We gonna do this here? Why not inside?"

"Because I don't want anyone to walk into the office and wonder what we're doing, so unless you want to ride all the way out to my place, let's do it right here. Plus, it'd be best to stay in the city if you want to run somebody down before sunrise."

"That's fine with me." She opened the book and began scanning. "Good grief. This was one well-organized lady. She's got names, numbers, email addresses, and the physical addresses of everybody she knew right here in the front. Where do we even start looking for a clue to these people?"

"Go to the place where you found the name of Jacob Statute. And what did the databank give you on 'Fortinus?'"

"'Bout like you said. I got the phone book – eighty-five thousand hits. Everything from graveyards to businesses to time-shares. It's obviously some old English surname. Probably somebody who founded Jamestown or something."

Five minutes later she said, "She doesn't have any more names in this section but she has some very strange looking email addresses. It looks like she was approaching this from every angle." She read. "I'm not sure whether these names are important. Some of them are scratched out like she checked on them and came up empty."

"Do the emails help us?"

"No."

"Why not?"

"Because it takes a court order to hack an IP address." She looked at Joe for a few moments. "An IP address is a computer address. You do remember computers, don't you? I mean, they *were* invented before you retired?"

"Funny. You know a good hacker?"

Jodi closed the book and started the squad car.

"I know 'the weirdest.'"

"Is he 'the goodest,' too?"

"The weirder they are, 'the gooder' they are."

* * *

Five sharp raps on the flimsy wood door of Elmo Gelaton's third-floor hovel located deep in Brooklyn was met with an explosive cry of panic on the far side of the panel. Then there was a frantic scrambling as someone began racing around the apartment.

Joe Mac effortlessly heard repeated whispered declarations of how they could never trace this back to him, how he was never going to share a cell again with one of those meat-eating, gun-crazy Texas bruisers who stole his blankie last time, how he didn't *actually own* a computer and how he hadn't *actually violated* his parole …

Jodi kicked the door in.

"*Elmo!*"

"Ho!" a young voice yelled. "These aren't computers, Officer Strong! These are actually my own personal experiment in –"

"Tell somebody who cares." Jodi closed the door behind Joe. "I need your help, Elmo. And you *are* going to help me."

"Of course!" Elmo replied politely. "Who's the blind dude?"

"A friend. And if you're really smart, Elmo, you'll make him a very *good* friend before we leave."

Joe Mac could almost hear Elmo smiling.

"Law and order! That's me!"

Jodi walked further into what was obviously a tiny room and said, "Look at these IP addresses, Elmo. Can you get me a physical address?"

Elmo didn't reply – at least not verbally – before Joe heard unbelievably rapid tapping at a keyboard. Meanwhile, Elmo continued his impassioned monologue with, "Now I do happen to temporarily possess a few *minorly* functional iPads. But you know me, Officer Strong. I don't hack anybody anymore. I can't even *remotely* –"

"Hack the hell out of these guys, Elmo."

"I'm on it." A moment more and Elmo said, "Well, I'm shocked. These guys are all using 'The Dark Net.' That's even harder to access than TOR, and TOR ain't no piece of cake." His mouth twisted curiously. "Let's see what they're trying to hide from law-abiding citizens. Like me." He typed for a while in unexpected silence. Then he said in a vaguely troubled tone, "Why are you looking for these people?"

"Why do you ask?"

"Because this person and his friends have some very strange fantasies. They're all part of some kind of underground, game-playing routine but it somehow … doesn't seem like a game … to me."

"Why not?"

"Because there's no scoring system for killing dragons or centaurs and stuff. And there's no really cool titles like *Swordblaster* or *Vampress the Pirate Queen*. And it doesn't look to me like there's any way to win." With that Elmo typed for two minutes before he said, "These people aren't playing any kind of game that I've ever seen."

There was the sound of Jodi leaning close to Elmo as she said, "Explain to me what they're talking about, Elmo."

"Well," Elmo began, "they seem to be anticipating … or preparing … for some kind of major event."

"An event to be held here? In the city?"

"Looks like it."

"Why do you say that?"

"Because all these IP addresses are inside New York, and they keep referring to meeting at 'the temple.' But none of them need any directions." Elmo paused. "It's like they're all talking about a place down the street."

Joe Mac asked, "What's this event all about?"

Elmo typed for two full minutes.

"They're using game code, but I get the drift," he said finally. "They seem to be talking about a temple, a sacrifice, an orgy, and a feast. They're using, like, 'Pizzagate' terminology for the sex stuff."

"*When?*" asked Joe Mac.

"If I'm reading this right, it's gonna be two nights from now."

"December 21?" asked Jodi.

"Yeah."

"Let me see that, Elmo."

Joe Mac heard a different staccato of typing on the keyboard and knew Jodi had taken over. Then she said, "That's it, Joe! December 21 is the Winter Solstice – the first day of winter. Didn't Marvin say that the Solstice is a crucial day for the Druids?"

Joe Mac's teeth gleamed, "Where is this meet gonna happen?"

"And what are they going to do?" Elmo asked as if he were suddenly part of the investigation. "I'm telling you, Officer Strong, these people are *not* refined. They're talking about a temple and drinking blood and cutting off somebody's head and having wild sex. And they keep talking about a 'sacrifice' and some kind of feast." Elmo became silent and still before he asked, "*Are these people talking about eating a human being?*"

Even though it was gentle, Joe Mac heard Jodi pat Elmo on the shoulder or arm, and then she said, "I want you to stay inside for the next few days, Elmo. Do you have enough food in this place?"

"You bet. I have twenty-four cans of Chili with beans and two boxes of crackers. I don't need anything else. Well, yeah, I need my *Legend of Zelda Marathon* discs. Forty-eight days! And I'm still winning! I'm about to –"

"Elmo!"

"Yeah! I got food!"

"All right." Jodi walked up to Joe Mac. "What do you think, Joe?"

Joe Mac lifted his chin.

"Get me the physical addresses for these goombahs."

* * *

"We can't just barge in on *these* people," Jodi said from where she'd parked the car to watch the first townhouse on the list. "Would you look at that?"

"I'm blind."

"Gee. Wow. No fooling? That place must be worth ten million bucks, Joe. If you go in there slapping people around like Lenny the Bruiser I guarantee you some ten-thousand-dollar suit will have our badges by morning."

"I ain't got no badge."

"I've got a badge! And you've got a pension!"

"Run him through NCIC," said Joe. "Find out if he's got relatives. Especially family. If we're lucky, he's got a sister or brother. More than likely, his folks are dead."

She began typing. "What are you gonna do?"

"If we can't go to him, we'll get him to come to us."

After ten minutes, she said, "Nope. No family that I can find. I checked him against everything we have, and there's nothing. So, calling him and telling him his sister is at the hospital is another lame-o idea."

A low moan rose from Joe Mac. When Jodi glanced over she saw his head was bent slightly forward, his face hidden in a penumbra.

"Well we can't just knock on the door," he said.

"I could shoot out the transformer and put this entire grid in the dark," Jodi offered. "Maybe he'll come outside to see what's happening."

"Yeah. You'll kill the electricity and probably kill a half-dozen people who are on life support machines. Plus, he'll have a flashlight. It's not like we're gonna ambush him in the dark, knock him on the head, and beat the truth out of him. And he'll probably have a gun, anyway. If we try and stiff-arm him, it'll more'n likely turn into a gunfight. And we don't want that because we found him illegally. It'd rebound on us, and we'll probably be the ones who end up in prison."

"How do you know he'll have a gun?"

"If I was kidnapping people, cutting off their heads, and eating them up, *I'd* sure keep a gun around. If some relative found out about my appetites, they wouldn't be calling the police. They'd come calling. At night. And they wouldn't come knocking."

Jodi sighed. "Yeah. Good point." She found herself staring at the front door. "Well, it looks like you're all out of ideas, Joe."

"Am I?" He opened the door. "Let's go."

He got out, and Jodi was one step behind him. As he came around the front of the squad car, he was tapping softly when she grabbed his elbow, guiding him across the empty street. She whispered, "What are you gonna do?"

"Take me around back."

"Oh, my lord," she moaned. But in moments Joe Mac was standing at the solidly locked back door. "He probably has a microwave alarm system, Joe."

"I ain't worried about the alarm. We'll be on top of him by then."

"How? The door is locked!"

Joe Mac removed a black case from his coat. He opened it, and Jodi saw multiple rows of silvery lock picks. "Any lights on?" he asked.

"No," she replied. "Okay, listen; once you open this door, I'll have ten seconds to find him before the alarm is activated. Which means I'll have to move fast, wake him up, and put a gun to his head before that phone rings. Then you'll have to make your way to me by the sound of my voice because I won't be able to leave him. Understand?"

"Yeah. Get your gun out."

"*It's already out.*" She watched him pick the lock with effortless skill. "How can you pick a lock when you're blind?"

"You don't pick a lock with your eyeballs, dufus."

Ten seconds later Joe Mac whispered, "Okay. Get ready. When I turn this lock, the alarm is gonna start ticking down, so you do like you said. You rush upstairs. Find him fast. Put that gun to his head. By then, the phone will ring. Tell him you're gonna blow his brains out if he doesn't give the right code. Then tell him you're gonna wait. And if someone shows up, you're still gonna blow his brains out. Don't worry about me. I'll find you." He turned his face toward her. "You ready?"

Jodi lowered her right gun hand to her side. She always shot with a solid two-hand grip, but in this situation she might need her left hand to throw open doors. Then she fell into a half-crouch like a football player preparing to charge the line.

"Uh huh," she said.

Joe Mac swung open the door.

Jodi was through it instantly noticing the red blinking light on the wall, and saw the staircase. She swung around the rail and took the steps three at a time, and when she reached the second floor she caught a faint glow in a room to her right. She went through it silent but fast and saw a man lying on the bed. Leaping to land solidly on top of him, she slammed the barrel against his forehead as he screamed.

"Shut up!" she shouted. "When that phone rings you give them the right code, or I'll blow your brains out! And if anybody shows up I'll still –"

The phone rang.

Like someone hesitant to stick their hand into a fire the man slowly reached out.

"*Answer it!*"

He snatched up the phone. His voice was tremulous, and his hand was shaking as he weakly asked, "Yes?"

A moment.

"*Sacrilege*," he said. "No. Everything is fine. I was just a little late punching in the code. Yes. Thank you."

He set down the phone with almost as much caution before he raised both hands to each side of his head and asked, "Do you want money?"

"What kind of code is *sacrilege*?" Jodi whispered with more confidence. "Yeah. You're the right one. Is your name Austin Phillips? Don't lie to me."

He whispered, "The right one for what?"

"*Is that your name!*"

"Yeah! I'm Austin Phillips!"

The room light was turned on, and Jodi didn't need to look. She heard Joe Mac lightly scraping the carpet with his cane as he walked forward, and she saw the man's eyes widen as Joe Mac's melancholic shadow darkened his face.

"We want to talk to you," Joe Mac said in a low voice infinitely more alarming than the voice of someone who shouts.

Phillips' eyes switched between them. "About what?"

"About some dead people," Joe Mac declared. "We want to talk to you before you join them."

"Uh …" Austin Phillips slowly scooted up until he was lying against the head board. "I'm not sure you have the right place. I don't know anything about any dead people."

Jodi took the fore because she was afraid to leave it to Joe Mac. If Joe didn't get the answers, he expected he might very well leave a dead man on this bed. And if they did happen to have the wrong address, that wasn't a burden of conscience Jodi was willing to bear. She leaned forward: "Listen to me very carefully. I'm going to ask you some questions. If at any time I think you're lying I'll step aside and let him have you. And you don't want that."

"No!" Phillips agreed. "I don't!"

"Are you part of some kind of weird Druid cult that meets in this city?"

"*What?*"

Joe Mac took a step.

"Yeah! Sort of!"

"You talk to this group online, don't you?" Jodi continued. "Don't you and your friends meet at some kind of game site and exchange messages?"

Phillips didn't remove his eyes from Joe Mac as he said, "Yeah. But so what? It's just a game. We get together and play dress-up like priests and have anonymous sex." He stammered as he added, "I mean, yeah, I guess some people take it a lot more seriously than others. But it's just a game! I'm a lawyer! I don't know anything about any dead people!"

"So why do you dress up like Druids?"

"Because that's the game!" Phillips took a second, visibly calming. "Look, this is how it works. We all get together and dress up like Druid priests with these long robes and hoods and masks and stuff, and we have sex. We just find someone we like and do our thing. It's so dark nobody knows who's who, so there's no guilt. You can see 'em the next day at work and nobody cares because you don't have any idea. It's just … uh …"

"Sick," said Jodi.

Phillips shrugged. "I can't exactly argue with *that*. I mean, it's not for everybody, that's for sure. But nobody ever gets *hurt*." His hands remained in a holdup position. "Listen, I'm being honest with you. It's just a game. It's just stress relief."

Jodi asked, "They why does your website talk about human sacrifice and cutting off people's heads and eating them?"

"Oh," Phillips shrugged, "well, that's just part of the fantasy."

Joe Mac said, "Explain that."

Sweeping a hand down over his face with a sigh, Phillips continued, "Okay, it works like this. We get together, and some of the guys are responsible for bringing a 'victim.' But it's not a 'real' victim. It's just someone who wants to join the group. A newbie. A first-timer. Being the victim is sort of like an initiation. Then we have this huge, fake ceremony where we play this bizarre music and dance around in our robes and play like we're doing all this kind of ancient Druid stuff. Some of them do a little cocaine, get all worked up. Maybe smoke a little weed. Whatever cranks your tractor. Then we get down to picking partners and ... well, you can guess the rest."

Resisting the impulse to lower the gun Jodi, asked, "Do you know anything about all the dead people that have been attributed to 'The Hangman?'"

"Yeah. I'm a lawyer. I follow the news."

"Do your people have anything to do with any of that?"

"What!"

"*Answer me!*"

"*NO!*" Phillips searched the room as if there might be someone who could save him. "Is that why you're here? You think I had something to do with all the people that have been killed in the last four years? Are you crazy? I only got stationed in New York two years ago! I wasn't even here then!"

"Aren't you people having a big meeting in two nights?" asked Joe Mac.

"Yeah!" Phillips nodded fervently. "Two nights from now. It's called the Winter Solstice. That's the first day of –"

"I know what it is," said Jodi and found herself staring down, her rage abating like a wave washing out to sea.

She actually believed this guy was telling the truth. In the first place, he was too scared to be a serial killer. He was also cooperative and obviously inexperienced at deadly encounters, and the psycho they were after was neither of those. Then she did lower the gun and sat slightly back on her heels, staring through narrow eyes.

She cocked her head toward Joe Mac. "The man we're looking for murdered this man's grandson. So you know what we're going to do when we find him, right?"

"Uh huh," Phillips nodded slowly. "And I'd do the same thing. Can't blame you. In fact, now that you've told me, I won't even mention that you've been here. That's as good a reason as any to bury somebody under the bridge. But you're not looking for me. *You … have … the … wrong … man.*"

"You seem like an idiot," said Joe Mac.

"I am *not* an idiot."

"The man we're looking for isn't an idiot, either."

"Oh! You were talking about *me.* Yeah, yeah, *I'm* an idiot. I don't know how I ever passed the BAR. Failed it three times."

Jodi pulled Phillips up by the hair of his head.

"Show me your Druid stuff," she said.

"It's in the closet."

"So get it."

He pointed. "But … it's in the closet."

Jodi smiled sweetly, "That means you're not showing it to me yet."

Phillips stared. "And that means …?"

"GET IT!"

Phillips jumped up, ran to the closet, reached in, and pulled out a long, black robe. Then he walked back and laid it across the rumpled bed with a gesture. "That's it. We all wear the exact same thing, so that you don't know who's who."

Jodi studied the robe, and it was identical to the one found in Jacob Statute's house. It had the same circular half-moons with twenty-one stars and a line of seven pentacles. Even the golden embroidery and the distance between emblems were exact. And, for Phillips, yeah, it was just 'a costume.' But to their killer this was *a robe.*

Anything worn to shed blood is a robe. Not a costume.

"I've checked every costume shop in town, and nobody sells a robe like this," Jodi said absently. "Where'd you get it?"

Phillips was eager to volunteer, "An old man makes them for us. And, no, he doesn't have a shop. It's just something he does, like, to supplement his social security, I guess. But he's supposed to be some kind of genuine expert on the Druids. And everybody wants to look authentic, you know?" He nervously looked at Joe Mac, who had begun moving forward. "I mean, the people I'm with are just playing a grownup version of Dungeons and Dragons! But you want to *look* the part, right?"

"It's the same robe, Joe," said Jodi. "Exactly."

"You sure?"

"I'm sure." She didn't look at Phillips. "What's this man's name?"

"Ben Chamberlain."

"You know him pretty well?" asked Joe Mac.

"*No.*"

"Then you'll introduce us."

Joe Mac stepped *perilously* close as Phillips quickly replied, "Yeah, man! I'll take you to his shop first thing in the morning!"

Jodi: "You said he didn't have a shop."

"Well, I meant that he didn't have an 'official' shop. He doesn't have a sign up or anything. He just works in a place that's above an old magic store in Brooklyn. And he only accepts cash so – needless to say – he's not 'on the books.'" A pause. "Actually, it's not a magic store *per se.* It's more like this huge archive of 'magical artifacts.' It's got Egyptian and Babylonian and African staffs and mummies and shrunken heads from the Amazon or the Congo or whatever godforsaken part of the world still shrinks the heads of human beings, God help me for even looking at it. I don't even know how they got that stuff into the country. It's *gotta* be illegal." He blinked. "Expensive, too."

"Sin isn't expensive," said Joe Mac. "In *this* world."

"It's expensive if you want to buy it from him. These robes cost a bundle."

"You'll take us there," said Joe Mac. "Soon as it opens. You're gonna introduce us as a couple of friends who want robes just like you got."

"You bet."

"Until then," Joe Mac added ominously, "we'll stay here. With you. And nobody's leaving this room until we leave together." He lifted his face, chin jutting. "I know I don't need to tell you that I'll kill you with my bare hands … real slow … if you try to hurt this little lady. Or don't do exactly as I say."

Phillips slowly lifted a trembling hand to his head.

"Glad to help," he said.

SEVEN

"I want ya'll to know that I'm not real comfortable with *any* of this."

"Phillips, shut up," Jodi sighed. "If brains were dynamite you wouldn't have enough to blow your hat off."

Seated behind the steering wheel of her squad car with Joe Mac beside her, Jodi didn't remove her eyes from L'Megra Relics, which seemed like a nondescript and unimpressive dime-store Hobby Lobby located deep in the south side of the Bronx. There was certainly nothing evil about the exterior although Jodi was becoming well accustomed to the mask of polite civility hiding the depths of human depravity.

From the back seat Phillips hesitantly asked, "What are we waiting for?"

"For an expert."

"On Druids?"

"Yeah."

"But you already have me."

Jodi briefly closed her eyes; "Phillips, you don't know any more about Druids than you know about a man on the moon. You're just some pervert who dresses up like a priest and has sex with strangers. At best, you're irresponsible. At worst, you're a walking bubonic plague. If you used good sense for five minutes you'd probably go insane."

The roof thumped.

"Hey, Poe," mumbled Jodi and looked at Joe Mac. "How long has he been around?"

"He never left."

"Should have known. Just 'cause you can't see him ..."

A rap on the window made her turn, and Marvin Mason was standing there dressed in a leather bomber jacket, khaki pants, boots, and a cowboy shirt. Flanked by the Kosiniskis, he was wearing a New York Yankee baseball cap.

Jodi opened the door and got out. She stared him up and down before she asked, "What? No bullwhip?"

Marvin smiled, "I'm undercover."

"Yeah. Nobody would ever mistake *you* for an archeologist."

Jodi smiled at Ronnie and Bobby Kosiniski. Ronnie was carrying a trombone case; Jodi had wondered how he would conceal his truly massive combat shotgun. She smiled, "Thanks, guys. And, just so you know, those guys you hit at the old lady's house are in potter's field. No prints. No ID. Nobody claimed them. Nobody cared. We just named 'em John Doe and planted 'em."

"Good," grunted Ronnie.

"I ain't sheddin' no tear," echoed Bobby. "We'll never be able to repay Joe Mac for what he did for our daddy. We feel the same about you. You know we won't let you down. We'll bag 'em and bury 'em just like Joe Mac did for our daddy and us."

"I know," Jodi smiled. "And I'll always cover you guys. But for right now I want you to disappear. We'll take it from here."

"If you need us, just call."

"You bet."

They turned and vanished in the crowd.

Poe squawked, and before Jodi even thought about it, she fearlessly reached over the roof to smooth the raven's feathers. With a short hop, Poe closed the distance, so that she could touch his entire body and Jodi realized – with a surprise – how humanlike he truly was.

He was more human than most humans.

Exiting ponderously, with a slight resettling of the car, Joe Mac stood on the other side and stated, "Advise Marvin what we got ... Poe, come here."

The raven lifted off and with a single collapse of its wings settled on Joe Mac's shoulder. With a gentle hand, Joe Mac smoothed its wings as he opened the counter-locked back door and Phillips stood on the street, straightening his tailored suit.

It took Jodi thirty seconds to explain the situation to Marvin, and then the archeologist gazed at the shop before he said, "So this guy made the robe for whoever was killed out on Long Island? And you know for certain that he was part of the coven that's responsible for all these murders?"

"Uh huh," said Jodi.

Joe Mac stepped onto the sidewalk with, "We want you to check him out, Marvin. We want you to see if he might be involved in this, or if he's just some kind of psycho suit-maker." He waved at Phillips without turning his head. "He made a robe for this idget, too. And he's no more a Druid than Poe."

Marvin narrowly searched the street. "Poe?"

"The raven," said Jodi and turned. "Let's do it, Joe."

As they began walking four-wide toward the store Jodi said, "Phillips, all I want you to do is tell this old man that we're all part of your sick little group, and we want robes, too. Then let Marvin do the talking."

Phillips muttered, "Whatever. I don't even wanna be here."

"If you don't mess this up, you'll be free to resume your sad little life."

"I resent that remark."

"You *resemble* that remark."

As they reached the store, Joe Mac shrugged, "Go on, Poe."

The big raven lifted off and settled on an easement at the edge of the door, immediately staring through a window.

Poe's quick head jerked left to right almost too fast for the human eye to follow, and Jodi knew Poe saw everything; the raven was worth a hundred guard dogs.

A doldrum bell droned as they entered the shop, and they stood hands in pockets as Phillips walked to the counter, which was staffed with a single middle-aged woman; she had short-cut, black hair and wore a gleaming silver pendant of a half-moon. She smiled quaintly as Phillips said, "Hey, Seka. How's business?"

Joe Mac angled his head as if already listening to something Jodi couldn't hear, but he didn't raise his face. Still, his mouth turned down and nothing could have fully concealed what deep purpose had abruptly condensed within him.

"These are friends of mine," Phillips lifted a hand toward them, and Seka nodded politely. "They, uh, are part of our group, and they want to order some robes from Ben. Would he happen to be around?"

Seka's gaze *searched* them this time and to Jodi's electrifying horror focused for a longer moment on Joe Mac.

As if he felt the concentration, Joe Mac removed a fist-size roll of bills from his coat and suddenly seemed harmless as he said, "I'd like to pay in cash if that's all right. I don't trust banks. Never have."

Still, Seka hesitated.

Jodi stepped forward with, "That's a beautiful pendant! Do you have any more like it? Or did you get it somewhere else?"

"Oh, yes, we have more," Seka smiled. "We can talk about it when you're finished with Ben." She picked up the phone and a moment later said, "Ben? You have customers! You free? Okay."

Lifting a counter door and stepping aside, she stretched out an arm toward a staircase that rose behind the desk. "Go on up. Ben's at the top of the stairs."

Jodi smiled, "Thank you."

Leading Joe in their now-normal manner, Jodi ushered him to the staircase, which he climbed with casual confidence. Then, when they entered the upper room, she saw a slightly bent old man. He was about five-seven with long, brilliant white hair and a wispy build. But his shoulders and arms seeming disproportionately developed as if he had once made his living cutting stone or steel, and the strength had endured the years.

"How do you do?" he smiled. "I'm Ben Chamberlain. How can I be of service?"

The near-dark room was equipped with three machines of dissimilar design, but each was obviously manufactured for sewing. The walls were exclusively draped with voluminous sheets of sheer, black cotton cloth obviously hung in preparation. There were no other colors – no red, green, blue or any disparate hue. From the blackened windows to the blackened walls the room was devoted to darkness.

Phillips smiled and hailed the old man with a raised hand. "Hey, Ben! These friends of mine would like to order robes just like the one you made for me." He gestured. "This is Joe, Jodi, and Marvin. Guys, this master craftsman is Ben Chamberlain. There's nobody like him. His work is 'perfecto.'"

With no discernable expression, Chamberlain asked, "Did my friend remember to tell you that I routinely require payment in advance?"

Joe Mac curtly nodded, "We're prepared to pay today if you'd like. I'll even pay extra if you could put a rush on it. We'd like to have them by the Solstice."

With raised eyebrows Ben Chamberlain turned slightly aside and took a single step, hand cupping his chin. "Hmmm," he began, "I don't know if that's possible at my age. I'm not sure I have the strength."

Jodi expressed disappointment. "But we were told you do such beautiful work."

"Thank you," Chamberlain nodded. "But the embroidery takes time. And the embroidery is everything."

"Because of the imagery within the thread," Marvin said solemnly. "I know. I am a *Manteis*." He respectfully laid a hand on Joe Mac's brute shoulder. "And although my friend is blind, he is an *aes dana* of the first order. And Jodi, who usually doesn't say much, is a *Filid*. And she has never been wrong."

Chamberlain was abruptly scowling. He stared for a long moment at Phillips before focusing with unconcealed confusion on Marvin as he asked, "And you want to join *his* group? How long have you known Mr. Phillips?"

Marvin bent his head. "We met two days ago at an *oppidum*."

"Oh, no," Chamberlain lifted his eyes to the ceiling before walking forward, gesturing to the stairway. "Mr. Phillips? Would you please be so kind as to leave me alone with your friends? You can rendezvous with them later."

"I'd love to, but I have to get to work!" Phillips waved and Jodi cringed as he did an exceedingly poor job of hiding his haste. "Ya'll have fun!"

He was gone.

Chamberlain shook his head with a sigh as he walked to a chair and sat, "Why do you not have your ornaments?"

"They were confiscated by Customs," said Marvin.

Chamberlain's eyes narrowed. "Why?"

"Because the gold used in our embroidery was genuine gold thread. My father is a jeweler at *Saluvii at D'entrement Province*, and he provided it for us. But when we arrived at LaGuardia for the Solstice, the men at Customs inspected our luggage and found our ornaments. Then they discovered they were crafted with real gold and detained us as suspected gold smugglers. They eventually released us, but kept our robes as evidence until they finish their investigation. Now we're not prepared."

Chamberlain looked at Jodi. "You are a *Filid*. How is it you could not divine that you were dealing with a fool in Mr. Phillips?" He lifted an arm. "Mr. Phillips is not a member of the family! He is only a degenerate lecher who likes to play dress-up!"

Marvin looked at Joe Mac. "He's the real thing."

Jodi removed her badge. "Because I'm not a *Filid*, Mr. Chamberlain. I'm a detective with the NYPD." She nodded to Joe Mac. "And this is Joe Mac Blake. He's a homicide detective. Can you guess why we're here?"

Chamberlain laughed lightly and nodded, "Yes."

Joe Mac stepped forward.

"Wait!" said Jodi, raising a hand. "Who are you, Mr. Chamberlain?"

"I am a *Ri*."

"A king," Marvin stated. "It's Gaelic. He's the king of a group of Druids."

"I have been expecting someone like you for many years, detective," Chamberlain said easily. "I'm surprised it took you so long. Why don't you all sit down? I am not reluctant to speak with you." He raised a gaze to Joe Mac. "And violence, my large friend, is not necessary. I am not the man you seek."

Jodi and Marvin pulled up wood chairs and sat.

"I'll stand," said Joe Mac.

"As you wish." Chamberlain focused on Jodi. "You seek the *Ri* who is ordering the deaths of these innocent people. Am I right?"

"You're right," said Jodi.

"As I said, I am not the man you seek. Nor do I know his identity. I only know he is very savage and very smart. He has concealed himself from me all my life."

Joe Mac asked, "How do we find him?"

"I don't know." Chamberlain's arms hung tiredly at his sides. "I gave up trying to find him years ago."

"Why did you try to find him at all?" asked Jodi.

"Because he's evil. Because his group has been committing human sacrifice in this city for decades." Chamberlain paused. "I presume that at least one of you knows something about the ancient Druids?"

"Yeah," Marvin answered. "I do."

"Well, they indeed follow the path of the ancient Druids. And they have killed many, many people." Chamberlain nodded solemnly, "For years I tried to discover the name of their *Ri*, so that I might inform the police. I even took great personal risks. But I learned nothing. And if I had continued – with my lack of skill – they would have discovered me and killed me along with my entire family, and so I stopped." He paused. "To be honest I didn't want to die horribly doing something that was doomed to fail, anyway."

Jodi: "What haven't you told police what you do know?"

"Because I don't know anything that would help the police." Chamberlain waited, staring patiently. "What do you think I know, detective? A name?"

"Someone picks up the robes, don't they?" asked Joe Mac.

"No," Chamberlain shortly shook his head. "No one picks up their robes. They have always placed an order through a foreign re-mailing service that can't be traced. Then I return the robes in the same way. I've never met one of them."

Jodi asked, "If all this is done through a remailing service, how do you know we're talking about the same group?"

Chamberlain shrugged, "I assume you've finally killed one of them doing something horrible and traced his robe back to me." His gaze revealed no surprise. "Am I right?"

"Yeah," she replied, "you're right."

"I expected as much. But the delivery system for the robes is of no consequence. I have known for years that these Druids were located in this city."

"How did you know that?"

"Because I saw them in a graveyard when I was much younger. It was from a distance. And it was dark. But even in the dark I recognized my own work." His frown deepened. "Every great artist recognizes his own work ..."

Joe Mac took a step. "What graveyard?"

"I'm obligated to tell you something else before I tell you that."

"*What graveyard!*"

"Please, Joe!" Jodi leaned forward, elbows on knees, hands clasped. "What do you want to tell us, Mr. Chamberlain?"

"These people will kill every one of you," Chamberlain said frankly. "They have survived eight millennia because they have always been more savage than any enemy that has come against them. They are more dangerous than anything else you will ever face in this world. And you should know that before you begin."

"But you were going to give them up," said Joe Mac.

"I changed my mind."

"Why?"

Chamberlain hesitated. "I guess I just decided I'd rather be a living dog than a dead lion," he said finally.

Marvin leaned back and swept a hand down over his face.

Jodi didn't even need to look at Joe Mac to know his answer; he would rather be a "living lion" but dead was just as well. She felt a fear she knew she couldn't deny. She was impressed, and the thought of walking away dulled her mind like smoke dulled the walls of a cheap hotel not built to last. She felt inadequate. And there was something about the old man's emotionless words that inspired hopelessness.

Joe Mac finally said, "Maybe you two should go home. There's no reason to start a fight you can't win."

Barely raising a gaze Jodi asked, "You gonna go home, too, Joe?"

With a slight frown Joe Mac shook his head once to the left, right.

"Then I'm not going home, either. So, Mr. Chamberlain, where is this graveyard? And what's so special about it? And why were you there?"

Chamberlain's brow rose in surrender as he began, "It is a graveyard containing pre-American Celtic gravestones. It is believed to be one of the first habitations of the Gaelic peoples on this continent because, as you probably know, Columbus did not discover America. It was discovered and indeed occupied by Celtic people centuries before Columbus set foot here, so this very old cemetery is believed to be sacred Celtic ground. And in a more practical sense, it is quite isolated, if not entirely forgotten, by the modern world, so it was once a safe place for us to hold ceremonies.

"However, one night, as I was wandering through the woods after our ceremony, I saw a separate meeting and crept closer to understand. And I saw soon enough that it was a gathering of Druids, and they were wearing robes of my design. Then I saw them sacrifice a human being on a stone altar and realized they were of an ancient sect avoided if not condemned by those of my Order. After that, we were astute to avoid the place altogether. We certainly did not want to be discovered by them. They would have shown us no more mercy than they would have shown their worst enemy."

"Why not?" asked Jodi.

"Because they must protect their secrets."

"And who do they consider their enemy?"

"They have plenty of enemies," Marvin answered for him. "Greeks. Romans. Christians. Jews. Basically the entire modern world. Even modern Druids."

Joe Mac asked sullenly, "Why do these folks always get together in graveyards? Why don't they have a temple?"

"We surmise it's because they don't believe god dwells in any temple made by man," Marvin continued. "That's one thing that scared Julius Caesar to death when he first discovered the Druids in Upper Gaul. When Caesar saw their places of worship – places in the deepest, darkest parts of what was then one of the most haunting forests on the planet – he was unnerved. He even wrote about it in his letters. And you can tell from his writing that the Druids scared the life out of him."

"Why?" asked Jodi.

"It's like the professor said. Gathering in the gloom of the deepest forest for ghostly ceremonies was a concept totally alien to the Roman mind. It was barbaric. And when Caesar discovered the murderous nature of their ceremonies like the *Wicker Man*, he was even more unnerved and launched a campaign aimed at the extermination of the last Druid *and* their religion. And some say he succeeded. And some say he didn't. But I guess we've learned the answer to that one."

"Marvin," Jodi said gently, "I'm gonna call you a cab. You're not trained for this."

"I'm staying," Marvin curtly shook his head. "I've studied this my whole life, and now I'm face to face with it, and I'm not running away. Anyway, you might need me. You don't know these people."

"Neither do you! Nobody even believed these people still existed until today!"

"Hey, old man," said Joe Mac.

Chamberlain raised a gaze. "Yes?"

"We have a theory that some of these victims all share the same genealogy, but we can't confirm it. The records don't go back far enough. But if we're right, and these people targeted these children for that reason, how would they know they're related?"

"Because these Druids would have continued the traditions of their ancestors," Chamberlain shrugged. "The Druids committed everything to memory. Including their genealogies that reach back thousands of years. Just as Hebrew genealogies reach back to the beginning of recorded time, so do Druid genealogies." His gaze grew distant. "Everything an ancient Druid knew was learned by oral tradition, and it generally required someone twenty years to learn all that needed to be learned, and so it's quite possible, even likely, that your victims were related before this country was ever formed. Even before England was formed. But only a true Druid – a man or woman who has committed the totality of their long genealogy to memory – would know who is related to who because nothing was ever written."

With irritation Jodi asked, "Why didn't you know all this stuff about their genealogies, Marvin?"

"How would I know that?" Marvin responded. "I dig up bones! I mean, I knew they didn't write anything down! But I didn't know the part about genealogies because they're *dead* when I dig 'em up! It's not like I've ever *talked* to one of them."

"Would you two knock it off?" said Joe Mac. "And why would these Druids go after these children because they're related?"

"Obviously because they fear this bloodline."

"Why would they be afraid of a bunch of children just because of their bloodline?"

Chamberlain appeared curious before he said, "The ancient Druids – and this group is certainly comprised of their most direct descendants – feared nothing. But the old ones did have a *resentment*. And over the centuries that resentment might have devolved into fright in the minds of those made of lesser stuff." He paused. "I don't hesitate to say that these children of the ancient bloodlines do not possess anything like the merciless determination or the iron will of their forefathers regardless what modern advantages they may enjoy, so what their fathers only resented, the children may actually fear."

Joe Mac eased to the desk. "I want to know why they fear this bloodline. I want to know why they're killing these kids."

"I am answering your question, detective." Chamberlain leaned forward, hands folded. "The last of the ancient Druids were exterminated in the first century. But they were not vanquished by Julius Caesar – as many believe. No, they were vanquished by an *idea* that God had come to Earth in the form of Man and revealed himself to all Mankind as Savior of the World. They were defeated by the idea that the only Son of the Living God had finally come to redeem Mankind and that other gods were not only unnecessary but were indeed evil. They were defeated by the strength of a faith in Christ Jesus of Nazareth long before they were defeated by the unconcealed, whole-souled contempt of the world." He nodded slowly, "And so the old Druids escaped the slings of Mankind which had begun progressively persecuting their ancient ways in the light of this new and more powerful God. Yes, it was the rise of the god-man, the Messiah, that defeated the ancient Druid kingdom of blood."

Chamberlain paused, his forehead rising slightly as he sighed, "Although the old Druids did not fear the Christian god, they did hate him. But the ancient Druids were made of incomparably stouter stuff than these puny modern versions. These contemporary Druids are but a pale reflection of their ancestors who trampled down both the strong and the weak with a remorseless inveteracy of purpose that made Julius Caesar himself fear their retaliation. But to finally answer your question in a manner fitting to your choosing; I believe these flimsy descendants of those original ironmen of the Druid Empire do more than resent the Messiah. Rather, *they fear the Messiah*. And by some celestial event, they have divined that another Messiah has been born of a bloodline mingled with ancient Druidic blood and the blood of the original Christ. And so they are killing these children to make certain the Messiah does not rise again and destroy their empire as he did before."

Jodi asked, "Could an astrological event like a Venus Transit, which happens only once every hundred years, be the catalyst for selecting these children? It's when Venus passes between the Earth and the sun, and it looks like a giant star in the sky – like the star that was seen over Bethlehem."

"Yes," Chamberlain nodded without reservation. "Then these descendants would listen to their *Manteis* – their 'Diviner.' And if their *Manteis* told them that this celestial event had revealed the second birth of the Christ, they would initiate their plan to kill all the children of this much-feared bloodline." He swept out his hand as if clearing a board. "There would be no other considerations. They would disregard all morality and law. In their mind, there would only be the celestial event, the bloodline of these children, and the fact that the child must be utterly destroyed from the face of the Earth."

Joe Mac frowned, "I thought Jesus was only going to come one time."

Chamberlain shrugged, "The test of a mythology does not lie within logic or ancient documents. The ultimate decider of mythology is the fear or the hope of Mankind. Men believe what they choose to believe."

Joe Mac's frown was deep.

"You don't seem like a Druid," he finally muttered.

With a laugh, Chamberlain said, "I consider myself a scientist, detective. But my god is not a cold and dispassionate figment of physics. Nor is my god a result of overly nuanced theology or the fantasies of metaphysics because I do not believe the myopic vision of Man can ever fully comprehend the vastness of god regardless which road a man walks. And so, as to whether I am what you so quaintly refer to as a Druid, well, I think the path of Nature has the same paltry chance of comprehending a small measure of god as well as any other. But my way is at war with no one. And my god does no harm to anyone else or their preferred path. I simply believe there is ultimately a last decider of all things, and it is omnipotent, omniscient, eternal, just, and quite beyond the ability of Man to fully understand. All we can do in this world is become one with it as honestly as we know how. And the truest path to that understanding is not dogma, but a contrite and humble heart."

Joe Mac said nothing.

Jodi couldn't contain herself anymore to immobility. She stood and walked across the dark room, arms folded, before turning back; "And so these descendants of the ancient Druids have inserted themselves into every level of society? They have access to police records and communications? To our credit cards? Our medical records? Our bank accounts? *Everything?*"

"Of course," Chamberlain stated, "they are mayors, senators, doctors, lawyers, governors, presidents and priests and cardinals and popes. Over the centuries, these Druids have covertly and cunningly made themselves indispensable to the highest strata of every global society that wields either influence or affluence." He lifted a finger. "And they also have a very formidable army of highly trained soldiers who will exactingly execute orders without any hesitation whatsoever. They are not without the means to purpose their will by force if they cannot do it by more subtle means."

"Like money," said Marvin.

Chamberlain waved; "Money. Power. Fame. Land. Security. Howard Hughes reportedly said every man has a price, and he could double it. That would be their motto, as well. But, if all that fails, they are not hesitant to leave a trail of dead bodies that would encircle this world. Because one commonly suspected factor about the original Druids was true then and there is no reason to believe that it is any less true today: They are ruthless. And human life is of no concern to them whatsoever."

Joe Mac asked, "What *is* their concern?"

"Secrecy," Chamberlain said frankly. "That should be obvious to you by now."

Tapping slowly, Joe Mac found an empty chair, and sat. He leaned forward, elbows on knees – a black-draped, hulking shape.

Jodi watched him as he turned his head to the right as if staring. Then he reached into his coat and removed the paper he'd taken from the house of Jacob Statute. He offered the paper to Chamberlain, who received it.

"Can you tell me what that is?" asked Joe Mac.

After staring over the paper, Chamberlain muttered, "This is a map to their place of ritual." He waved a hand at the page. "These are means of measurement used before metrics were invented. You see these signs? Each sign is one league. A league is an ancient Celtic unit used to measure distance. One league equals three miles." He pointed. "This is the spine of a wagon. Twenty feet. And there are six of them used here, so you're talking about one-hundred-twenty feet. And all this leads to a modern replica of Stonehenge – something I have long believed they had rebuilt."

"Here?" asked Marvin. "In New York City?"

"Yes."

"But Stonehenge wouldn't serve its purpose in the United States," Marvin objected. "Stonehenge only works because it's set at the fifty-first parallel. And the fifty-first parallel doesn't even pass through the United States. It passes through Canada." He raised a hand into the air. "*Way up in Canada.*"

Chamberlain frowned as he shook his head. "They would not require it for celestial purposes. They would only need it for ritual – especially for the *Wicker Man*, the most savage of all the sacrificial horrors of the Winter Solstice.

"My father told me thirty years ago that this sect had begun building a replica of Stonehenge in some kind of abandoned bomb shelter located beneath New York City for the *Wicker Man*, and that is exactly what I believe they have done. And tomorrow night I can promise you that there will again be the most hideous sacrifice of human life when they surrender another poor soul to that cursed idol. Even more, if they kidnap another child, they will not hang him from a tree. They will surrender him to the flames. Their evil ritual is far too precious for them to waste it if they have a Messiah. They will rejoice forever if they can surrender Christ to the *Wicker Man.*"

Jodi blinked, "I'll get back to that in a second, Mr. Chamberlain. But are you telling me there's a bomb shelter beneath New York that's big enough to contain Stonehenge? And we're not actually using it as a bomb shelter? Like we don't *need* a bomb shelter?"

Joe Mac mumbled, "After the Cuban Missile Crisis, the government began hollowing out big caverns under New York to make them mass bomb shelters. They cut out quite a few but some of them didn't fit the bill, so they abandoned them. They eventually built one that worked out but it's under heavy guard."

"What happened to the caverns that didn't work out?" Marvin asked.

"Nothing," Joe Mac shrugged. "The Army just left them. So if these fools found one of those old caverns then, yeah, they could have built something as big as Stonehenge. And it wouldn't matter that it's underground because – like Chamberlain says – they wouldn't need it to read the stars. They'd only need it for rituals. And it'd be perfect for that. You could murder people all day long and never get caught. You wouldn't even have to worry about disposal of the bodies. Just drop it in an old pit and throw in some dirt." He looked at Chamberlain. "You said they started building this thing thirty years ago?"

"Yes. They waited until the government abandoned a few caverns. Then they waited an additional period until they felt it was completely forgotten. After that, they moved in and began building their version of Stonehenge."

"And your daddy told you all this?"

"Yes, my father told me of it shortly before his death." Chamberlain nodded slowly. "But he didn't know its location because he was not one of them. He was only close enough to remain aware of their activities."

Marvin raised a hand. "How did they lift forty-ton stone slabs twenty feet into the air in an underground cavern? We don't even know how they did that when they built the original Stonehenge. But we're sure they used a lot of people. And these guys don't have a lot of people, do they? I mean, what do they have? A couple hundred? They'd need a thousand."

"They would have used construction equipment," said Joe Mac. "When the Army abandoned the shelters, they left the bulldozers and forklifts and front-end loaders in the caverns. It wasn't cost effective to take all that stuff back to the surface. So, if you knew how to use the equipment, you could build anything you wanted. It wouldn't even be hard to do. One good man with a dozer and a front-end loader could build a modern version of Stonehenge in a couple of months. He'd just need somebody to tell him where to put this or that. And I'm sure they got plenty of those guys."

Jodie walked to the desk and regarded Chamberlain. "Mr. Chamberlain, do you know where the entrance to this cavern might be? I mean, according to this map?"

He lifted the map. "This seems to indicate that the entrance is underground. Perhaps a subway tunnel. But there's nothing to indicate which tunnel."

"Do you know anybody we could talk to that might be able to help us out?"

"No," he said frankly. "Anyone familiar with these particular Druids will be far too terrified to help you." He nodded, "You can put them in jail, yes, but these Druids would still kill them in the most horrible ways imaginable – even in jail. And everyone knows it. And that's why no one will cooperate."

Joe Mac stood. "Take me to this cemetery."

With no reluctance Chamberlain lifted his coat and stood.

"It's your funeral," he said.

EIGHT

"How long ago was it that you saw 'em here?"

Joe Mac's truculent question seemed unnaturally absorbed by the deep mossy softness beneath their feet, and Jodi couldn't help but wonder what obscene sustenance fed this overgrown jungle of a graveyard.

"Twenty years ago," Chamberlain answered as he pointed. "They were over there when I saw them. It was night. And they were walking toward the road."

"Where were you at?"

"I was over there inside that tree line."

"How did you recognize your robes if it was night, and you only saw them at a distance of two hundred feet?"

"There was a full moon."

"Did they have lights?"

"Yes. They had lanterns and flashlights."

"But they wouldn't have needed lanterns and flashlights if it was a full moon, and they were on top of the ground," Joe Mac said slowly. "They would have only needed flashlights if they'd been *under* the ground."

Jodi leaned forward, staring close into Joe Mac's dark glasses. "Are you thinking the entrance to this tunnel is in this graveyard?"

"I'm thinking that it's inside one of these tombs." Joe Mac nodded once. "That'd be an underground entrance. Let's take a look around."

"There's no reason to look around," Chamberlain commented. "There is only one mausoleum, and it's back in that ravine. That's where people used to bury family members that they were ashamed of."

Joe Mac: "Marvin!"

Marvin stepped up. "Right here, Joe."

"You got a gun?"

Hesitation. "What?"

Joe Mac pulled a .45 from his coat. "Take this. I ain't leading you back in there without you being able to defend yourself. We don't know what we might run into. Do you know how to use this?"

"Just point and pull the trigger?"

Joe Mac reached out, found Marvin's hand, placed the .45 in his grip.

"I'll only say once, so listen up. This is a semiautomatic .45. This is the safety. You push down this safety, and this weapon is ready to fire. Then all you do is pull the trigger, and you've got eight bullets before you're empty. But *do not* push down this safety unless you are ready to fire this weapon. And never use this weapon unless you seriously mean to kill somebody. You understand?"

"Uh," Jodi began, "Joe, I'm not sure this is such a good –"

"He'll do fine," said Joe Mac. He clapped Marvin on the shoulder. "I got faith in you, kid. Just remember: Don't use this thing unless you mean to kill somebody. You don't aim for somebody's arm or leg." Joe Mac placed a hand over his own heart. "You aim center mass. Got it?"

"Got it."

With a shrilling screech, Poe landed on Joe Mac's shoulder, and instantly the raven's jet black head was turning in every direction, clearly searching. He seemed to see something every tenth of a second, evaluating and dismissing, before he sighted something else in the next tenth of a second. And it was never ending, never ceasing.

Jodie laughed; it was amazing how much sheer physical and mental energy it took this gigantic raven to remain so alert to every movement and sound both near and far and at such a relentless pace. Poe seemed to hear and see everything for miles and miles – everything behind them and everything in front of them. He was like a guardian spirit that never sleeps and never reveals fear or fatigue.

Joe Mac reached up to briefly caress Poe's head before he said, "Stay alert, boy."

With a shrill, Poe exploded into the air. In seconds he was circling, and at his low altitude – just slightly above the trees – Jodie could see that the magnificent raven was searching, always searching, and she *did* feel safer with him up there.

Joe Mac began walking.

"Come on, Chamberlain."

* * *

Before the tomb, they stood.

It was a square granite and cement crypt built into the side of a slope that rose on the east side of the hollow. Wide, brown steps led up to the black gaping entrance framed by two marble lions green with gloom.

Above the door was written a single name …

… *FORTINUS* …

"Yep," said Jodi. "This is where the map begins."

Joe Mac frowned, "Or ends."

Gazing down, Jodie wasn't surprised to see that there was a well-worn, weedless path up the steps much the same as the path they had soon discovered in the woods that led them to this very spot. It was more than obvious that this was not merely a mausoleum; it was almost like a subway station.

Shrilling, Poe settled above the mausoleum door, perched on the lintel. He glanced into the door before jerking his head up, searching the woods behind them, the sky, the path they'd walked. Jodie knew she didn't need to look back; if there were something behind her, Poe would let her know.

She took out her Glock as Joe Mac used his cane to climb the steps. He rose with strong, fearless, balanced strides and entered the tomb with absolutely no hesitation. But Jodie needed a moment, standing close, before she stepped into that corporeal darkness. Then she was standing beside Joe Mac, her hand tight on the pistol.

"What do you see?" asked Joe Mac.

She removed her flashlight from her coat and saw that the upright crypt was as well-worn as the door to her apartment. If there was a dead man in there, he sure had a lot of friends.

"Well?"

"Over here." She guided Joe Mac to the crypt. "It's right in front of you. It's the door to a crypt. But it's straight up and down like they buried him standing up." She paused. "I've never seen a grave like this before."

"Any other folks buried in here?"

"Nope. Just this guy."

Leaning his cane against the wall, Joe Mac began feeling the door with both hands pressing and pulling and searching. He pried at the crypt as if it would open like a normal door but it wouldn't budge. He struck it with his fist. Then he struck the wall beside it.

"It's hollow, all right."

"Aren't all graves hollow?"

"Not as hollow as this one."

Joe Mac lifted his nose. Then he stretched up his arm, holding it aloft without attempting to touch the crypt or the wall. And he slowly began to move his hand through the air, shuffling forward. Finally, he reached a place on another wall and by now Jodie understood; she could feel a faint draft from a niche in the stone.

Joe Mac stuck his hand inside the crevice and jerked.

The crypt behind Jodie clicked and she whirled, gun raised.

The door to the tomb swung open.

Trembling, Jodi raised the flashlight.

"WOW!"

Jodi screamed as she leaped into the air. When she came down, Marvin was standing where she'd been, peering into the tomb. She landed on her feet and it took her several seconds to recover before she shouted, "Jesus, Marvin! Don't do that!"

Marvin turned toward her. "This is great, Jodi!"

Shifting from foot to foot Jodi breathed, "Oh, man. Oh, man …"

"Look at this!" laughed Marvin. "This is an archeologist's dream! Hey! Can I borrow your flashlight?"

Marvin reached for her flashlight, and Jodi found herself in an amateur wrestling match. "Wait a minute!" she shouted as she pushed him back. "Marvin! Think about what you're doing! We're looking for *murderers*. Do you understand! *We're looking for murderers*! This is not archeology!" She pushed back her hair from her face. "I'm sorry, but I can't let you go in there alone."

He smiled, "Come with me."

Jodi found herself staring.

"We're going in," said Joe Mac.

Turning, Jodi looked up into Joe Mac's fearless, frowning face. Although Joe Mac couldn't see what was before him, it obviously didn't matter.

"What do you see, Marvin?" he asked.

Marvin stretched out his hand. "Jodi? Please?"

"Oh, man," Jodi moaned. "I give up. Here."

Taking the flashlight, Marvin smiled spectacularly before he said, "I'll be right back." In seconds, he was swallowed by the gloom.

Jodi knew this was her big chance to talk some sense into Joe Mac. She gathered herself, then said, "Joe, great job. Now, let's go back to the station, and we'll get some men and equipment. We'll come back here with SWAT – those guys *live* for this kind of thing, ya know – and we'll go get these heathens. Whattaya say? Sound like a plan?"

"We're going in," said Joe Mac.

Jodi leaned her head back, hand on her forehead. "Joe, we can't go in there without backup. This is extremely *un*safe."

"Why is that?"

"Why?" Jodi stared. "Why? Are you kidding me?"

She turned as Marvin emerged from the tunnel brushing off dust. He clicked off the flashlight as he turned to Joe Mac. "The tunnel runs straight as an arrow toward the city, and it's been used so much that there's not even any footprints. The path along the floor is smooth as stone, so if we use this tunnel and come back out this way they'll never even know we were here."

"Joe," said Jodi. "Listen to me. Please."

"Go ahead," he said.

"We are 'unarmed.'"

Joe Mac removed another .45 from his coat. "I got another .45. Marvin's got his .45. You've got your Glock. We're packing."

"Wait, wait, wait, wait!" Jodi held up both hands. "Hey! *Look*! We are *not* that well-armed! I've never been in a single gunfight, and Marvin's never even shot a gun! And you're blind! We're like the gang that couldn't shoot straight! What if we go in there and run into a whole coven of these guys? We're gonna die and blow this entire investigation! And I wanna catch these guys!"

"I just wanna take a look around," said Joe Mac.

"You're blind! What are you gonna look at?"

"Chamberlain!"

Realizing she had forgot all about Ben Chamberlain, Jodi turned as the old man stepped forward as calm as the dead surface of a pond without fish.

"Yep?" he asked.

Joe Mac presented the map, "How many … what did you call them?"

"Leagues?"

"Yeah."

Chamberlain accepted the map and walked to the light of the door. He gazed down a full minute before he returned. "If I'm reading this right –"

Jodi: "*If?*"

"… it's less than two miles to the place where they've built this thing. But don't get off the path. Just go straight on. You'll know it when you see it. Then come straight back the same way you go in." Chamberlain nodded. "You should be fine."

Jodi: "You're not coming?"

"You crazy? I'm not getting killed in there."

Joe Mac stepped forward. "Listen, Chamberlain, I need you to make me two robes, and I need 'em ready by tomorrow morning."

"I guess I can do that if I have to. I can do two robes. I couldn't do three but I reckon I can do two of them."

"Have them ready for me."

"It'll be ready."

Joe Mac turned back to them as Chamberlain sauntered toward the mausoleum's gaping door, which never seemed more like the mouth of a skull than it did to Jodi in this moment. Seconds later he was gone, and Poe descended from the lintel to land where Chamberlain had stood, staring into the crypt.

With a heavy breath, Joe Mac said, "Jodi, you stay beside me. Marvin, you take the flashlight and lead. You've done this before, haven't you?"

"All my life, Joe."

"All right. You know what we're looking for. Let's get to it."

Jodi was beside Joe Mac with Marvin in front as she heard a rushing sound and ducked as Poe flew over her head, diving as it reached the entrance of the tomb, and in a flash the gigantic raven disappeared into the darkness before them.

She began, "Poe just – "

"I know," said Joe Mac.

"What's he doing!"

"He's a raven."

"What does that mean?"

"He's protecting us."

"How does he know we're in danger?"

"He knows death when he's near it."

* * *

It was a thoroughly unremarkable two miles, and then the tunnel opened up into a gigantic floor as smooth as finished cement and a ceiling that the flashlight could not even reach. But before them, as they continued to walk forward, Jodi began to see something rising from the floor like a leviathan rising from the sea in the midnight dark.

Monolithic flat stones began to stand – seemingly one by one – as the flashlight slowly illuminated their majesty, and even Jodi, despite her fear, felt thrilled to be inside this fantastic, beautiful work. She had a passing thought that streets so far above their head, so proud of their towering architecture, paled in comparison to this triumphant display of stone wrought by the hand of prehistoric man.

"Oh, my god," she whispered.

Marvin had stopped and was slowly staring from one pillar to the next. Then he retreated to Jodi and said, "Sit right here. You and Joe. And don't move. I'm going to walk around a little bit and do some measuring, okay?"

Jodi nodded, "Okay."

Marvin stood and turned.

"Hey," said Jodi.

He stared down.

"Don't go too far, okay?"

Marvin smiled, "I'll be right here."

Jodi watched as the flashlight moved in the dark. She couldn't see Marvin, just the light, but suddenly it would move along the floor, slow and measured, before the blindingly bright beam rose along a stone slab. Eventually Marvin left the circle of stones and wandered far into the distance – so far that Jodi felt compelled to call out to him in case he'd forgotten where they were waiting. But then she saw the light returning, and she blew out a series of breaths and wiped a tear from her eye.

Joe Mac laid a massive hand on her shoulder.

"What's the boy doing?" he asked.

"I have no idea."

Jodi screamed as something huge – *Poe!* – landed on the floor before her. She almost swatted him before she gained control and hissed, "Poe! Stop it! You scared me!"

Poe cawed and walked to her, nudging her with his head. Then he lifted and settled on Joe Mac's shoulder although they were in total darkness. Jodi could see nothing, but she heard Poe shuffling and Joe Mac laughing.

"What?" she asked.

Joe Mac chuckled, "He's just running his beak through my hair checking for bugs. He does that." He grunted. "Might as well. He might find some."

Marvin had been walking steadily toward them and the light had been growing and now he arrived and knelt before Jodi. "You okay?" he asked.

"Yeah. You?"

"I'm fine."

Marvin tilted the flashlight so that the beam bounced off the wall to their right although the slope was a hundred feet away. But in this complete darkness it was amazing how much difference a little light could make. Even though Jodi had only been sitting in total dark for a few minutes, she had to squint.

"What'd you find?" asked Joe Mac.

Marvin sat cross-legged on the floor, took a heavy breath, and said, "Okay. Yes. It's a replica of Stonehenge as near as memory serves. Stonehenge is not exactly my area of expertise. But I know how many pillars, how many lintels, the sacrificial stone, and the outer posts, which nobody understands. And my best guess is that this place was built by an expert. I mean it was built by somebody who duplicated Stonehenge down to the smallest ditch, hole, and line. Only, there's one difference."

Jodi scowled, "What's that?"

Raising a hand, as if for patience, Marvin said, "This is Stonehenge as it was at the height of Stonehenge. You know what I mean?"

"No" said Jodi. "What do you mean?"

"I mean that this is Stonehenge as it probably looked when it was 'perfect.' When it was used every day by that powerful, genius nation that originally built it for whatever kind of ritual or whatever astrological purpose it served. This isn't a replica of today's Stonehenge in Salisbury. That one's broken down. That one's a skeleton. This is the Stonehenge that dominated Salisbury for eight thousand years. This is Stonehenge before it crashed. Before it was abandoned and disintegrated into ruins. And *long* before it was discovered by the so-called 'modern world.'" Marvin stretched out an arm toward the architecture. "This is Stonehenge at the height of its glory. When it was feared by the entire world. When it was worshipped by the entire world."

"Huh," Joe Mac grunted, "which means these people aren't trying to duplicate Stonehenge. They're trying to bring back whatever empire built it."

"Exactly," said Marvin. "This isn't 'honor.' This is *'resurrection.'*"

"God!" shouted Jodi.

The entire subterranean cavern was sharply illuminated by spotlights that Jodi couldn't identify because she couldn't see at all. She found herself twisting away from the brilliance as Marvin rushed forward and threw an arm around her waist fairly picking her up as they crashed into Joe Mac.

"Hurry!" Marvin hissed and Jodi staggered a half-dozen steps before she gained a blinding white view of the smooth cement floor. Then she saw that Marvin was rushing her along with his right arm and had his left arm wrapped around Joe Mac and they were all charging toward a jagged pile of broken rock.

Poe swooped across their path shrilling and then disappeared.

They reached the rubble in a staggering, confused tangle to stumble and crawl over the crest before rolling roughly down the far side where the faintest shadow fell over them. Dust rose above the pile of shattered stone as Jodi threw herself against the gravel and dirt. Her face was toward Marvin and Joe Mac and she saw that both of them were in similar positions – flat against the rubble, heads down, utterly unmoving.

Voices rose in the cavern.

"Fill the lamps!" someone shouted.

"Get this place ready for tomorrow night!"

It was a second voice, but Jodi heard at least ten or maybe fifteen people talking. Then, "Hurry it up. Come on. You know your jobs."

Only then did Jodi notice a black blur at her feet and rolled her eyes to see Poe perched beside her legs. His wings were closed tight, but his head was ever twisting with that quickness that indicated he was hearing and following everything he couldn't see. And she wondered what marvelous and fearful intelligence this raven possessed that allowed it to somehow understand that it could not make a sound.

She was too frightened to smile. And her greatest fear was that the uncontrollably fast beating of her heart was so loud that it would give away their position although she hadn't even moved. But how could they *not* hear the pounding of her heart so big inside her chest when it was all she could hear herself?

It was impossible they wouldn't hear her!

"Uh," Joe Mac grunted as his foot slipped on a stone.

Jodi's breath caught.

"Hey!" she heard someone. "Did you guys hear that?"

"Hear what?"

"I heard a sound. Over there. Hey, Andre! Check that out, man!"

"Check it out yourself! This is New York. It might be way *underneath* New York but it's still New York. There's all kinds of rats and zombies and alligators and everything else down here. Just fill the lamp, man."

"Fine. I'll check it myself."

"Man, do your job, so we can get outta here!"

"Just a second! I swear I heard something!"

Jodi couldn't hear the approaching steps, but she reached for her Glock and *si-lent-ly* drew it, holding the pistol tight. She knew they didn't stand a chance in this situation if they were discovered. She closed her eyes, concentrating, as a voice suddenly erupted on the close side of the shattered stone.

"It was right here …"

Jodi clenched her teeth and began to rise.

With a screech Poe erupted from the floor and landed atop the heap instantly flapping its enormous wings in the face of whoever stood there.

"*God Almighty!*"

A chaotic sound of crashing and falling down the distant rubble.

Poe stood its perch screaming. Then it exploded into the air and began flying to and fro across the cavern as some of the intruders howled in laugher at something Jodi couldn't see, but it was clear from the upheaval that the men were no longer concerned about whatever might have lain on the far side of this broken stone.

"It's just a crow, man! Forget it!"

"That's the biggest crow I've ever seen!"

"That ain't no crow, fool! It's too big to be a crow! *Look out!*"

She heard Poe diving and rising and diving again and each swoop was following by a curse, and then a gunshot boomed. Then other shots were fired and more curses rolled over the rubble. "Stop shootin' at that bird!" someone bellowed. "You can't hit that bird with a nine millimeter! You're gonna hit one of *us*!"

Poe continued his harassment and Jodi heard stones clattering across the hard floor. Then the voices faded and the lights disappeared and, in the distance, she heard a steel door clang solidly shut.

No one moved for a long, long time. Jodi didn't hear Poe. She didn't hear Joe Mac or Marvin. She heard nothing. But, finally, Poe settled on the crest of the rubble and cawed softly as if to tell them he was here, and Jodi knew they were safe.

A moment later they were on their feet and over the broken stone as if emerging from a tomb. And Jodi stood bent, hands on knees, trying to breath. After five minutes Marvin switched on the flashlight, and they were again alone with the monument.

Jodi felt Marvin's arm around her, and she turned as he embraced her and said quietly, "It's okay. They're gone." He held her until she stopped trembling, and, as she separated, she gazed up with an affection she had never anticipated.

"Thank you," she managed. "That was brave."

Marvin smiled, "I'm an archeologist. I was born brave."

Jodi laughed.

"Let's go," said Joe Mac. "We got what we need."

As they walked toward the tunnel Poe settled on Joe Mac's shoulder. And when the gigantic raven leaned forward Jodi saw his powerful profile against the backlight; he was still searching and fearless and faithful unto death.

She wiped a tear from her cheek.

* * *

It was early daylight when they arrived at her squad car without incident and with Poe circling low to follow their every twist through the overgrown jungle fed so voraciously by the inevitable cold crucible of all flesh. And when they reached the road, Jodi simply sat on the bumper of the car leaning forward, elbows on knees, hands over her face.

Jodi had been in alarmingly dangerous, stressful situations before. But she had never been in a situation where she was so totally outnumbered with no chance of backup or even an eventual ambulance if she were shot or cut into living, bloody pieces. In a way, she was trying to chalk this one up as a "learning experience" but it was a learning experience she would have gratefully missed. Nor did she value what she'd learned. If anything, she'd only learned not to tear off into the wild blue without a decent plan or adequate backup should things go south but, then, she'd already known *that*.

She resisted the impulse to believe Joe Mac was a bad influence. She had come to genuinely love Joe; she felt like her father was alive again. And, to be honest, they *were* making headway with his impetuous if not downright suicidal commitment to disinter the truth beneath this literal and figurative graveyard.

She knew Joe Mac was standing stoically to the side patiently allowing her to regain her balance mentally and emotionally. And she was actually a bit peeved that Marvin seemed so unaffected.

Marvin didn't have the training to handle high-stress situations. He wasn't some world-famous gravedigger experienced at dealing with assassins and chains rattling inside the walls as the lights go out. But here Marvin was, standing at her side as easily as if he'd changed a car tire in the morning sun. There was just something about it that ruffled her feathers.

"You okay?" Marvin asked with lamentable timing.

"I'm fine," Jodi answered from within her hands. "How are you?"

"I'm good. I thought it was sort of exciting."

"You would."

The radio cracked and Jodi turned her head as they listened to an Amber Alert released for a four-year-old boy – his name was Tommy Childers – who had been kidnapped from a daycare center by an offender dressed as a fireman. They released a description of the man, his car, then detailed his last known direction of travel, and Jodi lowered her hands to gaze over Joe Mac.

Yeah, he'd heard.

"Let's go," said Joe Mac. "We've got 'till tomorrow night."

"How do you know that?" she asked.

"They won't waste the precious blood of this 'Messiah' the day before their *Wicker Man* ceremony." Joe Mac was a monolith of judgment that could have blotted out the noonday sun. "They're gonna give him to the Wicker Man, so they'll keep him alive and well until tomorrow night's ceremony."

Jodi rose and got into the squad car with Marvin climbing into the back. As they fastened seatbelts, she glanced at the rearview mirror.

"You sure you're okay, Marvin?" she asked again.

"Let's get ready for tomorrow night," he muttered. "If you guys don't come back here with me, I'm coming back alone and crashing this party by myself. But I won't let them sacrifice that little boy." He lifted the pistol. "Joe? Can I keep this .45 until tomorrow night?"

"It's yours," said Joe Mac. "You earned it."

Marvin nodded.

"Good enough."

NINE

The war room at the precinct was the last place for chaos, but that's exactly what Jodi measured when they walked through the door.

Almost immediately Brightbarton saw the three of them and turned. "We've lost another four-year-old boy!" He placed hands on hips. "This one was taken from his kindergarten class at a preschool during a fire alarm!"

Jodi wasn't sure what to say since so much of what they'd done so far was downright criminal, and any evidence not legally obtained was fruit of the poisonous tree, which meant it was not only inadmissible in court but could land them all in prison on everything from breaking and entering to theft, obstruction of justice, kidnapping, coercion and conspiracy to commit murder. She had no doubt whatsoever that a determined prosecutor could win them all a good one hundred years apiece.

Brightbarton walked over with an expression of distinct irritation. "What do you two have?" He stared between them. "Joe? You know something. What is it?"

"We're close," said Joe Mac.

"Uh huh," Brightbarton nodded a long moment. "I'll see the three of you in my office. Right now."

Jodi grasped Joe's elbow. "The professor's here."

Across the room, moving with decided concentration over a long conference table, was Professor Augustus Graven. He was handling the robe they'd recovered on Long Island, studying it closely. Then he seemed to feel the focus of Jodi's stare and lifted his face. In seconds he saw them and dropped the ornament; he quickly made his way through the milling crowd until they stood face to face. His frown was grim as he said, "I believe I've discovered something you need to know."

Brightbarton spun in stride and pointed. "Professor Graven! I want both you eggheads in on this!"

"Of course," the professor nodded.

When they'd convened in the office, Brightbarton solidly shut the door and moved behind his desk. He sat and leaned forward, hands flat, and took a moment before he said, "I am bone tired of you guys keeping this investigation to yourselves. And don't lie to me, Joe. You're onto this crew. You've been onto them since you started."

"How do you know that?" Joe Mac asked.

"Because I've got five dead witnesses, and the only thing they had in common was the fact that you guys were on their trail. So you're either gonna tell me what you've got, Joe, or I'm taking both of you off this case. You've got ten seconds."

The five of them stood in silence until Professor Graven offered, "Might I, perhaps, tell you what I have gleaned from the evidence?"

With a sigh Brightbarton crossed his arms. "This better be good."

Without knocking, Special Agent Jack Rollins suddenly entered the room and stopped in place staring curiously from face to face although he seemed to linger longest on Jodi before he directly addressed Brightbarton: "I need a moment with you, captain, to coordinate some search grids."

Brightbarton stood and spoke on his way out the door. "I'll be back in a minute, and you better have some answers." He leaned close to Jodi. "And you need to know your job is on the line, rookie. If you've been withholding critical information that resulted in the kidnapping of this little boy, I'll have your badge."

When he was gone, Joe Mac turned to Jodi with, "We need to get our hands on that robe," he said.

Jodi blinked. "What?""

"The robe that the FBI confiscated on Long Island."

There was an even longer moment before Jodi blurted, "Are you talking about the Druid robe that's lying on that table out there in front of fifty FBI agents?"

"That's the one."

Jodi stared from the table to Joe Mac before she replied, "You're not just blind, Joe, you're insane. How am I supposed to steal that thing from the FBI? They haven't even finished processing it. And you do realize that stealing evidence from the FBI is a federal crime, don't you?"

"We need it," Joe Mac shook his head. "We gotta have it."

"Why?"

Joe said, "Because old man Chamberlain can only make one more robe for us before tomorrow night. But we need three robes so we can all sneak into this midnight mass and arrest every single one of these goons." He raised his face. "You hear me? We're gonna walk in there with the rest of them because we'll be dressed for Halloween just like everybody else. Then, when they start on this little boy, you'll pull your gun."

Jodi was nodding as if in agreement. "And then they'll murder us like dogs and throw our bodies into one of their death pits."

"They call it a 'ritual pit,'" said Marvin.

"Are you dead when you hit the bottom of it?" asked Jodi.

"Yeah."

"Then it's a death pit!" Jodi focused on Joe Mac with, "I don't mind telling you, Joe, that I'm not going back in there tomorrow tonight. I'm not going back in *there*! Period! I'm gonna tell Brightbarton that we've found their little prehistoric frat house and he can send every SWAT guy we've got to mow 'em down like the heathen scum they are!"

Joe Mac shook his head, "That won't work."

"Why not!"

"Because they'll see SWAT coming a mile away and they'll just fade into those tunnels, and we'll won't catch a single one of them. Then they'll build another one of those monuments somewhere else and start all over again."

"That's too bad," Jodi shrugged, "because I'm not going back in there just so we can all get butchered by a bunch of devil-worshipping cannibals. This is what SWAT does, Joe! They're pros at this! It's their job to take down heathens like this when they're going to sacrifice the life of a little boy in some kind of ungodly *Wicker Man* ceremony tomorrow night!"

"What manner of monument?" asked Professor Augustus Graven.

"They've built an exact replica of Stonehenge somewhere beneath the city," answered Marvin. "We found the entrance, but the tunnel ran for several miles, so we don't know the exact location. Jodi's best guess is that it's somewhere west of the city."

"And you are certain about this ceremony?" Graven followed. "It is the *Wicker Man* and it is tomorrow night? The Winter Solstice?"

"Yes."

Professor Graven was ashen as he said, "Then I'm afraid Detective Joe Mac is correct. The only chance you have of saving this little boy's life and apprehending this *Ri* is to seize him during the *Wicker Man* ceremony."

"Why don't we just capture one of these guys on his way to the meeting and make him give us some names?" suggested Jodi. "You can even torture him, Joe, and I'll hold him down." She added, "We might as well. I mean, illegal imprisonment and aggravated assault are the only laws we *haven't* broken."

"No," Professor Graven shook his head. "It will do you no good to merely capture a member of this group because he will not know the true identity of this *Ri*."

"They don't know who he is?" asked Jodi. "How is that possible?"

Professor Graven glanced at Brightbarton, who was still busy with Rollins, before he said, "The high priest of a Druid sect wears a red death mask during rituals, and so it is highly unlikely that any member of this group has ever seen his face. And you've probably surmised by now that these are not social people. They only gather for ceremonies where there is no need for conversation or names. So, not only do they not know the identity of their *Ri*, or their chieftain, they probably don't even know the identities of one another because they each wear a mask and say nothing but incantations."

Marvin said, "How difficult will it be to get close to their *Ri*?"

"It will be very difficult," Professor Graven answered. "He will have well-trained bodyguards who will not hesitate to kill at the slightest provocation. But if you can kill his bodyguards and put him under arrest before he can flee, then you won't have to worry about the rest scattering and escaping through the tunnels. The *Ri* will know their names, and you can arrest them later."

Joe Mac asked, "How is it that this chief knows the names of his people, but they don't know his name?"

"Because the *Ri* must approve every member. But the *Ri* himself comes from a royal bloodline, so no one can either disapprove or approve of him. His title is inherited, and there is no dispute."

"So we don't have a case unless we capture this one man?"

"You will have slaves. But you won't have the master. And the master is the one who organizes the slaughter of victims. He is also the only one who can rebuild the coven should he escape."

Joe Mac turned to Jodi. "Well?" He waited. "We don't need a whole SWAT team just to take down one man, do we?"

Jodi responded, "Joe, we'll be outnumbered hundreds to one. And I shouldn't have to remind you that they carry guns, too. Yeah, sure, we could make a play for this king of theirs, but even if we get past the bodyguards, what makes you think we can survive the rest of them when they all pull a piece?"

"You got a better idea on how we're gonna capture this guy?"

Jodi found herself nervously tapping her foot. And she didn't want to say anything, but she eventually muttered, "We need two more guys."

"Why do we need two more guys?"

"*If* ... and this is a big '*if*' ... *if* I can get close to this king of theirs, and put him under arrest, I'll have to concentrate on keeping him under control. That means I won't be able to concentrate on what's in front of me or behind me. And I can't trust Marvin with that. He doesn't have the training. And I can't trust you with that, either. You're blind. So how am I gonna cover the chief and the Indians, too?"

"I will go with you," Professor Graven volunteered.

Jodi found herself studying the old man. "You have a lot of experience at gunfighting, professor?"

"I gained a very unfortunate amount of combat experience during the Vietnam War," answered Professor Graven. His brow rose, "Yes, I have not always been a scientist. When I was young, I was a soldier."

Jodi grimaced and looked to the window, fighting the urge to fidget. "What a crew we got – two archeologists, a blind man, and a rookie detective. There is no way this is going to end well." She took a moment. "So how are we going to steal that robe?"

"Leave that to me," said the professor. "Dr. Mason? I'll need your help.

Marvin nodded.

"Come."

Brightbarton reentered the office as they moved toward the door.

"Where do you two think you're going?" he asked. "I want some answers."

"We have learned something critical about the identity of these Druids," said Professor Graven without hesitation. "And the secret lies in the documents we found in the dead man's house. But we'll have to take the documents to the museum to compare them with ancient Gaelic letters that are under glass – items that cannot be removed because they will disintegrate if exposed to the atmosphere."

If suspicion had a physical face, Brightbarton would have personified it. Then he looked at Jodi who did her best to appear innocent before he focused on Joe Mac, who said, "I'll have some answers for you after they check those documents, Steve, but you gotta let them translate that stuff. All I can tell you right now is that we're close." He paused. *"Real close."*

Shaking his head with a grimace, Brightbarton motioned for the door. "Get out of here. And if you don't get back to me by this afternoon, Joe, you're off this case. And so are you, hotshot. Your detective career will be as dead as Julius Caesar."

As Jodi guided Joe Mac from the office, she saw Marvin energetically searching through papers on the conference table with Professor Graven gazing on.

Marvin was creating quite a stir at the far end of the room speaking rapidly about ancient locations and Druidic practices with Rollins and every other FBI agent catching each word as Professor Graven slowly opened his leather briefcase and slid the robe surreptitiously into the open gap. Then he quietly closed the case and slowly made his way across the squad room. He didn't look back. Didn't speed up. Didn't slow down. He simply sauntered through detectives until he disappeared out the door.

When Jodi and Joe Mac emerged onto the street, Professor Graven was standing at a far corner and waved. Then he stepped into the street, hailed a cab, and was gone.

Jodi didn't have to be told where to find him.

They waited another ten minutes before Marvin bounded off the stairs carrying another briefcase. His face was pasty and pale and covered with sweat. "Holy Mother!" he whispered, a hand on his chest. "That was rough! They realized the robe had gone missing before I even got out of the room."

Jodi's eyes widened. "What did you tell them?"

"I told them the robe is just a Halloween costume. I said the documents hold the answer they're looking for. I got the papers right here. Then they asked Brightbarton about the robe, and he said someone probably inventoried it."

"Did they buy it?"

"For now, yeah."

"Good."

Jodi hailed a cab and they climbed in.

"The Museum of Natural History," she said. "And hurry it up. We're half out of time and clean out of luck."

* * *

Marvin explained the entire layout to Professor Graven who sat with a stare as unrevealing as a stone Buddha. Graven had also said nothing as Marvin described in detail the layout of the monument they'd discovered, and when Marvin finished Graven merely stood and walked slowly across his office, an arm across his chest, one hand cupping his chin.

Finally, he asked, "You say this would be a replica of Stonehenge at the height of its glory? Before it fell into disrepair?"

"Yes," Marvin nodded.

"Yes," Graven murmured and stopped strolling before a picture window. "What they have done is no more than guesswork because no one knows the original architecture of Stonehenge." He paused. "But the original design is inconsequential. We can confidently infer that it was the locus of great and horrific human sacrifice. And that is not surprising. Animal and human sacrifice were commonly practiced during the fifth millennium BC by practically every people group on the planet. What is more important is this: What are they trying to accomplish that was originally the intent of Stonehenge? What is their end cause? What is the motivation for recreating the locus of such a savage empire? And what is the cause of these seemingly random murders not committed on the sacred ground of this new Stonehenge but in trees and warehouses and the homes of everyday people?"

Jodi said, "We think they're afraid that the Christ child has been reborn, and they're trying to kill him before he destroys their movement like Christianity destroyed their movement in the first century."

Graven nodded, "Yes, the arrival of Christianity sounded the death knell for the Druidic Empire – the beginning of the end. It destroyed them on the level of ideas, and that is always the purest, strongest way to destroy a movement. For when you defeat the idea, you defeat the people behind the idea. They would obviously not want the Christ child to be born again and set them back another two thousand years." He gestured to a book shelf. "Forget that the Christ was prophesied to be born only once. Theological and mythological inaccuracy is always the greatest weapon of a religion's opponent."

Joe Mac was sitting with a stoic, displeased expression as he commented, "Where do these people come from?"

"From everywhere," Graven replied plainly. "From the staffs of museums, police departments, fire departments, universities, corporations, and hospitals. The appeal of immortality gained through a metaphysical belief is in every suburban home and every bank and military institute and temple. It was the same with Egypt, with Israel, with the Aztecs, the Mayans, and the Saracens. It has been thus throughout history, and it is the same today with the most ennobled president or the lowliest peasant. Every human being wishes they could live forever, and that is what the mythology of the Druid promises."

Marvin remarked dryly, "It makes for motivated followers."

"Indeed," Graven nodded. "That is why we must not concern ourselves with capturing a mere member of this group. They will tell us nothing because all they know is the mythology that binds them. They don't know the identity of the chieftain who leads this movement to resurrect an empire so savage that the Romans obliterated it not to annex their land but to destroy the horror of what the Druids had so mercilessly inflicted upon the world. When Roman Centurions saw the Druids perform their ceremony of the Wicker Man they immediately killed every Druid in the valley of *Pies de Martel* out of sheer revulsion."

"So what's the plan?" asked Jodi. "I don't mind saying that I don't fancy Joe's idea of just walking in there wearing these Halloween costumes. We'll be outnumbered and outgunned and these people are not shy about killing. If we make a single mistake, it'll be our last. I promise you."

"Then I suggest we do not make a mistake," said Graven. "There is simply no other way to apprehend the *Ri*. Nor, I might add, do you presently have a *reason* to apprehend him. Like everyone else in this country, these people enjoy the freedom of religion. They are protected by the Constitution and so to pursue them is to violate every constitutional and civil right on the books. That is why you must catch them in the act of murder. Then you can connect them to the other murders, and you will have your case for the District

Attorney. Otherwise this is merely an academic debate on ancient mythologies – something that belongs to the realm of archeology and not police work."

Joe Mac looked distinctly unhappy as he said, "All right. We're gonna need a place to hole up until tomorrow night. I can't go home with them knowing I'm onto them. You shouldn't either, Jodi. Even if you live alone. It's not safe. And the same goes for you, Marvin."

"I have an adequate home," said Professor Graven. "I am not connected to this in any 'official' way because my advice has been totally off the record – so to speak. I think you would be safe with me."

"All right," said Joe Mac. "Jodi? Get Captain Brightbarton on your cell."

"The captain? Why?"

"Just do it."

Jodi hit '1' and Brightbarton answered on the first ring. Then she simply gave it to Joe Mac who said, "Steve, listen quick. I've found one of 'em. Yeah, I'm on top of him right now." He paused. "I'm at the south end of Central Park beside the fountain. I'm gonna be here until he comes out of this townhome. Got anybody who can back me up? No, I don't want any uniforms. Has to be undercover."

Joe Mac gave the phone to Jodi.

"What was that about?" she asked.

"I'm gonna try to find out who blew our rendezvous with Montanus," said Joe Mac. "If things go bad tomorrow night, we'll have to call for backup whether we like it or not. And I'd like to know who we can trust."

"I thought you said we could trust the captain."

"It's not him I'm worried about. Brightbarton is gonna talk to somebody. Maybe Rollins. I don't know. But if somebody shows up to kill me, then we'll know where it's broke."

"But why did you pick a place out in the open?" Jodi pressed. "They could hit us from a dozen different directions."

"I want Poe with me." Joe Mac extended his cane. "He'll let me know if something's coming." He nodded, "You go with them. I'll catch a cab to the park, and I'll call you later if things work out all right."

"You gotta be kidding." Jodi grabbed her coat and turned to Marvin. "I'm going with him. Call me with the professor's address. If nothing happens, we'll be there in a few hours. But I'd feel better if you were off the street."

"She's right," said Professor Graven. "The museum is not secure, and these are the most dangerous of all people. We need to retire to my home where I might arm myself. And I have a very good security system. We will be safe there."

Jodi grabbed Joe Mac's elbow, "Let's go, Joe. If we've got a date to get ourselves killed there's no use being late."

* * *

Standing beside an oak tree Jodi found herself gazing up at the expansive canopy still thick with the full gamut of autumn color. Although tomorrow was the first day of winter, this towering arboreal giant was lasting far longer than most to shed its glory.

Joe Mac was standing on the far side of the trunk, one hand in a pocket, his other hand holding his cane. And before them, perched on a limb, Poe was doing his normal thing – watching everything, catching everything. Jodi was sure that nothing moved within their sphere of safety that Poe did not notice and evaluate.

"Do you think Poe knows what he's saying when he uses his words?" Jodi asked.

Although she tried to make it sound like casual conversation, the truth was that she needed to talk to defuse her fears; she'd never been in a gunfight before, but she was learning the fear before the fight wasn't exactly a cake walk.

"Of course," said Joe Mac. "Why do you think he talks?"

"I don't know. Sounds a little far-fetched. If he knows what he's saying, then he's almost human ... or something. I don't even know how to describe it. What has he ever said to you that makes you think he understands the meaning of words?"

"I saw him harassing a dog."

"You saw him do what?"

"Harassing a dog."

"How was he harassing the dog?"

"Well," Joe Mac began slowly, "there used to be this big ol' black hound dog down the street. I hated the thing. It used to tear up my garbage and bark at me every time I went outside. Then Poe vanished for about a week. A few days later the dog came back around and Poe came back around with it. I heard Poe in the trees. Then the dog came close to me, and Poe said, 'Zeus! Come inside!'"

When Jodi peeked around the tree, Joe Mac was smiling.

"When Poe said that, the dog ran back home," Joe Mac continued. "Then every time the dog came around Poe would get above it and say, 'Zeus! Come inside!' And the dog would run off." He chuckled. "Poe kept that up for weeks. He wouldn't let that dog alone. Every time it came into the yard Poe would be telling it to go back inside, and it'd run home again. It might be back in fifteen minutes, but Poe would still be telling it to go inside. Finally, it just stopped coming around. It couldn't get no peace."

Jodi laughed, "That's incredible."

"Believe it or not, but it's true. Poe knows what he's saying. At least, most of the time. It might take him a while to catch on, but he catches on. He catches on to what we're saying a lot faster than we catch on to what he's saying."

"He's your friend, isn't he?"

"Ah, he's more'n that."

"What do you think he is?"

"I don't know," Joe Mac said more slowly. "He is what he is. I am what I am. Poe don't ask no questions. I don't, either."

After a moment, Jodi said, "I think Poe's your Avatar."

"What's an Avatar?"

"An Avatar is a spirit that takes physical form, and it comes to someone for a reason."

"What reason?"

"Only the Avatar knows that." Jodi noticed Poe staring directly at her. "But an Avatar isn't just flesh. It's inhabited by a powerful spirit. And only the Avatar knows why it chooses who it chooses."

Joe Mac laughed, "My old grandma used to say a raven on your porch means somebody's about to die."

"Well, I have to say, Joe; I've never felt closer to death than I have since I've been hanging out with you. It must be your happy attitude. All your funny jokes. At least you're not dark and serious and suicidal all the time. It'd be terrible if you were the kind of man who would follow a secret tunnel from a graveyard where families only bury those they're ashamed of to an even more awful graveyard where they cut off people's heads and eat the rest. And then you'd want to go *back*. That'd be rough on me."

"Aw, you'll be all right." Joe Mac tapped the grass with his cane; his other hand remained buried in his coat. "But if anything happens I want you to just hit the ground behind a tree. You know the difference between cover and concealment, right?"

"Yep. I remember the course. Cover is something that stops a bullet. Concealment means they can't see you, but they can still shoot you. Concealment is a bush, a curtain. Cover is something like a tree, a rock wall, a cement barrier. Maybe that water fountain out there. But since I don't really have any experience at gunfighting – and hoped I never would – what's the most likely kind of ambush out here in the park?"

"A drive-by. Something fast. They don't want a standup gunfight in the park in the daytime."

Jodi paused. "But in the late afternoon there's a billion witnesses. And it's not like we don't have a thousand cops within a few blocks of here. Do you really think they're gonna try a drive-by in a high-profile area like this?"

"The chances are slim that they'll try anything at all. That's why I picked this spot. I mostly just wanted to see who comes to us. I want to see who Brightbarton is talking to when we call in a report. Who he might be under orders to talk to."

Jodi took a moment. "Are you thinking it's Rollins?"

"Could be."

"You do know FBI agents have to past a psychological fitness test, don't you?"

"So do we," Joe Mac replied dryly. "And look at us."

"That's … true."

Poe was constantly spinning and his head was twitching and switching from sight to sight – something that left Jodi in constant amazement. She said, "Have you ever thought about how much sheer physical energy Poe burns up doing what he does? He never stops moving. I wonder if birds ever sleep."

Joe Mac shook his head. "Birds don't sleep like we sleep. Our whole brain goes to sleep. Only half their brain goes to sleep. That's how they can keep flying in their sleep. Kind of amazing, if you ask me."

"How'd you learn these little tidbits about birds?" Jodi laughed. "I didn't figure you for a bird expert."

"They call 'em 'ornithologists.'"

"Wow. Excuse me, doc."

"That's all right. Anyway, my son-in-law ordered one of them audio books on birds a while back. He noticed Poe hanging around and staying inside the barn with me and thought I might find it interesting. He was right. It was pretty interesting stuff."

Jodi noticed a car stop in the middle of the block – directly across from their position – and three doors opened.

"Heads up, Joe."

"How many?"

"Two so far."

"I didn't think they'd try anything in broad daylight. Remember what I said. Solid cover and then get out of here. But remember their faces in case they're cops."

Poe whirled the instant Jodi's gaze locked on the car, and now Poe's gaze was locked on the car, too. He was bent, his head aimed like a bullet, and his massive, blue-black wings were partially unfolded like a black jet ready for takeoff. Then Brightbarton got out on the far side, and two other figures exited the vehicle before it sped off.

"It's Brightbarton," said Jodi. "Two more guys got out, and they're walking in opposite directions. And it looks like they've got cut-down AR-15s under their coats. Hard to tell. They're good at concealment. But they've got some kind of rifles."

Holding his overcoat close – Jodi glimpsed a shotgun underneath it – Brightbarton walked up until he was at Joe Mac's side. Then he stood gazing in the opposite direction – the direction at their back – as Jodi continued to watch the street.

"Seen anything, Strong?" Brightbarton asked.

"Just you."

"How about your bird, Joe? Has he seen anything?"

Joe Mac grunted, "How'd you know about him?"

"Are you kidding me?" Brightbarton replied, and Jodi glanced over to clearly see the standard Remington 870 pump-action shotgun under his coat on his right side. "That bird's a legend, man. The forensics guys at the crime scene said it led them all the way through the woods to where that psycho parked his car. No lie. Led them all the way from that dead cat to the end of this road where he musta' parked. Said that bird's like a human being. I'd give him a badge if I could." He gazed across the park in a slow one-eighty. "Strong, you just worry about your side. I'll handle this side. Isn't that what you guys are expecting? An ambush? You wanna find out who it is inside the department that blew your rendezvous with Montanus? Who set you up to die at Mrs. Morgan's place?"

Jodi wished too late that she hadn't reacted as she said, "Captain? How'd you know we thought someone set us up?"

"Kid," Brightbarton grimaced, "I may have fallen off the turnip truck, but I didn't land on my head. And you need about thirty years of experience before I can't predict every thought that passes through that rookie brain of yours. You think me and Joe Mac ain't seen it all? And *done* most of it?"

Jodi had never felt more like a rookie – not even when she was fresh out of the academy and really had been a rookie.

"Who'd you tell?" asked Joe Mac.

"I told Rollins."

Joe Mac was silent. "That's it?"

"That's it."

"Why didn't you tell somebody else?"

"'Cause I ain't trusted Rollins since this thing started." Brightbarton muttered with obvious displeasure. "I've never seen how this Hangman could murder twenty-four people and not leave any DNA. Not even any 'touch DNA,' which is almost impossible not to leave. And if these FBI crime scene people are covering something up then Rollins is covering *them*. Or he's an idiot. And I don't think he's an idiot."

Jodi asked, "You really think Rollins is one of them, captain?"

"I think Rollins is too smart by half, Strong. And that's a mistake because true believers always think nobody is smart enough to see through their lies." Brightbarton shook his head with a sneer. "That's the mistake all of them make. They think peons like us ain't smart enough to see through all that fancy footwork. And that's how you find them." His teeth glinted. "The first thing a liar does is act real smart and helpful. Then, if that don't work, he acts real dumb and useless. He goes from smart to useless in a heartbeat. Now, listen up; they don't always do it. But they do it often enough, so when someone goes from sincerely being helpful to being completely useless in the ten seconds, you keep looking at them real hard."

"Just don't let them *know* you're looking at them," added Joe Mac. "Let them believe that you think they're too stupid to have done this. Tell them that you don't have any clues. That this crime will probably never be solved."

"That's right," Brightbarton continued. "If you let people talk long enough, Strong, they'll hang themselves. But, if they don't, then look at what they *do* after the crime. 'Cause what a person does *after* the crime is gonna give him away, too, if you just let him go on down the road thinking he's safe. But he'll be ten times more careful if he thinks you're looking at him, so don't let him know you're looking. Tell him that you don't have a clue, and whoever did this probably got away with it. Then watch him like a hawk."

"Watch him like Poe would watch him," nodded Joe Mac. "You know what that means, don't ya?"

Jodi glanced at Poe scanning everything dead or alive. "Wow. Hanging around you two is like getting a college degree in Killer Elite. I bet you guys have solved ten thousand murders in this town."

"More'n that," Brightbarton muttered. "And Joe Mac's probably got the all-time record if there *is* such a –"

Shots erupted on the street from unknown directions – Jodi had instinctively ducked behind the tree, and all she glimpsed were shots and smoke exploding on every side as bullets hit the oak tree. She knew that all the training in the world could have never prepared her for this moment as she hit the ground with her heart in her throat. Her brain went white with adrenaline and she screamed as she ripped out the Glock.

She sensed a black shape beside her and knew it was Joe Mac as he rolled awkwardly behind the tree. And on the street there was staccato gunfire too fast to count or even locate. Then she somehow – incredibly – gained a knee with an unsteady shooting stance and leaned out praying she could lock on a target.

Shapes were running along the sidewalks and more bullets hit the tree. By instinct alone Jodi jerked back flattening her back against the oak as the trunk vibrated with the impacts. Then there was rapid, frantic shouting and cars squealed in various directions. As she ducked out again she saw people lying face down on the street and sidewalk, and she searched violently for a target but saw no one firing a weapon or even armed.

Everybody on the street was down.

She glanced to the side to hear Joe Mac moan painfully and for the first time noticed Captain Brightbarton lying motionless on his face, the shotgun half-hidden by his body; she realized he'd tried to clear the gun from his coat but failed before he was shot in the back. Then Brightbarton made a sudden move with a single arm, and she knew he wasn't dead. But that's all she had time for as she jerked her radio from her coat and began shouting, "Officer down! Officer down!"

She gave her designation and location and didn't wait for a confirmation as she stood and moved around the tree toward the street, her knees threatening to give way beneath her. She hadn't taken three steps before she had to stop and blink to clear her vision, also gathering her will to steady her legs. Then she continued forward and saw two shapes lying utterly motionless on the sidewalk.

Brightbarton's backup officers were covered in blood. Finally, someone on the street leaped to their feet and began running and within seconds a dozen people who were obviously horrified civilians were up and escaping the scene.

A sharp crack made Jodi raise aim, and she saw windows being slammed shut on every surrounding building. Then squad cars came streaming from every direction with sirens flooding the air, and she heard even more sirens approaching. And for the first time since it began, she consciously drew a breath, amazed she could breathe at all.

With a cry she ran forward sweeping the street with the Glock, trying to follow her training – to shoot anyone using deadly force, to make sure backup was on the way, to call an ambulance, to secure the scene …

Even before Jodi reached the first fallen officer, she knew he was dead. And she only needed to glance at the second officer to know he was dead, too. Then the first patrol cars skidded to a stop with uniform officers jumping out bearing shotguns.

"Get me an ambulance!" Jodi screamed, and one officer lifted the microphone, calmly calling in the scene. Only then did Jodi turn and run back to where Joe Mac and Brightbarton were just now struggling to rise.

Joe Mac was the first to gain a knee but remained bent, a single hand over his chest. Jodi slid to a halt beside him and struggled twice to speak before managing, "Joe! Joe! Can you hear me? Are you hit?"

Joe Mac groaned painfully as he shuffled off his heavy overcoat; he ripped open off the Velcro straps of the bulletproof vest and reached beneath it, feeling his chest. Finally, he pulled out his hand and there was no blood.

"Any blood?" Joe Mac asked.

"No," said Jodi.

"All right … It held. Check Steve."

Brightbarton still hadn't moved, and Jodi knelt at his side, leaning close. She saw an impact crater in the back of his coat, but there was no blood.

"Captain!" she shouted. "Captain! Can you hear me?"

"Of course I can hear you, Strong! I'm shot! Not deaf!"

"Are you all right?"

With a moan Brightbarton slowly managed, "Strong, with your powers of analysis you ain't never gonna make sergeant. Does this look all right to you?"

He put a hand on the ground and pushed himself to a sitting position. Then Jodi helped him remove his coat and undo the straps of an identical ballistic vest before she pulled it around so he could look at the marks; two bullet scars stood out, the white Kevlar fibers blasted and torn, and Brightbarton said, "Did it get through?"

Jodi turned him, gazing at his back.

"No," she said more calmly. "You're not hit."

With a curse Brightbarton slumped forward.

"Joe Mac?" he asked. "You all right, son?"

"I'm all right," Joe Mac answered in obvious pain. "But we need to get to the ER and get checked out."

"Tell me about it."

Ambulances filled the street within two minutes with EMTs scattering to the fallen officers and then to Joe Mac and Brightbarton. Jodi stepped back, letting them do their job without her in the way until the EMTs walked them to the ambulances. In less than a minute they were gone.

Jodi knew she wouldn't have to make a statement just yet. First, the last ambulance would take her to the hospital for some oxygen. Then she'd be given until tomorrow morning before she had to sit down with investigators and detail what happened. Blinking back what focus she could manage, she prayed that Joe Mac would be there beside her. But all the control she could muster didn't stop her tears and she swiped a hand over each eye. She was consciously trying to conceal her shock or fear or whatever this hellacious thing was that had obliterated her control but failed completely.

Vaguely, she realized that a much older cop came up to her, wrapped an arm around her shoulders and was ushering her to an ambulance saying over and over, "Come on, kid. I know. It's tough. Just get in the ambulance. They'll take you to the hospital and give you some air. Get in there now. Go on."

She didn't pass out on the way to the ER.

But she prayed all the way that she would.

* * *

It was three hours at the ER and long after X-rays before the doctor returned to tell Jodi she could put her clothes back on. Afterwards she asked about Joe Mac and found him in another cubicle. He was in a blue gown and lying on his back, two white patches on his chest. He also had an IV in his arm and an oxygen tube on his face.

"Hey," she said. "You all right?"

"I'm all right," Joe Mac tiredly replied. "How's Brightbarton?"

"I asked the doc about him. He said he's got some contusions. 'Bout like you. But the vest held. No blood, no foul."

"You ain't hit?"

"Nah, I'm good."

"Good," Joe Mac nodded. "They give you some air?"

"Yeah. Same as last time. Calmed me down."

"That's how it works." Joe Mac inhaled deeply before grimacing, "I didn't really expect that. Not in broad daylight. And not in a public place." His frown deepened. "I never meant to bring you into this game."

"We knew that already."

"That's not what I'm saying."

Jodi scowled. "What are you saying?"

"I'm saying it's over for you. You're off this case. If you don't go home on your own, I'll have Brightbarton put you on leave for being involved in three shootings inside one week."

It took Jodi a minute to reply, "But it was justified."

"You're still off the case."

"Why!"

"'Cause you ain't ready for this yet!" Joe Mac took deep breaths. "Maybe in a few years. But you ain't got the time for this kind of hammering. You ain't got the experience. You got heart, but you're still too green for this stuff."

"I'm not letting you take me off this case, Joe!" Jodi stepped forward to stand directly over him. "Have you not thought that these people know who I am by now? That they might not care that Brightbarton sends me home? That *I'm dead* if we don't finish this? And that *is* the case, you know! If you send me home, they'll just kill me at home where I won't even have any backup! How is that doing me a favor?"

Joe Mac's lips moved, but there was no audible reply. Rather, he only seemed to be breathing in some deep sorrow. Then, finally, he moaned, "I'm sorry I got you into this, kid. I really am. It's my fault." He paused. "All of it."

"Joe, I was in this before you ever showed up at my desk," Jodi said with more composure. "And without you I'd be dead already. But you've taught me how to stay alive. And I don't think you need to apologize for that."

It was shocking that Rollins spoke from behind her. "I'm glad you two are all right," he said as he closed the curtain.

A thrill surged through Jodi, and she expected Joe Mac to come off the bed, but he didn't even move. Then he calmly asked, "How many dead?"

"Just the two officers," said Rollins. "I'm sorry. Their families have been notified, and my guys are in on the manhunt. We found the cars a few blocks away. They'd been torched the same as the others. Crime Scene is working it, but I don't have much hope for prints or anything else. How you feeling?"

"Ah, it's like getting hit by a sledgehammer." Joe Mac revealed no indication of suspicion; Jodi tightened her lips. Then Joe Mac added, "Brightbarton told me you guys were gonna back us up."

Rollins glanced down as he shook his head. "We were only ten minutes from your position when it went down." A pause. "They hit you pretty quick after Brightbarton got there, didn't they?"

"They hit me about five minutes after Steve got on site."

"How long were you guys there before he arrived?"

"About ten, fifteen minutes."

"You think they followed you?"

"I think they knew where we were going."

"How would they know where you were going?"

Narrowly watching Rollins's expression Jodi couldn't determine whether he was being deceptive. Even with all her training to detect a lie she couldn't read anything in his body language. He didn't glance to the right, which would indicate he was accessing his imagination. He didn't direct a stare, which would indicate what the polygraphists called "over emphasis," also the sign of a lie. He didn't look away, either, which everyone knew was avoidance. For all Jodi could determine, he was being honest.

Or she just flat wasn't any good at this stuff.

Joe Mac said simply, "We're compromised."

Rollins brow hardened, and he was silent for five seconds before he said, "Maybe. I'll look into it. You guys were smart to wear your vests."

"I wasn't hit," said Jodi.

"You were still smart to wear your vest."

"She was lucky," muttered Joe Mac. "But I'll take luck over smart any day of the week and twice on Sunday. Listen up, Rollins; someone blew our rendezvous in the park same as they blew our rendezvous with Montanus. Or Mrs. Morgan. But our security's compromised. And until you run down who it is, we can't keep going to people just to see them gettin' blown away. We're gonna have to lay low until you figure this out."

"I understand," Rollins nodded. "I'll put some men on each of you until we're all convinced you're safe. And

I don't think that's gonna take long. I'm convinced we're closing in on these guys. I don't know who or how many, but I know they wouldn't pull a stunt like this unless they're in a panic. And that means we're getting close."

"Good enough."

Rollins moved out the curtain but held it open, staring back. "I'll have some guys take you home when you're ready."

"Thanks."

When he was gone, Jodi walked to the drape to see him halfway across the emergency room. Then she glanced into flanking cubicles before she whispered, "What are you talking about? Rollins is the only one Brightbarton told! He's the only one that could have set us up! And you're gonna trust him to guard us? Are you insane?"

"What'd I tell you about letting people hang themselves?" Joe muttered.

"What about hanging *us*!"

With a groan Joe Mac pushed himself up to a sitting position. "Look around and find my clothes. We ain't waiting for no doctor's release. And make it quick. We need to get to a safe place before they even know we're gone."

Spinning on a heel, Jodi marched toward a nearby chair loaded with Joe's clothes. She heard herself talking although she didn't consciously choose the words.

"Like my grandma used to say ... I pray you get to heaven before the devil knows you're dead ..."

* * *

"Good lord!"

Marvin half-caught Joe Mac as they stumbled together through the door of the palatial home of Professor Graven. In the same split-second, Jodi spun to search the road before she slammed the door and turned to see Marvin struggling to lower Joe Mac into a large leather chair positioned before a fireplace.

Marvin glared at Jodi. "What happened!"

"Haven't you been watching the news?" Jodi gasped, swiping off her coat to throw it across a chair. "We were ambushed."

"*By who?*"

"Who do you think?"

"How would I know? Did anybody get killed?"

"Two cops got killed." Jodi said as she walked forward and collapsed on a matching leather couch. "Brightbarton and Joe got hit. But they were wearing vests. The bullets didn't get through,"

Marvin hesitated. "Weren't the other cops wearing vests?"

"We were *all* wearing vests, Marvin. But bullets don't always hit you in the vest. Sometimes you get hit in the leg or the head, and then you're dead." Jodi raised her face, swallowing hard. "And, sometimes, even vests don't work. But they worked today. That's the only thing that matters."

Jodi lifted her hands before her face, fingers spread. "God," she whispered, "my hands won't stop shaking."

"It's just adrenaline," said Joe Mac from the chair. "It'll go away in a little while. Trust me; it ain't no big thing. You'd be crazy if you *didn't* have adrenaline."

Marvin had been gazing between them, and asked Jodi, "How about a drink? Think that might help?"

"Yeah. Make me a dirty martini, please. Dry. Very dry." Jodi gazed around the opulent Tudor home. "Good grief. The professor lives large, doesn't he?"

The professor's house wasn't exactly in the country, but it wasn't in the city, either. Rather, it was in that comfort zone that rich people inhabit when they're far from the maddening crowd but still close enough to town to avoid inconvenience. It was located on a very well maintained two-lane road north of New York City proper and every estate was at least ten acres with manicured grounds and elegant mansions. Jodi was no good at real estate, but she estimated thirty or forty million for the whole shebang.

A sweeping array of heads and the complete bodies of stuffed animals were hung on every wall and stood along every side of the vast front room. There was the head and shoulders of a gigantic boar, then the entire majestic body of a Siberian tiger, and a Grizzly bear that touched the ceiling. Two enormous curving ivory tusks of an elephant formed a circle around the mounted body of a gigantic black panther. And there were other, smaller trophies displayed which Jodi somehow sensed had been the last of their kind.

Finally, she noticed an exquisitely designed rifle case. It was obviously the work of a master craftsman who ornamented wood with the same exacting detail some gun lovers gave to engraving firearms. And she didn't need to be told that the double-barrel shotguns inside the case were worth years of her salary – apiece.

She said quietly, "He's really into hunting, huh?"

Marvin glanced at the wall. "Yeah. There's obviously more to the professor than meets the eye."

"Where is he?"

"He went out to get what he calls provisions. I assume he was talking about food, but I'm not sure." Marvin pointed. "He might have been talking about what's in the gun case. I think he's low on ammo."

Jodi leaned forward; "Are those double-barreled shotguns?"

"Those are very expensive, English-made double-barreled *rifles*. The professor took one out and loaded it for me before he left. I didn't tell him I already had Joe's forty-five." He threw off an afghan and reached down to lift an oversized cannon of a rifle. "I don't see how they carry this thing around all day long. It's gotta weigh fourteen or fifteen pounds."

"That's huge!" exclaimed Jodi. "What caliber is it?"

Marvin shrugged, "I don't know. I'm not a hunter. He did mention something about a four-five-eight Weatherby. Whatever that is. And he's got a six-hundred Nitrous … something. I don't know guns. But, whatever it is, it can knock down an elephant." He gestured to the wall. "Obviously."

"Hey," Jodi stated, "you said you were gonna make me a drink."

Marvin walked across the room. "The professor – I might add – has also got one of the better-stocked bars I've ever seen. I'm not even sure that some of this stuff is legal." He began mixing. "That's funny. I never took him for a drinker. He's always so proper."

"So are you, Marvin, and I never took you for a gunfighter." Jodi inhaled, calming. "But I'm glad you weren't there today."

Marvin began pouring ingredients as he glanced at Joe. "You seem to be doing okay, Joe. You been shot before?"

"Once or twice," Joe Mac groaned. "But that don't make it no easier. I'm as upset as she is. I'm just used to it. How you doing, kid?"

Jodi closed her eyes. "I'm settling down." She was silent with her thoughts before she asked, "Is it usually like this?"

"It's usually a lot worse." Joe Mac paused. "But that's because you usually get shot yourself. As it turned out, we didn't. And getting hit in the vest don't count. What counts is that we're not laid up in critical condition right now with the chief and the mayor standing out in the hallway. Believe me, that's worse. By far."

"What do they want?"

"They want to talk to you."

"About *what*?"

"The same thing Internal Affairs wants to talk about every time you use your gun. Why did you feel your life was in danger? Why did you shoot him forty-five times?"

"I fired until the aggression stopped," Jodi muttered mechanically. "Yes, I felt I was in immediate, life-threatening danger. I then called for an ambulance and secured the scene. No, the scene was not disturbed and, yes, I want to speak to my PBA representative before making any further statements."

"There you go," Joe Mac rumbled. "You don't talk, you walk." He grunted in what seemed like a laugh. "Reminds me of my first shooting statement."

"What'd you write?"

"I wrote, 'I told him that if he moved I'd shoot him. He moved. I shot him.'"

Jodi stared. "That's it?"

"That's it."

"Was Brightbarton your supervisor then?"

"As a matter of fact, he was."

"What'd he say?"

"He said, 'That's more than I'd write.'"

With total surprise, Jodi laughed, "I like the captain."

"He likes you, too. He believes in you. Thinks you're gonna make a real good cop one day. He wouldn't be getting personally involved – not with two months out – if he didn't think you were worth it. And I expect he'd like to pass on what he knows to somebody that he believes can carry it forward."

A calm had risen inside Jodi like a blue pond in twilight. Then Marvin arrived beside her bearing a large blue glass. Jodi took it; "Thank you."

"You're welcome." Marvin turned with a steady gaze. "Anything for you, Joe? Sorry. I should have asked sooner."

"A bottle of water if he's got one," said Joe Mac.

"Coming up."

The front door opened, and Professor Graven entered bearing large bags beneath his left arm and dangling from his left hand. His eyes opened wider before he turned and secured the door with three large locks. Then he walked forward, sprawling the bags without order on a coffee table. With that done he straightened, staring over them.

"They got there the same time you two got there," the professor stated as if he needed no confirmation. "They have someone on the inside. I feared as much."

Marvin delivered a bottle of water and Joe Mac sighed, "Thank you."

With a weary expression, the professor turned and began removing ammunition, food,

and a bottle of wine. He also laid a series of smaller containers in a tight group seeming to separate them according to purpose.

"I picked up some ammunition since I don't intend to go into that cavern unless I'm fully armed. And I picked us up some dinner. I hope you like Chinese. There's a wonderful restaurant down the block. I use it all the time."

He picked a sack and set it down on the table positioned between Jodi and Joe Mac. After placing Styrofoam plates with plastic forks and spoons alongside half a dozen boxes, Professor Graven generously gestured, "Bon appetit."

Jodi watched as he walked to the gun case.

"A couple of people got killed, professor."

Without looking back Graven unlocked the case. "I assumed."

"You don't ask a lot of questions, do you?"

The professor returned bearing a double-barrel rifle. Frowning, he took a seat beside Joe Mac in a duplicate chair. "No, Detective Strong; I don't. I suppose it's because I've been an archeologist almost my entire life."

Joe scowled, "What does that have to do with not asking questions?"

"Archeology, my dear." Professor Graven expertly broke open the rifle and began cleaning. "As an archeologist you spend your entire life either presuming or just plain guessing. You don't ask a lot of questions because all the people you'd like to question are dead. So, you look at what's in front of you and take your best guess. And I suppose the habit of looking and taking my best guess has translated itself from my professional life to my private life." He seemed to laugh. "I'm as surprised as you are that I didn't ask a question. I hadn't noticed that about myself. But I suppose not asking questions has become a part of my personality and not just my work."

Jodi actually found that interesting; she didn't allow herself to contemplate whether it was for future reference involving Marvin.

"Is that what archelogy is all about? Guessing?"

"I'm afraid so." Graven began cleaning the rifle like a pro. "It works like this: An archeologist accidentally discovers a piece of metal that's been buried in the mud for ten thousand years. Needless to say, there's not much left of it, and so he cleans it up. He carbon dates it. He references what he knows of the geology of the region to coincide with that carbon dating. He references what he knows of the immigration and exodus salient to that period. He talks to meteorologists about what the weather was like during that epoch. He talks to biologists about what animal life was prevalent during that period. Then he shakes it like dice and takes a guess as to whether this was a king or a slave or a warrior. Whether this was a great nation or one of many tribes or just a single family. Whether this was someone who died naturally or whether he was sacrificed in some mysterious ritual." He shrugged, "He makes the best guess he can make based on little more than a piece of metal that just happened to be tough enough to have survived being buried in the mud for ten thousand years. The rest is whatever you want to call it. Assumption. Presumption. Guesswork. Imagination. Sequential logic. You name it. But it's not '*knowledge*.' That would be the greatest assumption of all."

Jodi had noticed that Joe Mac seemed to have been listening with keen interest and was surprised he didn't follow the professor's dissertation with a question. She glanced at

Marvin, who nodded as he said, "The professor's right. As a rule, archeologists don't work with knowledge. We just go where science leads. And sometimes science leads us to a very tentative conclusion that dispels everything we've ever believed about who built the sphinx or the pyramids or the Nazca Lines. We still don't know how the people of Baalbek moved this stone that weighs over a thousand tons into their temple and set it down with a precision we can't duplicate even with today's technology. It would have taken a hundred thousand men, and they never had a hundred thousand men. And there's always the gold standard of mysteries – the Shroud of Turin. That thing has defied every scientific theory that has ever been proffered. There is simply nothing known to science that could have produced that image. And I mean *nothing*. Not radiation. Not heat. Not light. Not any kind of chemical reaction. There is nothing in the known universe that could have made that image, so archeology is full of mysteries. The Druids are just one of them."

Using a long aluminum rod to clean a barrel, Graven frowned, "But now we must deal with today. And what we do know. What happened at the rendezvous?"

Taking a moment, Jodi said, "We were waiting. Captain Brightbarton showed up with two more men. Then a car pulled up, and some guys got out and starting shooting. I'm not sure who else might have been shooting from a roof or window. Brightbarton's men were caught in the open. They're dead. Then Joe got hit. Then the captain got hit."

"You were not injured?" Graven asked with a gaze.

"No. I was behind a tree. Then they piled into some vehicles and tore out of there." She paused. "They torched the cars a few blocks away and either switched cars, caught the subway, or just faded into the crowd. Nobody knows. They picked one of the few places that isn't on camera."

"It sounds as if they were prepared," Graven announced. "They had a target, a time, and a location. You are both lucky to be alive."

"We sort of figured that out."

"What is the next course of action?"

"There isn't one," said Joe Mac. "It means we can't trust anyone in the police department or the FBI. It means we're on our own. It means we stick to the plan and crash this party."

Jodi stressed, "We don't have enough men, Joe! We need at least one more man. Maybe Marvin could cover my back, but somebody else has to cover what's in front of me. I can't keep this leader under control and watch the crowd, too."

"I can do that," said Professor Graven. "As I said; I have experience. I was often the point man in my platoon. But I assure you these people will be armed and will do everything within their power to kill us before we escape that tunnel. They will follow us. And they will be waiting for us when we reach the graveyard."

Graven stared as if expecting Jodi to say something.

"Do you understand?" he asked.

"Yeah!" she nodded. "*Do you?*"

"I understand that we are going to die unless you call for backup when we are on our way out of this model of Stonehenge," Graven stated with a dead expression. "We will never survive a walk through those woods without a thousand police officers searching every shadow." His frown deepened. "I know you feel you were betrayed today but –"

"'Feel' has got nothing to do with it," stated Jodi. "We *were* betrayed."

"Forgive me." Graven momentarily bent his head. "What I meant to say is that I know you have been betrayed, but you were very likely betrayed by a small group. Or perhaps only one man. You will surely be safe if you call in an entire battalion of police officers." His brow hardened. "Surely not every one of them can be compromised, so the greater the number, the safer we'll be. That's all I'm saying."

Joe Mac said, "Tell me something, professor."

"Yes?"

"Just what is this *Wicker Man* ceremony?"

Professor Graven frowned as he said. "It was the most hideous of all Druid ceremonies. It was a ritual where the Druids imprisoned both animals and human beings inside a wooden replica of a man. They referred to it as the *Wicker Man* although it was not, of course, made from 'wicker.' No, wicker burned not half so hot for their intended purpose. Then, at a predetermined time, the high priest of the Druids would set the *Wicker Man* on fire and all those trapped within the *Wicker Man* would slowly be roasted alive in horrible, horrible agony – both animals and men. It was wholly barbaric – as savage a ritual as has ever existed in the history of the world. And it played no small part in Julius Caesar's decision to wipe the Druids off the face of the Earth.

"And these people plan to put Tommy Childers inside this Wicker Man and set it on fire while Tommy's still alive?" asked Jodi,

Professor Graven nodded.

Jodi eyes were wide. "Well, they're gonna die."

"I'll drink to that," said Joe Mac. "Think you could get me that whiskey now, Marvin, if it's no trouble?"

Marvin rose. "Be a pleasure, Joe."

The subject matter hadn't interrupted Professor Graven's gun cleaning. "It should be noted that the Druids were not the only ancient culture that sacrificed living human beings to the flames," he continued. "In Carthage, they threw living children into the burning belly of a giant bronze idol named Molech. It was supposedly a demon. And in Babylon they threw both living children and adults into the fires of Ba'al. But the methods used in those rituals insured an almost instant death for the victims – something which was literally 'civilized' compared to the bestial savagery of the *Wicker Man* used by the Druids. Supposedly, a victim sacrificed to the *Wicker Man* could survive for as long as half an hour in the most hideous, unspeakable agony before he finally succumbed to the flames."

"Just who *are* these animals?" asked Jodi.

Professor Graven shrugged, "Two thousand years ago, the Druids were the social elite of their world. They were diplomats, priests, soldiers; they were actually quite well organized and had tribal leaders who were called – as you already know – a '*Ri.*' They were the only class of people that could travel freely between territories without the threat of being captured and killed. The Druids were everything to the world they dominated. They had an inexplicably vast knowledge of all things involving nature. They were renowned for their knowledge of elixirs and drugs and sedatives for every purpose. And they were known to invoke genuine powers in their rituals to an extent that even the Knights Templar came under their influence, which was also the beginning of the end for the Knights."

"How is that?" asked Joe Mac.

"The Knights Templar were a formidable Christian fighting force that reached the apex of their power in the thirteenth century. Then they were destroyed by Pope Clement and the Army of Rome when Clement deemed them guilty of heresy and witchcraft. Although the true reason for their destruction was that Clement had come to fear the immense wealth and extraordinary influence the Knights had come to command. But, in any case, many believed that the Knights had long ago crossed paths with the old, surviving Druids and absorbed many Druidic ways consequently forming a hybridized form of Christianity and paganism that was not well understood at the time and remains something of a mystery even today."

Marvin silently delivered a whiskey to Joe Mac as the professor became pensive, staring into the hearth. "I myself believe that the two great powers – the Druids and the Knights Templar – merged to form an entirely new order that the world had never seen or imagined. It was not Christian. It was not pagan. It was, in its true sense, a uniting of the power of Nature with the power of the cosmos, and yet it served neither Nature nor God. Rather, it used the powers of both worlds for whatever purpose it decreed. Yes, and so the old world of the Druids and the new world of the Knights were forged into a new order that went underground with its vast secrets, its unknown magic, and its immeasurable wealth. And just as all true stories end in death … nothing more was said."

Jodi found herself staring into the flames. She didn't know what to say for a long, long time. Then she felt like she had to speak and began, "Whatever they were, or whatever they are, they didn't have the right to kill even *one* innocent person. That's why we should kill every one of them."

Gravin scowled, "For ten thousand years, armies have tried to destroy the Druids and the Knights and now whatever New Order they have forged in the crucible of their mutual persecution. And yet here they are. As dangerous as they ever were. They have even rebuilt the womb of their empire – the mega-monolith of Stonehenge. Only God knows what dark magic has been vomited forth from that temple, but I assure you that their magic is real." A pause. "Teleportation. Time travel. Crossing dimensions. It's possible. I know. I've seen it. And I don't doubt what I've seen with my own eyes. And this New Order knows the secrets of that power." He was breathing shallowly. "That is why they have prevailed. You can slaughter them all day long, but they will ultimately survive and even thrive. The most you can hope to do is destroy a single family. A single tribe. A single temple."

"That's the captain," said Joe Mac.

Jodi blinked. "What?"

"Captain Brightbarton's about to knock on the door. Let him in."

Jodi turned her head as there was a knock at the door. She pushed herself to her feet and walked forward not bothering to draw her Glock. She opened the door and stepped back.

"Been a while," she said.

"Uh huh." Brightbarton walked in carrying a long black rifle case in each hand. "Make sure you lock that thing."

Jodi meticulously set all three locks and followed him into the den where Brightbarton simply stood gazing over all of them together before he said, "I confidently predict that absolutely none of this fiasco is going to end well in any way. But after today I really don't care too much. One of those young boys was my nephew. That's why I called him. I knew that he could be trusted. And he vouched for the other one, and that was good enough for me. Jodi, move that food, would ya?"

She took a moment to clear the coffee table, and Brightbarton laid out one rifle case, unzipping it. He threw it open to reveal five Glocks with extra clips and a lot of ammo. He laid the second gun case on the floor and opened it to display two more shoguns, more ammo, flex ties, and Jodi's eyes widened as the saw the final item in the arsenal.

There were a dozen stun grenades, but she was familiar with those; she'd used them in training. But beside the gray cylindrical stun grenades were at least twenty black military "hand grenades" that Jodi recognized only by shape.

"Captain?" she began, "are those real –"

"You bet they're real, rookie." Brightbarton lifted one of the black spheres. "This, boys and girls, is an M61 tactical fragmentation grenade used by every meat-eating, heat-seeking branch of the United States military. It's crammed with Composition B and a tetryl booster to insure a detonation that will cut a car in half. It's has a prenotched inner liner to guarantee a spread of shrapnel that is certain death inside a six-foot radius. It has one safety. You pull this pin and you have three-point-five seconds before it goes boom."

"But," Jodi followed, "where'd you get them? That's a military weapon, and we don't keep military weapons." She paused. "*Do we?*

"I boosted them from the evidence locker," Brightbarton grunted.

"Where'd the evidence locker get them?"

Brightbarton shrugged, "The FBI asked us to inventory the armaments they confiscated at the house of that fool, Jacob Statute. It seems the FBI's local storage facility for explosive materials is under repair, so they asked us to take these off their hands and hold them for a while. Anyway, when I decided to join your little excursion tomorrow night I made a withdrawal from the evidence room – namely these babies." He nodded with a frown. "I think we're gonna end up needing them."

Brightbarton reached into the paper bag plastered under his right arm, and when he withdrew it he tossed a Druid's robe to Marvin.

Marvin caught it and held it up.

"Where'd you get this?" he asked.

"From that fool, Phillips." Without invitation Brightbarton walked to the bar. "And he was none too happy to see me. But he was overjoyed to let you have his robe once I told him you were gonna come back and visit him if he didn't cooperate." He waved it off. "I don't wanna know what you did to him. I'm sure he deserved it. Joe, how many times have you ever heard me say I need a drink?"

"Never."

"Anybody else want one?"

"I'm way ahead of you," said Jodi.

Joe Mac: "Got one."

"Yeah, boy, I need this." He tilted his head to swallow the whole glass. Then he began filling it again. "Those were some good boys out there today, and they didn't deserve to get killed like that by these lowlife bushwhacking psychos. I hope you ain't planning on bringing any of them back alive, Joe."

Kneeling, Marvin gently lifted one of the deadly M61 grenades. "So you pull this pin and you've got three and a half seconds?"

"That's it."

"Do you mind if I take some?"

"Knock yourself out, Einstein. That's why I brought 'em." Brightbarton pointed to the grenades. "You just remember that once you pull that pin you have three-point-five seconds. And *nothing* can stop it."

Marvin's eyes narrowed as he slowly turned the grenade in his hand.

"Joe?" Jodi ventured. "Does the captain know this is *extremely* dangerous? What about Florida? What about naked women and the beach?"

"He knows," answered Joe Mac in a bored tone. "This ain't his first rodeo. And they killed his nephew, so he wants his payback." He was silent. "Good grief, girl. I'm more worried about *you* than him."

Jodi threw herself back into the couch. "I'm going with you whether you like it or not. I might be a rookie, but if I walk away from this I might as well turn in my badge. Things like this are why I joined the force in the first place."

Brightbarton raised his glass. "That's the spirit, kid. You gotta get your feet wet sooner or later. Might as well be sooner." He burped. "Just think of it like prom night. You go in all nervous and scared and before it's over you realize that all that fear about Don Juan was a thousand times worse than this ignoramus who can't find his butt with both hands in his back pockets. Same with a firefight. The anticipation is usually worse than the fight. At least, that's been my experience."

Jodi almost laughed; the prom joke was closer to the truth than she wanted to admit. She asked, "So you've been in on a few of these?"

"A few." Brightbarton savored a sip. "But it was Joe who was involved in – forgive me – 'the father of the mother of all shootouts' back in eighty-six." He burped. "He was only seven years on the force back then, but they'd put him in organized crime. In any case, he got himself caught in a warehouse with fourteen Mafioso goons who suddenly decided Joe needed to go the way of all flesh."

Brightbarton cocked his head once, then nodded, "Yep, I don't think I've ever seen so many bullets fired in such a small space in such a short period of time in my whole life. They even shot the cat and the pigeons up in the rafters. And when we finally broke down the door we found Joe sitting all by himself on the floor. He'd been shot eleven times. That's gotta be some kinda record."

Jodi balked. "You were shot eleven times!"

Joe Mac muttered, "It was a few."

"How did you *live*?"

He shrugged, "A lot of it's just attitude. Most of the time whether you live or die is in the mind. If you stay calm and don't panic –"

"What's panic got to do with it?"

With a grimace Joe Mac added, "Because you gotta stay calm, kid. If you get all excited and panic, well, you're probably gonna die. I've seen officers get shot in the hand and die from shock. And I've seen officers get shot six or seven times and walk to the ambulance, get patched up, and go home."

Professor Graven glanced at Jodi, "He's right. I saw a lot of that in Vietnam. The ones who fought to stay alive usually lived. But the ones who gave up died. Faith can access great powers – powers that are almost entirely neglected by modern Man, but ancient Man used them all the time."

"How do you know that?" asked Joe Mac. "I thought it was all guesswork."

Graven frowned as he shook his head; "Not every civilization was as oblique as the Druids. Some wrote quite generously about magic and numerology and how to summon or even control cosmic forces. King Solomon wrote extensively on sorcery."

Jodi was gaping. "You actually believe in magic?" She shook her head. "Listen, I believe in Druids. I believe they are an ape-crazy sect of secret psychos who get together to do some very evil stuff. But I don't believe in *magic*. That's crazy! And I can't believe that a man with your education would believe in it, either."

"He who judges before he listens is a fool," contested Graven. "And I have seen things that I cannot explain." Unexpectedly, he seemed to surrender somewhat. "Now, I can't say with empirical authority that there is such a thing as magic. I'll give you that. But I can say that I have seen things that have no logical explanation – things that I've studied and studied, and I still can't explain, so I can't say that it's magic. But I can't say that it's not magic, either." He took a moment. "It reminds me of what one scientist said after they'd run every test known to Mankind on the Shroud of Turin, and they still didn't know how to explain it."

Brightbarton grunted, "What'd he say?"

With a subdued laugh Graven answered, "He said, 'If it's real, we don't know how it was done. If it's a fake, we don't know how it was done. So, don't ask me if it's real or fake or how it was done. All I can tell you is that I came here with a pure, scientific mind. But when I get home I think I might pick up my Bible and give it a look."

Finally sitting beside Jodi, Marvin smiled. She returned the expression as he said, "What the professor is trying to say is that the sum of what we don't know is greater than the sum of what we do know. Or, in other words, all serious scientists are also humble people. They don't claim to know the answers to the secrets of the universe. They just claim to know some of the questions."

After a moment Brightbarton said, "Well, that's all very interesting. But that doesn't have much to do with tomorrow night because we're not going in there to arrest a bunch of wizards and scientists. We're going in there to arrest a bunch of murderers. And, magic or no magic, they ain't gonna survive no twelve-gauge."

Joe Mac asked, "You staying here tonight?"

"Yeah. I went through too much work to sanitize myself before I came here. I'm too tired to do it again."

"You got enough room for the captain, professor?"

"Hmm?" Professor Graven lifted his face. "Oh, yes, of course. I have four bedrooms plus the couch."

Joe Mac continued, "Then we'll have some drinks, relax, and get some sleep. We'll go over the plan first thing in the morning when we're fresh. And I'd suggest that everyone sleep with their piece close. We don't know how much they know."

"Do you think it's Rollins?" asked Brightbarton.

Jodi venomously interjected, "*I* think it's Rollins! Who else could it be?"

"I don't know," Brightbarton said frankly. "All I know is that whoever it is will be there tomorrow night, so I guess we'll find out together."

"If we live," the professor added soberly. "Don't underestimate these people. We will not be the first enemy to attack them during one of their rituals. Armies have attacked them day and night for ten thousand years, and yet they've prevailed." He gazed over all of them. "If you think we have the advantage, you're a fool." A pause. "They survived Julius Caesar. They survived the armies of Rome. They survived the Black Plague and the Dark Ages and centuries of war and persecution. You can slaughter them until you rot. But they were the first to master the powers of Nature. And I see nothing to indicate they won't be the last."

Jodi commented, "If you think these people are so unkillable why are you even joining us? It seems stupid to fight something you don't think you can beat. In fact, sounds like suicide. And I'm not into suicide. I'm into taking these people down even if it costs me my badge." She paused. "Or my life."

"You're gonna make sergeant yet," Brightbarton frowned. "If we were in the station house I'd promote you right now." He focused on Professor Graven. "Look here, old man, magic or wizards or Halloween costumes or whatever, these people are going down. And if you come with us you'd better be ready to pull the trigger on that buffalo gun. Or I'm gonna take it away and do some trophy hunting myself."

"The professor's right," rumbled Joe Mac, facing the fire. "It'll be a mistake to underestimate them. We have to plan for the probability that they already know we're coming." He grimaced, "They've been ahead of us at every turn. I don't see why any of that would change now."

"They don't know we're coming because we haven't told Rollins!" Jodi said fiercely. "I'm telling you, Joe! Rollins is wrong! He's been selling us out! That's the only way we could have been ambushed! *Twice!*"

"Take it easy, kid." Joe Mac's dark glasses melted into the shadow of his heavy brow, so the top half of his head was hidden. "We're still going in. That's not gonna change. And you're not a gunfighter, yet, but you will be before this is over – I promise you – so you ought to be grateful. This is gonna be a great learning experience for you. But we have to go in there with an edge – something they won't see coming even if they see *us* coming."

Jodi threw herself back into the couch and slapped her leg. "And how are we gonna do that, Joe? We are outmanned and outgunned in every way by a bunch of psychopathic freak murderers in Halloween costumes! We can't trust *anybody,* so we can't use *any* backup! I don't see how in the world we're gonna go in there with 'an edge' when we'll be lucky to get in there at all! And we'll be twice as lucky if we come out alive!" She raised both hands. "Joe, this is like Thermopylae when Leonidas and his three hundred were surrounded by a million scumbag-Persians with elephants and rhinos and all the Spartans had were their spears and swords and shields. And look how *that* ended."

Marvin: "They died hard, though."

"I'd rather make *them* die hard."

"You should have been at Thermopylae."

"*I am.*"

"For somebody that ain't never killed nobody you sure seem ready for a whole lot of killing," offered Brightbarton blandly. "Maybe you should try it on a little for size before you put it on your bucket list."

"I've been exposed to more killing in the last three days than I have in my entire life," Jodi replied. "If I survive this I'm going to open a flower shop. I'm going to surround myself with beautiful things that are pretty to look at." Her face grew stony. "Yep. This is it for me. I'm not cut out for this. I don't want to be sixty years old and the only thing I've ever looked at are dead bodies. Life is too short."

Brightbarton laughed, "You were born for this job. You've got integrity and you've got brains, and you've got guts." He grunted. "Put all that together with some good experience and you've got the perfect cop. Course ..."

Jodi waited. "Of course ... what?"

A pause.

"Well," Brightbarton continued slowly, "what I was about to say was that, of course, you don't 'own it' because it hasn't cost you yet. It's just been your job. I mean, it's a job you're good at, but, still, up to now it's just been a job." He was silent a long moment. "You don't own it until it costs you."

"Until it costs me what?"

"I don't know," Brightbarton shrugged. "It's not the same thing with everybody. But you'll know it when you get to it."

Joe Mac was bent slightly forward, and his face was totally hidden in shadow, not even half visible. Cloaked in his dark coat, only his massive hands resting on the forearms of the black leather chair were visible. And for a moment Jodi wanted to ask Joe Mac what it would cost but decided against it. She could tell by the silence inside the darkness that it was something terrible, and it would never, ever leave her once it was done.

"Why don't you let him in?" Joe Mac asked out of nowhere.

Setting down her glass, Jodi stood and walked to the back door of the home. She didn't need to be told who it was as she opened the glass panel and stepped outside. She lifted her face and listened and in moments heard the familiar thunder of great, wide wings, and Poe settled on a small patio table.

She smiled, "Hey there, boy! Why don't ya come inside?"

She stepped to the door and waited as Poe ducked and peeked through the opening beholding only what he could understand. Then he leaped and with a single flap sailed past her. After quietly closing the door Jodi walked back to the hearth to find Poe perched like a supernatural bodyguard on the chair beside Joe Mac's head.

No one expressed surprise, but Brightbarton grunted, "Good god! That's the biggest crow I ever did see."

"He's a raven," said Jodi. "His name is Poe."

Brightbarton lifted a toast. "Hello, Poe."

"*Hello,*" said Poe.

Brightbarton coughed up whiskey. "*It talks?*"

"Poe can speak very well when he wants to." With a surprise, Jodi found herself laughing; something about the situation made her feel like she was more of a veteran than Brightbarton. "Poe knows that words are important."

"Does he know what they mean?"

"Sure he does."

"I ain't *never* seen no talking crow before!"

"He's not a crow! He's a —"

"I know! He's a raven! What's the difference?"

Jodi blinked, genuinely offended although she wasn't sure why. "There's a lot of difference between a crow and a raven, captain. Ravens are different physically, and their brains are wired in a far more complicated way than any other kind of bird. Or any other *creature* as far as that goes. Biologists say they're the most intelligent creatures on Earth next to humans. They say ravens are even smarter than dolphins."

"No way!"

Jodi accepted the challenge before she even consciously recognized it as such. She glanced left and right, searching for a way to prove how smart Poe was. She grabbed a piece of chicken from the Chinese box.

Jodi said, "Poe can't get to this unless he uses one tool to reach another tool."

"Animals don't use tools," said Brightbarton.

"Sure they do. Apes use sticks to drag ants out of ant hills. But I'm making this so that Poe has to use one tool to get to another tool. Plus that, he has to figure out water volume and displacement, so we're talking about the same kind of mechanical thinking people use to build a boat."

"Ha!" Brightbarton burst out. "I wanna see this!"

Jodi picked up a tall glass, walked into the kitchen, and half-filled it with water. Then she tied the string around a piece of chicken and dropped the chicken into the glass; the chicken sank to the bottom, but the string floated on the surface.

Clearly, if Poe could reach the string, he could have the chicken. But the glass was tall and the string was floating well out of reach. Finally, Jodi walked to the back door, went outside, and gathered up a handful of rocks. Then she walked back inside and sat the rocks on the floor beside the glass.

Smiling as she knelt, Jodi locked eyes with Poe and whispered, "Poe! Hey there, my love! Here's some chicken! You hungry? Come and eat, okay?"

Poe glanced at everyone, then leaped to the floor. He dipped his head, studying the chicken at the bottom of the glass. He attempted to reach his head down and grab the string, but it was beyond his reach. He stepped back. He studied the glass. The water. The string. He looked at the rocks. Then he picked up a rock with his long black beak and dropped it in the water.

The water level – and the string – rose a fraction of an inch.

He studied the water level again.

Brightbarton was leaning forward, eyes wide. "Look at him!"

"Shhh ..."

Although Jodi had anticipated it, she was still fascinated as Poe dropped rock after rock into the glass until he finally decided the string was within reach. Then he stuck down his long beak and snared it. Within seconds he had used the talons of one foot and his beak to pull up the string, so he could grab the chicken.

"My god," whispered Brightbarton, "I would have never believed it. He's smart, ain't he?"

Joe Mac grunted, "He's more'n smart. He knows things." He paused. "Things that even people don't know."

"Like what?" asked Brightbarton.

Jodi said, "Like who has a good heart, and who doesn't. And he knows when things threaten the people he loves. And he does love. Don't ya, big guy?"

Poe continued tearing at the chicken.

"That is indeed a fascinating animal, but we are going to need all our strength tomorrow, so I am going to bed," said the professor. "By the way, we do have the option of using more police tomorrow night if we're in a truly life-threatening situation, don't we?"

"No," said Joe Mac. "Our security is compromised, so we don't have that option. I don't wanna have to worry about what's in front of me *and* what's behind me."

Jodi looked at Marvin. "You okay with all this?"

"I'm good," he nodded. "I'm in."

"You could get killed, Marvin."

"Or I could die of old age counting dinosaur bones. But I'd rather go out like this. With you." His smile was warm. "You're more fun."

"Yeah," Brightbarton stated, "that's what we used to say back in the war. We used to say that war is actually a lot of fun as long as you don't get killed."

Graven stood. "I'm sure you are all quite capable of making your own sleeping arrangements. But I must go to bed. I'm too old to stay up all night discussing a strategy which will probably go out the window thirty seconds after we implement it." He set down his glass. "It reminds me of a saying we had in Vietnam."

"What was that?" asked Marvin.

"We used to say that no plan, however perfect, survives the first thirty seconds of combat." He bowed to Jodi, nodded to the rest. "And with that, my friends, I'll say goodnight." He walked slowly to the door and turned. "Goodnight, Poe."

Poe stared without blinking.

Professor Graven was gone.

"There's no such thing as a perfect plan," muttered Brightbarton and took another sip. "You can trust me on that one." He raised a toast to Jodi. "Congratulations, kid. Remember what I told you?"

"Yeah," Jodi stared into the flames. "You said that I don't own it 'til it costs me. And Joe said that if I go up against something that is truly evil it might be something a lot bigger than me that pulls the trigger. But I'm not sure what either of you mean."

"If you win this," Brightbarton nodded, "you'll know."

Poe rose with a single tremendous flap of his wide, wide wings and settled once more on Joe Mac's chair. And, very slowly, Joe Mac reached up and the huge raven pensively dipped its head so that Joe Mac could smooth its feathers.

And for a moment, as Jodi studied it, it seemed like they shared something spiritual. But, whatever it was, it was certain that no one else in the room shared it with them.

Brightbarton swept his glass over the two open gun cases. "Grenades. Masks. Extra ammo. Rifles. Feel free to take your pick. I reckon we could smuggle in a howitzer under these robes."

"I've got my Glock and two clips," said Jodi. "I'm good."

"You'll carry as much ammo as you can carry," said Joe Mac.

"Why do I need more ammo, Joe? I've got sixty rounds."

"First rule of combat. If you know that the chances are good that you're gonna get into a fight, then you carry as much ammo as you can carry."

"Why is that?"

"Because as long as you've got ammo, you've got options. But when you run out of ammo, you run out of options."

Jodi swallowed a sip of wine and replied, "Okay, then."

Marvin was frowning at the gun cases. "Well I don't know about the rest of you, but I'm gonna carry a rifle, four or five pistols, lots of ammo, some grenades, a bulletproof vest and … we got anything else?"

"That's about it, chief," said Brightbarton.

Marvin lifted his glass to Poe.

"On a wing and a prayer."

* * *

Joe Mac didn't move from his chair.

Jodi knew it because she didn't move from the couch.

The only action Joe Mac took was to push up his utterly black glasses. And Poe stayed perched beside his head as motionless as Death as the hours slowly passed with the flame of the hearth casting strange spectral shadows.

Jodi felt they were thinking the same dark thing or beholding the same dark vision. But nothing could be read in Joe Mac's black glasses that hid eyes that saw nothing – just as nothing could be read in Poe's black eyes – eyes that saw everything.

She wondered if Poe ever dreamed.

"You don't own it 'till it costs you ..."

Sleep came to her far too slowly ...

Then she dreamed of Death.

* * *

Jodi noticed she was half-way between dream and sleep for a long time, and then she slowly rose from the couch, pushing off the afghan. She stared about the flame-shadowed room wondering what had awakened her before she saw her cell phone pulsing on the coffee table; she picked it up.

"Hello," she murmured.

"Jodi! It's me!"

Jodi blinked rapidly; "Rollins?"

"Yes!"

It took her a split-second to orient, but even before she was fully conscious she knew that this was terrible. She reached down to pick up a shoe to throw at Joe Mac, but when she glanced up she saw that he was fully awake with his face turned in her direction. Even Poe was watching her.

"Rollins?" she asked. "What's wrong?"

"I'm in a bad way, Jodi." His breathing was rapid and panicked. *"The only person they're letting me call is you."*

Jodi stood, automatically sliding on her shoes. "Where are you, Jack? We're on our way." She hesitated. "That's what they want, isn't it? They want us to come to you?"

"Yes!"

Jodi realized she was expecting to feel alarmed, and five days ago she knew she would have been, but she was dead calm. "Fine. Tell 'em we're coming. Where are you?"

"*I'm at Pier twenty-three,*" he said. "*I'm at the end of the pier.*"

Jodi clicked off the cell, and Joe Mac was already shoving extra .45s in his coat. "I'll wake up Marvin and the captain," she said and started across the room.

"No!"

Jodi stopped. "Why not?"

"Because they're luring us into a last-minute ambush," Joe Mac stated coldly. "They want all of us to show up so that they can kill every single one of us. That's why we can't bring Steve and Marvin. If this goes bad, which it probably will, there's gotta to be somebody left who can stop them from sacrificing that little boy tomorrow night. We can't afford to get everybody killed trying to rescue Rollins."

Jodi didn't like the logic but knew he was right. If they were all killed in this gambit there wouldn't be anybody to stop these psychos from cutting off the head of a four-year-old boy which meant that the two of them would be walking into an ambush with no backup.

"Why do they have him on a pier?" she asked as she picked up extra clips.

"Because there' ain't but one way in and one way out," said Joe Mac, chambering a .45. "Once we get out on that pier, we're sitting ducks. One man with a rifle can kill all three of us – no sweat. That's why they'll have Rollins wired or chained down real good."

She threw on her coat. "You think they've got him strapped to a bomb?"

"Probably something like it."

"Great."

"But we've got backup."

"What backup?"

"Take a guess."

"Oh, yeah. The Brothers. Almost forgot."

Jodi picked up the keys to Brightbarton's car from a table beside the front door. In moments, they were leaving the beautiful grounds of the subdivision and angling down the hill toward a violence that was becoming more a part of her with each second. She hit the exit cruising with a calm control she didn't expect and didn't say a word as she merged into traffic, still amazed that she was feeling so calm.

"Is this what it's like?" she asked in a low voice. "You play this game every night, cheat death, and don't think anything about it?"

"If that's what you're made of," said Joe Mac.

"Is that what I'm made of?"

"Yeah," he said. "It is. Here, dial Ronnie at this number." He gave her a card, Jodi dialed the number and Joe Mac took the cell. A second later he said, "Yeah, Ronnie. It's Joe Mac. Listen, I got a situation on Pier 23. Yeah, your back yard. Same goombahs. They want me and Jodi to go out on the pier so they can ice us. I need you and the boys to find them before we walk out there. Yeah, snipers." A pause. "Yeah, kill every one of them. Don't worry about the paperwork. There ain't gonna be any. We're gonna wrap 'em in razor wire and sink 'em. Our ETA is about a half-hour. Yeah, call me back on this line. We're not gonna move until you give me the all-clear."

He clicked it, and Jodi muttered, "The brothers do come in handy."

"Put that thing on vibrate. I don't want it sounding when we're close to the pier. It'll give away our position."

She switched off the sound.

"The brothers must owe you big-time, Joe."

"We owe each other." Joe Mac turned his face to the window. "I've covered for them a few times. Nothing serious. A few Mafia bulls trying to horn in on the teamsters." He paused. "It wasn't actually 'murder.' It was more like self-defense."

"So why did you have to cover for them?"

"Because some things are about justice, not law."

"Why do you say that?"

"Because court rooms are all about money and expensive lawyers and nuances and technicalities that could send a poor, innocent man to prison for the rest of his life but let a rich man walk just because he can buy his way out of what he damn well deserves." Joe Mac cleared his throat, settling into the ride like it was just a midnight run. "There's a big difference between law and justice. You'll see."

"So what are we in this for?"

"What do you think?"

"Justice."

"You're getting cold-blooded, kid."

"It must the company I keep."

* * *

Jodi parked a full block from the pier, and they walked slowly through the mostly darkened alleys until they neared the entrance to the docks. "Okay, we're here," she said quietly, pulling back on Joe Mac's elbow. "The gate's open. Imagine that."

"Take your binoculars and scan the roofs."

Jodi raised the glass and began systematically searching the skyline but saw only shacks and chimneys. Finally, she said, "I don't see anybody."

"Don't look for bodies. Look for *movement*." Joe Mac bared his teeth. "If a person ain't moving you're not gonna see them in the dark. Or in the jungle. Look for a chimney that gets wider for a split-second. That's somebody leaning out to get a better look."

Two minutes later she was still looking at shacks and chimneys.

"They must not be moving." She froze the binoculars at the corner of a shack that abruptly widened. "Wait a second. I got something. There! The far end of that warehouse! He's behind a shack at the end of the dock. He just leaned out."

"There's gonna be three of them."

"How do you know?"

"Standard operating procedure. They'll form a triangle on the pier, so they'll have us in a kill box with all three sides covered."

"So where are the other two snipers?" Jodi asked as she began randomly searching surrounding rooftops.

"That guy is on the west. The other two will be to the north and south."

"Why not the east?"

"Because he's not a fish."

Jodi blinked. "Oh. Yeah. Sorry."

She scanned to the north when shots suddenly rang out on the closest rooftop. She swung the binoculars back and saw at least six figures running frantically around the roof with muzzle flares streaking through the dark from every direction. Then the shooting abruptly ceased and shadows gathered, staring down. They bent out of sight.

"That's one," she said.

The phone rang and Jodi answered. She placed it in Joe Mac's hand, and he lifted it to his face; "Yeah?" A pause. "How about the others? Okay, good enough. Keep that rifle ready. We're going out on the pier." He shut it off. "They got eyes on all three. Let's go."

"Are you sure it's safe?" Jodi asked. "I'm not worried about us. I'm worried about Rollins."

Joe Mac's teeth gleamed in a grimace. "I know what I told you about not pushing a bad situation. But in this situation ..."

"We don't have a choice."

"Nope."

"Let's do it, then."

Five minutes later they were at the foot of the pier, and at the far end Jodi saw a diminutive figure crouching beside a pylon. She knew instinctively that it was Rollins but he was in a low, cramped, awkward position. Even in the moonlight she could determine he was severely bound.

"Yeah," Jodi said quietly, nervously. "Rollins is at the end of the pier, but it looks like he's chained to one of the pillars. I can't be sure." She squinted. "He's not moving, Joe."

Joe Mac inhaled deeply and nodded. "All right. Let's do it."

As they began walking Joe Mac was talking quietly. "Keep your eyes down for a trip wire. It'll look like fishing line. Real thin. Transparent. And look at the pylons as you get close. Look for duct tape. They might have a claymore or a hand grenade or something like it taped to a pilon with a trip wire running across. You hit the wire and that pulls the pin and we're dead."

It only took them two minutes by Jodi's calculation to reach Rollins; he was still alive but he was heavily chained to a pylon and he was wearing a vest that was obviously loaded with explosives. Jodi saw a host of wires and blinking red lights, but she didn't know any more about bombs than what she'd learned at the Academy, and that wasn't much. Very carefully, she lifted Rollin's face with a hand.

She whispered, "Rollins? Hey. Wake up."

Rollins blinked slowly and finally focused on her, but where Jodi had expected relief she saw only alarm. "Snipers!" he rasped.

"Don't worry," Jodi said quietly. "We took them out before they took us out. Is this thing a bomb, Jack?"

Closing his eyes, Rollings nodded with the most perilous exhaustion Jodi had ever witnessed. He whispered, "I can't move. They said … a mercury switch. If I even twitch, it's over. For all of us." He was barely breathing. "They didn't put this on me until after I called. I would have never called you if …"

"It's all right," said Jodi. "We're gonna get you out. Jack. I'm calling SWAT. I'm telling them to bring the bomb techs. Joe? Is that our play?"

Grim, Joe Mac nodded.

"Hang on, Jack. This'll be over soon." Jodi took out her cell and began to dial; she reached the first number when –

The pylon to Jodi's side exploded in splinters and one second later the crack of a gunshot rolled over the pier like a sonic boom; she was stunned at the force of the bullet that hit the wood brace of the pier and was flat on the boards. Looking across, she saw Joe Mac had fallen to the planks, too, and drawn a .45.

"Where is he!" shouted Joe Mac.

"I don't see him!"

"He's gotta be on another rooftop further out!"

Another bullet hit the pier directly in front of Jodi's face and she screamed as she rolled to the side knowing she'd been hit but not knowing whether it was splinters or a bullet. She smashed into a pylon still screaming and sweeping her face with a hand. In another moment she held her hand in front of her eyes glaring down.

There was no blood.

"Jesus!" she cried.

Another bullet hit the dock where she'd just laid tearing a long furrow in the planks. Then shots exploded from the nearest warehouse roof where the Kosiniski brothers and whoever else opened fire on the fourth sniper.

Jodi only knew one thing; Joe Mac was no good at all in this situation. He couldn't see, couldn't move. And Rollins had a bomb strapped to him.

She was on her own.

She shut her eyes; *"Come on!"*

She fiercely spun to her knees and was at Rollin's side ignoring a pylon that exploded behind her although she'd felt the concussion of the bullet as it tore through the air over her head. She screamed, *"Joe what do I do with a mercury switch?"*

"Find the wire to the blasting cap!" Joe Mac bellowed.

"What wire is that!" Jodi was leaning close, scanning everything. "There's three wires, and they're all leading to the same thing!" She instinctively ducked as the very pylon Rollins was chained to exploded in a shower of splinters. "They're all leading to this pack on his chest! Which wire do I pull?"

Training she couldn't even remember receiving sparked Jodi to rip her flashlight from her waist. She clicked the chest plate and saw three wires – red, green, blue; the red wire was in the center with the others flanking it. She searched and saw that the red wire fed into tubes of what appeared to be more than enough to destroy the dock.

"Joe!" she screamed. "I've got red, blue, and green! Which wire is it!"

Rollins bellowed as a bullet passed between his body and Jodi, smashing through his right arm, and Jodi screamed as she expected him to twist away, but Rollins didn't move. His eyes were wide and horrified, he was gaping, and, yet, he somehow didn't move even as the blood rained across the two of them.

"Get out of here!" Rollins shouted.

"No!" Jodi shouted. "I'm gonna get you out!"

"Jodi if you don't run you're gonna die! Get outta here!"

Another bullet hit the pylon beside Rollins' head. He twisted his face to the side, and when he looked back Jodi saw the realization of death in his face.

"Run!" he whispered.

For the briefest moment, Jodi stared into his eyes and knew it was over. There was no way to defuse this thing under rifle fire, and they realized it together. It was a moment that was both profound and brief, and then it was gone and Jodi leaped to Joe Mac's side, hauling him to his feet. "Put your arm around me!" Jodi screamed. "We have to run!"

They staggered thirty steps before the concussion of a supersonic bullet passed Jodi on the right, and she knew from that angle that –

TEN

White light ... white ... ceiling ...

Jodi blinked ... focusing ...

The walls of an ambulance.

She realized she was laying in the back of an ambulance, and then she weakly raised her right arm to see an IV tube. It took her a while before she also realized she was on a gurney; she felt, then saw, safety straps around her waist and legs.

An ambulance attendant climbed in the open doors and bent; he lifted her left wrist and felt her pulse.

Jodi whispered, "What ... happened?"

"I don't know," he answered. "All I know is that there was an explosion, and you guys were somehow involved. Some longshoremen fished you and another detective out of the water."

"What about ... Rollins?"

"He's in the other ambulance."

"No," Jodi shook her head. "What about Rollins? He was on the pier."

The EMT put a hand on her chest, pushing her down. "Hey, hey, hey, settle down. You just got blown up. You might have a concussion or something worse."

Jodi blurted, "But Rollins was on the pier!"

The EMT was her age, dark hair, and looked compassionate and competent and calm as he said quietly, "Detective Strong, there's nothing left of the pier. You and your friend were blown into the water, and you got rescued by dock workers." He hesitated. "But the harbor police are looking for survivors. Rollins might have made it."

Absolute exhaustion claimed Jodi and she laid back.

"No," she whispered, "he didn't make it ..."

She closed her eyes.

* * *

This time it was different.

A who's who of the FBI and the great city of New York arrived at the hospital within an hour, and Jodi finally understood what Joe Mac had meant about it being worse; she was in a room by herself, but the nurse told her it was standing room only in the corridor. From the mayor to the Assistant Special Agent in Charge of the New York City FBI field office, they were waiting to bury her with questions.

Jodi found herself staring at the ceiling.

"I gotta get outta here ..."

She closed her eyes trying to recall the last hour; she remembered the pier, the ambulance, the emergency room, X-rays, and then they had moved her in here and gave her a shot of something to help her relax. But they hadn't cut her clothes off, so they should be in the closet.

She ran a half-dozen scenarios through her mind trying to scheme up a way to escape this, but everything she conjured seemed doomed; it would be next to impossible to walk unobserved past a hundred law enforcement officers highly trained to observe.

A nurse entered the room and smiled encouragingly, "You feeling a little better?" She began removing tabs from her chest. "The doctor said you don't have a concussion, and your EKG looks normal. But he wants an MRI. You up to it?"

"Yes!"

It took another few seconds to "unplug" her, and then the nurse spun the bed around and pushed her into the corridor. As they moved down the hall Jodi pretended to be staring blandly at the overhead lights, but she was in fact stunned at the politicians, cops, and television crews that were wall to wall. Two minutes later they were on another floor, and she asked the nurse, "Where is the other officer who came in with me?"

"He's getting his MRI," she smiled. "I have to tell you: He's not a happy camper."

Jodi grunted, "I'll bet." She began to calculate. "What hospital?" she asked hoarsely.

"You're in Lennox Hill."

Lennox Hill happened to be the one hospital she had never been to in her life. She only knew it had the reputation of being a stellar teaching medical center with a five-star rating from patients. And she only knew that much because some of her friends had joyous memories of their deliveries in this place. Then her mind moved on, and she knew that if they put her in the same room as Joe Mac they were as good as gone clothes or no clothes.

"I need to see the other police officer," she said weakly.

"I'll arrange for you to see him right after your MRI," said the nurse.

Clearly it was best to be cooperative, so Jodi said nothing more until the nurse stopped the bed, put on the brakes, and patted her arm. "It'll just be a few minutes," she smiled with what seemed like genuine concern. "Just try and relax."

"Okay."

The nursed walked from the room and Jodi sat up. She threw off the sheet, stared down, then ripped the IV from her arm. She swung her legs over the edge and hit the cold floor only to collapse clumsily against the bed, knees buckling.

Groaning, she took deep breaths trying to focus as wide white circles passed before her eyes. It took longer than she liked but, finally, she recovered and studied her surroundings; it was a waiting room with a large glass window allowing a clear view of the MRI tube; they were just now removing Joe Mac.

Joe Mac was in the same shape – an IV, a hospital gown, and a large bandage on his forehead. Jodi simply pushed open the door to the room and grabbed him by the arm.

"Joe!" she said sternly. "It's me!"

Joe Mac straightened as if he'd been hit with a shot of adrenaline.

"We gotta move!"

"What are you doing?" asked the nurse. "Wait! You're both hurt!"

Jodi didn't slow down as she hit the corridor with Joe in tow. She wasn't going to wait for them to call security who would in turn call a stampede of police officers stationed outside their rooms; they had maybe one minute to get clear of this hospital.

The elevator was directly beside the room, and she hit the button. The doors opened immediately, thank god, and she fairly fell into it and hit the first-floor button. They must have only been on the second floor because five seconds later the doors opened and she dragged Joe into an open lobby teeming with people who turned as one to behold what Jodi knew what must have been an amusing sight.

The security guard at the exit raised a hand as if to demand an explanation but Jodi said sternly, "This is a police matter! Stand down!"

If she'd had her badge and gun it might have worked but it was impossible to appear authoritative when you're near-naked and bent and dragging an old blind man through a crowd of gaping onlookers.

The guard patiently raised both hands.

"Hold on, lady. I think you need to see a doctor before you –"

"*Marvin!*" Jodi gasped.

The doors opened, and Marvin came out of the night; he seemed to understand the situation perfectly and took a single decisive stride before he lashed out and connected with a left fist against the side of the guard's head. With a shout the guard spun around and collapsed.

Marvin leaped forward and grabbed Joe Mac, hauling an arm over his shoulders. He surged back through the door with Jodi following fast.

"Hey!" someone shouted. "Stop!"

Marvin stopped and whipped out the 45; his aim was dead steady and another security guard half-way across the lobby froze.

Marvin shook his head.

"Go!" he said without looking at Jodi.

As Jodi rushed past him, she was aware that he was backing out with her. But it took her a second to realize Captain Brightbarton was driving the squad car waiting outside the doors. He was glaring over the front seat, a single hand on the wheel.

"Hurry it up!" he shouted.

Pushing Joe Mac ahead of her into the back seat, Jodi piled in as Marvin slid into the front and slammed the door.

Brightbarton didn't need any direction. He floored it, and they cleared the parking lot in seconds. Then they were flying, and Jodi stared back to see how many squad cars were in pursuit but after two minutes she saw nothing and twisted back again and collapsed.

For a while she wasn't certain whether she was conscious or unconscious.

"You all right?" Marvin finally asked.

"Yeah," she moaned. "Ah … Yeah … I think so." She leaned her head back. "How did you …"

Marvin shook his head, "I woke up worried, so I went downstairs to check on you. Needless to say, you weren't there. I didn't know what else to do, so I woke the captain up, and he started listening to radio traffic."

"Yeah," Jodi nodded. "Yeah …"

"We heard the call go out from the pier," Marvin continued. "The captain made a couple of calls and verified that one of you were involved. We figured out the rest." He cleared his throat. "We knew we had to get you out of the hospital if you're weren't too hurt. But it looks like you were doing pretty good by yourself."

"We wouldn't a' made it," Jodi managed and swallowed hard. "He had us." She focused on Marvin's sweating face. "Thanks."

"No problem." He passed a white plastic bag over the seat. "Here's some clothes. We picked them up coming into town. I figured that they probably cut your other clothes off in the emergency room, and you couldn't hardly make a run for it naked." He gestured. "The fat ones are for Joe."

Jodi would have laughed if she'd had the energy; "Thanks."

It was a perfect fit, and she was genuinely touched that he'd guesstimated her size so astutely. It took Joe Mac a good five minutes of struggling, but he finally managed to slip on his sweatpants and sweatshirt, as well, and when they cleared the city they tossed the hospital garb out the window.

"What about Rollins?" Jodi asked.

Marvin's eyes narrowed, but he revealed nothing. "They didn't say anything about him on the radio. Was he involved?"

Closing her eyes, Jodi bowed her head. Her lips came together in a painful grimace, and she inhaled deeply before she said, "Yeah ... he was involved."

Marvin seemed to understand.

"I'm sorry," he said.

Jodi found herself staring out the window.

"Me, too."

* * *

It was almost sunrise when they reached Professor Graven's house.

Although Marvin had literally risked his life to rescue them, he made a concerted effort not to complicate the situation with any display of affection, and Jodi found herself feeling both respected and moved.

He fetched blankets for them as they took places in the front room, and then he loaded a Glock for Jodi and wordlessly set it within her reach. He loaded a .45 for Joe Mac, slid it in the pocket of his coat and laid it over the arm of his chair. He brought them bottles of water and two small bowls of fruit, and then he took a seat in the second lounge chair staring idly at the flames in the hearth.

Jodi found herself quietly gazing upon the archeologist with an affection she could hardly remember possessing in her whole life.

It had been ... *a* ... *long* ... *time.*

Although he didn't say anything, Marvin was acutely alert to her every need, and after they had calmed from the fight and flight of the night, Jodi stood and walked to where Marvin was seated. Without saying anything, she lowered herself into his lap and laid her head against his chest; he wrapped an arm around her and said nothing.

She never remembered falling asleep. She only remembered waking for a floating, dreaming moment as she was being carried in cable-strong arms. Then she was laid in a bed and the covers were pulled to her chest.

A kiss touched her forehead ...

* * *

Jodi awoke surprisingly early – she'd expected to sleep until noon, but it was far from noon – but still wasn't surprised to see Joe Mac already cleaning a .45. He raised his face as she descended the stairs and wandered into the front room.

"How you feeling?" he asked.

"Like I've been blown up. How about you?"

Joe Mac cocked his head once. "About the same." He sighed. "Rollins didn't make it. Brightbarton called to check his status."

Jodi winced; she wanted to say something, but there was nothing to say. She had been over her head and knew it would be stupid to feel guilty or even responsible, but she felt both. Rollins had been difficult at times, but he had died bravely, and that meant more to her now than it ever had in her life. She was beginning to think that death wasn't something far off; it was here and now, and whatever time anyone gets is just blind, stupid luck. She dropped into a chair, staring numbly at nothing.

The words of Tony Montanus suddenly returned to her; *"I resolved a long time ago to leave nothing unsaid, undone, or unsung ..."*

But it's so hard to open up, so hard to share, so hard to trust.

Her voice was a whisper. "Where's Marvin?"

Joe Mac ceased cleaning the .45. His eyebrows rose and then fell before he chuckled and said, "Ya know, I met my wife when I was working the docks. I used to unload thirty tons of fish a night – one at a time – by hand."

Jodi said, "Yeah?"

"Yeah," Joe Mac continued, "that was some tough work, boy, unloading them big, ol' flounder by hand one at a time all night long 'till the sun came up. Then, every morning, I'd walk out to the parking lot the loneliest man in the world. I'd have a torn tendon or something in my arm. My feet would be killing me. My hip would be killing me. My back would be killing me. And I'd walk to my car same as always day after day. I didn't like nobody. I didn't trust nobody. I was scared of people 'cause you never know when somebody's gonna turn on you. You never know when they're gonna stab you in the back." He paused. "Anyhow, I'd go home and try to get some sleep. But you can't really sleep when you're in all that pain. It's just too much pain all the way 'round to sleep."

Jodi glanced to either side. "Uh huh?"

"Yeah. Anyhow, I came home one day, and I met my neighbor coming down the stairs, and we started talking. And I kinda liked her." Joe Mac raised his face with a smile. "I think she kinda liked me, too."

Jodi nodded, "Okay …?"

"So she made me breakfast one day, and we sat together on my little ol' balcony and talked, and then she went home. Then, after that, when I'd come home, she'd come out while I was climbing the stairs, and we'd talk, and she'd cook me breakfast, and we got to know each other real good. And then she'd go home again, and I'd go to sleep."

Jodi was staring, mouth open.

"The funny thing was …Well, it was funny to me when it finally occurred to me … The funny thing was that I found myself going to sleep every mornin' after she cooked me breakfast, and we sat for a little while and talked." Joe Mac nodded a long time. "Yeah, talking to her made me forget all about all that pain. Then she'd go home, and I'd go to sleep without even thinking about it." He frowned. "Finally I decided that this was working out so good, and I was feeling so good about it, that maybe I should try and keep her around a little more. So I married her. And even though I'd been so miserable and didn't trust nobody … it worked out all right." He lifted his face. "Know what I mean?"

Jodi smiled.

"Yeah … I know what you mean."

* * *

"It will happen thusly," Professor Graven began like a Sunday school teacher, "at midnight they will gather within the inner circle of this replica of Stonehenge. If there are too many priests to gather within the circle, which is quite likely, then they will form a concentric circle outside the lintels. Then their ceremony will begin. Now," he looked at Joe Mac, "you say they have kidnapped this last child?"

Joe Mac raised his face and paused.

"His name is Tommy Childers," he finally said. "He's four years old – the only child of a single mother."

"Very well, then. After these Druids complete an incantation, they will present Tommy Childers upon the central stone of the Stonehenge monument. It is called the Bloodstone, and, according to legend, it is where the chief priest of the Druids – or the *Ri* – would bind the victim. Then the victim is carried to the *Wicker Man* and imprisoned within it. After this, the *Ri* will simply set the *Wicker Man* on fire and this child will slowly be burned to death while still alive." He stared. "So what is the plan?"

Brightbarton muttered, "Kill 'em all. Let God sort 'em out."

"When they put Tommy on this Bloodstone and start to tie him up, I'll draw down on the chief priest," said Jodi. "You guys cover my back. It doesn't matter that you're blind, Joe; I don't see how you can miss since we'll be surrounded. And – at that point – if this high priest makes a move to hurt Tommy, I'll kill him. And we'll be in the biggest gunfight of our lives."

"If you do that, we die," Marvin observed. "Including this boy."

"Do you have a better plan?"

Marvin frowned for a long time. Then he said, "Nothing of any great tactical merit comes to mind."

"There's a better way," said Joe Mac.

Jodi: "What way?"

Joe Mac continued, "As soon as we get there, the professor puts me beside this high priest. The second we even see Tommy Childers and this priest at the same time, I grab the priest and put a gun to his head. At the exact same second, Jodi, you grab Tommy. And if some other priest is holding Tommy, just kill him where he stands. The main thing is that you get your hands on that boy at the same second I take down the chief priest." He shook his head. "We don't have to wait for them to put this boy on that rock and start tying him up. All we need to prove is intent. Isn't that right, Steve?"

"Just these psychos showing up with this kid proves intent, conspiracy to commit murder, kidnapping, and attempted murder," stated Brightbarton. "I say we take this bird down at first sight. There's no reason to let this ritual go to the matt."

Jodi nodded, "Then that's our plan." She gazed around the room. "Well, we have enough robes and masks. We have all the weapons we can carry. Do we have need anything else?"

"I could use a little Dutch courage," said Brightbarton. "But since we're sure to be in a gunfight, and we'll all have to make official statements, it won't bode well if I'm drunk when it goes down, so I'll wait."

"Let me finish," Joe Mac stressed, lifting a hand, "Professor, you stay right beside me. You're the best one to identify this priest. Then, when I take him down and Jodi grabs the kid, the rest of you have to cover that entire crowd. I can't cover them because I can't see, and Jodi will have her hands full protecting this boy, so it's up to you three guys. Then we make our way real slow and cautious back to the tunnel." He sighed heavily. "Once we're inside the tunnel, we'll be fairly safe. One guy with a rifle could hold that tunnel against a thousand men, so we won't have to worry about anything until we get outside."

Marvin hesitantly asked, "What happens when we get outside?"

"There's more than one passage out of that chamber," Joe Mac said slowly. "After we take out their chief, they'll move ahead and set up for us outside. Their first plan will be to kill us with snipers before we clear that graveyard. Their second plan will be to wait for us at our cars and ambush us like Bonnie and Clyde."

"That means they'll also kill their high priest," said Jodi.

"At that point they won't have any choice. They can't let us take him alive. He knows too much. He knows their names."

Marvin: "Are you sure about that?"

"Yeah," Joe Mac grunted. "They can't let us take him alive, or they'll all hang. And self-preservation is gonna take precedent over ritual or respect."

Poe lifted himself to soar past Jodi. He landed on the mantle of the fireplace and turned to stare down. He looked at each one of them with that quick analysis and then lifted off again to land beside the back door.

"He's got something on his mind," said Joe Mac. He turned his head as if listening. "You better let him out ... with the others."

Jodi rose and walked to the back door. When she set Poe free a strange dark movement as wide as the sky caught her attention, and she looked out to see every tree filled with what seemed like living leaves of black.

It was crows and there were thousands of them.

It was more crows than Jodi had ever seen in her life. Yeah, she had seen hundreds of crows flock together, but she had *never* witnessed such a storm cloud of blue-black forms. If they had taken flight together they would have blocked out the sun.

"Hey, Joe."

"I know," he said.

She turned her head. "You know?"

"Yeah."

"How?"

"Poe knows what's going on."

Jodi turned again to study the thousands of wings moving in concert making the trees flock like living leaves of black.

And their calls were all the same as if they were all sharing the same thought or planning the same thing.

Jodi scowled, "What do you call a flock of crows?"

"A 'Murder of Crows.'"

"What do you call a flock of ravens?"

"An 'Unkindness of Ravens.'"

"Then we have a real unkind murder coming this way."

Joe Mac revealed nothing.

"I know," he said.

* * *

"Where did Brightbarton go?" asked Jodi. "And where did the professor go? And where in the world is Marvin?" She lifted and dropped her hands. "Am I missing certain need-to-know information?"

Joe Mac opened his mouth to reply.

"Wait!" She raised a hand. "Is this gonna put more stress on me? I only ask because my body – *literally* – can't handle any more stress. We have five hours before sundown and the big 'showdown,' and I don't want bad news. Or, let me say 'more' bad news."

With a laugh Joe Mac said, "I sent Brightbarton out on an errand. He'll be back soon enough. And the professor and Marvin went to the museum to do some last-minute research on these guys. The professor said he wanted to double check some stuff because one mistake on our part will probably be our last mistake."

"Well, that's prudent." Jodi collapsed on the couch just as the front door opened, and Joe Mac said, "'Sup, captain."

Jodi turned and saw Brightbarton walking forward with a gym bag.

"What's in the bag, cap?"

"I borrowed some throat mics from the SWAT guys," Brightbarton answered simply. "If we pull out a radio while we're surrounded by a bunch of power-mad psychotic priests, I'm sure it'll be a bad day all the way 'round." He reached into the bag and set a handful of mics on the table. "I also picked up some ammo for Joe's .45. The NYPD doesn't use .45s, so I had to do a little shopping. You guys okay?"

"I'm scared," said Joe Mac.

"Yeah," grunted Brightbarton. "You look it."

"I'm just trying to be professional," said Jodi and glanced between them for a long moment. "You guys have done an awful lot of this stuff, haven't you? Because I've never been in anything like this. I've *read* about it. But I've also read about giant squids and Bigfoot. *Seeing* it is something else. And *experiencing* it is even worse."

Brightbarton shrugged, "Over a period of thirty years you work a lot of weird cases, kid. Serial killers. Cannibals. Crazy people who think they're god." He fixed her with a ponderous glance. "And there's really nothing unusual about psychos practicing human sacrifice, either. Or even cannibalism. I mean, look at that crazy freak Jeffrey Dahmer. He practiced human sacrifice and cannibalism at the same time. Made it a hobby. He should have been given an Oscar for lunacy. So there's nothing all that unusual about this. In fact, I'm surprised you haven't seen more of it yourself with three years in the field."

"You don't meet a lot of cannibals doing administrative work," Jodi muttered. "I've spent half my career filing papers for the holy men downtown. But I've got enough street time to make detective. I just never ran into any cannibals."

"Give it time," said Brightbarton. "You'll see more weirdness in this city than you will in any ten cities in the world put together. And that's saying something."

Jodi relaxed deeper into the couch. She closed her eyes, leaned her head back, and took long, deep breaths. Then she fixed a gaze on Joe Mac and said, "I guess you think we've got god on our side, huh?"

She never understood how Joe Mac always knew when she was speaking specifically to him even when she didn't use his name. But he did know because he said, "I can't say we've got god on our side. But we've got the next best thing."

* * *

The door slammed, and Jodi leaped for her gun before she saw Marvin rushing forward trailed by a much calmer Professor Graven.

"Stop that!" Jodi exclaimed and took a moment, hand on her forehead. "We're about to be in a gunfight! My nerves are shot!"

He presented a fistful of papers with a smile, and as she mechanically took them he pointed to a specific page. "You see that?"

Jodi stared. "A bunch of numbers. What about them?"

He pointed again. "There was a Venus Transit in 2 BC. That's the true year that Jesus of Nazareth was born. So, if they use some kind of symbol for Venus tonight, we'll know why they're doing it. We won't be caught off guard or confused." Marvin stepped back. "What do you think?"

Jodi was gaping. "Was this necessary?"

"Yeah!"

"Why?"

Marvin leaned close, hands on her shoulders. "Because now we know that we're right. They're killing these kids because they're afraid one of them is the Messiah. And if they want us to participate in some kind of crazy ritual, we'll know why. We won't be caught off-guard. Plus, if someone tries to talk to us about it we'll know what they're talking about. We'll know what to say."

It took Jodi a second to compose, then she said, "Yeah, well, I seriously doubt these people are into conversation. I mean, they're coming to decapitate a little boy and then eat him. There's not gonna be much to talk about."

Marvin shook his head once. "Maybe not. But I guarantee you there's gonna be some kind of mondo-bizarro ritual and we'd better be prepared for why they're doing it because if we make a mistake we're dead." His voice grew softer. "You understand, Jodi?"

Jodi stared up into his face.

She blinked, then smiled tightly.

"Yeah," she said.

"Marvin is correct," announced Professor Graven. "There will be a complex ritual that will involve items that are obliquely symbolic and even celestially symbolic. But you must not reveal confusion. You must understand why these symbols are being used and not hesitate to participate properly."

Joe Mac asked, "Is this why you went to the museum, professor?"

"No," he answered curtly. "I went for another reason. But my young protégé had an instinct and discovered this information while he was waiting for me. And I do agree that this is critical information."

"So what'd you go down there for?"

Graven frowned, "I had to reexamine early literature depicting how Druids gathered for their rituals."

Jodi said, "I thought Druids didn't write anything down."

"They didn't. But they did draw pictures." Graven bent his head as he added, "They are simple black and white drawings, but they are the only source of reliable literature we possess of the ancient Druids."

"What did you learn?"

"I confirmed that Druids gather in three concentric circles inside and outside of Stonehenge. No one knows why. And nobody knows if a priest's place in the circle was decided by rank or something else. Also – and this is rather grisly – they all wore belts decorated with their various … uh … *trophies*."

No one spoke until Jodi asked, "Trophies?" She waited patiently as Graven failed to reply. Then she added, "What kind of trophies?"

The old man shook his head. "They drape themselves with human skulls and other medieval relics that only a madman would bear." His teeth gleamed as he continued, "There were barbaric images of some Druids decorated with human heads not even decayed. Many were wearing necklaces very obviously made from finger bones. And almost all of them carried a long butcher's knife. But my point is that we might be discovered very quickly indeed if we go in there wearing nothing but a robe. I'm suspecting that our disguises won't last longer than it will take them to strike us down."

Marvin: "We *are* going to be armed, professor."

"So are they, boy."

Brightbarton simply stood and walked to the bar. "Forget what I said about not having a drink before tonight, Joe, but I don't think we're gonna be around to make any statements. And I'd rather not die sober."

Joe Mac leaned forward in his chair, hands firmly clasped. "Jodi, listen up; I want you and Marvin to go out and find Old Man Chamberlain. He's got shrunken heads and finger bones and God only knows what in that Persian Bizarre shop of his. I want you to load up with everything we need to look like we're just as crazy as the rest of them. Then hightail it back here so we can get ready. That should take care of that because we're going in there tonight whether it's a last chance suicide run or not."

Without question or hesitation Jodi snatched up her coat and grabbed Marvin's arm. "You ready, Marvin?"

"Wait a second," he said.

"What is it?"

Marvin bent over a rifle case, and Jodi could see he was working quickly. Then he stood and walked swiftly forward.

"Let's go," he said.

In a moment, they were gone leaving Joe Mac alone with Brightbarton and Professor Graven. In a shaken voice the professor uttered, "They're monsters. This is just death for the sake of death. I don't understand it."

Joe Mac's words held no compassion.

"You will."

* * *

Two hours later Jodi parked the car at the same street corner, and Marvin was at her side as she barged together through the side door into a strangely silent shop.

Sometimes you simply know that something is terribly wrong even when there's no obvious reason to know or feel anything at all, and Jodi knew something was deathly out of place as soon as she stepped through the unlocked side entrance. Marvin was also becoming attuned to combat situations because he immediately drew his .45 as smoothly as she drew her Glock. Then, silently and slowly, they stepped deeper into the shop, turning and searching.

"What's wrong in here?" asked Marvin.

"I don't know," Jodi replied. She leaned out to look over the counter. "They wouldn't leave the door open like this. Not with nobody at the cash register." She stared up the stairs that led to the professor's shop. "Professor! Are you up there! It's Jodi!"

Silence.

Marvin whispered, "We need to get out of here, Jodi."

Jodi took time to gaze across the cluttered shelves that ran up and down the length of the little shop. "First, get what we need," she said. "Do it fast. I don't like this." She looked over her shoulder. "This has 'bad' written all over it."

Without holstering the .45 Marvin snatched up a basket-weave and began to scoop items into it. Without any apparent system, he went down a shelf picking up shrunken heads, threaded beads, carved bone, leather belts, and whatever was within easy reach. Then he turned to Jodi and lifted the basket with a single hand.

"I got it. Let's go."

The floor creaked above their heads.

The door slammed at their back.

Marvin shouted at the same time Jodi screamed, and they were pointing their guns in opposite directions; Jodi was aimed at the ceiling; Marvin was aimed at the door. And they held positions but there wasn't another sound above their heads, nor did anyone charge through the door; Jodi found herself hyperventilating.

"Are you okay?" she asked quietly.

Marvin grated, "Let's get out of here!"

"No! Don't move!"

Jodi had taken one cautious step toward the door when the ceiling above them exploded downward in a white storm of shreds that lanced everything in the room.

Before Jodi made a conscious decision, she was firing straight through the ceiling; she knew from her training that someone had fired a shotgun through the second floor. She also knew that the shooter had been aiming to hit both her and Marvin. And she knew that this wasn't finished. Not by a long shot.

Another blast tore down through the ceiling, and Jodi and Marvin moved in separate directions not by any coordinated plan but because the shotgun rounds were tearing up the floor between them; if they had remained close they would have both died because whoever was wielding the riot gun was uncannily accurate despite the fact that he couldn't visibly identify the target.

Jodi was only aware of Marvin firing upward – the same as she was – and that the blasts from the shotgun moved across the ceiling in a continuous stream.

"Come on!" Marvin shouted and leaped to the door.

"*No!*"

With the reflexes of a cat Marvin jerked his hand from the knob and twisted to the side as bullets tore through the door, fired from the alley.

"I knew it!" screamed Jodi.

Steps rushed down the stairs.

Jodi spun and began firing before she even saw the attacker. She unloaded a full clip from the Glock – seventeen rounds – and aimed at the wood panels that obscured the upper steps from view. In the next split-second they heard a smothered groan, and a body rolled down the remaining steps, a shotgun clattering beside him.

With remarkable calm Marvin had turned and was holding a rock-solid aim on the side entrance. But Jodi was still focused on the stairway.

If one attacker was up there, two could be up there.

Or three.

Or four.

Angrily wiping sweat from her face, Jodi narrowly risked a glance at the door, waiting for light to vanish behind the torn fragments of wood. Without fully removing her attention from the stairway she waited and waited and finally something told her to *move*.

Jodi charged up the staircase as Marvin shouted; she saw two newly-sewn robes lying on the old man's desk, but Mr. Chamberlain was nowhere in sight. Scanning the room, she snatched up the robes and leaped back down the stairs.

"Time to go!"

"Wait!" Marvin snatched her by the arm. "Are you sure?"

"I'm sure," said Jodi. "They know people have already called this in. They're not gonna hang around for police."

"How long do we have?"

"Maybe thirty seconds. We gotta move."

With a deep breath, Marvin walked to the door.

"Stay behind me," he said.

He jerked the door open and stepped outside, gun raised.

Although Jodi couldn't see the alley from her position, she saw Marvin's posture suddenly relax as he gazed in either direction. Seconds later he seemed to almost faint as he said, "They're gone. Come on."

Jodi snatched up the basket of relics and rushed forward, pushing him forward. She turned to the right. "Walk. Don't run."

They cleared the alley before squad cars came into view, and then they casually faded into a nearby grocery as cops leaped out racking shotguns. Inside the store, Jodi snatched up a burlap bag and unceremoniously poured the contents of the basket into it as Marvin handed the stunned clerk a twenty-dollar bill.

He nodded with a smile, "Thanks."

They reemerged onto the sidewalk walking efficiently but without any appearance of agitation or even concern. In the nearby alley, they heard more sirens approaching, and then tires squealed to a stop.

"Not too fast," Jodi whispered. "Just keep it steady."

"Are you sure you don't need your friends?" asked Marvin.

"I'm sure."

Marvin was dutifully matching her stride for stride with a discipline Jodi sincerely admired; she didn't know how he was acclimatizing to this so quickly, but Marvin was showing more courage and more brains than any partner she'd ever had.

"How could they know we were gonna be here?" he whispered.

"I don't know," Jodi shook her head, breathless. "They're probably just trying a shotgun approach."

"What's a shotgun approach?"

"It's when they go to every place on the map. They go to our homes. Where we work. Where we might have been. Where we might be going. They just cover the entire city and hope for the best. The same way cops look for somebody."

"Like that guy firing through the floor," Marvin muttered. "He didn't know where we were. He was just hitting everything in the room."

"Same principle," Jodi said and then grabbed his arm pulling him toward a cab. "Come on. We have to leave my car."

"Why?"

"If they saw us drive up, we've been made. We'll have to take cabs from here. Then a bus. Then we'll have to walk."

Jodi climbed into the cab as Marvin opened the door, setting the bag down between them on the back seat. She leaned forward, speaking to the driver; "Just drive! I'll let you know where to go in a minute!"

They slowly made their way from the increasingly busy store which belonged to Ben Chamberlain when Marvin said quietly, "You think Chamberlain's dead?"

"Yeah," she said tiredly. "He's dead."

"Do you think they know we're coming tonight?"

"Yeah, I expect they do."

"We should assume they know everything. We might live longer. They probably even know we're at the professor's house."

Jodi's eyes flared as she clutched the headrest in front of her.

"Oh, god," she whispered. "Joe Mac ..."

* * *

"Do you think something has happened to them?" asked Professor Graven as he strolled across the den.

Joe Mac slowly removed the .45 from his coat, and sighed. "They're not going to attack us here." He turned his face to the professor. "Not yet."

Professor Graven's foot made a grating sound of turning.

"Why do you say that?"

"Because we're ready for them, and they're mostly just bushwhackers. They don't want a standup fight. Not in broad daylight. They'll wait until they can isolate us."

"Do you think they ambushed Marvin and Jodi?"

"Probably."

"You are not concerned?"

Joe Mac's face bent. "Jodi's got good training. She knows what to look for. She's well-armed. And she's made up her mind. She'll kill if she has to, and I don't think she'll hesitate."

"And if she dies?"

"That ain't up to me."

Professor Graven paused a long time before he stated, "You seem a little tense, detective. Are you always so alert and on guard?"

"I don't make mistakes," said Joe Mac.

"What does that mean?"

"It means I don't trust people."

With a short laugh the professor made his way to one of the leather chairs and sat. From the sound of it Joe Mac knew he had lifted the double-barreled rifle and was either loading it or cleaning it. Graven spoke; "I suppose that being a homicide detective for thirty years makes you suspicious of … well, basically everybody."

"Being a homicide detective was easy," said Joe Mac. "There were good guys and bad guys. It was clean." He grunted, "It was life that taught me not to trust people. And age helps a little. It teaches you that people can hide true colors for a long time."

"I'm far older than you," Professor Graven stated, "and I still trust people. Although I admit that it's always a risk. And I do find myself forgiving people more often than I'd like. But I don't see how a life without trust … or love … is worth living."

"I didn't say it was," said Joe Mac.

"So why are you still hanging around this place, detective?" Graven clicked the breach closed on the rifle. "I'm surprised a man as cynical as you would waste any more time in this old world than he has to."

"I'm just waiting for what's coming," said Joe Mac.

"What would that be?"

"Justice."

"Justice and death often go hand-in-hand."

"Does it matter?"

"I suppose not." Professor Graven was silent. Then, "You are a strange man, detective. You see all life against the background of a graveyard. It must be a terrible thing to live your life in fear."

Joe Mac turned his face to the flame.

"It ain't the graveyard you should fear," he said.

* * *

Jodi scowled over the seat at the cab driver.

"Hey," she said. "This isn't the right route."

The driver – apparently Irish – half-turned his head and raised his right hand. "Let me tell you something, lady. We got construction going on all over town. We got dump trucks shutting down half the streets. I'm taking the fastest route, believe me."

"But this is taking us south of 42."

"I ain't got no choice, lady! Dump trunks have shut down everything north of 44."

"Stop the cab!"

The cabbie glared over his shoulder before he reached down and suddenly the locks on either door to the back seat snapped shut, and a glass partition sharply rose to separate them from the driver. At the same second the cabbie floored it, and they descended an off-ramp leading to the long gray sand of the Hudson River.

Marvin exclaimed, "*What*!"

"Forget this!" shouted Jodi as she whipped out the Glock and aimed it over the seat. "We are *not* civilians! Stop this thing or I'll blow your head off!"

The cab gathered speed.

Jodi rapid-fired five rounds into the partition and blinked, stunned that the driver wasn't dead. In fact, he wasn't even hurt because the bullets had impacted without effect against the glass. With a shout, Jodi fired five more rounds, but they were equally useless because the thick panel held.

The driver slammed on the brakes, bringing the cab to a halt on the sand. Then he did something and leaped out the door, quickly running.

Thick gas assaulted Jodi.

"Exhaust!" she shouted. "He's got this thing rigged, so the exhaust comes into the back seat! We gotta get out of here!"

Marvin shouted, "Is your door locked?"

"He's got it counter locked!"

Marvin ripped out a tube from beneath his coat, and Jodi saw it was a stun grenade. Then he jammed it into the door handle on his side of the seat and pulled the pin. In the same breath he twisted into Jodi, putting his back to the grenade, and pushed her down, covering her with his body as the grenade exploded.

The detonation would have been normally stunning at such close range, but it was even more stunning because the force was amplified by the close confinements of the back seat. Then through the flame tearing at the door Jodi saw that the interior panel had been destroyed by the explosion. In the next moment, Marvin managed to reach inside the ravaged door, unlock it, and they crawled onto the sand.

Rolling, gagging and spitting blood, Jodi slowly began to regain her mind as her hearing and vision returned. She didn't attempt to wipe the sweat and blood from her face as she laid a hand on Marvin who had finally reached his hands and knees.

She coughed, "Are you okay?"

"No," Marvin shook his head. "That hurt." He paused. "*A lot.*"

"It's supposed to hurt," she replied. "That's why they call it a stun grenade." She searched the beach. "Where's the guy?"

"He's gone." Marvin gained his knees, leaning back, and shook his head. "Who was that guy? How did he know we were gonna grab a cab at the –"

Jodi spoke in broken fragments as she slowly and painfully caught her breath. "They probably had a dozen cabs in the area … in case we grabbed one. This isn't the first time these guys have done this – I guarantee it. They've killed other people the same way."

"*Who are these people?*"

"Psychopaths who think they're god."

"I've never seen god run for his life."

Jodi gritted her teeth; "I'd kill him if he was still here! Just out of principle!" She inhaled deeply. "What made you bring a stun grenade?"

"That ain't all I brought." Marvin opened his coat to reveal his belt laden with stun grenades and the deadly M61 hand grenades and two extra pistols. "It's like Joe said. If you think you might be going into a fight, carry all the ammo you can carry."

Jodi nodded, "As long as you've got ammo …"

"You've got options."

"Right."

With difficulty, Jodi stood and Marvin followed. When they were steady, she turned toward the road with, "Let's get back to the house. If they know where we are, they might know where Joe is, too."

As they walked, Marvin asked, "Why don't they just shoot us with a high-powered rifle or something simple like that?"

"They tried that already. But I'm also betting they had a lot of faith in their cabbie back there, too." She swept back her hair. "Carbon monoxide is actually a pretty effective way to kill somebody. We'd have been dead in thirty seconds if you hadn't brought that stun grenade with you. That was smart."

Marvin muttered, "Well, I'm starting to get the hang of this." He looked over. "I can't believe you do this for a living."

"Oh, make no mistake." Jodi almost laughed, "I've been on the job three years, and I've never even pulled my gun. But hanging out with Joe has changed the balance of my universe." She sighed. "I guess death comes knocking when you're on a 'vision quest.' Or whatever you'd call it."

"Is that what Joe's doing?"

"I don't think Joe even knows. But Poe knows."

"How does Poe know?"

"Poe just knows."

"How?" Marvin pressed.

"Personally?" Jodi cast a glance. "I think it's spiritual."

They reached the pavement as Marvin said, "As far back as history goes, ravens have always had a reputation for things like death or resurrection. According to the Bible, a raven was the bird that god used to feed Elijah when he was in the desert. A raven is also the bird Noah sent out from the ark to find land after the flood." He grunted softly as he added, "The Egyptians used a raven to symbolize resurrection. And the Cherokee thought a raven was death itself. The raven is always used to represent either death or a new life."

Jodi asked, "What do you think?"

"Poe saved our lives, so I don't care if he's a spirit or just a real smart bird. Saving my life is enough for my respect."

Jodi walked into the street and hailed a cab.

As they opened the doors, Marvin got into the front seat and smiled at the surprised driver. "I like it up front," he said.

The driver melted into traffic, and in a half hour they caught a bus. In another hour, they were a half mile from the professor's home. Then they spent an hour walking before Jodi looked around and said, "Okay, I think we're clean. They may be dedicated, but they're not that smart."

"Let's get back," said Marvin. "Joe needs to know about all this."

"He already knows."

"Why do you say that?"

"He just knows." Jodi found herself walking with her head bowed when she finally added, "Like I know."

Marvin was watching her. "What do you think you know?"

"I know Joe is going to die. And so am I."

Marvin grabbed her shoulders and turned her, angrily glaring down. "What does that mean, Jodi!"

She gazed up. Blinked softly.

"It means that what's always been coming has finally come," she said. "It means I'm not in control of my life. It means I never was."

ELEVEN

A thunderous, flowing black cloud of crows commanded Jodi's attention when they were still a quarter-mile from Professor Graven's sprawling home, and when they arrived she merely stood and stared at the hypnotic rising and diving.

"Let's go to the patio," she said. "Joe's out back."

Marvin draped an arm over her shoulders as they rounded the corner of the home , and she immediately saw Joe Mac sitting at the small glass table with Poe perched before him. Joe lifted his head as they neared, and he said, "Have some trouble?"

"A little," Jodi said casually.

"Kill anybody?"

"Yep. You?"

"Not yet. You all right?"

"First time for everything."

"It took you long enough."

"You been hanging fire for something?"

"Just … a little worried."

"Well, I'm fine. Thanks for the concern." She took a seat and extended a hand to Poe who crept over and lowered his head. "I got bad news. Mr. Chamberlain is dead. They killed him, and they probably killed that woman, too. But we still managed to get the stuff."

Joe Mac sighed, "All right. Well, I'm thinking that maybe I need you in a command center. I don't need you in that cave."

"I'm going in, Joe."

"You're lettin' me down, kid."

"To repeat myself: You don't need me in any 'command center,' Joe. You just don't want me going in there because you think I'm gonna get hurt or killed. But I'm going in. It's too late, as they say in the song, to turn back now." Jodi stared more seriously. "If I back out now, Joe, I'll never be a real cop. And you know it."

"Not everybody's meant to be a real cop."

"*I* am."

Upon the table, Joe Mac's hand clutched, fingers curling as if they held the main strength to crush stone. Finally, he nodded, "All right, then. We all go. But I want you loaded up with all the ammo you can carry. And stick close to Marvin and the captain. Don't stay close to me. No matter what."

"Why not?"

"Because I'll be close to the professor."

She glanced through the sliding back door and didn't see Professor Graven as she curiously asked, "Is there something I should know?"

"Just stay away from me and him. It's gonna be a dangerous place to be." Joe Mac blew out a breath. "The *most* dangerous."

Poe jerked his head to the side and spread his gigantic wings with a shrilling caw as the door opened and Brightbarton stepped out holding an M-4 – a short-barrel version of the AR-15. He slammed in a clip as he walked forward and appeared totally relaxed as he stated, "You ready for this, rookie?"

"Are you?"

"I was born ready, kid."

Joe Mac mumbled, "Just like 'The Wild Bunch.'"

"I sure hope this has a happier ending," said Brightbarton.

Joe Mac stood.

"Let's do it."

Jodi narrowly cut her eyes to catch Marvin's worried gaze and didn't waste a second understanding more than that. She stood and followed Joe Mac into the house where they began to arm themselves.

Marvin used the time to prepare each cloak. He decorated them with beads, shrunken heads, iconic talismans and anything else he'd lifted from the shop before the shootout shut them down. He also made subtle slits in the sides of every cloak so they could covertly reach within it to grab their weapon without laboriously dragging the one-piece drape over their heads and off their bodies to fight. When Marvin was finished, they were able to appear fully covered, yet they had access to any weapon.

Brightbarton also had the much-appreciated prescience to bring bullet proof vests with solid steel shock plates in front and back. The ballistic vests weren't bulky because they were composed of interwoven Mylar, a material not unlike a stiff blanket. But the solid steel shock plates, while guaranteeing protection from any bullet that might hit them at any range, added considerable weight.

Jodi had worn a vest every day in uniform, but, like most officers, she didn't carry the extra slabs of steel. Twenty extra pounds of high carbon steel was simply too much weight to haul around in the burning sun for eight hours. Tonight, however, she snugly fit the slabs in place and resolved to live with the added stress.

Each of them had their own preference for how they wanted to carry their weapons. Jodi elected to carry the Glock and extra clips in the front of her belt; it would be her only weapon, and she wanted fast access for reloads. She decided to forego any hand grenades since she would probably be carrying Tommy Childers, and she ultimately didn't trust the unpredictable pattern of shrapnel.

Joe Mac used the simplest preparations. He just jammed three .45s in his belt and slid extra clips in the front pockets of his pants and shirt. He did elect to wear one of the vests, but he declined the shock plates – a decision that worried Jodi but she remained silent.

Marvin took the deadly M61 grenades and shoved the levers into his stiff leather belt so that his entire waist was a solid line of hand grenades. When he was done, he was bearing a solid arsenal of M61 grenades and three stun grenades. Then he made room on either thigh for a .45 and put extra clips in every pocket. He also resourcefully stuck extra clips for the .45s in the top of each boot. Last, he taped three clips together for the M-4 so that he only needed to eject an empty clip, flip it, and slam in another without searching for the extra magazine. All in all, the M-4 setup provided him with 90 uninterrupted shots and when that was done he would just drop the weapon and pull the .45s.

Brightbarton was old school; he only carried his duty pistol and the M-4. He stuffed clips for his Glock in every pocket and stuck magazines for the M-4 inside his belt front to back. Then he pulled on a steel-reinforced vest. Last, he dragged the Druid-robe over his head and, like Jodi, spent ten minutes walking around the room developing a technique for surreptitiously grabbing his weapons.

Jodi was certain she could put her hand on her Glock without moving suspiciously, especially in a half-shadowed environment. She wasn't quite as confident about her ability to find the extra clips. And she had a nagging fear that, once the fighting started, she might become so entangled in the cloak that she'd be forced to haul it over her head and fling it aside.

There was an upside and a downside to keeping or losing the robe. The upside of retaining the robe was that it would at least temporarily confuse the Druids. In the chaos of combat, the priests would have to wait for Jodi to fire to determine whether she was an enemy. The downside was that the huge cloak was not at all congruent to battle; agility was severely compromised and lightning-fast speed was out of the question.

At the last, Jodi glanced over the room and tried to gauge the emotional temperature; Joe Mac was easy to read.

He seemed the same as he always seemed. He could have been preparing for a funeral or a wedding – no difference. Brightbarton was a bit tighter with micro-expressions hinting at anger or, perhaps, dread.

But Marvin was the most difficult to decipher. His movements were slow, methodical, deliberate, and careful. He appeared neither eager nor reluctant. Rather, it was as if he were simply preparing another doctrinal dissertation on some archaic civilization. But most encouraging was the aspect he projected of being merciless without being cruel. While he did not seem to loath killing, neither did he exude the aura of a man eager to shed blood. Instead, he was behaving as if this was just business as usual.

When they were finishing, Jodi glanced at Joe Mac.

"Any last-minute advice, b'wana?"

"Yeah," Joe Mac answered gruffly, "shoot until the aggression stops. It don't matter if you have to shoot him a hundred times. Don't worry about that. He could be wearing a vest, too. You just keep shooting until he goes down. Second, don't let yourself get tunnel vision. Keep your eyes open to what's happening on all sides. And always keep moving forward and turning, so nobody can sneak up on you from behind. The trick is to not have a blind side. And if somebody rushes you, rush them back. Don't' retreat. Ever. If someone comes straight into you, you go straight into them. And if you get shot, get up. Don't think you're gonna die or you probably will.

"Now, listen up, kid. If it gets bad – and it will – go straight into it. Don't ever run. Not ever! If he charges at you, you charge at him. If you're gonna die, you get it in your mind that he's gonna die, too. 'Cause the most important thing in a gunfight ain't your gun: It's your mind. You gotta be willing to get shot to pieces and know that you're still gonna kill whoever this is trying to put you in the dirt. You can't let your fear cripple you. You can't let fear cripple your thinking. It don't matter if you're shot or if the situation is absolutely doomed. Yeah, maybe you do die. Maybe we all die. But, by God, he's gonna die, too. And you stick that in your mind because your mindset is gonna be worth more than all the training in the world. Got it?"

Jodi nodded, "Got it."

"I'll be watching your back," Joe Mac added. "But if I go down, you keep moving. You're gonna have the little boy with you. Your priority is getting that boy clear of that place. I can take care of myself."

"All right."

When they were ready, Professor Graven descended the stairway dressed in what Jodi could only summarize as the ultimate safari wardrobe. He wore a sleeveless leather vest with bullets already packed, khaki shirt, cotton pants, and knee-high leather boots that looked to be ridiculously expensive if not downright unaffordable. He walked forward, lifted the double-barrel Weatherby, checked the chambers, and shut the breach.

"How many cars are we taking?" asked Brightbarton.

"Two," said Joe Mac. "And we ain't driving either of them."

"We ain't?"

"No, I got the Kosiniski brothers dropping us off at the graveyard. Then they'll stay close, and we'll call 'em on the cell phone when we get out. I don't want our cars on that road. Might make somebody suspicious."

"Don't you think there's gonna be plenty of cars on that road?" asked Brightbarton. "We ain't the only ones gonna be using that graveyard."

"Nothing wrong with caution."

"Caution!" exclaimed Brightbarton. "If we were using caution, we wouldn't be going out there at all! We'd let SWAT do this."

Joe Mac shook his head. "Our security's compromised. I don't know if it's Rollins or somebody else. But that's how they hit us at the park. Somebody set us up. And I'm not gonna run that gauntlet again."

"Yeah, yeah, I know. We got a fox in the hen house. But don't bring up 'caution.' If I was using caution I'd be sitting on a beach. Not following you into a showdown that's gonna make the Alamo look like a Billy Graham tent revival."

"Everybody check your throat mic," said Joe Mac, and they did a series of counts. "All right. We're good to go. Each one of us will hear every word you say, so if you get into trouble just talk like you're talking to anybody else. Give your position. Stay calm. And somebody will come. Okay?"

Nods.

Graven asked, "Any last-minute changes?"

"Same plan," said Joe Mac. "You stick close to me. When you see this high priest, you put me next to him. Then I'll grab him, Jodi will grab Tommy Childers, and we'll make our way out of there. If anybody looks sideways at you, kill him."

Movement caught Jodi's eye as she was loading a clip and she noticed Poe perched on the fireplace mantle watching each of them with lightning-quick attention. Then something prompted her to look to the patio, and she saw a hundred crows and ravens perched on the fence, the table, the chairs, the deck. With a curt laugh, Jodi spoke to Joe Mac, "Looks like Poe brought friends."

"Yeah," he raised his face, "he knows what's happening."

Graven had followed Jodi's gaze. "Do you truly believe that that … bird … understands the gravity of the situation?"

"He understands a whole lot more," said Jodi. She reached out and Poe fluttered from the mantle, landing on her hand. She brought him close and kissed his forehead before softly adding, "Don't ya, big guy?"

Joe Mac slid a third .45 into his coat and stood for a second with both hands shoved deep in his pockets. He turned his face to Poe and the raven cawed softly. Then he lifted his chin in Jodi's direction. "You loaded?"

"All I can carry."

"Got your vest on?"

"Yep."

Joe Mac tossed his cell phone. "Keep that 'till it's over. Just hit 'one' when you need to get picked up. But the Kosiniski brothers will be thirty seconds out, so be prepared to hold your ground for thirty seconds. Think fast. Move fast. Kill anything that even looks at you." He paused to take a deep breath. "Let me ask you a question, Detective Strong. How do you fight a thousand men?"

Jodi blinked. "How?"

"One at a time."

Jodi bowed her head. "*Yeah* ..."

Brightbarton lifted the M-4. "You ready?"

Joe Mac chambered his last .45.

"I reckon so."

* * *

In the shadow of midnight Jodi could almost hear the doom, doom of drums as she stared upon the shadows of gravestones – shadows that reached to the very edge of the dark tree line, but no further as if even shadow was afraid of touching what this forest held.

Wearing the dark robes of the priests, they had stood within the blackness of the jungle gloom watching people emerge from the cemetery trail to silently enter the crypt and disappear into the hidden tunnel. They had watched for hours without revealing their position and Jodi had begun to wonder what sign Joe Mac needed to decide that it was time. But she had said nothing. She had only occasionally glanced into the Cimmerian darkness of the triple canopy of trees hearing the soft caw of Poe.

Yes, Poe had followed them from the house, as always, but this time it was different. The magnificent raven had not come alone.

She had glanced back as they traveled here.

Behind them the sky had been lost to innumerable black wings that followed with that familiar shrill Poe used when he sensed danger. To even make an intelligent estimate of the raven and crow would have been foolish. Safe to say they were as numberless as the grains of sand in the sea. And they had followed them down that now familiar trail from the dirt road to the cemetery, and the entire forest had bent beneath the weight of wings when they settled on every branch.

Joe Mac asked quietly, "Jodi, has anyone entered the tomb in the last twenty minutes?"

"No," she whispered. "Nobody."

"Remember what you know."

"I will, Joe."

"All right, then. Let's do it."

In seconds they reached the tomb and Joe Mac mounted the long granite steps with Marvin's hand on his elbow. Jodi led the way with both hands wrapped around the grip of the Glock – a grip that now brought a familiar comfort.

She had borne her weapon every day, on duty and off, for three long years and yet she had never found comfort in it. Rather, every time she'd drew it, held it, cleaned it or even qualified with it on the range she had been afraid of it. But it was wrong to say she had hated the gun. Rather, she had hated *herself* for her lack of commitment ... or courage.

Now her weapon was her friend, although she knew her truest, most dependable, most spiritual friend was perched above her in a tree watching the whole night with that supernatural prescience she had come to trust with all her heart.

Poe was a bodyguard who would never know fear, who would never flag or fail, who would always watch over her, who would never sleep, who would see in others what they couldn't see in themselves. She had truly come to believe that the raven knew things beyond the reach of the human mind. Poe simply had the God-given ability to look into someone's soul. She couldn't explain it, but she knew it was true and that was enough.

They stood within the crypt.

"Professor?" said Joe Mac.

"I am here," he replied.

"Stay beside me. We'll follow the others."

"As you say."

Joe Mac's brick-silhouette turned minutely toward Marvin.

"Marvin?" he said with a voice next to silence. "Marvin, you lead the way. Steve, you stay behind him. And you're next, Jodi." His barrel chest expanded with a breath. "When we reach the cavern just walk out amongst them but stick close to each other. Professor, you'll lead me to the inner circle of those stones."

"I don't know if that's possible," the professor objected. "I don't know how they choose those who enter the inner circle. They may have rules we don't understand, and, if we violate those rules, they'll know we are intruders and promptly attack." He raised both hands as if to form a box. "You must not underestimate the suspicions of these people. They have remained hidden for a thousand years. They know how to detect an enemy."

"We have to take our chances," Joe Mac said. "Put on your masks." After masks were in place he said, "Find a large stone and prop it in the door."

"Why?" asked Professor Graven.

"To keep the door open," said Joe Mac cryptically. "Prop the stone in the door, so it can't shut behind us."

A shadow made Jodi turn, and she saw Marvin walk out the entrance of the tomb. He returned carrying a section of branch she remembered seeing when they'd come here in the daylight. Marvin pushed the crypt fully open and wedged the wood in the joint where the lid of the sarcophagus joined the wall; it was the same principle as wedging a pencil in the hinge of a door, although the pencil is small it could defeat a door a thousand times its size just by where it was set against the joint.

"I fixed it, Joe," he said. "And it looks like it could have happened naturally. Nobody will be suspicious if they come up behind us."

Joe Mac nodded, "Good enough." He stared over them. "Listen. Sometimes plans go to Hell. If that happens, just remember that your priority is saving this kid. So just keep shooting, keep moving. Kill anybody that gets in your way. And forget mercy. They ain't gonna show *you* none." He took a slow breath. "Remember, winning ain't always living. Dying ain't always losing. On the last day, you can die and still win all there is to win." He lifted his face, as if looking into another world. "All right … it's time."

The long walk through the tunnel, uphill and down, felt all too brief to Jodi, who was hoping the walk was all they would face tonight. Then, in the distance, she began to hear the quietest murmur and knew they were almost at the cavern. She resisted the temptation to reach within the cloak and grip the Glock.

They were all fully armed beneath the robes, but no one would know until the last moment. The professor had easily concealed the elephant gun within his robe simply by slinging it across his back; the priestly cloaks were so voluminous that the old man could have borne three rifles without any revealing ridges. Marvin and Brightbarton were similarly armed with the M-4s, which were ridiculously easy to conceal.

She had only brought the Glock, but the pistol fired seventeen-round magazines, and she had ten extra magazines. If that wasn't enough to see them safely out of this mess another forty magazines wouldn't make any difference. On some level that she barely understood, Jodi sensed that firepower wouldn't be what saved them tonight, anyway; this night belonged to a power she felt but didn't understand. She only knew it was as real as the wind that lifted Poe into the clouds or lowered him to the Earth.

Marvin entered the chamber.

They followed, and the scene was hellish and despairing.

At least three hundred soundless, melancholic shapes draped in black robes with human skulls tied to their knife-bearing belts crept through the oppressive tombstone shadows of Stonehenge. Demonic masks concealed their faces, but their eyes glinted, red, in the flames. Uncountable sheep and goats dangled dead on black rope strung lintel to lintel, gaping throats choked with blood. Then Jodi saw human skulls strung like ornaments for the most unholy holiday; they were elaborately suspended, staring with empty eyes. They were piled in four pyramids as high as a man. And they were laid in a continuous connecting circle around the innermost stones as if to curse all who enter here.

If the gates of Hell do exist, they look like this, thought Jodi.

Only then did Jodi reflect that Marvin had entered this nightmarish gathering without revealing the most minute doubt. By now the archeologist had reached the rim of the crowd and was threading a casual path through them as if this was his most familiar ground; one would have never guessed that only three days ago this man had been consigned for life to a dungeon of dry bones and dusty rock.

By reflex Jodi began searching for whatever figure might be the high priest of this underground field of cannibals, but she saw no one noteworthy. They all seemed the same; they were all savagely adorned like barbarians after a feast of rape and theft and murder; they each wore demonic masks of horrific distortion.

When they reached the Stonehenge monument Marvin stopped with his head slightly bent. He waited until the rest reached his side and began walking to the right, slowly circling the tiers. Glancing to the side, Jodi saw the Bloodstone positioned directly in the center of the pillars. It was flat like a table and reddened by whatever ghastly rites had preceded them to this night. But at the same time she saw something else that overwhelmed her mind.

In the middle of the inner circle stood a wooden figure of a man.

The Wicker Man ...

It was ten feet in height and pieced together with what looked like thousands of dry tree limbs. It was a boxlike representation of a human being with square arms that stuck straight out from the shoulders. Its legs were built from thicker sticks and the torso was only a rectangular box; the head also appeared to be a box but Jodi wasn't certain because they had draped a black shroud over the face and neck.

In the wavering light of rising flames Jodi determined that the wood wasn't painted or in any way refined for the creation of a work of art. Rather, the whole of the Wicker Man was crude, ugly, and savage. It was a god of the base wickedness of the human soul and not meant to represent anything in the way of life. It was a god built to satisfy the most obscene hungers of the most primitive mind of Man.

At the base of the grotesque idol was a massive circular mound of firewood that might burn for days and days – long after the idol itself, and whatever had been imprisoned within it, was reduced to ashes.

Jodi shivered and prayed no one noticed. She resisted the temptation to look back; she had to trust that Joe Mac and Professor Graven were close.

Don't turn ...

Trust your instincts ...

Before she could stop herself, Jodi turned her head and confirmed they weren't more than three strides from her, and they appeared harmless and at home.

Jodi had no doubt that if she had removed her mask her horror would be vividly displayed for all to see, and the game would instantly be up. She was thankful for whatever bizarre and arcane reason dictated they conceal their identities; it was the only thing keeping her alive although she was certain that Marvin could have seamlessly wound his way through this cannibal coven without raising an alarm if he had cast away *his* mask.

She began to study the room from a tactical angle. The monument of Stonehenge stood one hundred yards from the tunnel. The rest of the chamber was empty and flat. There were no granite blocks they could use for cover once the fighting started. The only protection would be the pillars of Stonehenge itself, and those would do them no good because they had to make a hasty retreat from it once Joe Mac grabbed the high priest.

Overall, it was a tactical nightmare; the only way to get clear of the gunfire would be straight through it.

Even in her considerations Jodi had not lost sight of Marvin and Captain Brightbarton. She saw they had positioned themselves very close to the *Wicker Man* and were standing with heads down and hands clasped as if in meditation. But from the angle of the Brightbarton's head Jodi perceived he was measuring the place for tactics, as well. Then she noticed black-draped shapes filtering through the pillars and turned her face to Joe Mac and the professor as they simply walked into the inner space of the monument.

Gazing steadily over those who were entering the inner sanctum, Jodi saw nothing notable about the shapes that would designate them for some solemn possession not granted to others. In the identical black robes and interchangeable masks, it seemed like anyone could approach *The Wicker Man* and so she stepped forward. Then she was standing as close as she dared and saw that Joe Mac and Professor Graven had done the same; they stood a short four strides from the idol.

Although Jodi had feared they would be called upon to participate in some incomprehensible ritual certain to reveal her as an imposter, nothing happened as they closed the circle. Then others formed a larger circle and, last, still others formed a large cordon around the entire monument.

Jodi had estimated three hundred of them, and now it appeared to be even more but it didn't matter whether it was three hundred or three thousand.

They had a plan, and they were committed.

She searched for guards but saw none and assumed everyone was armed and more than willing to kill an intruder. It seemed appropriate to assume that each would be as deadly as the other since they were universally bound to this most horrible of all rituals and this most savage of all sins.

An approach …

Moving only her eyes Jodi saw a large shape nearing the Bloodstone. She narrowly glanced at Joe Mac and saw the professor briefly tilt his head; he appeared to be giving Joe a play by play of the proceedings.

Joe Mac subtly turned an ear toward the figure.

With reverence the herculean Druid stopped before the Bloodstone. His mask was blood red and his sash was blood red with a long black knife slid beneath it.

"This child is the last," the *Ri* announced. "Never again shall we be forced to hide in the caverns of the Earth where we have been so wrongfully hounded and persecuted. Never again shall we be forced to conceal our birthright, which is rightfully ours. We will rebuild what was destroyed by hate and intolerance. And we will again worship in freedom and take our rightful place among the powers of this world."

A dozen Druids holding torches stepped to the *Wicker Man*.

"Remove the shroud!" he shouted.

A Druid tore the black shroud from the idol and Jodi gasped.

Within the *Wicker Man's* open head was the pale and innocent face of a helpless boy. Jodi saw red rope encircling his neck and more rope wrapped around each shoulder to tightly imprison him inside the idol.

He's already inside it!

Tommy Childers was unconscious; Jodi knew that much in the split-second she saw his small head bent forward just as she knew he would have been screaming if he were awake. But, even so, she was certain that whatever drug they had given him would be neutralized by the fire once it reached his body and his hideous screams would begin.

They would not deprive themselves of his agony and horror.

She cut her eyes to Joe Mac who had his ear turned to the Bloodstone as the High Priest raised his arms high. Then, moving with steps that were almost no movement at all, Jodi began to inch her way even closer to the *Wicker Man.*

"But first we must first purity our ritual!" the *Ri* shouted.

Jodi had no idea how she knew ... but she knew.

"Intruders are among us!" the priest cried and began to turn. "And they must be destroyed before we offer up our sacrifice!"

Jodi's heart was instantly so thunderously fast that she glanced to either side to see if anyone noticed. Then she realized with a shock that she had already slid her hand into her robe and was fiercely gripping the Glock.

If this maniac pointed toward anyone on the team, it was on.

Suddenly the High Priest spun and pointed at Joe Mac. "Seize him!"

Joe Mac ripped out the .45 and fired. The bullet hit the High Priest in the chest and Joe Mac continued from a classic shooting stance. He fired six more rounds and, unless Jodi lost sight in the ensuing rush, every bullet found its mark.

The priest staggered back and crashed across the cavern floor.

Jodi spun and shot the closest priest holding fire to the Wicker Man in the back of the head and, as a second priest turned, Jodi jammed the barrel of the Glock in his face and pulled the trigger. Then the other Druids hurled their torches into the mound of wood at the idol's feet and spun away, instantly running.

Jodi shoved the Glock into her belt and leaped to land on the chest of the *Wicker Man*, her hands gripping the open face. With a frantic scream, she surged back to rip the sticks away, but they were tied together tightly and in the split-second she realized she didn't have the strength to tear Tommy free.

Flames exploded, consuming the robe on her back, and Jodi screamed as she stumbled away. Then she was rolling across the cavern floor twisting frantically to tear the flaming sheet over her head; she finally ripped it off and hurled it to the side as she glimpsed a figure coming down on top of her.

An enraged Druid raised a butcher knife.

A muzzle flare erupted behind the Druid's head and he fell forward like a tree to hit the floor beside Jodi's face. She glared up to see …

"*Come on!*" Marvin shouted as he hauled her to her feet.

"I can't get him out!" Jodi screamed. "He's tied to it!"

Marvin's reaction wasn't a tenth of a second as he stooped and snatched up the dead Druid's butcher knife. He ran forward, over the blocks of wood that had begun to burn, and slashed fiercely at the ropes holding the sticks together while simultaneously tearing at them with his free hand.

Flames set Marvin's robe on fire as he wrenched the entire chest from the idol, and then he reached into the husk and, with three swift slashes, Tommy Childers's small body collapsed forward. Marvin caught him and turned, easily leaping over the flaming mound, and tossed him into Jodi's arms.

Marvin snatched off the robe going fully up in flame and hurled it aside with a reviling hand. Teeth bared, he ripped an M61 hand grenade from his waist, charged back to the face of the *Wicker Man,* and smashed the grenade into its guts.

Jodi heard his words ...

"Sacrifice this!"

Marvin leaped back and Jodi dropped to the floor, instantly bending to protect Tommy with her body. Then in the next second there was a cavern-shaking blast and a hurricane of flaming wooden shards exploded in every direction slashing through Druids to sever heads and arms and legs with what had been the Wicker Man.

Howls of agony erupted, and Jodi whirled to see a dozen priests rolling on the cavern floor with arms and legs broken and twisted. Even more priests were running wildly across the inner circle, their robes fully aflame. Then something told her to look back, and she saw a priest almost on top of her with an upraised blade.

Brightbarton came out of nowhere, firing over her body.

The priest was blown backwards.

"Protect the kid!" roared Brightbarton, and then he was forced to return fire with the M-4 as fast as he could pull the trigger.

"Down!" Marvin yelled again and flung one of the M61 grenades toward a crowd rushing from the far end of the monument. The grenade landed inside the racing wave of rising rifle barrels and the blinding-white explosion hurled black and red carcasses against the pillars of their resurrected Stonehenge like spatters of paint.

Thrown by the detonation, a perfect mushroom of fire hit the cavern ceiling, erupted outward and descended in a blast trapped by the granite to flood over robed figures who threw up arms howling with horror.

Jodi stood, placing a foot on either side of Tommy's body, and knew she wouldn't be moved; she decided that much in the moment and with remarkable ease just as she knew there would be no regrets. She chose in a single breath to make her last stand right here, right now, live or die.,

Priests were ferociously firing on them and Brightbarton bellowed as he was hit and slammed onto his back. With an enraged expression, he grabbed an edge of the Bloodstone with a single hand and pulled himself to his feet, firing the M-4 as he rose.

The cavern was a holocaust of gunfire with figures shooting in every direction, and then Jodi lost sight of Marvin and Brightbarton as she heard Professor Graven bellow, and she whirled; the old man staggered forward, dropping the elephant gun, and fell on his face. Beside him Joe Mac collided with a knife-wielding Druid.

Joe Mac raised the .45 between them and fired three times. The attacker collapsed forward holding his chest. Then a half dozen Druids leaped atop Joe Mac bearing him to the cavern floor, and Jodi raised the Glock for a shot but was afraid she'd hit Joe Mac. In the next moment gun blasts exploded in the center of the pile, and the attackers began to shout and fall back one by one until Joe Mac surged up, the .45 in his hand.

Jodi glanced down to make sure she still straddled Tommy's small body. Then a bullet cut across her cheek knocking her off balance; she rolled with the impact the same way a boxer rolls with a punch and when she came around she was already firing. She saw her rounds hit two of them.

Both twisted, leaping, before going down to the floor.

Jodi dropped to a knee, spinning again, and swept the room firing until the slide locked. She didn't try to make sense out of who was firing at her; she changed clips and returned fire at any muzzle blast she sensed or saw.

Some instinct made Jodi turn, and she saw Marvin racing along the outer edge of the monument with M61s in each hand and he dropped one moving fast but before it exploded she knew he dropped another one, and still Marvin flew along the edge dropping another and another and another and another before diving behind a pillar. With a wild cry Jodi pulled Tommy tight into her chest and swung her back to the grenades.

Six near-simultaneous explosions detonated along the far edge of Stonehenge where a hundred priests were rushing forward; it was a cataclysmic event, but Jodi wasn't watching. She was bent tight over Tommy, both arms holding him hard against her chest, and although Jodi didn't see the carnage she *felt* the sonic impact as it rolled over her – a physical wave of fire and force that would have blown her from her feet if she'd been standing.

Get down!" bellowed Marvin.

Jodi fell flat across Tommy as the explosion of a stun grenade lit up the space not more than six feet behind her with mushrooming fire, and priests staggered across the circle screaming and howling, their robes aflame, leaving scarlet ribbons in their wake.

Breathless, Jodi gasped, "*God help us!*"

Two figures staggered into the circle, and Jodi saw that a gigantic Druid had grabbed Joe Mac by the throat and they were locked in a contest of brute strength. The Druid had both hands wrapped tight around Joe Mac's neck as Joe Mac drew another .45 from his cloak; he placed the barrel flat against the man's chest and pulled the trigger.

In an explosion of flesh and blood the Druid fell back.

Jodi heard Brightbarton bellow in agony, and then she saw Marvin running forward from the far side of the monument. He leaped to hit the Bloodstone, leaping even higher from that, and came down on a half-dozen Druids who were slashing wildly at the captain. But as Marvin landed he fired the M-4 into one, two, three Druids and then a fourth priest as they all whirled with knives rising.

Standing coldly in place, Marvin simply raised a hand holding an M61 grenade. With a frown, he released the lever.

Shouting wildly, the priests scattered.

Marvin hurled the M61 grenade after them and grabbed Brightbarton before twisting to throw both their bodies to the floor; the stunning explosion sent arms and legs spinning across the smoking air.

Jodi was so deafened, stunned, and off-balance from the condensed concussions of the grenades that she could hardly stand.

She rose but staggered wildly to the side.

Marvin was suddenly there and caught her. Then he stooped to pick up Tommy before thrusting the boy into Jodi's arms.

He was in her face; "*Stay close to me!*"

Cradling Tommy, Jodi followed, her gun hand extended. She swung her whole body at once as gunshots erupted to her left and she emptied the clip; she saw three priests fall back, weapons clattering to the stone floor.

"Wait!" Marvin yelled as he held up a hand. "I have to get Joe!"

She screamed, "Go!"

Marvin was gone as quick as something hit Jodi hard in the back and she went sprawling on her face, Tommy cascading beside her. She didn't know what hit her – a bullet, a knife, a fist – but she rose with her hand tight on the Glock.

As she reached a knee she turned to see a Druid on top of her with a shotgun but he had her cold; she couldn't acquire aim and fire before he pulled the trigger. Then he was hurled through the air by something that hit *him* in the back so that he came down on the ground beside her. She raised her eyes to see Brightbarton frowning down, the M-4 smoking.

"These punks ain't that tough!" Brightbarton sneered. "Get up, kid!"

Suddenly Marvin returned dragging Joe Mac and shouting over the colliding sounds of gunfire and wounded screaming. He dropped beside Jodi and hauled her hard to her feet; "*Jodi we gotta get outta here now!*"

A Druid leaped on Marvin's back and they staggered forward.

Marvin spun and *surged* backward smashing the Druid into a pylon. The Druid's grasp was weakened, and in the next split-second Marvin spun placing the barrel of the M-4 against his chest; Marvin fired the full clip into the black robe that was immediately transformed into a ragged shroud of red. Then he ripped out two grenades and hurled them outside the pillars along the path Jodi knew they had to take; the blinding twin explosions lit the entire cavern from end to end in billowing shades of fire.

Marvin turned to Jodi bellowing, "*They're blind! Come on!*"

She didn't need any incentive.

Her only priority was getting out of this place with Tommy Childers alive in her arms. As they rushed through the crowd, Marvin threw another grenade every twenty feet like a man might throw rocks to scatter dogs. Jodi simply stayed as close as possible while trusting him to identify anyone targeting them.

They surged forward and the one thing that should have been an advantage for the Druids – their superiority of numbers – was turning out to be their *dis*advantage because they couldn't gain a clear shot without hitting one of their own; the priests continued to surge back and forth across the chamber clearly in a panic as Marvin led Jodi with an unerring and remarkable sense of direction toward the tunnel.

Suddenly Brightbarton surged from a wall of colliding priests with the M-4, blasting apart anyone who raised a weapon.

"What are you waiting for!" Brightbarton roared. "Get out of here!"

With Brightbarton leading the way emptying clip after clip they rapidly gained steps on the tunnel. Then Joe Mac bellowed and was smashed to the floor on his face. At the sound of the shot Brightbarton turned and swept an entire line of Druids, blasting them up and back or spinning them into the wall. After that he reached down and hauled Joe Mac to his feet shouting at him to *move-move-move!*

Marvin suddenly jumped back with a shout and Jodi knew he'd been hit. Rising from his knees, Marvin hurled the M-4 aside and drew both .45s, instantly firing. He glared over his shoulder, "*Stay with me!*"

Something caught Jodi's attention and she spun.

In the waving torch light she saw dozens of the dark priests rushing into tunnels that she hadn't noticed until now. Some had clearly chosen self-preservation over valor and Jodi sensed that those unknown exits would put them outside far faster than their own escape route.

Joe Mac had been right; the priests would be waiting for them with rifle fire if they ever reached that now-faraway graveyard.

"*They'll cut us to pieces,*" she whispered.

She heard Marvin shouting at her and clutched Tommy tighter as she turned again into their escape. Although Jodi couldn't see the entrance to the tunnel in the confusion of rushing bodies and the blinding staccato light of gunshots she knew they had to be close. Then something stood before them; she sensed it before she could identify it ...

Then she knew what it was ... and her heart sank.

At least sixty of the more self-possessed Druids had formed a firing line between them and the tunnel and were vengefully raising rifles.

Jodi grimaced in pain for all of them; they had fought so hard against so many; it was so tragic it was going to end like this.

Marvin angrily snatched two M61 grenades from his waist and hurled both; the grenades landed dead-center of the line and exploded to howls and screams. Then they were rushing forward again as Marvin snatched the .45s from his belt and began firing. But, Jodi realized, there were so many;

if Marvin killed one with every shot he'd run out of bullets before they ran out of men; Jodi clutched Tommy tighter, bowing her head.

And then she heard something …

… *Coming* …

It wasn't the rushing of wind that made Jodi suddenly focus on the tunnel. It wasn't the rolling thunder of explosions. And it wasn't the rising, howling tide of the wounding and dying that thickened the subterranean darkness like cold blood in dirt.

"*Poe*," she whispered.

Suddenly the granite corridor behind the implacable firing squad vanished in a living darkness that rose above the Druids and dove into them with screams and shrieks and struck like the Hammer of God.

Instantly the Druids whirled erupting with howls and screams and began firing wildly into the air. One began bellowing like a man on fire as he charged across the cavern shooting blindly at a hundred crows that were tearing him apart with murderous savagery and horrifying determination. And the others – those who attempted to stand their ground – were staggering first this way and then that as the ravens rose and fell diving again and again to tear their masks into bloody shreds and rip robes into ragged strips.

Joe Mac shouted, "Go straight through 'em!"

Marvin and Brightbarton hesitated as Jodi whirled and screamed.

"*COME ON!*"

They ran enclosing Tommy Childers in a fluid box formed with their own bodies and then they collided with the swirling, screaming cordon of Druids. At the impact they began shooting Druids seemingly at random but they were simply killing whoever was closest. Jodi kept waiting for the first talon or beak to slash her head or face not believing the ravens would be able to differentiate friend from foe in the howling cloud of blood but the attack never came and then they reached the tunnel.

At the entrance, Marvin turned and threw three more M61 grenades into the disintegrating block that had been so determined to prevent their escape, and although Jodi heard the explosions, she didn't look back to measure the damage.

She knew it was devastating; that was enough.

"*Run-Run-Run!*" Brightbarton was shouting. "*Keep running!*"

They fled down the tunnel together and then Marvin caught up to Jodi and tore Tommy Childers from her arms.

"Give him to me!" Marvin gasped. "Keep moving!"

The long run up that tunnel was the greatest labor of Jodi's life but she was so fired with blood and sweat and adrenaline that she wasn't even aware of how dead her body had become until they approached the exit. Then they were through the open door of the sarcophagus and into the cold air of the tomb.

This is where we die ...

She knew there would be fifty priests in the forest before them, and they'd be cut to pieces by rifle fire long before they could reach safety.

Shots erupted in the trees.

All of them fell to the floor of the tomb as rapid gunfire continued in the wood line and beyond. Then the shooting began to move away from the crypt as eight tall figures wearing military BDUs and holding automatic weapons rushed inside. One man knelt beside Marvin and shone a light on his chest. The man spoke sternly into a microphone at his collar, "SR-2! We're in the tomb! I need EMTs Code Three! I've got multiple shooting victims!"

Rising on a single arm, Marvin coughed violently; "Jodi! Are you all right!"

"Yeah!" she gasped. "I think so! ... Are you?"

"I don't know," he shook his head.

"Both of you stay calm," the SWAT leader said. "EMTs will be here in a second. We've got to secure the woods first."

Only then did Jodi finally realize that it was the New York City SWAT guys, and they were rapidly securing the graveyard and forest. Her mind was on autopilot as she turned her face to Brightbarton, gasping, "What! I thought you said that we didn't have any –"

"Joe cooked it up," Brightbarton groaned. "He told me he knows who sold us out. And it wasn't Rollins ... and it wasn't no cop ..."

Jodi grimaced, "But you guys were talking about how we wouldn't have any backup when we got to this graveyard!"

"Joe cooked that up, too ..."

"*Why?*"

Brightbarton only shook and bowed his head.

Vomiting blood, Joe Mac staggered out of the tunnel. His chest was soaked black and Jodi saw three bullet holes cut through his vest. Joe Mac angrily ripped down the Velcro straps, hauled off the armor, and flung it against the wall.

He gasped, "Give me that cell phone!"

It took Jodi a moment to orient. Then she snatched out the cell phone and placed it in his hand. Joe Mac raised his face and nodded at EMTs rushing into the tomb hauling two gurneys; the EMTs instantly lit up the crypt with flashlights and lamps as they began stabilizing Marvin and Brightbarton.

With a groan, Joe pushed off the wall and impatiently waved away attempts to tend to his injuries, although Jodi saw he was gravely wounded; he staggered to the door clutching a .45 in a bloody fist.

"Joe!" she cried. "You're hit! What are you doing!"

Covered in blood, Joe Mac paused in the door of the tomb and slowly turned his head. "You're a good kid," he smiled, and nodded. "You're gonna be all right ..."

He was gone.

Jodi whirled to Brightbarton. "Where's he going!"

"He's going after whoever did this," Brightbarton groaned.

"Who is that?"

"I don't know … I don't know …"

Jodi lifted Tommy Childers from the floor and set him gently on a gurney before surrendering him to even more EMTs who rushed into the tomb. After that she stepped back and let the technicians do their work to stabilize wounds. She held Marvin's hand tight as they began slamming bandages onto numerous bullet wounds that had ripped him up head to foot. She didn't count the shots; she only felt amazement that Marvin could have continued for so long with so many wounds.

With Brightbarton already ordering SWAT into the cavern and dispatching orders to anyone else in the vicinity, they moved in a ragged, bloody procession toward the road. When they cleared the hollow and entered the forest, Jodi was stunned at the number of police jerking zip-lock cuffs on dozens of Druids.

Rifles were scattered across the forest floor.

"Get me out of this thing!" Brightbarton bellowed as he unhooked the belt holding him fast to the gurney and crawled off, to stand. He raised an arm in what seemed biblical wrath; "I want every one of these scumbags booked for *murder!*" he roared. "Tell the magistrate they're going down for murder, for attempted murder, for the attempted murder of a police officer, for the kidnapping and murder of an FBI agent, and the kidnapping and attempted murder of a little boy! And that goes for every one of them by God!"

It was almost five minutes before they stabilized Marvin and lifted the gurney into the back of an ambulance with Brightbarton still bellowing commands that Jodi finally remembered Joe Mac. But at the thought she spun and walked toward a squad car.

"*Strong!*" Brightbarton shouted. "Where do you think you're going!"

"I'm going after Joe."

"You can't go anywhere! You're involved! You have to go to the hospital!"

Jodi didn't look back. "I don't need a hospital, captain."

"Strong! If you walk, it's your badge!" Brightbarton was breathless, and hesitated. "You don't even know where Joe's gone!"

"Yeah," Jodi grimaced, "I know where he's going."

"How do you know!"

"I just know, captain."

Brightbarton staggered toward her. "Don't do it, Jodi! You're a great cop! You're throwing away your badge! You're throwing away your career!"

"So be it," Jodi said and stood with one foot inside the squad car, her hand on the door, as she gazed. "Thank you, captain. You were right. You don't own this job until it costs you. And sometimes it's not always you that pulls the trigger. But Joe's gone after Professor Graven. And I'm going after Joe."

She shut the door.

In seconds the squad car was sailing into a low half-sun rising to her side casting the blood and the black of the forest in an azure haze. And when Jodi left the dirt road to hit the tarmac she floored it so that the sunlight was streaking through the trees casting her in the light, then the dark, then the light and then the dark as if revealing the heart of good and evil and lies and truth that this horrifying journey had become as she rushed toward what she knew would be the darkest truth of all.

* * *

Sitting in the front room, Joe Mac rested a forearm on the table clutching the .45 in a blood-soaked hand. He was dragging deep burning breaths, and the enraged Kosiniski Brothers had all but refused to let him get out of the truck but Joe had prevailed.

Joe Mac had smiled and said goodbye but the brothers simply bowed their heads and drove away.

A sound ...

... Yeah, it's him ... He's moving with strong steps ... No hesitation ... A key in the door ... The door opening, closing ... Steps approaching ... The click of a light switch and ... no more movement ... He's standing there staring at me ...

"Glad you made it, professor," said Joe Mac.

Professor Graven took a single step, and Joe Mac thumbed back the hammer of the .45. "I wouldn't do that," he said. "I may be blind, but I'll still get you." He tried to smile, but pain and exhaustion ripped the guts out of it before it began.

Professor Graven said slowly, "Why aren't you in a hospital, detective? You certainly look like you need one."

"How'd you make it out of there?"

"Luck."

"I'll bet." Joe Mac took a shallow breath and wasn't surprised that the next breath didn't immediately follow. He said, "They didn't know who you were, did they?" He paused. "You know who they are. But they don't know who you are. Because only the high priest knows everything. That's how you got somebody to stand in for you tonight, wasn't it? You made a phone call."

"You are bleeding very badly, detective." Professor Graven hadn't moved again. "You are seeing things that are not there."

Joe Mac removed his glasses to reveal eyes white and opaque and translucent. "I see just fine," said Joe. "I see you."

"And what do you think you see?"

"I see a murderer." Joe Mac grimaced. "Some might call you a psychopath. But I like to call 'em like I see 'em." There was a dark, possessed silence. "You killed my grandson. You killed all of them. You gave the word, and they were dead. It doesn't matter if you didn't pull the trigger. You gave the word, and it was done. And that makes you a murderer. And that means you're gonna die."

Stillness.

"Are you feeling cold, detective?"

Freely Joe Mac nodded, "Yeah."

"That's because all the blood is leaving your body. Now you feel cold. Soon you'll be dead." He was taking his time as if waiting for Joe Mac to fall. "I understand why you might be suspicious of me. But I am not the high priest of those savages. I was with you tonight, and they almost killed me, too. Remember? So why would I have put my life in such danger? What you are inferring makes no sense."

"That's exactly why you did it," said Joe Mac. "Because it makes no sense."

"Why are you convinced that I am the man you seek?"

"You made mistakes."

Professor Graven hesitated. "What mistakes?"

"The police department never knew that me and Jodi were going out to Long Island to talk to Montanus. But you knew." Joe Mac finally smiled knowing it was a ghastly sight. "You're the one that gave Marvin the name. And then Marvin gave it to us. But Marvin didn't know any better. He didn't know you were setting us up to die." He let that settle. "You deceived Marvin like you deceived everybody else."

"Marvin told others, as well."

"But the others didn't know we were meeting the captain in the park. Only you knew. That's two strikes."

"Agent Rollins also knew."

"Rollins is dead, so he's not a suspect. And since you killed him just so you could lure us to that dock, I don't think Rollins ever sold us out. I think you sold us out. All of us. Then you told us we'd never make it out of that graveyard, or that tunnel, alive."

"So?"

"I hadn't said anything about that tunnel. Or that graveyard. But you said we'd never get out of that graveyard alive."

Professor Graven hesitated. "Of course you mentioned it."

"No," Joe Mac shook his head. "I didn't. But you knew all about it because you knew about that entrance. And you knew that Jodi and Marvin had gone to Chamberlain's place because you were there when I sent them. That's how they got ambushed so fast. You told your boys where they were going."

"You're delirious, detective. This is nonsense."

"And you didn't go to the museum yesterday to look at any black and white pictures. You went to make arrangements for your imposter because you couldn't very well preside over a ritual – not like you usually do – and fight beside us at the same time." A pause. "Did your substitute know he was going to die for you?"

The professor said nothing.

"That's how your high priest knew we were in the crowd," Joe Mac continued, a slow breath. "He knew because you told him." A nod. "Yeah, you led us into an ambush hoping we'd get killed, and then you could slip away unnoticed, and that was a mistake. And then you said that the high priest wore a red death mask."

"I knew that from the drawings."

"The drawings are in black and white. But you knew the mask was red because that's the mask you've always worn for the Wicker Man." Joe took a deep breath. "Yeah ... But your greatest mistake was that little boy."

Professor Graven muttered, "How was the boy a mistake?"

"You said that that little boy was the last one."

Silence.

"Only someone who made the list could know that that boy was the last one," Joe Mac said with a hoarse breath.

"Of course, I couldn't confirm that he was the last one. But then your imposter said the same thing. *He* confirmed it. And I knew."

A stillness joined them superimposing a silence that lasted and lasted until, finally, Professor Graven spoke solemnly.

"For a blind man ... how much you know."

Joe Mac didn't blink.

"If you were so convinced that I was this *Ri*, then why didn't you arrest me yesterday?" asked Professor Graven. "Or the day before?"

"Because you weren't my priority," whispered Joe Mac. "Saving that little boy was my priority. I wasn't gonna let him die like the others. And if I'd arrested you, or killed you, your people would have still killed him. They would have just done it in their own time." He paused for breath. "Killing you wouldn't have stopped them from doing that."

"You put your friends in great danger," Professor Graven in an accusing voice. "You care so little for them that you would risk their lives for this lunacy? They might have all died in what you fantasize is a grand conspiracy between myself and those barbarians. It is difficult for me to believe you care so little for them."

"I care enough to keep them out of this."

Professor Graven's grunt with clearly contemptuous.

"You know, of course, that no one will believe you?" Professor Graven stated very calmly. "It is a fantastic theory. And there is no one who can testify that I am the *Ri*. Also, you have no evidence. No proof. All you have is your word against mine. And you will need far more than that to level charges of kidnapping and murder."

"We'll see." Joe Mac had to shift his numb grip on the .45. "When this started, I was gonna kill you when I found you. But somewhere ... somehow ... I passed from revenge ... into justice. Now, I think spending the rest of your life in a prison will be a thousand times worse for a man like you."

Graven paused. "You're going to die tonight, detective."

Joe Mac laughed weakly.

"*I know* ..."

A car screeched to a stop outside the front of the house and someone began banging on the door. Graven didn't move and then shots thundered at the front step and there was a crashing sound. In the next moment, Joe Mac heard a familiar voice ...

* * *

"*Joe!*"

Jodi instantly raised aim at Professor Augustus Graven as she saw Joe slumped forward on a stool at the counter, blood soaking his entire body.

"Don't move!" she shouted and quickly, cautiously began to make her way across the room toward Joe, who seemed barely able to hold his head up.

His .45 was in his right hand, his forearm resting on the counter. He was breathing with deep, labored breaths and faintly lifted his face as she drew closer. Then Professor Graven hesitantly leaned to his right as if to take a small step and Jodi froze with her aim hardening on his chest; "*DON'T! MOVE!*"

The professor settled in place.

Jodi was at Joe Mac's side and she knew he was moments from death. Shifting the Glock to her left hand, she placed her right hand on his shoulder and leaned close, "Joe? We're gonna get you to an ambulance, okay? Can you hang in there for me?"

She was still watching Professor Graven with her peripheral vision and was oh-so-ready to pull the trigger if he made a move. She wasn't worried about the paperwork or even the right or wrong of it. She only knew that he was responsible for all this and – one way or another – she was going to make him pay.

"Uh!" Joe groaned and fell to the side.

Jodi twisted to catch him.

Professor Graven moved and Jodi fired following him by inches across the room as he dove over the couch. She instinctively caught Joe Mac in both arms as he pitched fully from the stool and put her back to Graven as she quickly dropped Joe Mac to the floor. Then she spun as she stood, searching with a level aim.

Jodi was ready to kill but she needed a target and the professor was nowhere to be seen. Moving quickly to the couch she glared down, her finger taking all the slack out of the trigger, her breath racing.

He wasn't there.

She backed up, scanning the second-floor balcony. She spun toward each open door primed to fire at the first shadow or silhouette. She blew out a hard breath trying to reduce the oxygen that was making her vision white and narrow.

Her brain was simultaneously calculating a dozen factors – the distance he could have traveled in that split-second; the location of the gun case; the sound a hunting rifle makes when it's loaded; the certainty that he would never surrender ...

From the floor, Joe Mac groaned, "You have to kill him ..."

"I know!"

A thunderous blast caused a huge section of wall to disintegrate in front of Jodi's face, and her first reaction was to twist away throwing her arms over her head. Then she realized it was one of the elephant rifles the professor kept in the gun chest as she dove over the couch, rolled across the floor, and reached her feet to charge through an open door.

She barely glimpsed – at the very last – the professor as he leaped into a door frame and fired another deafening round from the rifle, and then she was running full-out; the rooms were all interconnected, and Jodi fled through three before she threw herself against a wall trying to gain control of her emotions and breath.

Somewhere in the house she heard the crack of a breach viciously slammed shut and knew the professor had rapidly reloaded.

" ... *Think*! ... *He's only got two shots at a time*! ... *Make him shoot and hit him before he reloads*! ... *And get him away from Joe*! ..."

Blowing out a focused breath, Jodi bent her head ...

Listening.

She heard nothing but the echoing thunder of the elephant rifle.

In her mind, she began scanning and throwing off blueprints of the house – all she knew – calculating angles and connecting corridors and steps and doors trying to select the best place for an ambush because she was absolutely going to blow his brains out from the back of his head if she got the shot; there would no warning, no chance to surrender.

Get him away from Joe!

She visualized the closest corridor before she yelled, "I'm in here, Graven! What are you waiting for!"

Jodi launched herself into a run at the last word but barely made the corridor as the wall where she'd been standing was blasted into dust by the incomprehensibly powerful double-barreled rifle; she didn't know if Graven quick-loaded another round in the next split-second because she was charging down a cobblestone walkway that ran along the long back wall of the house.

She already knew there was nothing in this mansion that would serve as "cover." That elephant gun packed enough punch to blow a hole through a concrete wall, so blasting apart wood or marble was nothing.

The wall to her right was stone, and Jodi knew Graven had to be on the other side so she didn't worry about sound. Even he couldn't hear through a stone wall. Then she reached a pair of French doors and stopped quick to see if –

Stone exploded from the wall in front of her chest at the same second she heard the titanic eruption of the rifle, and Jodi was again running all-out along the wall as another blast tore through the space where she'd been standing. She calculated how many seconds it'd take him to reload both barrels as –

She dropped to her knees raising arms over her head.

Jodi didn't know why she ducked, but she did as the granite above her head was vaporized by two near-simultaneous blasts. Then she threw herself forward knowing even Graven couldn't reload *that* fast; she chose to bypass the French doors, and then the only place to go was a door that led back into the house; she charged through it expecting a bedroom but it was a library and she kept running.

She needed distance. She needed time to think. Time to set up. Time to find the right angle and wait for Graven to come around the corner so she could hit before he could acquire her as a target. But as she went through the next door she stopped.

It was a bathroom.

Jodi spun.

A shadow was approaching along the outside walkway; she saw it along the cobblestones at the base of the frame. She whirled in every direction, searching.

A previously unseen door came into focus on her left and Jodi quietly moved to it. She gritted her teeth as she turned the knob, and as a rifle barrel moved into the entrance she silently slipped through, closing the door.

She was inside the house again and knew this hall connected to four rooms on her left. If she moved to the right she would be adjacent in the kitchen. If she moved through the kitchen she'd be back in the front room. If she …

For god's sake just move!

She crept down the hall and stepped into the third room on her left. She didn't pick the first room because it wouldn't give her enough time to acquire Graven as a target if he was in her tracks; she needed more time to take a solid aim.

Inside the door she dropped into a crouch, switching the Glock to her left hand. Then she laid the slide against the frame for a bench rest, closing her right eye. When Graven emerged from the door of the library, she had a clear line of sight, a clear shot. She'd put one round in his chest, run, call for backup and let him bleed out.

Jodi stilled her breathing. Then she remembered that Graven wasn't only a famous African butcher, he also had trigger time in Vietnam, and so he was no fool. He might very well anticipate an ambush like this and retreat to come at her from another angle.

She waited …

The door didn't open.

Her eyes darted left searching for any shadow that could be coming up on her from her blind side but saw nothing. Then, very warily, she lowered her head to look down the hall that led toward the front of the house.

If Graven –

She screamed as a bullet exploded from the wall.

Jodi didn't know she was on her back until she rolled into the hall and frantically began scrambling backwards. Then she flipped to her feet and began running, ignoring the commotion she was making with screaming and smashing into tables and portraits and everything else that served as high-priced décor for the mansion.

She didn't have to think about it: Graven had fired straight into the wall from the library and the bullet had smashed a hole through that wall and every other wall in front of it and probably exited through the brick exterior at the driveway and kept traveling even beyond that until it hit a tree that might have finally stopped the buffalo round. And he had very intelligently aimed so that bullet had skirted the inside wall – the very place she'd taken for the ambush. But Jodi had been on her knees – something he *didn't* anticipate – and the round had only brushed her hair as it ripped past her head.

She couldn't help visualizing what would have happened if she'd been hit; they'd have to bury her in a soup can.

She waited, her back against the kitchen wall. She was trying to listen but the blood in her ears and her heart thundering in her chest was all she heard. She blinked, trying to focus, but that didn't work either. She was hot, hot, *hot* and swept sweat from her face as she glimpsed a shadow move on the face nail flooring outside the kitchen.

The shadow fell across the threshold.

Jodi lifted the Glock and began firing through the wall to the left of the entrance. She fired a full clip and then frantically leaped to the side as Graven surged into the entrance with the rifle already level at his hip.

She charged through another doorway as Graven pulled the trigger and the kitchen was filled wall to wall and ceiling to floor with a muzzle blast that replicated the detonation of a stick of dynamite. But it was something Jodi sensed and didn't see because she had hurtled a couch. Still running, she knocked over a chair and rebounded off a table as a second shot disintegrated a marble statue at her side.

Her thoughts were coming too fast for conscious terror but she realized she was almost out of places to run and then she saw what had to be the garage door; she ripped it open and leaped past the steps to land on the smooth cement floor as she saw a second stairway that rose along the opposite wall.

It connected to the second floor – it had to. There was no other place it could go, and she was going to take it because there was no other place she could go, either. She swung around the rail and charged upward only to smash into the door.

It was locked.

Jodi took one step back and fired three rounds through the lock, then threw her shoulder into it; the door was blasted open and she was through. She slammed it but knew she had to move fast because now Graven knew exactly where she stood and he'd be maneuvering to fire straight up through the floor to quite literally blow her to pieces.

But then – with a control that shocked even herself – Jodi began *easing* down the hallway. She was barely lifting her feet – not even raising them a fraction of an inch – and trying to orient her position to the bottom floor layout.

She knew she had to be between the library and the kitchen, and Graven's last shot had come from the door leading into the kitchen, she aimed the Glock at the floor. If he shot up, she was shooting down. Although the nine millimeter Glock wouldn't smash a hole through a stone wall it would still go through a sheet of plywood.

Suddenly a devastating wave of exhaustion washed over her, and she eased her back against the wall abruptly afraid she was going to faint; she closed her eyes tight, concentrating on all her horrifying fear to keep herself alert and energized. Sweat was dripping from her nose and lips and she shook her head to throw perspiration from her face but it wasn't enough. She quickly swept her right forearm down her face trying to clear away the sweat burning her eyes blind with every blink.

Where is he!

In an even more vividly alarming moment Jodi thought that Graven might have gone back to the front room where Joe was lying helplessly on the floor. But in the same instant she knew he hadn't.

No, now he was in this for the kill. This was a hunt to him, and he was a hunter. Whether Graven was aware of it or not, he was following his insatiable instinct to hunt her down and kill her the same way he hunted and killed any other endangered species.

Swallowing, Jodi realized that Graven had every advantage.

He had incommensurately superior firepower. He knew the layout of this house far better than she did. He was a world-class hunter and experienced at stalking and killing the most dangerous game. He even had more experience at killing *people*. And despite his age he seemed to have lost none of the killer instinct or skill that had seen him alive through war and hunting and murder after murder …

Grimacing, Jodi raised the Glock with both hands wrapped around the grip and she pressed the barrel to her forehead; she was horrified that the very drops of sweat falling from her face and hands would give away her position.

Jodi knew in her soul that this paralyzing fear was defeating her, and she was going to die because she was too afraid to do what she had to do, and that's why she was going to die because she was too afraid …

She closed her eyes as tears fell …

"Come on, Joe," she silently cried. *"Talk to me …"*

An old blind man … in her mind …

"… Listen up, kid … If it gets bad – and it will – you go straight into it … Don't ever run from it … Not ever … If he charges at you, you charge at him … If you're gonna die, you get it in your head that, by God, he's gonna die, too … And you stick that in your mind because your mindset is gonna be worth more than all the training in the world …"

Jodi opened her eyes.

With a frown she ejected the half-spent clip from the Glock and slid in a fresh one with seventeen full rounds. She stuck the used magazine in her back pocket. Then she gripped the Glock tight in her right hand and turned to walk straight down the hall. She would have a clear view of the front room in seven steps. She angled to the left side of the corridor so she could fully extend her right arm and the Glock.

She emerged onto the open balcony.

Professor Graven was crouching at a distant doorway holding the double-barreled rifle close and Jodi didn't give a warning. She began shooting on sight and rapid-fired a full clip from the Glock; the shots were so tight it was like machinegun fire.

Graven howled, twisting and raging at the impacts, before he staggered through the open door and then Jodi reached the front staircase. She vaulted the last of the railing and hit the stairs once before landing on the first floor, instantly changing magazines.

She moved forward holding the Glock high for a fast first shot. If Graven stepped out she would unload a full clip into him before he could even acquire aim.

"Drop it!" the professor screamed.

Jodi spun, instantly falling into a crouch, her aim dead steady on an open door.

The voice had emerged from an unseen room; the professor wasn't visible. For a flashing split-second Jodi considered firing through the wall beside the frame but something caused her to hesitate and then a rifle barrel began to protrude from the opening.

The barrel was aimed at Joe Mac.

Professor Graven limped from the frame and he was holding an aim solidly on Joe Mac. He didn't remove his eyes from Joe Mac as he repeated his command, "I said drop the weapon, Detective Strong!"

In the moment, Jodi saw that she had hit him at least five times with the Glock – his arm and both legs were covered in blood – but they weren't mortal wounds; he would eventually die, yeah, but he wasn't dying anywhere near fast enough.

"*Kill him!*" gasped Joe Mac.

Teeth clenched, Jodi didn't look at Joe Mac; she didn't have to. She focused on Professor Graven's right hand and saw that his finger was on the trigger of the elephant rifle. She glanced along the barrel and saw that there was no trembling, no fear, no doubt; he would pull the trigger, and Jodi knew he wouldn't miss.

Although there was only faint chance that Joe Mac would survive his present injuries, there was still a chance. But if Graven pulled that trigger, it was over. Joe Mac wouldn't survive even one round from the hunting rifle.

"I won't tell you again," said Professor Graven in a shaken voice.

His hold shifted on the rifle.

Jodi tossed the Glock to the floor.

"It's down!"

Finally, Professor Graven turned his gaze from Joe Mac to focus on her and swung the aim of the rifle toward her chest. His mouth was a bitter line of disappointment. Or perhaps it was frustration.

"Both of you have interfered in something that is quite beyond you," he stated with bizarre formality. "You haven't saved the child. The child will still die. Not today, no, but he will die." A pause. "There is nothing you can do to stop a power that conquered nations before nations were even born."

He shook his head as he could not believe their arrogance.

"*Fools*," he muttered. "Your god only rules sheep that I've sacrificed to the *Wicker Man* my entire life." A sneer. "If your god loved you, he would protect you. But he doesn't protect you! Look at you! All of you!" He took a labored breath. "All of you will be led away like sheep to the *slaughter*."

Jodi defiantly muttered, "So why are you so afraid of the child?"

"Because he's not a child! He's a god! But he's a defeated god! Rome defeated him last time but we will defeat him this time! *You* and your friends are testimony to that! Yes! His kingdom was for a day when Rome hung him from that tree! And it will be even less when we do the same!"

Sirens in the distance …

Closing.

"You hear that?" whispered Jodi. "It's over, professor. They know. That's why they're coming. Are you going to kill a cop? Do you know what they'll do to you? Or do you plan to talk your way out of two dead police officers on your floor?"

Professor Graven's gaze angled high and to the side as if he could see the approaching patrol cars. They were closing fast and Jodi estimated one minute before they stormed through the door; it wouldn't matter if the professor still held them captive. After the bloodbath in the cavern, they wouldn't waste more than a second on negotiations. If Graven didn't give them the answer they wanted, they were coming in, and Brightbarton would be leading from the front in no mood to take prisoners.

Jodi smiled, "You're out of time, professor. It doesn't matter now whether you kill us or not. It's over. You lose."

Professor Graven's lips drew back in a snarl. He raised the stock of the rifle to his shoulder and aimed dead at Joe Mac.

"So do you!"

It was a flicker of black that caught Jodi's attention and then the sunrise beyond the great picture window at the back vanished behind a wall of black and the glass was blasted into shining white shards sent spinning across the room. The shrieks of a thousand ravens and crows fairly lifted the entire house into the sky as flashing jet-black forms flooded through the broken window filling the entire room.

With a shout Professor Graven lifted the rifle and fired a single impotent round into the lethal slicing sea of lightning-fast predators who were instantly cutting him from head to toe and then he raised both arms over his head howling.

Jodi was frozen in that split-second but she saw Joe Mac rise on his knees, his right arm extended, the .45 in his hand. His teeth came together with a supreme expression of determination as he fired a single round and the professor bellowed as he brought the rifle down also firing a single round.

Both fell to the floor.

"*GOD!*" cried Jodi and ran forward ignoring the black bolts of fury slashing through the air with immeasurable rage. She reached Joe Mac and dropped to his side, rolling him on his back; it took only a glance to know he was dead.

"Oh, no, no, no, no …."

She was aware of nothing else.

Then, slowly, she became conscious of the flood of black birds of prey flying toward the broken window. In another moment the room was empty, and she saw Joe Mac's .45 on the floor slightly beyond his hand.

Numbly she lifted it, and stood.

Uncountable patrol cars skidded to a stop outside the house, surrounding it. One second later Jodi heard Brightbarton shouting through a megaphone.

"*Professor Graven!* You are ordered to step outside!"

With an enraged groan Graven rose from the floor. He had an arm wrapped around bloody ribs; Joe Mac had hit him but not killed him. Graven would live, and he turned his face to the shattered window. Then he focused steadily on Jodi, and grinned, "I am unarmed, detective. And now I'll go to court and you can't prove a thing! It looks like I won't die today after all!"

Tears fell, and Jodi slowly lifted her gaze to Poe who was staring upon her, unmoving, from the mantle.

Poe didn't blink.

"Professor?" Jodi whispered.

Graven hesitated. "Yes?"

"Do you know why God sends a raven?"

A long hesitation as more sirens closed.

Graven frowned, "Because a raven means death?"

"Death is just a beginning," Jodi said quietly. "God sends a raven because he wants you to repent before …"

Silence lasted between them as Graven swayed, and an anger began to visibly build … and build. He bared his teeth, pushed himself away from the wall, and stood glaring with fingers hooked like talons.

"*Say it!*" he cried. "*Before what!*"

Jodi raised the .45 and fired.

She watched as Professor Graven's body fell back, his forehead leaving a bloody trail in the smoking air; he hit the floor hard and didn't move again as thunder rolled into the crimson dawn. Gazing down, Jodi lowered the gun.

"Judgment."

Head bent, Jodi turned to Joe Mac lying on his back, so still, and movement caught her eye. She lifted her face as Poe soared without sound from the mantle, wings spread wide as he settled on Joe Mac's chest.

Poe stretched out his magnificent wings, lowered his head to Joe Mac's face, and draped both wings over Joe Mac's head as if to comfort him … and receive him. And he remained like that with his head bowed, wings embracing, for a long time. Then Poe raised his face and with a single move rose into the air to soar silently through the shattered window.

And was gone …

Jodi sighed, then slowly crossed the room walking toward the open front door, and when she emerged into the light she saw Brightbarton standing with the megaphone in his hand and police armed with shotguns and rifles. As she reached the patrol cars Brightbarton stepped out. For a long moment he stared over her face, and then he grimaced.

"Joe?" he asked.

Jodi shook her head and Brightbarton lifted his face toward the mansion. He stood staring, and then he nodded and gazed down into Jodi's face once more.

"Now you own it, kid," he said.

Wiping away a tear, Jodi walked past him and down the long road, head bowed, gun hanging in her hand, as a great shadow darkened the whole world behind her, and the shadow descended … and descended … and descended until …

The raven settled softly on her shoulder.

THE END

*For More News About James Byron
Huggins, Signup For Our Newsletter:*

http://wbp.bz/newsletter

*Word-of-mouth is critical to an author's long-
term success. If you appreciated this book please
leave a review on the Amazon sales page:*

http://wbp.bz/darkvisionsa

INTERNATIONAL BESTSELLING AUTHOR

JAMES BYRON HUGGINS

"Pure entertainment"—Publishers Weekly

SECOND EDITION

HUNTER by JAMES BYRON HUGGINS

http://wbp.bz/huntera

Read A Sample Next

CHAPTER 1

"Vicious little beasts, aren't they?"

The words, spoken with ominous disaster, came from a white-haired old man in a white lab coat. Seated patiently, he watched as a host of red army ants, some as large as his thumb, attacked what he had dispassionately dropped into the aquarium. The ants overwhelmed the rat in seconds, killing it almost instantly with venom, then devouring it. In three minutes a haggard skeleton was all that remained.

Dr. Angus Tipler clicked a stopwatch, staring down. "Yes," he frowned, "utterly vicious."

He turned to others in the laboratory of the Tipler Institute, the leading crypto-zoological foundation in the world. His face portrayed consternation. "What are we to do with them?" he asked, almost to himself. "They kill with venom long before they dismember their prey." He looked back. "Yes, and so we must therefore devise some type of ... serum, if for no other reason so that people will stop bothering us all the time. Has anyone concluded the molecular weight of the poison?"

A woman bent over an enormous electron microscope positioned neatly in the center of the room muttered in reply. "Not yet, Doctor. I need another minute."

Dr. Tipler said nothing as he turned back to the aquarium where the ants were safely—very safely—contained. The rest of the laboratory was filled with virtually every poisonous animal in the world, insect and mammal and reptile. There were black scorpions, Indian cobras, adders and stonefish, brown recluse spiders and the lethal Sydney funnel web, the most dangerous spider in the world. A single unfelt bite from the tiny arachnid would kill a full-grown man within a day. It was Tipler himself who had created the anti-venom.

"It seems this venom is neuromuscular in nature," he said in a raspy, harsh voice into a recorder. He waved off the video technician who had recorded the grisly episode. "The venom, no matter the location of injection, seems to infiltrate the ligamentum denticulatum, thereby bridging the pons Varolii to decussate the involuntary respiratory abilities of the medulla oblongata. Now, if we can—"

"Dr. Tipler?"

Tipler raised bushy white eyebrows as he turned, seeing a young woman scientist with long black hair. The Asian woman was obviously apprehensive at the intrusion, despite the old man's well-known patient nature.

"Yes, Gina?" His voice was gentle. "What is it?"

"There are some men to see you, sir."

Tipler laughed, waving a hand as he turned away. "There are always men to see me, lass. Tell them to wait. The commissary should still be open. They serve an excellent roast chicken. It is my best recommendation."

"I don't think these men will wait, sir." She stepped closer, lowering her voice. Her eyes widened slightly. "There are three of them, and they're wearing uniforms."

Tipler barked a short laugh. "Uniforms! What sort of uniforms?"

"Army uniforms, sir."

Tipler laughed again and shook his head as he rose. "All right, Gina. Assist Rebecca in discovering the molecular weight of this venom. And, also, if you would be so kind, extract venom from, oh ... let's say fifty of these infernal creatures. Just sedate them with chloroform and use the electroshock method—the same procedure we use for the black widows." He removed his glasses with a sigh and stood up. "And I will deal with these impatient men in uniforms."

"Yes, sir. They're waiting in the observation room."

"Thank you, lass."

Upon seeing the three, Dr. Tipler stopped short. He had been told often enough that, upon first impression, he was not an imposing figure, so he had no illusions. At seventy-two years of age he was short and thick with a wide brow and snowy hair laid back from the forehead. But he knew that his eyes, blue like Arctic ice, distinguished him from other men both with their startling color and their equally startling intelligence. And equally their quickness to perceive the heart of a mystery. And it was that perceptiveness, a blending of art, science and intuition that had made the world's eminent paleontologist and crypto-zoologist.

Crypto-zoology was in itself an almost unknown area of biological expertise. Fewer than a dozen distinguished scientists in the world practiced it with any measure of dedication. And, for the most part, few scientists realized that it was practiced at all. But, in essence, it was a systematic and highly rigid system of investigation designed to determine whether species thought to be extinct still inhabited the planet.

Tipler had known significant success in various stages of his career, discovering the last surviving Atacama condors in the Andes Mountains of Chile in 1983, and later discovering a species identified as the blind stone-fish, off the northern coast of Greenland. The deep-water fish had been thought extinct since the Paleolithic Period, but Tipler had pieced together a theory that they still existed in the south-flowing East Greenland Current, which drew directly from the Arctic Sea. He held even further suspicions that the fish existed higher in the Arctic Circle, protected by the vast ice caps of the pole. But a lack of funding had prevented further exploration.

However, his startling discoveries had earned him a modest measure of global recognition, which consequently delivered the attention of several wealthy philanthropists who deemed his unique nonprofit enterprise worthy of endorsement. So, with significant funding and a larger, better-trained staff, he had founded the Tipler Institute. Now, a decade later, he was recognized universally as the world's leading expert on unknown species, and their extinction or survival. Along the way he had also gained significant exposure to deadly snakes, fish, and spiders and discovered, to his own surprise, that he had a remarkable acumen for pinpointing the molecular characteristics of each type of venom.

Studying venom was, at first, simply a means of aiding those few medical institutions already overwhelmed trying to keep apace with the new strains of poison. But through a working relationship with the Centers for Disease Control, Tipler also joined the crusade, synthesizing over a dozen effective anti-venoms over the past decade. Nor did he find it distracting. Although he was an increasingly sought-after author, lecturer, and researcher, his greatest pleasure remained the simple pursuit of biological science.

From time to time, however, agencies not academic had sought his aid. And he had assisted. Once the Central Intelligence Agency had requested that he do what their physicists could not; develop a counteracting agent for a deadly poison in use by Middle Eastern countries. Tipler had succeeded and consequently heard no more of it. And last, the U.S. Army had asked him, rather sternly, if he could not identify a substance in their own anti-germ warfare serums that tended to incapacitate soldiers. In this, too, Tipler was successful, and modifications were made in the synthesis of the serums. Again, he heard no more of it. Yet he knew they would return, as they had.

A thin smile creased his squared face.

Before him, he knew from his World War II days as an infantryman, was an army lieutenant colonel, whose rank he identified from the silver oak leaves on his uniform. There was another man in uniform, a major, and an unknown representative who wore nondescript civilian clothes. But, as always, it was the man in civilian clothes who commanded

Tipler's attention, for he was accustomed to subterfuge. Tipler greeted them as the man in the rear silently lit a cigarette, settling into a chair.

"Dr. Tipler, I'm Lieutenant Colonel Bob Maddox," the short, gray-haired man said distinctly. "This is Major Preston Westcott. And that "— the colonel gestured vaguely—" is Mr. Dixon. He's a liaison with the Department of the Interior."

Tipler smiled as he weighed the colonel; the army officer carried himself with an air of indisputable authority, as if his self-worth relied upon his rank. His insignia were so highly polished they couldn't be overlooked, even by civilians. His face was slightly pudgy and his stomach strained against his uniform. He held his hands behind his back as he spoke. "Thank you for seeing us on such short notice, Doctor. I assure you that we won't take up too much of your time."

Something in the voice intimated to Dr. Tipler that he had no choice in the matter, but he revealed nothing as he moved to sit at a table directly opposite the mysterious Mr. Dixon. "Oh, I am always ready to assist the military, Colonel," he said with exacting courtesy. "In fact, as you are probably aware, I just finished working with an army research team to design new protocols for Arctic survival. So please, continue."

Maddox was obviously in charge, Tipler realized, and Prescott was present to verify the meeting or take mental notes. He hadn't yet concluded a purpose for Dixon.

"That's part of the reason we're here—your experience in the Arctic. We also understand that you're the world's leading authority on crypto-zoology." Maddox strolled before the table. "So we hoped you'd be able to help us with ... a situation."

Tipler decided to play their game for now. He did not look at Mr. Dixon. "Perhaps," he replied casually.

Clearly, Maddox was proceeding with caution. "Doctor, we would like to ask you some questions about species of predators found in the Arctic Circle. Specifically, species that inhabit the deep interior of Alaska and the North Face region." He stepped forward, almost delicately. "Recently we lost several members of an elite military training squad to an animal. They were killed. And we want to determine what manner of animal it was."

Tipler absorbed it without expression.

"Surely," Tipler said finally, "Alaskan wildlife officials can be of more use to you than an old gaffer such as myself. And I am not certain in what aspect my credentials in crypto-zoology are related. Crypto-zoology is the study of animals long presumed to be extinct but which are, in fact, not. Such as some of the marine reptiles like the one the Japanese fishing vessel, the Zuiyo Mam, snagged on a line nine hundred feet below the surface of the Pacific near Christchurch, New Zealand, in 1977. Or," Tipler could not resist adding, "perhaps like the beast of unknown species that attacked the U.S.S. Stern in the early 'eighties, disabling its sonar system with hundreds of teeth driven deeply in the steel. It was documented with the Department of the Navy and the ship was examined by the Naval Oceans Center. They reached the fascinating conclusion that damage to the sonar was caused by the attack of a large and unknown ocean-dwelling species."

Maddox stood in silence. His face tightened. "Yes, Doctor. We are aware of those incidents. It is certainly verification of...something. But those cases are not why we have come."

"I presumed." Tipler smiled. "So, shall we get to the reason? I am a bit overwhelmed by my work."

Gravely, even apprehensively, Maddox laid a gory series of full-sized color photographs on the table. And Tipler precisely set glasses on his nose, leaning on broad hands to examine them. So total was his concentration, it was as if, in seconds, he had physically removed himself from the room.

The old man made no sound as he studied the photographs, but his brow hardened frame by frame. His lips pursed slightly and he began to take more time with each, returning often to the first, beginning over. Finally he lifted a single eight-by-ten and studied it inches from his face, peering at the details. "Colonel," he said, casting a slow gaze over the massacred bodies. "These wounds, were they all inflicted by the same creature?"

There was no hesitation. "Yes."

"You are certain of this?"

"Yes, Doctor, we are certain."

"And how can you be certain? In science, certainty is determined by exceedingly strict criteria."

Maddox grimaced slightly. "There were obscured video images. Nothing too revealing, but it gave us glimpses of whatever this was. We couldn't make out the species. And, despite what I said earlier, we can't be, uh, absolutely certain on whether it was one or two of them. It's just that the evidence, except for some of these photographs, seems to indicate that."

Without reply, Tipler shifted several of the photographs of massacred soldiers until he had the most vivid, the ghastliest. He placed a hand on it and touched the image of wounds as delicately as if the soldier were before him. Finally, he mumbled, "This is not the work of Ursus arctos horribilis."

Clearly, Maddox was trying to be patient. "Could you be more specific, Doctor?"

"This is not the work of a ... a Grizzly." Tipler was again staring at the photo he had lifted, a close-up image of tracks leading across hard sand. The elongated footprints moved in a straight run down a strand to disappear in the distance, but some of the tracks were disjointed, as far as three feet to the side. It was not a straight line of tracks, though clearly the creature had been running straight. Rocks littered the stream.

"Now ... " the old man continued in a genuine tone of confusion, "this is somewhat curious."

"What?" Maddox asked.

"The way that the tracks are broken."

"That's what our own trackers said, Doctor. I mean, despite the cameras, we want to know about this. Do you think there could be two of them?"

Tipler took a long time to consider. "I am not an expert in tracking, Colonel Maddox. I cannot say. But I do not think that there were two creatures involved in this ... this catastrophe."

"Then how do you explain the way some tracks are so far to the side from others?"

"As I said, sir, I cannot explain such a phenomenon."

Maddox concentrated. "You're certain this isn't the work of a Grizzly, Doctor? Or maybe a polar bear? A tiger, maybe?"

"No, not a Grizzly, nor a brown bear," the professor expounded in a low tone. "For one matter, a Grizzly has five claws. And whatever did this had four predominant claws, and a smaller one. But the paw print is distinctly ...humanoid. Now this," he paused, "is damn peculiar." A long silence lengthened. "No, gentlemen, not a bear of any kind. Perhaps a tiger could have caused this much carnage to your team, but the tracks are ... just ... they just appear to me to be somewhat too manlike. In fact, far too manlike."

"But clearly no human being could do something like this, Doctor." Dixon spoke for the first time.

Tipler raised his eyes, gazing over bifocals. "I would not make a determination of any fact until I had obtained the information necessary to make the determination of that fact, Mr. Dixon." He smiled. "That is the discipline of science."

Dixon leaned back, smoked in silence.

The army officials were, indeed, leaning forward as Tipler raised a magnifying glass from his pocket, studying the photograph more closely. Finally he lowered it with the glass, but continued to stare profoundly. His voice was quiet. "These tracks ... how far did your men follow them, gentlemen?"

"Why?" Maddox asked.

"Because they do not 'register.' "

"Register?" the colonel asked. "What does that mean?"

"They ... they are not in line." The scientist gestured. "A tiger, which is the only terrestrial beast that could have struck with such fury, registers when it walks or runs. Which is to say that both paws on the left side are in a line, as they are on the right. There should be two paw prints set closely together, in a straight line, left side and right side. And, clearly, they are not the tracks of a Grizzly, though they resemble one in size."

"Yes," Maddox said. "Our military trackers told us that. But they lost the trail when it moved to high ground. They said no one can track across rock. This animal seemed to know it was being hunted."

"Most creatures are more intelligent than we presume, Colonel," Tipler replied, casting a narrow glance at Dixon, who was smoking quietly. "No," Tipler added finally. "It was not a tiger. The fury of the attack is commensurate with a tiger, but it is not feline or canine. Nor is a larger species of Ursus. No. Whatever did this ... was distinctly bipedal."

They waited, but the old man merely placed his glasses back in his lab coat pocket. Then he bridged his fingers, capping them, allowing them to continue the conversation.

"Bipedal?" Dixon asked without friendliness. "Does that mean what I think it means?"

"Quite probably," Tipler smiled. "It means that whatever killed your men walks on two legs, Mr. Dixon."

"That's preposterous." Dixon leaned back again. "Humans are the only animal that walks on two legs, Doctor. What do you suggest left these tracks? Bigfoot? This thing must have been registering! It's just that the tracks are too difficult to read."

"Difficult, yes," Tipler scowled. "But not impossible. Is that why you called me here? Because your men have already told you that they know of no creature that could have done this? And now you wish to know if, perhaps, there is an undiscovered species?"

"To be honest, I'll admit it occurred to us," Maddox replied. "And let me add that this is a situation of some seriousness, Doctor. We've got dead soldiers near secure facilities and we want to know how they died. We want to know why they died."

Tipler gazed over the photos of carnage. "I cannot give you the answer, gentlemen," he said finally. "There were species of beasts that are presumed to have been exterminated hundreds of thousands of years ago, yet we still find evidence of their continuing existence. But I am not familiar with this paw print, or footprint." He paused and strolled a short distance away before turning back. "In order to answer your question—to even attempt to answer your question—we would need a scientific expedition, saliva samples, blood samples, plaster casts of the prints, hair samples, video surveillance records. If you are willing to fund an expedi-"

"We can't do that." Dixon stood up. "There are factors which preclude that option. We just wanted your best opinion, Doctor." He paused for effect. "We still do."

Tipler held the stare.

"My best opinion, Mr. Dixon, is that whatever did this has the strength of a Grizzly, the speed of a Siberian tiger and, quite probably, the stalking skills of a tiger. Which happens to be the most skilled predator on Earth. Further, if it managed to evade the initial pursuit of your military, I would confidently surmise that it has unnatural intelligence."

"So," Maddox asked, asserting some kind of vague authority, "what do you think it is? I want your best guess."

Tipler sighed once more and glanced at a photo of the tracks. "Your best guess will be revealed by these tracks,

Mr. Dixon. But I don't understand why some of them"—he pointed at several—"are so far to the left of these others. It makes no sense that I can see."

They exchanged glances as the old man stared over them. Then, after a moment, they began wordlessly gathering papers.

"Will you be hunting this beast again?" the scientist asked, interested.

"Yes," Maddox replied solidly. "We will."

"Then I suggest you find a man who can possibly track it," said Tipler.

He hesitated, as if scientific passion and personal loyalty were competing with something more hidden, staring at the photograph.

"I know the man," he said softly, "who could do this? If anyone could. But I do not know if he will cooperate. He has his own reasons ... for why he does things."

Maddox stepped forward. "Who is he?"

Tipler stared slightly to the side, brow furrowed.

"His name," he said finally, "is Nathaniel Hunter."

CHAPTER 2

The sunset breeze carried a sweet tang of mountain laurel. Nathaniel Hunter was emptying his simple leather pack onto the table. The door of his cabin was wide open, allowing the green sound of rushing water to move over him. And yet it wasn't sound, but a sudden silence, that made him lift his head.

Where there had been a communicative chorus of bird surrounding his backwoods home, there was now an unnatural quiet. He turned to stare out the door, listened, and heard a car coming slowly up the one-lane dirt road. It was still a mile away.

It took them more than ten minutes to arrive. He met them on the porch wearing old blue jeans, a leather shirt, and knee-high moccasins.

One of the contingent—a portly army colonel—spoke first. But it was the man in civilian clothes, standing in the rear that drew Hunter's sullen attention. Quiet but close, the man was dressed in a suit you would have forgotten without even trying, and dark sunglasses protected his eyes from any probing. Hands clasped behind him, he followed the others like a schoolteacher ensuring that the students perform the assigned task. It was clear who was truly in charge.

"I am Lieutenant Colonel Maddox of the United States Army," said the man in uniform. "We would like to speak with Nathaniel Hunter, if that's possible."

"I'm Hunter," he said, his voice low.

"Well." The colonel stepped forward, an ingratiating smile on his lips.

"We'd just like to get your opinion on some photographs, if you don't mind. Of course, if there is a problem, we can arrange a more formal appointment."

Hunter took his time before turning toward the door, motioning vaguely. "Come into the cabin," he said.

It took only a few minutes for them to recount their story of blood and death in the snow. Then they displayed a series of photographs on the cabin's crude wooden table. They wanted his best guess as to what the killer was, they said, and they wanted to know if there was more than one of them. Hunter bent over the photographs and studied them for a moment. His eyes narrowed as he examined the tracks, as well as the terrain.

Maddox began, "We want to know why these tracks here are so far from the others."

"Wind," Hunter said simply.

Hunter heard the man introduced as Dixon step forward. But Maddox only stared as he said, "Excuse me, did you say 'wind'?"

"Yeah." Hunter had expected this confusion. "These tracks to the side were in a straight line with these others. But the wind moved them, inch by inch. The other tracks weren't moved because they were shielded from the northeastern breeze by this boulder."

Maddox seemed astounded. "Wind can do that?"

Hunter pointed to the tracks. "These to the side were originally over here, like the others. You can see the gap that was left when they were moved. The wind just edged them to where they are here." He shrugged, gave the picture to Maddox. "It's a common phenomenon on sand like this. Is that what you wanted to know?"

"Uh." Maddox started. "Uh, actually, no. We wanted you to—"

A sudden, silent atmospheric change in the cabin stopped him short. It was as if the room had been instantly charged with a primal force, something utterly savage. Hunter watched as Maddox slowly turned his head. He almost smiled at the nervous expression on Dixon's face as he began to sense what was behind him. Slowly, moving only his head, Dixon managed to look down stiffly. Hunter saw sweat glisten suddenly on his forehead.

Massive and menacing, Ghost stood less than a foot behind Dixon and Maddox, slightly to the side. The gigantic wolf was almost entirely black, touched with gray only on his flanks.

Ghost's jet-black eyes seemed to possess a primal and predatory glow. Black claws clicked on the wooden floor as he took a single pace forward, head low, again unmoving. Ghost's uncanny silence seemed more terrifying than a roar.

Hunter made them suffer for only a moment. With a slight smile he snapped his fingers.

"Ghost," he said.

The wolf glided innocently through the men and sat beside Hunter.

Hunter spoke politely. "You were saying, Colonel?"

Maddox had trouble speaking. "I, uh, I was saying that... uh, we wanted you to help us with ... with ... something."

Hunter smiled at the trembling tone and noticed that Major Prescott's fists were clenched. All of them were sweating, and Maddox's face was pasty, whitening by the moment. He knew this would take all day with Ghost in the room. He looked down, speaking so low that none of the others could catch the word.

"Outside," he said.

Treading with an air of shocking animal might, the wolf moved fearlessly through the three of them. Then it reached the door and angled away, disappearing with haunting silence and grace. The air silently trembled with the wildness, the power, the very scent of it as it was gone. But Hunter knew Ghost would remain close, just as he knew they wouldn't see the wolf again—not ever—unless it wanted them to.

"Good Lord," whispered Maddox as he took out a handkerchief, wiping his face. "Is that ... is that your dog?"

"He's a wolf."

"Yes ... yes, of course." The colonel cast a nervous eye to the doorway and involuntarily backed up. "But ... but what does it do?"

Hunter stared, almost laughed, but suppressed it; there was no need to mock them, even incidentally. They weren't at home in his world, though he had managed to become both prosperous and respected in theirs. He added, "He does whatever he wants to do, I guess. He comes, he goes."

"I mean, do you own him?" Maddox added. "Is he trained? Does he always come and go like that?" All three of the men had repositioned themselves so they could keep an eye on the door.

Hunter half-shrugged. "No, he's not trained, Colonel. And nobody owns him. He comes when he wants. Goes when he wants."

"But ... but how much does the thing weigh?" Maddox asked. "I didn't think wolves got so ... so huge."

"That depends on bloodline," Hunter answered, continuing to unpack. "Most male wolves go a hundred or so. Ghost is about a hundred and fifty, more or less. He won't get much bigger."

Maddox began to recover degree by degree and Hunter tried to move it along. He knew they were still dancing around the central issue. He continued quietly. "Now, gentlemen, if you're ready to talk, maybe we can get down to why you wanted to see me. What do you want?"

Fortifying himself, Maddox stepped forward. He pointed at the photographs of slaughtered soldiers.

"We want to know," Maddox said in a stronger tone, "what kind of creature could have done this? What kind of creature could have walked through an entire platoon like this, killing such heavily armed men?"

Frowning slightly, Hunter shifted the photos and finally shook his head. "Maybe a Grizzly," he muttered, but with obvious uncertainty. "But I doubt it."

"Why do you doubt it?"

"Because a Grizzly will usually maul its victim," Hunter answered, more certain. "It'll hit over and over, tear off your scalp, your face. And whatever did this struck once, maybe twice, with each kill." He pointed at a photo. "This man was killed with one blow. So whatever did this didn't attack out of fear or rage." He paused, eyes narrowing. "Whatever did this ...had a reason."

Get the book at: **wbp.bz/huntera**

ONE
Westchester, New York

"Is he dead?"

Father Stanford Aquanine D'Oncetta shook his head patiently as he casually removed a cigar from the darkly-illuminated Savinelli humidor.

"No, Robert, he is not dead," replied D'Oncetta calmly. "But there is no need for emotion. He will be dead soon enough."

"Not soon enough for me."

Stately and imperious, D'Oncetta laughed. Drawing steadily upon a vigilance candle to light his cigar, the priest leaned back against a mahogany desk, slowly releasing a stream of pale blue smoke.

Separated from D'Oncetta by the length of the library, Robert Milburn regarded the priest in the dim light. Reluctantly impressed by D'Oncetta's authoritative appearance, Milburn noted the deeply tanned hands and face of a man who had actually spent little of his life in dark confessionals or chapels.

The face of this man commanded true power and feared nothing at all.

Above the clerical collar and the black, finely tailored robe, D'Oncetta's straight white hair laid back smoothly from his low forehead, lending him the demeanor of an elder statesman. Everything about the priest was richly impressive, dignified, cultured and refined - an investment banker wearing the robe of a holy father.

"What are you so afraid of, Robert?" D'Oncetta laughed in his voice of quiet authority, a voice accustomed to controlling and persuading. "How many men is it that you have stationed outside?"

"Eleven." Milburn met D'Oncetta's steady gaze.

"And is that not enough to guard a single, isolated mansion in Westchester, especially with the noble assistance of New York's vaunted police force that even now has a priority patrol on surrounding streets?"

D'Oncetta smiled reassuringly and exhaled again, savoring. Then he looked down at the cigar, turning it in his fingers with familiar approval.

"A Davidoff," he remarked fondly. "Rich and complex. Always the result of superior breeding. And it's not even Cuban, as one might presume, but a product of the Dominican Republic."

D'Oncetta's satisfied gaze focused on Milburn. "Would you like to try one?"

"No."

Turning his back to the priest, Milburn moved to the uncurtained picture window. He stared past the mansion's carefully manicured lawn and into the shadowed night beyond.

"I just want that old man upstairs to die, so we can all get out of here." Control made his voice toneless. "I don't like this, D'Oncetta. If Gage is really out there, like your people say he is, then we should just leave the old man alone. Because if Gage claims the old man as family ... If he's put Father Simon under his protection, then Gage will come for him. And if that happens..." Milburn paused, turning coldly toward the priest. "You don't have any idea what you're dealing with."

"But that is why you are here, isn't it, Robert?" D'Oncetta responded tolerantly, and Milburn suspected a faint mocking tone. "It is your solemn responsibility to deal with such matters. And there is much that remains, for this is simply the beginning. There are even more delicate tasks which will require your skills in the near future. Tasks which, through the centuries, have always demanded men such as yourself. Men deeply inured and intimately familiar with the higher arts. Men who can insure the success of our plans while simultaneously protecting us all from this individual whom you seem to respect, or fear, so profoundly."

Milburn's face was stone.

"Yes, Robert, that is why we need superb field operatives such as yourself. And that is why you and your men will remain here, guarding us all so efficiently, until Father Simon is dead. We do not want him disturbed in his final, tragic hours, do we?"

Milburn took his time to reply.

"I'm retired," he said finally.

D'Oncetta nodded magnanimously.

"Of course."

Milburn looked again out the window. Shadows completely cloaked the darkened wood line, untouched by the security lights illuminating the surrounding lawn. Training told him not to look for the faint outline of sentries concealed within the obscured trees, so Milburn allowed his gaze to wander, unfocused, receptive to discerning movement where shape could not be seen.

But there was nothing.

He turned nervously toward D'Oncetta.

"How much longer will it take?"

Black and stately, the priest shrugged.

"An hour," he said with supreme composure. "Perhaps less. The chemical is quite painless and, I might add, undetectable. Not that we shall have to worry. Validating documents have already been executed. There shall be no confirmation of peculiarity. So it will be tragic, but natural. For, as you know, Robert, all of us are destined to die."

D'Oncetta released another draw from the Davidoff and smiled again, this time plainly amused. And Milburn made a decision, releasing some of his tension by taking a slow and threatening step across the library.

Toward D'Oncetta.

The priest watched Milburn's measured step with calm detachment. And when Milburn was face to face with D'Oncetta, he stopped as if he had always intended to stop, emotions tight once more. But as Milburn stood close to the priest he felt a sudden strangeness in the moment, in the tension, and he heard the question coming out of himself before regret could silence it.

"Who are you, D'Oncetta?" he asked quietly in a voice of unbelief no matter what the answer.

D'Oncetta laughed indulgently.

"I am a priest, Robert."

Milburn's face was a rigid mask. Slowly he turned away and lifted a small radio from his coat: "Command post. Perimeter check."

One by one, unseen guards responded.

"Position one, Alpha clear ... Position two, Epsilon clear," until finally the code words, "Position eleven, Omega clear," emerged from the radio with startling clarity.

"Command clear." Milburn lowered the radio to his side, refusing to look at D'Oncetta again. But he knew the priest maintained his air of amused calm.

"There, you see, Robert. We are all quite safe."

TWO

The pale figure lay silently beneath the white shroud that stretched, thin and veiled, from the vaulted ceiling.

Darkness cloaked the room, leaving the dying man within a single white space claimed by the lampstand, a separate light that removed the old man from the shadows with a deep and glowing authority.

He laid with eyes closed, as motionless as he would lay in true death. But he was not dead, for the ashen face would sometimes tighten, stirred from within some abysmal pain, to release a low moan.

Watching in silence, the stranger stood in the shadows, far from the dying man, sweat glistening on his darkened face. Only moments after the priest had departed the room, he had stepped from the curtained balcony, moving without sound to shut the wide, double doors behind him.

Now he studied the room. And after a few moments he slowly removed a thick, black visor from his waist-length coat and raised it to his eyes.

His head turned with a mechanical, trained precision as he scanned the room, concentrating longer on areas that separated him from the dying man. Then he placed the visor again within his coat and eased into a crouch, feral and wary, an animal approaching a trap baited with what could not be resisted.

A long time he poised, as if searching for something that should be feared but could not be seen. Then in a slow, fluid movement he rose and stepped lightly upon the floor. At home with the darkness, he threaded a careful path through the shadowed furnishings to approach the dying man.

With reverence, with tenderness, the stranger reached down to clasp the man's trembling hand. The dying man weakly turned his head to behold the ghostly image and through clouded eyes, he smiled. Then he returned the stranger's grip with a strength that made death seem suddenly more distant. For the briefest of moments the hands held strong, encouraging, delivering and receiving with the familiar measure of firmness known only to old friends. And the weakened eyes looked up warmly into the shadowed face.

"I knew you would come. My son ... I knew you would come ..."

Silently the stranger nodded. Then he lowered his head even more, his face close to the dying man, a strong hand on the white softness of the bed.

"I'm taking you out of here," he whispered.

The old man shook his head. "No, no, it is too late for me – far too late." He drew a painful breath. "Quite effective, this pestilence. And ..." He laughed softly, "I am too old to run."

The stranger searched the fading eyes. Then he shook his head and moaned softly.

"I know ..." The old man squeezed the stranger's hand. "But you will do well without me ... You are strong, now ... Strong! ... *You are not the man you were!*"

After a moment the stranger raised his head, but his countenance was changing with each breath, eyes narrowing slightly with a bitter frown turning the corners of his mouth. He gazed upon the pale hand held within his.

"What is happening?" He leaned closer to the old man, eye to eye. "Why have these people done this to you?"

The dying man shifted suddenly, remembering something that resurrected horror in the unseeing, widening eyes.

"It has been taken!" he rasped. "They have stolen the prophecy!" He rolled his head from side to side, grieved. "I cannot believe they would commit such sacrilege! Surely it is mortal!" Trembling, he paused. "Clement would have destroyed it in time. He scorns their secrets and has always stood against them." A mournful breath escaped the sunken chest. "*They will destroy us all!*"

"Who are they? Tell me! Who are these people?"

The old man stared blindly into the surrounding darkness. "No, no, I do not know who they are ... But I knew you would come ..." He focused again on the stranger. "Yes, it was ordained long ago ... And now the Hour of Darkness has come – the Hour where *you* must take your place!"

The stranger's brow hardened in concentration. "What would you have me do?"

"Destroy the prophecy!" the old voice hissed. "Destroy it! It has cursed us for too long!"

With compassion the stranger's hand settled on the old man's chest.

"Rest, old friend," he said.

"No, no, there is no time," the dying man whispered. "I wish I could tell you more. But there is no time ... no time. But I knew you would come, so I prepared a letter for you. It is hidden in the cathedral. You know where to look." A sudden thought and he found a defiant strength, struggling to rise. "Ah, only know this, my son. Their victory is not complete. For Santacroce repented of his sin! Yes! He repented! And he buried ... he *hid* the prophecy in the tomb of his father! You can find it before they do! You can destroy it before their Evil claims it once more!"

The stranger gently pushed the old man to the bed.

"Rest. I know what to do."

The dying man hesitated, staring, and was quiet. And the stranger watched as the thin, dry lips moved in an unknown supplication, before the prayer fell still.

"I've loved you like a father," the stranger said.

Old eyes laughed. "And I have loved you as a son. I am sorry that I did not tell you more. I feared that this would come one day. But I wanted you to forget that world. To forget ... I know you have seen too much ..."

"I have forgotten," the stranger said.

The old man shook his head. "I know better. I know the faces still come to you in the night. But you are not what you were! The Dragon is dead, my son ... He is dead."

Abruptly the old man stiffened, face pale with pain.

A frown hardened the stranger's face.

"Do what you can for Sarah," the old voice whispered, and the stranger perceived that he heard a faintness behind, or within, the words, as if they were spoken from within some invisible mist. "Malachi is prepared to die. He is a good man. But Sarah has done nothing! She does not even know their secrets!" He shook his head. "She was there when we found it. But she does not know what it contains!"

"No one else will be hurt, my friend." The stranger placed a hand upon the old man's brow, gently pushing back the wispy, white hairs now damp with sweat.

"I'll bring an ending to this."

Nodding, the old man began to speak again, but the thought was lost as the clouded eyes saw something in the surrounding shadows. The stranger didn't turn; he knew there was nothing there that human eyes could see.

"Yes... an ending," the dying man whispered. "At last ... an ending."

It happened quickly, peacefully. The stranger knelt in silence, waiting, holding the weakened hands until softness faded from the pale face beneath him, and a brittle coldness settled upon the brow. Then, breathing deeply, he slowly rose, stepping back from the light to gaze mournfully upon the still shape.

A long moment passed before the first, violent shudder stiffened him and his fist clenched. Though his gaze remained focused on his silent friend, his fist clenched tighter, trembling, bloodless, a force struggling to find release and he shut his eyes, fiercely resisting a hated passion.

Then, after a moment, the cold gray eyes opened again and turned to gaze, malevolent and measured, upon the bedroom door that led to the hallway, and to the stairs beyond that led downward.

To the library.

And finally, though the stranger continued to stare at the door, the trembling fist slowly relaxed, was lowered to his side. Frowning, breathing heavily, he turned back to the still form on the bed.

He nodded; "An ending."

Shattering the solemnity, static emerged from the radio concealed within the stranger's coat. An authoritative voice, tense and harsh, requested yet another perimeter check and unseen guards responded with clearances and codes.

Impassive, the stranger reached into his coat and removed the radio, along with the bloodied headset that he had chosen not to wear during the final, cherished moments with his friend. And he remembered the shocked expression of the guard now lying coldly beneath the shadowed wood line.

When it was the guard's turn to respond, the stranger engaged the device, speaking softly.

"Position eleven, Omega clear."

"Command clear," came the reply.

The stranger waited, gazing quietly upon his friend. Then he slid the radio into his coat, wearing the small, wireless earphone for silent monitoring. From his side pocket he removed a pair of black gloves and put them on, tightening a strap at each wrist. When he finished he was again completely cloaked in dark, somber hues.

He crossed the shadowed room with movements made profound by sadness, solid with purpose until he reached the balcony doors.

Was lost in the night.

THREE

Shadow in shadow, the stranger crouched on the balcony outside the room, opening his mind to the night to search by sound, sight, or scent. But he sensed nothing beside him in the dark. There was only the cool breeze, the sound of wind rustling the autumn leaves, distant traversing of traffic.

Moving slowly, carefully, the man reached back and removed the continuous circuit device that had bypassed the contact alarm on the double doors, placing it again within his coat. He turned, allowing his gaze to wander across the estate.

Almost completely concealed behind the balcony wall, he studied the surrounding grounds. He didn't center his gaze but scanned vaguely, knowing that in the darkness he would recognize shape by peripheral vision before he could discern it from middle focus.

He wondered if the slain guard, or the dog, had been quietly discovered and a trap set. He suppressed the violent urge to rush; it was always a mistake.

Soon.

He took a slow, deep breath and repeated the procedure to slow his pulse, waiting until the trembling stopped.

He shook his head.

Three years ... a long time.

Too long ...

Cautiously he took out the night-visor, a compact device resembling welding glasses that intensified ambient light sources for night-vision, and slid it over his head. Starlight luminosity registered sixty-four percent, easily allowing him to penetrate shadows of the distant tree line. He could also discern the faint outlines of three sentries, still holding the standard separation of one hundred feet.

No movement.

Suspicious, always suspicious, he attempted to scan along the tree line for other guards hidden behind the foliage.

He hesitated. Cautious. Uncertain. He initiated a switch on the upper right side of the visor, and the green-tinted screen was doubled over a thermal imaging detector that registered differences in air temperature.

Able to read through fog, windows, curtains, and rain, the heat sensor could detect heat variations as minute as one degree Fahrenheit. Instantly the three sentries were outlined in a reddish-yellow glow of body heat, while the remainder of the field was projected on the green rectangular screen in starlight, everything clear.

With the thermal imaging-starlight synthesis, he again scanned his field of observation. But he saw only the three sentries. He knew the rest would be stationed to the west and north of the estate, or roving.

That would make it more difficult.

Through an internal gauge in the night-visor, he saw that the batteries were nearly depleted and calculated that the double read-out mode was quickly exhausting remaining power. He switched off the heat index, leaving only starlight for visibility. Once more he scanned the layout of the surrounding terrain and streets, drainage pipes, hedges, and other areas that allowed limited visibility. And as he had done for the past night, he mentally familiarized himself with the architecture and landscape of the sprawling manor, preparing his mind for the instant rejection of any escape plan and the immediate selection of another.

Before entering the estate he had predesigned three various lines of retreat, with the last and most desperate being the initial line of entry. But he had never been forced to leave an objective along the path of entry. Never. It was an unbreakable rule, though desperation in past missions had taught him no rule was truly unbreakable.

On penetrating the security he had noted the roving patterns, the equipment, of the teams. He knew that whoever controlled the grounds had also hired military expertise for the job. Even after only a single night of surveillance he had determined that everything was done by the manual: listening posts directed outward, night-vision equipment and microwave transmitters for communications, patrol teams two by two roving interior grounds with dogs on the inside and perimeter.

Standard Operational Procedure ...

Night concealed his dark frown.

None of you can stop me ...

Automatically his mind locked into a familiar mode—fiercely focused, emotionless, concentrating his fear and rage and pain into physical strength and skill. A thousand calculations were formed, all turning intuitively in simplifying combinations: the mechanics of movement, light variations, background and cover, sound factors and noise discipline, tactics of evading detection while maintaining observation.

Then, remembering and ruled by the knowledge, he closed his higher mind. His training, sharpened and alive with instinct, would direct him. The science, the art would automatically select the tactic that his physical conditioning would reflexively execute.

Black gloves absorbed the moisture on his palms, but he wasn't accustomed to wearing gloves and unconsciously shook his hands, as if the cool night air would dry the sweat. Scowling, he noted the wasted movement, and his abrupt anger broke him from his heightened state.

Three years ...

I've lost my edge ...

Shut it down, he thought, shutting his eyes tight.

Concentrate on what you have to do ...

He expelled a slow, quiet breath, and focused.

Opened his eyes again.

No movement in the tree line, all visible listening posts facing outward.

Clear.

Silently, careful to keep his profile low, he moved slowly over the balcony, descending a thin rope he had lashed to the stone railing. When he reached the ground, he eased against the most advantageous background, a trellis of broken ivy and high shrubs that profoundly compromised security, partially concealing him from even ambient light devices. Then, patiently, he moved forward, coldly channeling feverish adrenaline and raging emotion into silent stalking.

An instinct, hot and fresh, that was the center of him, flowed through him. And he was hot with it; - thirsty, predatory, finding a familiar way with it.

But he knew he would not surrender to it.

Not like before.

Get the book at: **wbp.bz/reckoninga**

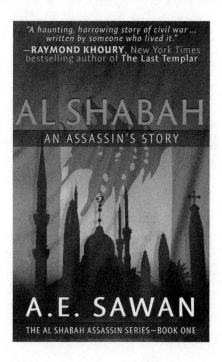